FATA
MORGANA

FATA MORGANA

STEVEN R. BOYETT
AUTHOR OF *ARIEL*

KEN MITCHRONEY

BLACKSTONE
PUBLISHING

Copyright © 2017 by Steven R. Boyett and Ken Mitchroney
Published in 2017 by Blackstone Publishing
Cover design by Kathryn Galloway English
Book design by Blackstone Publishing

Printed in the United States of America
First edition: 2017

ISBN 978-1-5047-5744-7
1 3 5 7 9 10 8 6 4 2

CIP data for this book is available from the Library of Congress

Blackstone Publishing
31 Mistletoe Rd.
Ashland, OR 97520

www.BlackstonePublishing.com

B-17F FLYING FORTRESS

"Fata Morgana"

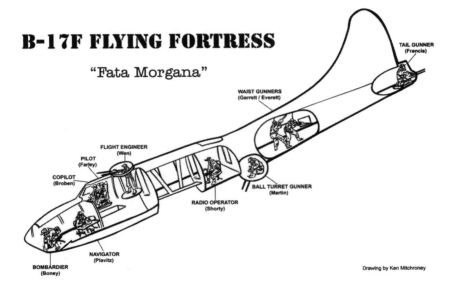

TAIL GUNNER
(Francis)

WAIST GUNNERS
(Garrett / Everett)

FLIGHT ENGINEER
(Wen)

PILOT
(Farley)

COPILOT
(Broben)

BALL TURRET GUNNER
(Martin)

RADIO OPERATOR
(Shorty)

NAVIGATOR
(Plavitz)

BOMBARDIER
(Boney)

Drawing by Ken Mitchroney

fata morgana, *noun*: an unusual form of mirage involving almost any kind of distant object, often distorted unrecognizably, and visible from land or sea, polar regions or deserts, at any altitude, including from airplanes. The name (from the sorceress Morgan le Fay in the Arthurian legend) derives from a belief that these mirages were fairy castles in the air or false land created by witchcraft to lure sailors to their death.

PROLOGUE

Two weeks ago in the *Voice of America* they had bombed an airplane factory in Brunswick and barely made it back. The Germans had that ground sewn up tight, flak so heavy the birds were walking on it. Even while you watched it shred the bombers in triple-group formation ahead of you, you found yourself admiring the precision placement. The krauts had a gee-whiz mechanical computer rangefinder that directed the 8.8-centimeter antiaircraft guns that fired a twenty-pound shell faster than the speed of sound. The shells went off at programmed altitudes like deadly popcorn kernels, spraying metal fragments that punched through aluminum sheeting, cut fuel and electrical and hydraulic lines, fouled props, and shredded engines and men.

And there was nothing to be done about it. The bombers had to stay level and on-course because the top-secret Norden bombsight had delicate gyros that wanted a Cadillac glide once the run over the Initial Point began. For maximum concentration of explosive damage, the bombers had to remain in tight echelon formation—which also maximized the devastation of the flak bursts. Once the bomb run began there was no deviating. No evasive maneuvers, no flying above or below the flak level. There was nothing you could do but ride it out and grab your lucky charms. The only good in that hot mess was that the flak kept the Luftwaffe out of their hair, because on the Brunswick mission the Messerschmitts had been on them like starving fleas on a fat hound.

11

Boney Mullen, their bombardier, had released with the lead bombardier's drop over the target, and they were just banking off the run to dive below the flak when they caught a close burst low on the right side. It took out Number Three engine and punched through the ball turret and shot chunks into the fuselage.

Voice of America was a hangar queen. She'd thrown a rod on the mission before this one, and Wen Bonniker, their flight engineer, had asked Farley if he could requisition a junked B-17 for parts. "Then we could fly that one instead," he'd drawled, straight-faced. "'Cause fixing this one's like taking a gator to the vet. You're just making it better so it can try to kill you again."

Captain Farley had feathered Number Three after it got creamed. Then he saw that it was leaking oil. At least the goddamn thing wasn't on fire. In the copilot seat beside him Lieutenant Broben called out the oil-pressure drop and reported that fuel was looking okay. He shut off Number Three fuel line and Farley upped throttle on the remaining engines. Higher RPM would eat up fuel, and the drag on Number Three would eat up more. It was a long way back to England, and now the bomber would be trying to turn right the entire way. TDB, too damn bad.

Farley got on the interphone for a status check. The crew reported that the bird was holier than the pope, but Number Three engine seemed to have got the worst of the damage. Handsome Hansen hadn't reported back from the ball turret and Farley told Garrett to go check on him. Garrett banged a wrench on the turret hatch and didn't get a return bang, so he cranked the turret and undogged the latches and swung the hatch down and stared into the tiny space for a moment. Then he dogged the hatch again and reported that the ball turret was out of commission and that Hansen had been killed by flak. He did not report the jagged, foot-wide hole in the side of the turret, or the bloody chunks of Hansen coating the inside in a kind of frozen stew that was in no way identifiable as something that, ten minutes earlier, had been a nineteen-year-old with big white teeth and a total inability to tell when his leg was being pulled.

With an engine out the *Voice of America* couldn't keep up with the flight group, so Farley had dropped out of the formation. He and Broben watched the other bombers pull ahead, stark silhouettes in the midday sun. They counted four B-17s missing from the group, apart from the *Voice*. Two of the remaining bombers were burning oil or worse, and trailed dark black plumes that would be a roadmap for any Luftwaffe pilots who sighted them.

Broben had shaken his head in disgust and said, "Why don't we skywrite directions to the airfield while we're at it?"

Farley nodded grimly and gave the homebound formation a wistful two-fingered salute. Then he told the crew to keep a sharp eye out for enemy fighters. Straggling alone apart from the bomber group the *Voice* was now a flying bullseye. The German pilots would go after her like wolves after a stray yearling. There'd be no help from other bombers, and the *Voice* was still hours away from picking up a fighter escort.

Near the coast north of Rotterdam they were spotted by four Bf 109s. Farley had taken the B-17 down below ten thousand so that the denser air would give the fuel more stretch and the crew could take off their oxygen masks. The yellow-nosed Messerschmitts broke formation and came at them from high and behind, four o'clock and eight o'clock. The *Voice* filled with staccato hammering from the .50-caliber Browning machine guns at the waist and tail and upper turret. The German fighters were going for the damaged wing. Oil had sprayed everywhere, and one good tracer round would light her up like a fuse leading straight to the fuel cells. Instant Fourth of July.

But Everett scored a hit on the Messerschmitts' first pass, firing from the bomber's right waist and carving chunks out of the canopy of the lead fighter. The Bf 109 veered off and corkscrewed down into the pale green Dutch countryside.

The other three fighters had immediately broken off the attack. That shot of Everett's had been the lucky first-round haymaker that ends the fight right then and there, and the remaining Luftwaffe pilots seemed only too happy to turn tail. Maybe it was dinner time.

Garrett and Everett usually went at each other like an old married couple, but when the 109s broke off, Garrett—a heavyweight wrestler in high school a few years ago—picked Everett up in a bear hug and carried him to the back of the bomber, laughing and yelling and calling him one terrific son of a bitch.

It had been great shooting, all right, but everyone knew how lucky they'd all been. There could easily have been forty fighters instead of four. And if the 109s had come from below, their pilots would have seen the wrecked ball turret and started working on gutting the bottom-blind *Voice of America* like a trout.

After the Messerschmitts had sped off, Farley took the *Voice* down to two thousand feet to conserve even more fuel. Number Four was leaking now and oil pressure was dropping. Wen reported that he could smell fuel near the bomb bay.

The North Sea was whitecapped and rough two thousand feet below. Farley didn't think the junkheap bomber was going to make it across. And he sure as hell didn't like the idea of his crew bobbing like corks in that cold rough water for however long it would take the Allies or the Germans to pick them up—assuming anyone picked them up at all. Turning back to bail out over Holland and Belgium was out, unless they wanted to ride out the war in a *stalag*. If they weren't shot after parachuting in.

Farley gave Plavitz their fuel situation and told him to find an English runway in range. The navigator stopped his constant drummer's paradiddles and hunkered over his charts and did calculations with pencil and paper and worked a ruler and compass on a chart and said he thought they could make the joint RAF/USAAF base at Horsham St. Faith outside Norwich. If not, there were RAF bases along the route—but they were all medium-bomber fields, and Plavitz wasn't sure about the runways. Farley told him beggars can't be choosers, and Plavitz sang out coordinates for the nearest field.

The bum-engined bomber took some nursing. They were losing altitude and speed and Farley couldn't get her to climb. Any slower than this and raising the nose would stall her. Farley told the crew they could either bail into the North Atlantic or take their chances on reaching an airfield.

There hadn't even been a pause. *"We're with you, cap,"* said Wen. The others chimed their agreement.

"All right, then," Farley told the crew, "let's clean her out. Everything that isn't nailed down goes out the window. We don't have room to be sentimental here."

"Sentimental, my ass," came Wen's gravel voice. *"I want to jack her up and slide a whole new bomber under her."* You weren't supposed to bad-mouth your aircraft, but Wen had pretty much given up by now.

The *Voice of America* had begun raining guns and gear into the North Sea. Brownings, ammo, parachutes, oxygen tanks, flak suits, helmets, binoculars. Boney wanted to activate the thermite grenade on the Norden bombsight, but Wen convinced him that no German was going to snag the thing on a fish hook before the war was over. Fuel was leaking everywhere and Wen was afraid that setting off the Norden would blow the whole damn aircraft. Boney acquiesced and then heaved the heavy apparatus out the front access hatch. Plavitz sadly patted his sextant and then chucked it out, followed by his entire chart table. He also quietly slipped his drumsticks into his flight suit. None of the other crew would have missed them, but Plavitz would rather go into the drink himself than chuck the pair of sticks he'd been beating since he was old enough to hold them.

Thirty minutes later the bomber was a hundred feet off the water and the English coast was dead ahead. Farley had the throttle shoved forward and his arms were aching from wrestling the control wheel.

"I'm open to suggestions," he told Broben.

"Set her down on the beach," his copilot offered. "I can work on my tan."

"In England?"

"It's still a beach."

Farley told the crew he was going to leave the wheels up and try to set her down in the shallows. He ordered them to throw out their heavy flak jackets and be sure they were wearing their mae wests, then take crash positions, which really just meant getting on the floor with a cushion and bracing themselves.

Number Four burped and cut out as Farley was banking left to line up the bomber over a stretch of narrow beach. He put all his weight into turning the control wheel, and he feathered Number Four and told Jerry to cut power to the remaining two engines. Jerry quickly powered down the engines and generators and shut off the fuel lines, and the *Voice of America* went silent for her last ten seconds of flight.

The North Sea blurred by on the left and England streaked by on the right. Farley kept the nose up and felt the tail touch water. The drag brought the nose down and Farley quickly raised the flaps to help her skim along the surface. They planed along the shallows off the beach like a skipping stone. The bomber breached the chop. The crew were jolted, then slammed forward as the fuselage touched bottom and hissed along the sand. Then the left wing's leading edge bit water hard and they were thrown around as the bomber slewed left.

The aircraft ground to a halt and yawed to port. Cold seawater poured through the wheelwells and bomb bay doors. The crew scrambled to their feet and got the hell out, each man picturing himself trapped in a huge metal coffin sliding to the bottom of a freezing sea. But the *Voice of America* had landed in shallow water, and her right half lay fully on the narrow beach as if her captain had ordered her careened.

Farley grabbed the flare gun, and he and Broben helped each other out the window. They slid down the hull and splashed into the cold water and slogged to the raw beach. Farley counted heads while Broben lit a Lucky and stood looking at the Flying Fortress half-submerged in the breaking shallows.

"Keep sailing like that and you'll make admiral someday, Joseph," he said.

Farley had scowled at the beached bomber. Waves gurgled against the hull. The water around her stained with leaking oil and fuel. He looked at Wen. "Think they can fix her?" he asked.

Wen spat. "I'm worried they might. She was a dog, I'da shot her five missions ago," he said.

Farley nodded. Then he handed Wen the flare gun. "Here," he said. "Put her out of our misery."

The RAF had picked them up. The Limeys in their fatigues regarding the huge American bomber burning on their shore.

At Horsham St. Faith they were debriefed about the Brunswick mission and then billeted in the most comfortably appointed barracks any of them had seen since joining up. Next morning they hitched a ride with a USAAF supply convoy back to Thurgood, where they found that their billets had been given over to new arrivals and their belongings had been divided up among the squadron, except for personal effects, which had been given to the chaplain to be mailed back home.

No one at Thurgood could believe it when the nine remaining *Voice of America* crewmen hopped off the Jimmy Deuce outside the mess tent. That night the crew were stood warm beers in the Boiler Room, and no one else realized the survivors were toasting the loss of the *Voice of America* every bit as much as they were celebrating having made it back alive. They left a glass full for Hansen and nobody mentioned him.

Every man got back every item that had been parceled out, except for the food that had been eaten. Zippos, paperbacks, playing cards, clothes. Francis, their tail gunner, even got back his *Shadow* comic books.

PART ONE: THE MISSION

ONE

Shorty perched on the A-frame ladder with six colors of paint in half-cut beer cans jostling on the top step as he worked the brush against the riveted aircraft hull. It was late afternoon on a rare sunny day in Thurgood, but the olive-painted aluminum was still cool and taking the paint well. The long fuselage of the B-17F Flying Fortress slanted down to Shorty's right, shadow stretching onto the recently constructed concrete taxiway. The Number Two engine propeller was a huge Y behind him.

"Her tits are too small."

Shorty looked down to see Gus Garrett squinting up at him. Blue eyes in a work-tanned face, hair the color of cornsilk. A worn ball glove hung on his left hand.

"Too small for what?" Shorty asked.

Garrett grinned. "For me, for starters."

Shorty shook his head sadly. "You just *remember* them bigger," he said in Jack Benny's instantly recognizable voice. "Because you haven't *seen* any in so long, y'know."

"I wanted 'em bigger then, too," said Garrett, and turned back to the game of catch going on around the bomber parked on its hardstand.

Shorty shook his head and went back to work painting the nose art. He'd already drawn the shape in chalk and then painted in the face, the flesh tones, the blue leotard, the gauzy windblown cape.

21

Flesh tones were hard, but at least he was working with oils, thanks to Corporal Brinkman's run into town for more art supplies.

Sunny days in June seemed about as common as rocking-horse shit here in southeastern England. Shorty was squeezing everything he could out of it, but soon he'd be losing the sunlight, and he still had to do the black ink outlines and final highlights that would make the whole thing pop and give it life.

Below him someone cleared his throat and spat. Shorty looked down to see Flight Engineer Wendell Bonniker squinting up at the painting in progress. Wen was a beefy, sandy-haired guy who was always looking at things as if he were trying to figure out how to fix them. People included. Four years ago he'd quit high school to run moonshine outside of Charlotte, and he'd outrun feds and sheriffs on endless miles of winding country road in cars he'd built and modified and repaired since he'd been old enough to reach the pedals. Wen claimed he could drive or fix anything with wheels on it, and given the magic he worked on a ship, no one had any reason to doubt him.

"That farmboy gettin' in your hair?" Wen called up.

Shorty wiped his forehead with the arm holding the brush. "Says her tits are too small."

"Sheeit," said Wen. He raised his voice. "That tractor jockey never saw tits on nothing he didn't have to milk at five a.m."

Shorty grinned and turned back to his painting.

"Legs could be longer, though," Wen added.

Shorty sagged. "For crying in the sink," he said. He glared over his shoulder and shook the brush at Wen. In Jack Benny's voice he said, "Don't you have a ball to throw, Cinderella?"

Wen smirked. "Man, you arty types sure are touchy." He touched the bill of his worn A-3 cap and spat tobacco juice and went to rejoin the game of catch.

The crew liked to go out to the bomber and throw the ball around after chow. It let them blow off steam and bitch about the Army and insult each other without it getting too personal. It worked pretty well.

Today they had another reason for their ritual game of catch. The B-17F heavy bomber that Shorty was painting was brand-new, delivered the day before yesterday and parked on a hardstand in the slot the much-reviled *Voice of America* had occupied for half a dozen straight missions.

At the moment the new bird was just a number, unchristened and untested. And even though her delivery had also been her shakedown cruise and she'd been checked out on arrival—and would be gone over again by the ground crew if Ordnance got the go-ahead tonight—Wen had told Captain Farley that a little tire-kicking session might be a good idea.

Farley had agreed. This was one of the world's most complicated machines, about to be loaded with four tons of coiled death and thrown into the sky with ten young men who squabbled like close brothers even though they had been strangers to each other the year before, and schoolboys the year before that. A successful mission and those ten lives could turn on a tightened oil gasket, a correctly loaded ammo belt, or any of the ten thousand other things that could go graveyard wrong. When that huge and intricate web could be undone at almost any strand, you bought yourself whatever insurance you could.

So today's game of catch served as a smoke screen to let the crew check out the ground crew's work without looking as if they didn't trust the ground crew. Because you had to trust the ground crew. The alternative was to worry that one link in that chain had not been done right, and go completely out of your mind. And the crew couldn't afford that, because doing their *own* jobs right could drive them foxhole crazy if they thought too much about what they were doing. USAAF hospitals were full to bursting with promising young men who had looked too long and too hard into the wholesale abattoir that was the new science of aerial warfare. Human brains might have invented it, but they sure as hell weren't built to endure it. As Lieutenant Broben put it, going daffy was the only reasonable thing a man could do in these conditions.

Somewhere behind Shorty a ball clapped into a leather glove and someone shouted a friendly insult. Shorty could listen to it all day. It sounded like home.

Every so often one of the men would take off his ball glove and jump up into the main hatch of the bomber. Sometimes the crew heard banging from inside. Sometimes swearing. They ignored both. They played catch and smoked cigarettes. Or, in Boney Mullen's case, a pipe. A few minutes later the missing crewman would hop back down to the concrete and put his glove back on and quietly rejoin the game, and the ball would come his way and he'd give a little nod.

At one point Shorty heard Plavitz yelling up at him, and he patiently finished painting a section and turned around to see the navigator shaking a finger up at him. "What are you doing with my sticks?" he demanded.

"Simmer down, Gene Krupa," Shorty said. "I saw them laying around and I knew you'd blow a gasket if they turned up missing, so I grabbed them. Here." He drew Plavitz's hickory drumsticks from a rear pocket and tossed them down.

Plavitz caught them up and twirled them in the same fluid motion. "I never," he said.

"You're welcome, I'm sure," Shorty said in Bugs Bunny's voice, and turned back to the painting taking shape before him.

"Yeah, okay, thanks," said Plavitz, and disappeared into the bomber. A moment later rapid-fire rolls and lazy paradiddles sounded from different parts of the aircraft.

Shorty mixed paints on a page torn from an old *Yank* magazine and leaned back to study the figure he was forming on the metal. He dipped his brush in a sheared beer can of black paint and pulled the wet bristles between his thumb and forefinger several times, testing the flow. Then he got to work on the black lines, starting with the legs, which were bare from ankle-strap high heels all the long way to the dark blue leotard at her pelvis. They were plenty long enough, thank you very much.

The drumming stopped and Plavitz hopped out of the aircraft. "It's still got that new-bomber smell," he announced.

Shorty made a pained face. "Your parents must be some very patient people," he said. "Or deaf."

Plavitz twirled a stick like a majorette. "You'll be laughing when I'm playing with Glenn Miller," he said, and hurried to rejoin the game of catch.

Shorty shook his head. Plavitz was okay, except when he wasn't.

Shorty's father, Howard Dubuque, owned a radio sales and service shop in downtown Grandville, Michigan. Little Wayne had grown up surrounded by radios and radio programs. He had learned to tell time by what show was on the air. In fifth grade he had built his first wireless radio with a piece of galena crystal and a safety pin, and he still remembered the thrill of hearing Fibber McGee's voice come over a speaker he had salvaged from a busted radio.

As he grew older he helped his father in the shop, troubleshooting ornate Gothic Hartcos, arched Philco cathedrals, cheap Sears Bakelite Silvertones. Eventually Wayne had his own little corner in the shop's back room. He'd repair the electronics, polish the wood with lemon oil, clean the Bakelite with dish soap. A Dubuque repair was good as new, and loyal customers and strong word of mouth helped carry Wayne's family through the Great Depression.

When Wayne's father asked him to spruce up the store's faded signage, Wayne went ahead and made all-new signs. He had a knack for drawing, and soon half the stores along First Street sported Wayne's lettering and artwork. Often he worked in trade for groceries or dry goods, one time even a month of free tickets at the Paramount.

Eventually Wayne became a ham radio operator, driving his mother crazy with the constant *"CQ, CQ, this is Grandville, Michigan, USA, come in"* that came from his bedroom. She would chase him out of the house, laughing and saying "Why can't you hang out on street corners like other boys your age?"

Radio Operator was an ironclad cinch for Wayne after Basic. His knowledge and experience pretty much guaranteed a slot on a bomber roster, and flying with the new Army Air Force and all that Buck Rogers gear was the cat's meow to the newly minted Pfc. Dubuque. After preflight training he was sent to Scott Field in Illinois for radio operator training. Wayne aced Morse Code, but he was surprised how much more than radio he was supposed to learn. Basic navigation, aircraft identification, gunnery, oxygen mask systems, generators. And radios, too—more intimately than even he could have imagined. By the end of training Wayne could assemble an aircraft radio by feel in a pitch-black room.

He'd been promoted to sergeant—all bomber crew were sergeant or higher so they'd be treated better if they were captured—and assigned to a B-17 crew under Captain Logan at Maxwell Field, Alabama. When the crew found out his hobby was shortwave radio, Wayne was Shorty from then on. When they found out he could draw, Captain Logan asked him to do the nose art for their new bomber, which he was calling *Voice of America*. Shorty painted a towering Uncle Sam shouting bombs through a megaphone at a cowering Hitler.

And now here he was, on the other side of the Atlantic, and Captain Logan had been killed by flak over Cologne, and Shorty was painting a new bird for a different pilot. Life worked out funny, when it worked out at all.

Shorty finished the black lines and stepped up a rung on the folding ladder and set a hand on the hull. He worked on the face again, adding contour and highlights, color to the cheeks.

"Hey, Shorty," a voice behind him called in a thick New Jersey accent. "How come you didn't make that little number look like Francis' sister?" Then a long low whistle, and a few laughs from below.

Shorty turned to see Lieutenant Broben sitting on the Number Two engine cowling. The copilot lit a Lucky and gestured with it. "That girl's a blue-plate special."

"Aw, jeez, lieutenant," said Francis, whom Broben had instantly dubbed "Saint Francis" because he was pure as angel piss. "I don't even have a sister."

"Whose picture were you showing these deprived apes the other day?" Broben demanded. "Your Sunday School teacher?"

Francis colored. He shaved once a month and had lied about his age when he'd joined up, and if anyone was going to get out of this war still a virgin, it was him. "Gosh," he said, "that was my mom. She does teach Sunday School, though."

"That dame was your *mother*?" Broben looked up at the clouds. "I wouldn't show these saps a picture of my great grandma. They get worked up when they see an overstuffed couch."

"You should make her look like Francis' mom," Plavitz called up. "It's good luck to have the mother of a saint on your bomber."

The others laughed.

"The captain was pretty definite what he wanted her to look like," Shorty said.

In fact, over beer in the Boiler Room the other night Captain Farley had gone into great detail about the girl he wanted on their bomber, nodding more and more enthusiastically as Shorty sketched on napkin after napkin, zeroing in on the face the captain wanted. Shorty had wondered why the captain didn't have a picture if the girl meant so much to him, but you didn't ask about that stuff. Whoever she was, Shorty wanted to do her justice.

Broben kicked his feet between the prop blades. "You're gonna be painting her by moonlight if you don't hurry up," he said.

"It'd go a lot quicker if everyone stopped giving me their expert opinion."

Broben spread his hands. "Everyone's an expert on dames."

"Well, you can have her fast, or you can have her good."

The lieutenant grinned. "Like I said."

"Why can't they be both?" asked Garrett.

Broben ignored him. "She's kinda pale, ain't she?" he asked.

Shorty didn't bother to look back at him. "Do I look like Michelangelo to you, lieutenant?"

"Well," a mild voice said, "you're painting on top of a ladder and you're taking orders from God."

27

They all turned to see Captain Farley standing with his hands on his hips, his crush cap raked back on his head as he looked up at the nearly finished painting. He wore his A-2 jacket despite the day's unseasonable warmth. A sergeant stood just behind him, a dark, small man with black eyes.

"What, you got demoted?" Broben asked.

Shorty shifted the brush to his left hand and gave the captain a casual salute, trying to gauge whether he looked approving or disappointed as he took in the artwork.

"I don't want to rush you, Shorty," Farley called up. "But I think she'll be happier if she's dressed up when we take her to the dance."

"So we're definitely going out tomorrow?" Everett asked.

Farley raised an eyebrow. "I don't know anything you boys don't. But if the order does come down tonight, it's a safe bet we'll be on the roster."

"If these guys'll leave me alone I'll have her done in half an hour, cap," said Shorty. "This crate'll fly out with the best nose this side of Durante."

Farley smiled. "That's what I want to hear." He glanced back at the new sergeant and waved him forward. "Gentlemen, this is Sergeant Proud Horse. He's our new ball gunner."

"Proud Horse?" Broben went to the trailing edge of the wing and slid off. He landed on the concrete with surprising grace for a man of his girth. "What kinda name is that?"

"Lakota," said the sergeant.

Broben cocked his head. Beside him Plavitz joggled the baseball in his hand. "Beats me," he told Broben.

Proud Horse nodded to himself. "Indian," he tried again.

"Well, why didn't you say so in the first place?" drawled Wen. He spat tobacco juice and held up a palm. "How, Chief."

The new man looked the flight engineer up and down.

Beside Wen, Everett put his hands on his hips. "You left your teepee to come all the way to England and shoot Germans?"

Proud Horse looked at him without expression. Then he pounded a fist against his chest. "Me heap big plains injun," he said. "Fly heap big planes. Droppum bomb, make-um smoke." He looked up and opened his hands to the sky. "Send Nazi devils to happy hunting ground."

Everett stared. Proud Horse kept looking up.

Shorty started laughing, and the crew took it up until they were whooping. Broben grinned and stepped toward the new crew member. "This circus needs all the clowns it can get," he said. He held out a hand. "Welcome aboard, sergeant."

The new guy may have been small, but he had a hell of a grip. "Thank you, lieutenant."

"Jerry Broben." Broben leaned in and lowered his voice. "There an Indian word for your name?" he asked.

Proud Horse looked up at him and shrugged a shoulder. He really was a little guy, about as close to 4-F as you could get and still qualify. "My first name's Martin, if that helps."

"Martin?" Broben shook his head. "Never mind. This bunch'll hand you a nickname in about two minutes anyways. Like it or not."

"I'm used to that."

"I guess so."

"Hey, chief," called Garrett. "They play ball out there on the reservation? You know, baseball?" He mimed swinging a bat.

"Some," Martin admitted.

"Well, don't worry, we'll show ya. First we gotta get you a glove." Garrett held up his own and flexed it. "See?"

"Mine's back at—"

"Hey, Shorty!" Garrett called up. "Loan Geronimo here your glove, will you?"

Shorty pointed with his brush. "It's by the wheel chock there."

Garrett fetched the wellworn fielder's glove and held it out to Martin. "Your hand goes in this end, chief."

Martin put on the glove and stood looking at it. Captain Farley looked as if he were about to say something but changed his mind.

Martin glanced at him, and Farley gave back a little smile and nodded. "Have fun, sergeant," he said. "That's an order."

Martin saluted with the glove. "Yes, sir."

Garrett jogged backward along the taxiway, away from the row of heavy bombers parked facing him. He nodded at Plavitz, and the navigator underhanded the baseball to Martin, who caught it in the trap and stood looking at Garrett.

The burly waist-gunner held his glove in front of his chest. "All right, Geronimo." He punched the glove, then flapped it. "Put her anywhere around here, got it? Just pretend you're throwing a tomahawk."

Up on his ladder Shorty shook his head. Being the new guy was hard enough without being the new guy and an Indian.

He bent and mixed up more flesh pink and was just stretching up to start on the face when a loud *pop!* nearly startled him from the ladder. It had sounded like a rifle shot. Garrett yelled and Everett hooted. Shorty turned as quickly as he could high up on the ladder and saw Garrett wringing his hand like he was trying to flick off snot. His glove and the baseball lay in the grass beside him.

"God *damn* it," said Garrett.

Everett put his hands on his knees and cackled. Wen laughed and slapped himself on the leg with his grimy cap. Broben grinned like someone had told a dirty joke, and even Boney smiled there behind his great stinking bulldog briar pipe as he sat in the shade of the wing. The captain folded his arms and tried to look above it all. He almost succeeded.

Martin remained in his follow-through, waiting to see what Garrett was going to do.

The big man turned his hand in front of his face as if puzzled that there was no blood. "I think you broke it," he said. "Son of a bitch feels like wood."

Martin straightened up and pointed to the trap on his glove. "It hurts less if you catch it here."

"Screw you."

"And the Proud Horse I rode in on," Martin agreed.

Everybody laughed harder, and Broben applauded slowly.

"Sergeant Horse was a pitcher for the American Legion team in Rapid City," said Farley.

"Post Twenty-Two, South Dakota state champs," said Martin.

"This just keeps getting better," said Broben. "You have a nickname when you played?"

Martin looked embarrassed. "They, uh, called me Red Man. Because I chewed tobacco."

"Good thing he didn't like Beechnut," Shorty chimed in from on high.

Everett chortled. "Hear that, Gus? Geronimo here's called Red Man."

"I don't give a shit if he's called General Jesus Roosevelt," said Garrett. "He nearly gimped my goddamn hand."

"You do all your pulling with the other one anyway," said Everett.

"Only when he sees an overstuffed couch," added Plavitz. He drummed a rimshot on the hull.

Shorty turned back to the riveted metal looming above him. Any other day he'd be in the middle of the fun, cracking jokes and doing voices and pulling faces. But tomorrow the aluminum he was painting would carry him across the English Channel or the North Sea in subzero temperatures, possibly through storms and definitely through enemy territory. It was thinner than the steel of a beer can, and it was all the shield he'd have between himself and fighter planes and antiaircraft shells. That shield would bear his artwork, and it had to be right.

Shorty came off like a goofball, but he was dead serious about his work. He was barely aware of what he was doing as he dipped a trim brush, borrowed from Corporal Brinkman, into half a beer can and pulled on the soft slick bristle and finished up the figure's face, adding shades and highlights.

Finally Shorty gathered up his paint cans and climbed carefully from the ladder. He set down the cans and moved the ladder aside and stepped back and looked up at her. Only dimly aware of his sore neck and aching back. The jibes and throws tossed all around him sounded underwater. There was just the parked bomber, angled as if already climbing in the air, the two small windows at the navigator's station in the nose, the painted figure prone beneath. The setting sun cast magic-hour light across the airfield.

He became aware that someone was standing beside him and he glanced at the captain. Farley wasn't smiling, he wasn't frowning. Shorty couldn't have said what the expression on his face was. Recognition, maybe. A man who saw some long-held notion given shape at last.

"Oh," said Farley. "Oh, she—she's fine, Shorty. Really fine. Just the way I pictured." Reluctantly he looked away from the painting. "You've outdone yourself on this one."

"*Sir.*" Shorty saluted.

Garrett's wolf whistle broke the moment. "She can wave my wand any time she wants," he said.

"A little respect, huh?" said Broben. "That's a lady you're talking about."

The ten of them were gathered around the front of the bomber now. Captain, copilot, navigator, bombardier, flight engineer. Left and right waist gunners, tail gunner, belly gunner. And Shorty the radio operator, who glanced among their faces, looking for frowns, knitted brows, cocked heads. He didn't find any. Even the new guy was looking on in open admiration, though he couldn't have fully appreciated what he was seeing.

The painting on the nose of the Flying Fortress showed a sorceress. Not a witch, not a hag. A long, slim, pale-skinned woman in a skintight navy-blue leotard. Long black hair and pale green eyes. She was posed like the figurehead on an old sailing ship, or the hood ornament on a Cadillac. Nearly prone, back arched, one arm back and one outstretched and raven hair windswept. As if diving through the water or the air. Long pale legs, one bent at the knee. A gauzy blue cape flowed from her shoulders. A black wand in her outstretched hand pointed toward the .50-cal cheek gun emerging from a clear plexiglas window. She was long and angular and strong, joyous in her flight but determined in her attitude. Her face was stern and regal and refined. Not a grin but the ghost of a smile. Her clear-eyed gaze was fixed on something beyond the aircraft. Always looking ahead, always flying to meet it.

This was no Betty Grable in a bathing suit. No girlish Vargas pinup. This was a da Vinci angel ethereal in metal, a Waterhouse nymph resplendent in flight. Beautiful and refined, magical and eerie and not quite of this earth.

In the background floated isolated clouds. Some of them looked oddly solid, like granite, and at least one looked suspiciously like a medieval castle.

The lettering beneath the flying woman was shadowed script, almost a signature. *Fata Morgana.*

The men were quiet, looking at her. Shorty realized that he had never once seen his crewmates together and quiet, except at mission briefings right before wheels-up. It made him nervous.

Then Garrett said, "Still needs bigger tits."

Lieutenant Broben took off his hat and rubbed his brush cut and sighed. He put an arm around Shorty and stood looking at the painting. "I apologize, ma'am," Broben told the flying figure. "An angel could play the violin, and some guys would only hear a horse's tail sawing on a piece of catgut."

"Well what else is it?" asked Garrett.

Broben dropped his arm from Shorty and turned to Farley. "I got an idea," he said. "Tomorrow, let's just drop Garrett on Germany. The Nazis'll be finished in a week."

"I think it'd violate the Geneva Convention," said Farley. "There are some things you just can't do in a war. Even to Nazis."

Broben sighed. "Bombs it is, then."

"Like civilized men," Farley agreed.

Martin shook his head. "I can't keep up with you guys," he said.

Boney pointed the stem of his pipe at the bomber. "Keep up in there," he said.

Martin looked at the bombardier. Tall and skinny and very pale.

Gaunt face impassive behind his fuming pipe. It was the first thing the man had said since Martin had arrived.

"Boney talks like he bombs," Shorty told him. "He doesn't drop one till he's sure it's gonna hit."

Martin pointed to the lettering. "Fata Morgana?" he asked.

"*Fay*-tuh Mor-*gon*-uh," Shorty corrected.

"What's it mean?"

"Tell him what it means, Joseph," said Broben.

"Yeah, tell him, cap," said Garrett. "I want to hear it again, too."

"Maybe it'll sink in this time," said Everett.

Garrett punched him on the shoulder.

"All right," said Farley. He looked around self-consciously at his attentive crew, then nodded at his new belly gunner. "Fata morganas are a kind of mirage," he said. "You see them under certain conditions in calm weather, when a layer of warm air sits on top of a layer of cold air. It acts like a lens. Sometimes they look like floating rocks just above the horizon." Farley paused. "Or castles in the air."

Broben waggled his eyebrows. "Castles," he said. "In the air."

"Say," Shorty said in his best radio announcer voice, "you mean like a ... *flying fortress?*"

"Why, yes, sergeant, I mean exactly like a Flying Fortress. Clever, no?"

"But why not call her *Mirage?*" asked Martin. "Everyone knows what a mirage is."

"A fata morgana's a special kind of mirage," said Captain Farley. "Technically, it's a complex superior mirage."

"Ooh, you got the fancy flight school," said Broben.

"The one for smart pilots," Farley agreed.

"So where does the girl with the magic wand come in?" Martin persisted.

"She's a girl," said Everett. "You need a reason?"

"Morgan la Fay was a sorceress in *King Arthur,*" said Farley. "She was Arthur's half sister."

Broben hooked a thumb at Farley. "College boy," he explained.

He mimed drinking tea with his pinky extended. "*Lih*-tra-choor, dontchoo know."

Farley nodded at the painting. "The Italians called her Fata Morgana. They named the mirages after her because they thought they were magic. Floating islands or castles that lured sailors to their death. Like the Sirens."

"Yeah, the air-raid sirens," said Garrett.

Martin squinted at the woman on the bomber. "So ... she's a sorceress ... and a flying fortress ... and a mirage?"

Farley nodded. "You've got it."

Martin looked thoughtful as he rubbed near the hollow of his throat. His intensity made the men glance among themselves, but they said nothing. "The Lakota have Heyoka Winyan," said Martin. "Thunder-Dreaming Woman. She carries lightning, and she's a great healer. She speaks in a voice like thunder."

"Well, this dame's gonna yell all over Germany when we take her up," said Broben.

"*Fata Morgana*," Martin said again.

Shorty nodded. "We weren't all that nuts about it at first," he said. He ducked his head apologetically at Farley. "But after the captain explained it, it was kind of hard to picture calling her anything else."

Martin nodded. "Names have power," he said. He became aware that they were all looking at him and he spread his hands. "Hey, you don't need *my* okay," he protested. "I'm the new guy."

"Tomorrow's our first time with her, too," said Boney.

"She'll be a good ol girl," said Wen.

"Lady," Broben countered.

Garrett shrugged. "Girl, lady. I'm still gonna see how far I can get with her and still be friends."

Broben shook his head. "Sergeant Garrett," he said, "you're a hell of gunner. But you are one hundred percent barbarian."

Whatever Garrett replied was drowned out by the crew's laughter.

TWO

Broben brought two mugs to the folding table and set one in front of Farley. "There you go," he said as he sat down across from him. "Nice and warm like momma used to brew. Cheers."

They clinked glasses and drank. The Boiler Room was full tonight, loud with chatter and thick with cigarette smoke. Kay Kyser played on the Armed Services Radio from the lone PA speaker on the wall. Beneath it were pinups. Beside Veronica Lake a well-lettered sign read KEEP 'EM FLYING! Groups of men, few in uniform, sat at folding tables or stood in clusters at the bar, talking shop and gesturing. It might have been a dive bar near a college somewhere, except there were no women, and the gestures weren't what you'd see in a college bar: One hand held level and the other diving under it, then the leveled hand slowly angling out to turn palm-up. Two hands struggling with an invisible control wheel. Two fists jerking in time as they swiveled an imaginary .50-caliber machine gun. Though technically it was an officers' club, there were plenty of noncoms. A few men had beers, most drank warm soft drinks.

Farley realized he could tell who was ground crew and who was flight crew without having to think about it. The flyers simply looked older. Dark circles under their eyes and a haunted, hunted look. They were nineteen, twenty, twenty-one. Whatever boyhood they had carried with them into service had been shot, shaken, blasted, burned, belly-landed, and grieved completely out of them. The boy in them had bailed out somewhere over the English Channel on his first mission. He was missing and presumed dead.

Farley knew that he didn't look any different.

Broben thumped his mug onto the table and wiped his upper lip and sighed. "Warm beer," he mused. "I'm turning into a friggin Limey."

"They're not so bad. They've been around a lot longer than we have."

"Yeah, yeah, they got socks older than us. I'll admit they're brave bastards." Broben raised his mug. "Here's to every milk-white one of 'em."

They toasted.

"They can keep their damn weather, though," Broben added.

"How in the world are you going to go back to driving a delivery truck after all this?" Farley asked.

"I ain't no truck driver."

"I thought that's what you did before you joined up."

"I'm more like a philosopher on wheels."

Farley snorted. "You're something on wheels, all right."

They were quiet a moment. Now it was Jimmie Lunceford on the PA. Smells of tobacco and beer and sweat. Steady hubbub and coiled tension.

"So what do you make of the Indian?" Broben asked.

"He seems all right. Handled himself pretty well after I threw him to the wolves."

Broben nodded. "If he shoots like he pitches, he'll clear us a path all the way to the IP."

"He was a ball gunner on another B-17," Farley said carefully. "Had to bail out when they took hard flak."

Broben whistled. "Why didn't they just hand his crew a new bird like they did with us?"

"He is the crew."

"Oh." The lieutenant nodded slowly. "That's a lousy break."

"It is that."

They were quiet again. Both men thinking of so many who had been here so briefly. A sad parade of unremembered names and faces and truncated histories. To talk about them was to conjure ghosts, invite bad luck, dwell on whether that dread country they had entered lay in wait for you as well. It was not discussed.

"So how'd a belly gunner make it out and nobody else?" Broben asked.

"Have to ask him."

"I might just do that. What was his ship?"

Farley took so long answering that Broben thought he hadn't heard him. Then he said, "*Ill Wind.*"

"Bullshit."

"That was his ship."

"Bull and shit. They were all dead on the *Ill Wind.*"

"*On* her, yeah. He bailed."

"You're telling me we got a guy from the *Ill Wind* on our brand-new bird."

"Yes, Jerry, that's what I'm telling you."

Broben frowned. "That's some bad juju, Captain Pilot sir."

"You sure you aren't just getting the heebie jeebies about going up in a new boat?"

Broben shrugged. "I dunno. Maybe."

"You'd rather be on the *Voice?*"

"Not on Hermann Göring's worst day. That heap of shit was the best weapon Germany ever had. I miss her like I miss getting crabs."

Farley nodded. He had inherited the *Voice of America* after Henry Alan Logan had been killed by flak, but he had never warmed to her. More important, she had never warmed to him. Farley liked the idea of a clean slate when it came to the bomber.

Broben leaned back in his folding chair. "So what happened on the *Ill Wind?*"

"I think it's better if Martin tells it. But go easy on the guy, Jer."

Broben waved as if shooing flies and glanced around the club. The pinups on the wall, a dartboard not in use, the men drinking and smoking and talking RPMs and pull-up speeds, hydraulic failures and flak patterns and Luftwaffe tactics. "So who's the dame?" he asked.

"What dame?"

"The one you're about to fly all over western Europe."

"I already explained who she is. The legend—"

Broben raised his hands. "Spare me the King Arthur stuff, Joseph. You handed Shorty everything but a photograph to work with. Come on, give. Whose puss we got plastered on our bird?"

"No one I know, I swear."

Broben studied him. "That's not exactly a straight answer."

Farley shrugged. "It's an answer."

The room went quiet. Frank Sinatra was suddenly loud on the wall-mounted speaker.

Farley looked up to see Major Delvecchio standing in the doorway. He did not meet anybody's gaze as he slowly raised a hand to touch his cap. He gave a little nod and then he left.

Broben's *Well, shit* seemed loud in the smoky room.

Men quietly finished their drinks and slipped out into the cold English night.

"Guess I better go join the conga line," said Farley.

"Why bother?" said Broben. "When *haven't* we been on the assignment sheet? Better I should grill our ground guys."

"The Ordnance boys don't know any more than we do."

"They may not know where we're going," said Broben, "but they know what we'll be hauling there."

Farley nodded. "I'll take what I can get," he said.

* * * * *

The flight line was a hive of activity. Farley put his hands in his jacket pockets against the cold as he walked along the row of Nissen huts to the operations room. He watched service trucks speed out from the bomb storage depot to the bombers on their hardstands, headlights taped over so that only narrow slits of light showed. Ground crew rode on the bombs in back like kids on a hayride. One of them was playing a harmonica, and the tones bent flat as the truck receded.

Farley tracked one service truck along the taxiway until it pulled up by the *Fata Morgana*. He nodded to himself. Ordnance would be assembling and loading bombs most of the night, and the ground crews would be working on the ships till dawn. They never seemed to sleep. Most of them had been mechanics before the war. Repairmen, some of them. They knew his bomber better than he ever would, and they worried themselves sick whenever their crate was out on a mission. Like parents loaning the car to a kid on his first date. They grilled you when you got back: How'd she do, what went wrong, how'd this or that repair hold up? And when ships didn't come back they sat on their bicycles along the runway and stared up at the sky like some stone age tribe forlorn at their god's abdication.

At the Operations Room a knot of pilots was gathered by the door. Farley greeted them as he worked his way toward the assignment sheet on a clipboard hanging on a nail.

In front of Farley, Hap Saunders turned away from the sheet in disgust. Hap was a scrawny little cuss who flew the *Dollar Short*. He shrugged at Farley. "Why don't they just list who *isn't* going?" he said. "It'd save a bunch of time."

"'Cause it'd be a blank sheet of paper," said Hernandez, beside him. Hernandez flew *Montezuma's Revenge*. As far as Farley knew, he was the only Latin-American pilot in the AAF. He nodded at Farley. "Ordnance tell you anything?" he asked.

"My XO went to get the lowdown."

"I heard it's mixed incendiaries and M44s."

"Munitions factory?" Farley wondered.

"I'm thinking."

Hernandez hurried away with Saunders. Neither had mentioned whether he'd seen Farley on the list. You found your own name on the assignment sheet. And if your name wasn't on it, you didn't mention that, either.

But of course it was there. *Farley, Joseph M., Capt.*

They never listed the other crew. They knew they'd be going with you.

* * * * *

A touch on the shoulder at 0430 brought Farley from a deep sleep on his cot in the officers' barracks. He always slept well the night before a mission. He had no idea why. Most of the others tossed and turned and called out in their sleep—if they could get to sleep. Farley went out like a light and stayed that way. Broben said that Farley could sleep on a meathook.

So when Staff Sergeant Boatman, the operations officer, came in quietly and went from cot to cot politely waking the officers on the mission roster—those who weren't already awake, anyhow—Farley had to swim up from the bottom when his shoulder was shaken and his name softly called.

"Morning, captain," said Boatman. "Briefing at oh five-thirty. Enjoy your breakfast." And then he was moving on to the next cot.

Broben was already getting dressed when Farley sat up. "Shit, shower, and shave, Joseph," Jerry said quietly.

Farley blinked. "The service at this hotel has really gone downhill," he said.

Broben nodded. "New management. I hear there's an outfit in Berlin interested in the property, though."

Farley rubbed his face, unfazed by the activity around him. "If there's no coffee around here," he said, "they can have it."

* * * * *

The crowded jeep slowed down but did not stop as it went by the dark shape of the bomber in the predawn light. Martin, Garrett, Everett,

41

Francis, and Shorty hopped off and shouldered their heavy Browning machine-gun barrels in their oily sleeves. They waved thanks to the driver, who sped off to collect the next crew. Garrett and Everett headed for the waist hatch, griping all the way. Their bright yellow mae wests flapped in the cold damp morning as the men heaved their parachute harnesses into the bomber and climbed in after. Francis went around to the other side, where he had his own little hatch at the rear of the aircraft for his tail gunner post.

Wen Bonniker was already doing a walkaround with Case Miller, the ground crew chief. Wen was not a small man, but he looked tiny beside the stern, bull-like Bostonian with pant cuffs half a foot above his ankles and sleeves halfway up his forearms. Case had been a company truck mechanic before the war, and Wen nodded as the huge man pointed a thick finger at Number Four engine and gave a detailed account of its most recent service.

Martin was layered up in thermals, wool uniform, leather trousers and fleece-lined jacket. Lined gloves stuffed in a pocket. He stood a moment and took it all in: Jeeps speeding crews to bombers, crewmen jabbering, trucks grinding through gears as they drove from the equipment shed for last-minute adjustments and repairs. Sounds of banging metal and tense laughter from inside the bombers.

Vestiges of night still lay upon the field. The sun a bad rumor at the horizon and dew blanketing the airfield. Tendrils of mist out near the fields, grassy mulch bordering the runways. A distant church spire.

The B-17F *Fata Morgana* was covered with dew that sparkled like a coat of diamond dust. It was as utilitarian as an aircraft could get. No comforts, no amenities. The cabin was not pressurized or heated. Interior ribs and metalwork were all exposed. There was barely even a floor—lengths of planking, and a bare metal catwalk to get across the bomb bay. The B-17 had not been built to deliver men, it had been built to deliver bombs. The men were provided what they needed to allow the aircraft to accomplish this and get back, and not one thing more.

And yet every man who flew in one loved her. Found a beauty in her aggressive form and purely functional design. A grace, even. They would fly in her, fight in her, bleed in her, curse her, even die in her. But they would never truly hate her. Any enmity a man expressed toward his bomber masked a profound disappointment, and was grudgingly given only after being insistently earned.

But unlike every other bomber here, the *Fata Morgana* was new. She was not patched or re-welded. She had never been shot at. Had never taken flak. Never burned an engine, blown a tire, dropped a bomb. She had yet to cross some remorseless boundary the other heavy bombers traversed like grim commuters, was not consecrated by the sacrament of blood and fear the other bombers wore like ghostly vestments.

Wen glanced at Martin as he came around the B-17 with Case. Maybe the flight engineer thought Martin was working up his nerve to climb aboard. Martin didn't really care. There would be no other time to take this moment in.

Finally he took a deep breath and lowered his chest chute and heavy .50-cal barrels to the ground, and he approached the ball turret that would be his home for most of the mission. The yard-wide sphere protruding from the belly of the bomber would hold a small man, barely. Not a small man and a parachute. Not even a small man in a full flak jacket. It had the best view in the house, and over pretty country it was awe-inspiring. In the middle of exploding flak and closing fighters and streaking tracer rounds it was terrifying beyond the telling.

Martin sat on the concrete with his legs on either side of the turret and made sure the brake was not engaged, then turned the ball until the ammo-can cover faced him. He unfastened it and checked the two belt feeds. They looked like a madman's roadmap, but his trained eye saw that they'd been loaded correctly. He sealed the cover and then screwed the heavy twin machine-gun bores into the gun assembly and rocked them on their cradle to be sure they were secure. Above him he heard Garrett and Everett banging around inside the bomber, joking and swearing and giving each other hell.

Martin glanced back to see Wen standing with his hands on his hips, watching him set up. Martin held his gaze and Wen nodded approval, then turned to talk to Case. The two men ducked under the fuselage to enter the aircraft from the opened bomb bay.

Martin spun the turret again until the hatch faced him. He undogged it and swung it down and saw that a lineman had placed a flak vest on the hard seat like some kind of Army elf. Martin checked the electrical cables and fuses, then backed out of the cramped space and sealed it up just as a crowded jeep drove up and slowed down to let Captain Farley, Lieutenant Broben, Sergeant Mullen, and Sergeant Plavitz hop off. They had just come from the storage shed after the mission briefing, and they wore their flight suits and mae wests and carried their parachute packs. The jeep sped off to the next bird in the line.

Farley gave Martin a two-fingered wave and set down his parachute. "All right," he called. "Everybody out of the pool."

Shorty, Wen, Garrett, Everett, and Francis came out of the bomber from different exits and gathered around Farley under the wing. "What's the word, cap?" Wen asked.

Farley surveyed his crew. "We're bombing a munitions plant in Zennhausen. Eastern Germany."

Garrett socked a palm with a fist. Everett held a hand out to him like an expectant bellhop. Garrett scowled and pulled out a wellworn fiver from his pocket. He held it by the middle and moved it up and down to flap it reluctantly into Everett's hand. Everett kissed it and tucked it into a pocket.

"Listen to the rest," Farley told Everett, "and you might even get to spend that." He nodded at Plavitz, and the navigator removed a recon map from his accordion case and unrolled it on the concrete hardstand. He weighted it with stones and a .50-caliber shell. The crew squatted to study it. All of them were smoking, except for Martin.

"Intelligence says Zennhausen's a major munitions factory," Farley continued. "Reinforced concrete, dispersed production. A rail line runs close by it. Good news is, it's not a heavily populated area. No schools, no civilian neighborhoods nearby." He pointed at the map. "We'll meet up with a flight group from the Hundred and Second Bomber Group out of Covent St. George off the coast near Norwich. We'll head northeast and come in across the north coast of Holland. From there we turn east and thread the needle between Bremen and Hanover. Those cities are heavily fortified, so we can expect flak."

"When can't we?" Garrett asked.

Farley pointed again. "We turn due south just east of Brunswick and drop on the target in a north-south line."

"What'll they have waiting for us at the target?" Martin asked.

"It's heavily defended," Farley said. "Eighty-eights and probably some one-oh-fives. Luftwaffe bases are here, here, and here." He tapped the map. "So they'll be dancing at this party, too."

"The weather's nice, though," said Plavitz. He smiled thinly. "So that's something."

"This is a pretty big facility covering a lot of ground," Farley continued. "Our flight group's carrying M44 thousand-pound concussion bombs. The boys from the Hundred and Second are carrying M17 incendiary clusters. They'll drop ten seconds after we do. The idea is to crack it open and then light it up." Farley surveyed the faces before him. None of what they were hearing was news, but it never got any easier to hear. Their thoughtful nods masked anxiety and fear. Farley would have had serious doubts about anyone who wasn't fearful of what they were about to do. "Any questions?" he asked.

They shook their heads, pulling on cigarettes and staring down at the map of the country over which they would find their reckoning.

"All right, then," said Farley. "Let's get on the bus and go to school."

Plavitz moved the weights off the map and rolled it up again.

Farley waited until the others had climbed into the bomber. Then he reached up and patted the fuselage just under the painting of the graceful figure flying prone. The drop-shadowed script of her name. The metal cold and damp in the early morning.

"Don't let me down, gorgeous," Farley whispered.

He wiped his damp palm on his jacket and then picked up his kit and ducked down to enter his new aircraft from the opened bomb bay.

THREE

The operations officer stepped onto the platform surrounding the tower and surveyed the thrumming airfield. The bombers rested on their hardstands with their engines idling, their combined rumble a veldt of waiting lions he felt deep in his chest. The drone of a vast engine of destruction. At least a hundred and fifty ground crew clustered near the operations building, sitting on the damp grass or watching on their bicycles.

The operations officer raised high a stubby M8 flare pistol and fired. A bright flare arced out into the misty morning—the soup, the pilots called it. Immediately the rumbling became a collective roar as engines throttled up. Ground crew yanked chocks from wheels, and brief shrieks sounded all across the airfield as brakes were released and two dozen bombers began to creep out onto the taxiway.

The operations officer thought about how odd it was that creatures built for flight so often looked ungainly on the ground. He glanced once more at the ground crews who would be sweating it out as they waited for their airplanes to return. A few of the men crossed themselves. He had heard that the waiting was as hard as the going. He wondered how that could possibly be true.

* * * * *

The crewmen all sat straight when the brakes squealed and the *Fata Morgana* lurched into motion. In the cockpit Farley craned to see Case Miller signaling directions from the mushy ground beside the runway, from which a Flying Fortress took off every thirty seconds. As if the airfield were some kind of factory that spat out laden bombers.

Farley inched the B-17 along the winding taxiway until finally he turned onto the runway. He scooted back into his seat and buckled himself in. Ahead of them the *Smoke 'Em Up* lumbered down the runway and picked up speed.

Broben lit a Lucky and kissed his lucky Zippo and tucked it away again. "Let's go, boys," he called out over the interphone. "Those Nazis aren't gonna bomb themselves."

Farley pulled up the brake and walked the throttle forward till the tachometers showed the engines at takeoff speed. The sound of it was all you could hear. The aircraft shuddered like a racehorse at the gate. As if eager to regain the sky.

Up ahead the *Smoke 'Em Up* lifted off. Farley let off the brake and the bomber surged forward. It always seemed to take forever to pick up speed. The fuselage shook and the outside world crept by. Then suddenly it was hurtling past and you were running out of runway.

Broben called out speed and RPM. At 80 Farley gave her some down elevator and brought the tail up off the runway. At 110 he eased back the yoke. The bomber lifted and the shaking calmed and the world filled with the resonant thrum of four powerful Wright Cyclone radial engines.

"Wheels up," Farley ordered.

Broben flicked back the wheel switch guard and flipped the toggle. "Wheels up," he confirmed when the gear indicators went off.

Below them England and the world they knew all dropped away. The Mission had begun.

* * * * *

The bomber group slowly formed up and gained altitude as it headed north to the assembly point just off the coast at Northampton. At his navigator's table in the nose, Plavitz continually consulted his charts and tables, compass and notepad, checking them against landmarks that revealed themselves through the haze below, and reported position to Farley at regular intervals. In short sessions between calculations he pulled out his sticks and drummed the edge of his wooden worktable. If it bothered Boney, the stoic bombardier never said so.

Boney got permission to arm the bombs, and he left Plavitz drumming in his imaginary swing band and went through the crawlway, gangly form unfolding like an accordion hatrack in the lower pit and stepping around the upper turret stand to stoop into the bomb bay. It was a tight fit. On the narrow catwalk between the V-shaped bomb racks he hooked up his safety line and held a grab line and pulled the cardboard tags that were sandwiched between the fuses and the bombs in their slanting racks. Eight thousand-pounders, four in each rack. Boney yanked the arming pin from the back of each bomb.

The catwalk between the bomb racks was nine inches wide, and the bomb bay doors above which Boney balanced his spindly frame would not hold a man's weight. If he fell on them without his safety line hooked up he would go right through. For all the expression on Boney's face he might as well have been playing checkers.

* * * * *

In the cramped radio compartment behind the bomb bay Shorty sat on his swivel chair before the radio stack, listening for transmissions from the lead bomber and scanning for the Armed Services Radio station. Taped to the opened and secured door was a hand-lettered sign: *Shorty's Shack: ON THE AIR.*

Shorty frowned at the crackling static. He cupped a hand against his headset and tried the Axis frequencies, but there was nothing all across the band.

* * * * *

In the waist, behind the radio compartment, Garrett and Everett checked their Browning machine guns and ammo boxes. The gun ports were offset so that the two gunners stood side by side while firing. The two big men had worked together enough that they didn't knock each other down when shooting back at enemy fighters, but they still got in each other's way, yelling and giving one another thirty kinds of hell.

* * * * *

Between the waist gunners and the little radio compartment, Martin knelt before the ball turret assembly bulging from the floor and fitted a Z-shaped crank into its slot. He hand-cranked the ball until the twin .50s were pointed straight down and the tiny hatch slid into view. He set the brake and turned and tapped Everett on the shoulder and pointed down. Wind through the gun ports, along with the vibration and drone of four twelve-hundred-horsepower engines, made normal conversation nearly impossible. Everett nodded and stepped closer to the turret.

Martin opened the hatch and looked down into the unbelievably small space. Two miles below, the dark English Channel sparkled through the plexiglas. The last time Martin had climbed into a ball turret was on the *Ill Wind*.

Everett took hold of the hatch while Martin knelt and reached into the turret and engaged the power clutch by feel. He stood again and nodded at Everett, then climbed down and fitted himself in. His knees were up by his shoulders and he was looking straight down at the English Channel. His position similar to a drowned man floating face-down on the surface. He hooked up his safety strap and yelled an okay. Everett patted his back and said, "Give 'em hell, chief," then sealed the hatch and thumped the turret. The closed hatch was now the upper part of Martin's seat, the only reinforced armor he would have.

Martin plugged in his interphone and put on his oxygen mask and checked the flow indicator. Smell of stale air and rubber. He hung the mask back up and powered up the turret and dialed the interphone to INTER. "Ball gunner checking in," he said.

Captain Farley's voice came over his earphones. *"I read you, Martin. How's the weather down there?"*

Martin glanced out the left windows. "Fog's burning off along the coast," he said. "Clear and sunny over the Channel. Nice day to bomb Germans."

"Roger that. Put her through her paces and keep me posted."

Martin grabbed the controls and pulled back. The turret pitched until he sat upright and the guns were level and facing the rear of the bomber. He checked the rotation: Hands left, and he swiveled right; hands right, and he swung left. The English coastline spun below.

* * * * *

Francis sat on his narrow saddle seat in the tail gunner position with his head sticking up into the angular canopy and watched the world recede before him. He was shoehorned into the back end of the bomber behind the rear wheel, nearly as isolated from the rest of the crew as Martin, and a lot less mobile. He could swivel his twin .50-caliber machine guns, and that was about it. He couldn't see where the bomber was going, or the ground directly below. He'd be able to see German fighters coming at them from the side, but he could only shoot at the ones coming in from behind. Lately those Luftwaffe pilots had taken to head-on charges, and knowing that was going on up front while he sat wedged-in here gave Francis an awful itch between his shoulder blades. It was a heck of a place to find yourself when you had never even seen an airplane till you joined up. He couldn't scratch his own foot if he wanted to.

He got permission to clear his guns. He aimed down and pressed both fire buttons. Loud chuddering drowned out the engine roar behind him, and bright tracer rounds streaked out as Francis swung the barrels left-to-right.

* * * * *

In the ball turret Martin heard Farley's okay to clear guns. He bent forward and crossed his arms to grab the metal rings to either side of his legs. He yanked them and heard the guns charge in front of him. He rotated to three o'clock, tilted toward the water, and fired a quick burst. Tracer rounds drew glowing lines toward the water.

Martin nodded, and then relaxed as best a man could inside an armed beachball with nothing but ten thousand feet of air between himself and the ground. He considered the length of the bomber before and behind him. The spectacular view. Himself inside a bubble pinched off from the world.

Memories of the *Ill Wind* flooded in, and Martin fought to steady his breathing. He fumbled past layers of thick clothing and fished out the leather medicine bag he wore on a thong around his neck. He held it under his nose and closed his eyes and breathed in deep. Whatever smell it used to hold was long gone. Now it only smelled like Martin Proud Horse.

* * * * *

Farley continually checked the instruments as the bomber climbed. At ten thousand feet he told the crew to put on their oxygen masks and check their flight suit connectors. The unpressurized cabin was already very cold. It would get much colder by the time they reached twenty thousand feet. A bare hand lost meat if it touched metal at forty-below. Twenty thousand feet wasn't very far, when you thought about it. Less than four miles. On the ground you could run it in thirty minutes, drive it in three. But go that far straight up and you might as well be on another planet—one where human beings did not belong.

Farley checked in with Plavitz and made minor course corrections as the navigator advised. Come nine a.m. they were right on the money at the assembly point. They met up with the bombers from the Hundred and Second Group out of Covent St. George and began the long, tedious, and nerve-wracking process of forming up into staggered echelons as the group turned east and began to climb. From here through the bomb run they would maintain this formation, wingtip to wingtip. It was dangerous and exhausting flying, but it made for tighter and more accurate bomb patterns, and concentrated the gunners' firepower while decreasing the chance that they would shoot other bombers in the formation. It also made it easier for German artillery to kill two birds with one shell, and for Luftwaffe pilots to create maximum damage with one good strafing run. But bombing missions weren't about getting men back safely. Bombing missions were about dropping bombs.

Ten minutes after the bombers began forming up, Boney reported incoming fighter planes at ten o'clock. The bomb group had picked up their little friends, a squadron of P-47 Thunderbolts that would escort them halfway across Holland—the farthest the fighters' fuel tanks would allow. Soon the front-heavy fighters swarmed like gnats around the bomber echelons, passing close enough that you could clearly see the pilots' goggled faces. The single-seat airplanes seemed small next to the Flying Fortresses, but they had a massive Pratt & Whitney R2800 power plant, and what wasn't engine on those things was gun.

Farley was happy to see them. Plenty of missions had proceeded after weather or some snafu prevented an escort squadron from meeting up with a bomb group, and the results could be pretty ugly.

A lot of bomber pilots swore that flyboys were arrogant and lazy country clubbers who didn't have a taste for the real war, but the truth was that many bomber pilots flew their heavy birds because they had washed out of fighter training. Farley had not. He could have gone on to be a fighter pilot—had even been urged to—but for some reason he had wanted to fly bombers. Perhaps because he had been smitten with the B-17 from the moment he first saw the Y1B-17 prototype in a newsreel. Big and ugly and beautiful and graceful and aggressive all at once. Farley had been seventeen, and even though he'd been an unusual combination of bookish studies and athletic competition—he was captain of both the debate club and the swim team at his high school in Los Angeles—he had a hankering to fly. When the silver bomber with the striped tail flew across the big screen on the *Movietone News* at the Orpheum Theater, Joe Farley had thought, *I'm gonna fly one of those.*

And five years later here he was. But the world above which he now flew his brand-new B-17F was not the world in which he had first wanted to. Careful what you wish for, his father often said.

Farley glanced out the window past Broben. *Fata Morgana* was number-two bomber in the lead echelon, just behind and off the left wing of *Wrecking Crew,* the group leader. Steady Eddie Harris was a good pilot with a first-class crew who'd go to the mat for him. He never took foolish chances and he delivered the goods. More than that, Eddie brought his crews back. A pilot could goose-egg every bombing run, but if he brought his crew back every time, they'd swear he was God's own aviator.

Farley adjusted the trim and tightened up his position. He nodded in satisfaction.

"So how do you like the new crate?" said Broben.

"I think we've got a lot better ride than our last one," Farley replied. In fact he'd known it the second she took to the air. You could talk about response time and climb rates and a hatful of numbers, but the truth could not be said in words or math, and it was something he'd never remotely felt flying the *Voice.* A kind of kinship. The *Fata Morgana* was never going to handle like a sports

54

car, but she wasn't a wrestling match, either.

The temperature gauge showed -30° Fahrenheit. Farley snugged his gloves and nodded at Broben, and Jerry got on the horn. "Let me hear you, fellas," he said.

The crew reported in, everything okay. Boney had the best forward view, in the bomber's station below and ahead of Farley and Broben, and he reported coastline ahead.

"That'd be Holland," said Plavitz. *"Right on time."*

"Hey, Shorty," came Garrett's voice, *"where's the music?"*

"There's some kind of magnetic disturbance in the ionosphere," said Shorty. *"Even the static sounds funny."*

"I love it when he talks dirty," said Everett.

"It means we're a little under the weather, *ya know,"* Shorty said.

"Gosh," said Francis, *"he sounds just like Jack Benny on the headphones."*

"Golly jeepers," said Broben, making fun of Francis' homespun talk, *"who'da thought we'd get to bomb Germany with a gosh-wow Hollywood celebrity?"*

"Don't encourage him," said Plavitz.

The bomber droned on over Holland. Still no antiaircraft fire. Farley checked the instruments, his position in the formation, the group's position on the map, the fighter escort. He scanned the clear sky for enemy aircraft.

"No one up here but us chickens," Broben said.

Farley nodded. He reached down and dialed up the suit heat and then knocked spit from his oxygen mask before it could freeze and block the on-demand valve.

"Shorty, isn't there anything we can listen to?" Everett pleaded. *"I'm about ready to cheer for Axis Sally."*

Farley muted his throat mike. "Sometimes," he told Broben, "I find out more about our mission from her than I do from our briefings."

Broben nodded. "I don't know how they do it. I'd sure like five minutes alone with whoever that dame gets her information from."

"I hear they've got one out in the Pacific islands, too. Tokyo Rose."

"You know how I know we're gonna win this war?" Broben asked.

"Because we're right and we've got God on our side?"

"Shit. We're gonna win because *they* play *our* records. Nobody plays theirs."

"Well, you can only listen to Wagner so many times."

Broben squinted. "You sure talk smart for an iron jockey."

"I prefer to think of myself as a philosopher on wings."

Broben cracked up.

* * * * *

Just past the German border their fighter escort had to turn back. The Thunderbolts waggled their wings and peeled off to head due west, canopies flashing in the noonday sun. Farley was sorry to see them go. Supposedly the Army was working on a long-range fighter. He wished they'd hurry up about it.

With the fighters gone the mood changed in the bomber. Everybody knew they were on their own now. Next crew check there were no wisecracks, no jokes. Just *"Navigator checking in," "Bombardier here,"* and the rest. Germany lay below them now and they had to get across most of it to reach their target.

A thought made Farley frown. He thumbed the "talk" button again. "Pilot to radio operator. Have you caught any ship-to-ship?"

"Frying bacon across the dial. It's been radio silence since we were over France, anyway."

"Roger, Shorty. Keep me posted if anything changes."

"Will do."

Everett's voice came on the interphone. *"Anybody heard any new jokes? Since there's no music or anything."*

"I got one," said Francis. He started to tell the one about the German paratroopers, but everyone yelled the punchline—*Zat vass ze*

pilot!—before he got two lines in. *"Gee whiz,"* he complained, *"a fella can't get two shakes in with you guys."*

"We better be nice to Francis, or he won't go to the next war with us," said Garrett.

"Anyone want to read a letter from his girlfriend?" Everett persisted. *"Tell a good story? I'm dying here."*

"Martin has a story I think we all want to hear," said Broben.

Farley looked at him sharply.

"I do?" said Martin.

"Sure you do," said Broben. *"The guy who made it off the* Ill Wind *has to have a story."*

"Beechnut was on the Ill Wind*?"* Everett asked.

"I heard they were all dead on board," said Plavitz.

"I heard that was all bunk," said Garrett.

"Why don't we let the guy who was there tell it?" asked Broben.

Farley muted his mike. "What the hell are you doing?" he asked.

"I'm giving him a chance to come clean. Anything goes wrong today and these guys find out our belly gunner was on the *Ill Wind,* they'll eat him alive. And they'll blame you for putting a jonah in the crew."

"There's not much to tell," said Martin. *"The bomber got shot up pretty bad and I jumped. The end."*

"Ill Wind," said Francis. *"Ill Wind. Say, wasn't that the ghost ship that landed in Jordan Abbey? Man, that story gave me the willies."*

"That's where I heard that name!" said Shorty. *"Holy jumping—You were on the ghost bomber, Beech—um, Martin? No fooling?"*

The engines droned for a while before Martin's voice came over the interphone again. *"Yeah, I was belly gunner on her last mission."*

"Well come on, chief, spill it," said Garrett. *"Everything I heard about that crate sounds like stuff we told around the campfire to scare the bejeezus out of each other."*

Shorty made a sound like a creaking door. *"Vell-kum to* Inner Sanctum*,"* he said.

"Can it," said Farley. He scowled at Broben. "How bout it,

Martin?" he asked. "We've all heard a bunch of different stories about it. You want to set the record straight?"

Droning engines filled the long pause.

"I'll set a record, all right," Martin finally said. *"But it'll be anything but straight."*

FOUR:
THE BALL GUNNER'S TALE

It was my eighth mission on the *Ill Wind*. We were bombing a big marshaling yard in Pleitzhaven, lots of oil and materiel, some troop transport. We'd hit it twice before, and the Germans always seemed to get it fixed up pretty quick.

The mission was a little bigger than the runs we'd made before, four squadrons carrying five-hundreds. It's a short run, right by Holland on the German border, but the Germans had it staked out. You could have mapped our route from the flak alone, just about. We took an awful pounding but we made the IP okay and dropped when the lead bomber dropped.

So the eggs are whistling down below me and dropping from the formation all around. They're right on the Aiming Point and it looks like they're going to mess up that railyard pretty good.

The bomb bay doors close in front of me, and Captain Ryan banks us down and picks up speed to run us under their ak-ak bursts, and then *bam,* we take a huge hit on the right side. I thought it was a 105 shell, so I swing around to look for damage. I think I'm gonna see the tail falling off, a broken wing or something, but there's not a mark on her.

Next thing I know it's raining B-17s all around me. I realize the Germans have moved their eighty-eights a lot closer to the railyard this time out, and they're firing almost straight up from the Aiming

Point. Some of their shells set off the bombs that just got dropped, and some of those went off right under the bomb bays and gutted those B-17s like fish. It was awful. I only saw a couple of parachutes. Mostly the bombers just broke apart and fell. We lost about a third of the squadron in less than a minute.

We turned out and got past the flak line and leveled off. We'd just re-formed about ten minutes later when the entire Luftwaffe showed up. There were more bandits than I ever saw at one time before. Me-109s, Focke-Wulf 190s. They didn't engage right away. They paced us out of firing range and then pulled ahead of us. When they were about a mile in front they turned and came at us head-on. They were wing-to-wing in groups of three and four, and they didn't start shooting till they saw the whites of our eyes. I could see them coming, but they were level with us and I couldn't shoot up at them. The only guy who could fire on them was the bombardier, up front, and he just had a thirty-cal, like Boney. That must have been scary as hell. They're coming in side by side, and they're close enough throw rocks at before they start firing, and even if you shoot the pilot his plane's probably going to plow right into you. Take you and your whole ship with him to Valhalla, or wherever. The very last couple of seconds they would open up with those twin .30 cannons. They sounded like a freight train going up a hill.

So this 190 comes in from one o'clock level and opens fire and then rolls off. He's still firing as he goes by. I could feel it stitching down the whole length of the hull, front to back. He's so close I think he'd have clipped us if he hadn't rolled. I had his whole silhouette not fifty feet away from me and I turned and fired, but he was already gone.

They came in one more time like that. This time the captain turned us away before they broke. It gave the navigator and the top turret a shot, but I wasn't expecting the turn and I missed by a mile when the fighter came by.

They peeled off after that. Two suicide charges at every Fortress coming off the bombing run, unload their thirties in a five-second burst, and then gone. They did some serious damage.

My interphone was out and I had no idea what the situation was inside the bomber. The engines weren't smoking up but the right stabilizer was chewed up something awful. You could see the tail waggling; the captain was having to zigzag to go forward. I'm hitting the talk button and saying, "Ball gunner checking in, anybody read me?" There's nothing. If it's just my connection, they'll know next time the captain calls a crew check. If it's the whole interphone, someone'll bang on the ball and I'll bang back.

So I sit tight and do my job. I've got about ten seconds of ammo left and I keep my eyes peeled in case those bandits come back. Pleitzhaven was burning behind us. Two more Fortresses went down, but I couldn't make out which ones. I counted eight parachutes. That's the most helpless feeling in the world, watching that.

After a couple minutes it's pretty clear the *Ill Wind*'s in trouble. The tail waggle's gotten worse, and every once in a while the right wing dips like she wants to roll.

Number Two engine cut out just as we got out over the North Atlantic. You could feel the drag trying to turn us, but the captain got the prop feathered and it wasn't as bad. But now we're out over the water and we're flying slower and losing altitude.

Well, that engine quitting made up my mind. I had to see what was going on upstairs. I could always get back in the turret if I had to, but I sure as hell couldn't always get out. So I rolled the guns straight down and I undid the hatch—and it wouldn't move. I checked the latches and stood into it and felt it give. Well, if it'll move, it'll open. The only place I can brace is the footrests, but at this point I don't give a damn about screwing up the range pedal, so I put my weight into it, and the hatch comes up and all this red just comes dripping down all over me. For a second I start to lose my noodle. Then I realize the hydraulics have been hit, and it's fluid leaking everywhere. But then I think that can't be right, either, because I was just moving the turret around like a carnival ride, no problem.

Something slides off the hatch as I stand up. I'm facing the back of the bomber, and the first thing I see is a line of holes big as dimes along the fuselage. There's light coming in and they're whistling loud as hell. There's a loud roar from up front and a lot of wind rushing through the cabin.

Then I see the blood. It's on the sides, the floor, the ribs. Like someone threw balloons full of red paint. There's a pile of rags up against a bulkhead and I realize it's Charlie Gower, one of our waist gunners. He's frozen solid and the blood everywhere is just red ice.

The bomber jerks and I catch myself on the hatchway, and that's when I see Eugene Walker, our other waist gunner. He must have been firing at the bandit as it came by, because he's shot in the chest. It knocked him back on top of the ball turret, and he's what was blocking my hatch. I've got his blood all over me and I feel like I'm gonna pass out, and I realize I've got to plug into an air tank pronto.

I pretty much fall into the radio room, and Bob Murray's dead at his table with his head on his arm like he's taking a nap. The line of bulletholes runs down the hull right beside him.

I plug into a walkaround and haul it back with me to check on the tail gunner. Past the rear wheel I can see Cantrell on his saddle at the tail gun, so I slide up a little more and I'm looking up at him and his face is blue. There's frost on his eyelashes but not a scratch on him I can see. I think his oxygen feed got cut.

I don't know why, but that gave me the creepy crawlies more than Charlie or Eugene. I guess because Cantrell never even had a clue. He just nodded off. Some people say that's better, and maybe it is. But I still want to be there when it happens.

I slid out of the tail and went up front. There was a lot of wind coming through the ship and it was loud as hell. The whole thing was shaking and shuddering. I got through the bomb bay and saw J.D. there on the floor. He was our flight engineer. Looked like he'd been standing behind the cockpit seats and fell backward and hit his head.

What had probably knocked him off was a hole a yard wide on the left side, near the pilot seat. The wind coming through was so strong I could barely stand up. Captain Ryan and Pepper Thompson were still up there in the cockpit, so I crawled into the nose. Louie Stoddard, our bombardier, was laying up against the plexi, and Ferguson was on the floor by his navigator station. Both of them just shredded. It was awful.

There was nothing I could do, so I backed out of there and climbed up to the cockpit. You could barely hold on, the air was so strong coming through the flak hole. Pepper Thompson had the wheel and he was staring straight ahead. Captain Ryan was just staring.

I yelled out to the captain, but no one could've heard me with all that wind blasting. I leaned down to yell in his ear and I saw that he wasn't even there from the waist down. The flak had just cut him in half. His seat was shredded and there was blood and foam everywhere. So it had to be Pepper Thompson who'd cut the feed to Number Two engine and feathered the prop. We called him Pepper because he poured Tabasco sauce on everything he ate. He was really struggling with the controls and I just stood there for a second. I didn't know if he even knew I was there. I wasn't sure what to do. Finally I put a hand on his shoulder. He nodded but he didn't look back or take his hands off the wheel. I yelled at him that everybody was dead. He just nodded again and said something.

I leaned in close so I could hear him, and that's when I saw about ten inches of metal sticking up out of his right side just as I felt his lips move against my ear. "We're *all* dead," he said.

I swear to god the hair stood up on the back of my head. I've had nightmares about it. His lips moving on my ear. That voice like it didn't even have any breath, telling me *We're* all *dead*.

I told him I'd stay with him but he just shook his head. I didn't need to hear him to know what he said next. He said *jump*.

I told him I'll get you a chute and we'll get you out of here. He kind of smiled at that, and a lot of blood ran out of his mouth. He stared ahead and grabbed the control wheel harder, and I understood that I wasn't going to be taking him anywhere.

We all have good luck charms. We don't talk about them much

because they have power for us and no one else. Pictures of girlfriends, letters from home. Pocket watches. I wear a medicine bag. My grandfather made it for me when I left the reservation. When he gave it to me he said that one day I would fight Wakínyan Tanka, the great bird whose voice is thunder. I can't tell you what's in that bag, but it has things that are part of my home. My people. So a piece of home is always with me. It's connected. Like a radio beacon. So that wherever I go, it'll help me get back home.

So I took off my medicine bag and I put it around Pepper's neck. I told him it would help him on his journey. I thought maybe the *Ill Wind* was the Thunderbird my grandfather meant. Pepper nodded and I put a hand on his shoulder. You don't wish a dead man luck. You say goodbye and you hope his spirit finds its way. So that's what I did.

And then I just climbed down. I grabbed my parachute and a ditch kit and I carried them to the forward hatch. The wind wasn't so bad right behind the radio room bulkhead and I squatted down and opened the hatch and put on the chute. We were up around three thousand feet, and there was nothing below me but a whole lot of North Atlantic. Dark and choppy and cold as hell. It looked hard as metal and I could see whitecaps even from this high up.

I inflated my mae west and grabbed the sides of the hatchway. I don't know why I didn't jump. I wasn't afraid to. Believe me, the idea of staying in that bomber was a lot scarier than jumping into the ocean. But I just watched the water go by underneath me and the wind was roaring through the flak hole like the bomber was screaming. I could feel it shaking all around me. I could feel the dead men all around me, too. Pepper up there looking for a landing no live man could see. Nine guys I'd had breakfast with that morning.

Then the bomber jerked right, and it threw me right out of the hatch. That air was like a wall. It spun me around like you'd throw a doll. I pull the cord and the chute opens and I'm hanging underneath it. I couldn't see the *Ill Wind* because of the canopy, but I could hear her. I still can.

I hadn't tied the raft to me, and it was still up there in the bomber. So I started worrying about what was below me instead of what was above me, because my cruise in the North Atlantic just got a whole lot worse.

Under me's nothing but whitecaps, ten-foot waves. I'm turning, and the coast comes into view—and I can't believe it. There's a boat, dead ahead. A big trawler. Like the bomber just spit me out right over it.

I came down less than a hundred yards away from that boat. The *Bonnie Marie.* Didn't need the raft, the flare gun, none of it. They'd seen the bomber and they saw me jump, so they were ready for me.

That was the coldest water I ever want to be in. I got tangled in my shroud lines, and they had to cut it all off me. I coughed up a gallon of North Sea, but I was on a deck and they were throwing blankets on me and yelling questions in some kind of English I couldn't understand. Someone put a coffee in my hand and someone else poured brandy in it, and I sat on that deck and stared up at the sky.

* * * * *

So the rest of the story comes from Clay Renick, our crew chief. The ground crews were all sweating out the mission back in Jordan Abbey, and finally the squadron started coming back in. Right away they knew it was bad. The ships are limping home like whipped dogs. Shot up, flakked up, smoking, leaking everything. There aren't enough medical teams for all the Fortresses that are shooting off red flares as they come in. The airfield looks like the Fourth of July. *Say Cheese* came in with the whole front bubble blown off. The ground crew are counting bombers, looking for ID numbers or nose art, trying to figure out whose ships are coming in, pedaling out to their birds the second they touch down.

Forty-eight B-17s went out. Thirty-two made it back. The orphan crews stayed on their bikes along the runway, staring up at the sky like they were wishing those bombers back. Like if they just waited long enough they'd show up. And you know, a couple stragglers did come through, toughing it out on two or three engines right above the trees.

Fifteen, twenty minutes after the last one touches down, the orphan crews start looking at each other. It's bad luck to talk about it, and no one wants to be the first guy to head back from the airfield. You don't give up on your ship.

Clay was the one who pointed first. I think he could have picked *Ill Wind* out of a whole sky full of Fortresses just from the sound. He knew those radial engines like a momma knows her baby's breathing. The rest of the crew couldn't see a thing, but he just set his jaw and shook his finger at the treeline and told them to hang on.

And a minute later there she was. The *Ill Wind,* no mistake. She was flying low and her gear was down and she was coming in on one engine. Two, Three, and Four were out and feathered. Right stabilizer just hanging off and the ship not able to fly straight. Flak hole on the left side of the cockpit, shot up like a bum-winged duck on the first day of hunting season.

And no red flare. Clay couldn't believe it. How could a bird get that shot up and not be firing a wounded-on-board flare?

Quarter-mile before the runway her Number One cut out. Clay said it was eerie as hell, watching that big, beat-to-death B-17 come gliding in dead quiet. She was fighting to line up on the runway and when she got it centered she just dropped, bam. Smoke from the wheels and a squeak of rubber and then she's sliding down the runway quiet as a ghost. You could see Captain Ryan and Pepper Thompson in the cockpit, but there was no brake, no crew chutes dragging her to a halt. She drifted off the runway and into the mush, and that's what finally stopped her.

Clay just shook his head when he told me about it. "All them purple-heart wagons limping in," he said, "and here comes the *Ill Wind* on no engines and held together with tape and spit, and she just glides in like a sailboat coming into the dock."

Well, the crew was out there like a shot. Clay was the first one on board. He was supposed to let the medics on first, but he said he just couldn't stand it. Said he knew something was wrong before he even got in the bomber. He was all set to give the captain grief about messing up the aircraft, but it just stopped up in his throat, even before he saw what was in there. Metal was pinging and creaking but there was no other sound. Nothing moved. He said it smelled like a butcher shop.

He came in through the front hatch, which was still open from when I bailed, so right away he saw J.D. there on the floor. He yelled for the medics and went looking around inside to help the wounded. He saw what I'd seen, the whole crew dead from flak and strafing fire.

But Pepper was dead, too. He had ten inches of metal sticking out from between his ribs and he was bone white. His hands were still on the wheel. Clay said he was staring out the windshield like he was still looking for a place to land.

The medics came in and Clay got out of the way. He came out of the bomber shaking his head, and all the air just went out of the ground crew. The *Ill Wind* had landed with no one alive on board, and that just can't happen. There's no place in the world for that to be right. They all stood outside the bomber and stared at it like it had just appeared there out of thin air.

When they took Pepper's body from the bomber, Clay told one of the medics he thought Pepper should get the Distinguished Service Cross for bringing the *Ill Wind* home. The medic looked at him like he was out of his mind. He had one end of the stretcher with Pepper in it and Pepper was frozen in place like he was still in his copilot's seat.

"Sergeant, this man didn't land this aircraft," the medic said.

"Well, the pilot sure didn't do it," Clay told him. "He was cut in two."

"The copilot couldn't have done it either," the medic said. "He's been dead for hours."

Clay told him to his face that he was full of shit. "The man's hands were still on the wheel," he said. He pointed at Pepper on the stretcher. "Hell, they still are."

"His hands were on the wheel," the intern said, "because he's getting *rigor mortis*. Which happens to a body after it's been dead for about three hours."

Clay stared at him. "Then who landed the goddamned ship?" he asked.

The medic shrugged and said, "Maybe it landed itself." And then him and the other medic loaded Pepper's body into the ambulance and went back for the rest of the crew.

Three days later I was back at Jordan Abbey. I got debriefed and I told them everything I've told you. No one said a word to me about me bailing.

The CO came in after my debriefing and said he thought it'd be a good idea if I transferred to Thurgood. He wanted me to know it had nothing to do with anything I'd done, or didn't do. "The real mystery," he said, "is what happened *after* you were off that bomber."

But even so, he told me, half the base had seen that Fortress come back home and land without a living soul on board. And that story was going to hang around my neck no matter where I crewed.

I don't know if it was me he was looking out for or the others, but I figured he had a point either way. So in the barracks I was putting my kit together to leave when Clay came in and gave me back my medicine bag. He said it'd been hanging from Pepper's hand when he found him. I don't know how Clay knew it belonged to me. I guess because, like I said, he knew everything about his bomber.

"One day ten years from now," he told me, "after this goddamn war is over, maybe you and me will meet in a bar somewhere, and you can buy me a beer and tell me how this got in Pepper's hand. But right now I don't want to know. Understand?"

I asked him why not and he said, "Because I'd like to sleep again someday. And I'm pretty sure you telling me what happened on that ship won't help that one goddamn bit."

And you know, I think he was right.

FIVE

The engines droned on for an uncomfortably long time before Farley looked over at Broben and said, "You happy now?"

Broben shrugged. "He tells a good story, I'll give him that."

Farley looked at his copilot a moment. "You're an asshole, Jerry," he said.

The laughter over the interphone was loud.

"You left your mike on, captain," said Garrett.

"Gee, ya think?" said Jack Benny's voice.

"Okay, pipe down," said Farley. "Plavitz, where are we?"

"One sec, captain," said Plavitz.

Farley muted his mike. "Don't sulk, Jer," he said. "It isn't manly."

"I'm not sulking," Broben said brightly. "I'm indispensable. If you didn't have an asshole, you'd be completely full of shit."

Farley barked a laugh.

"Anyway," said Broben, "I'm glad he cleared the air."

Plavitz came back on the interphone. *"Captain, we're almost directly north of Zennhausen. Wrecking Crew should be making her turn any minute now."*

"Time sure flies," said Garrett.

"Stow it," said Farley.

A minute later the lead bomber banked right and Farley immediately followed. The squadrons began their long southward turn in formation.

Farley got on the interphone again. "Time to roll the feature, boys. We're about ten minutes from the IP. Everybody put your work clothes on and do your job and we'll get back home fine."

"I hope you have a story for the ride back, chief," said Broben.

"If we make it out of here," said Martin, *"I'll make up another one."*

* * * * *

Garrett and Everett put on their heavy flak aprons and their helmets. All the gunners checked their guns again, hands clumsy in their thick heated alpaca gloves. The flight deck thermometer showed -30°. The weather was clear all the way to the horizon. Plavitz checked his chart against landmarks on the ground. Boney began calibrating his Norden bombsight.

After the broad turn south the formation tightened up again, and Farley concentrated on keeping the *Fata Morgana* straight and level and just off the leader's left wing. Broben reported the instrument readings. In their turrets Martin and Wen scanned the sky for bandits. In the tail Francis did the same.

The first flak bursts appeared about five miles off the Initial Point, wisps of black ink along an even line. The firing pattern took shape like a connect-the-dots drawing of a shoebox thousands of feet long. Each black wisp a blast of hurtling metal shards. The flak intensified, and in seconds the barrage became the thickest concentration of flak Farley had ever seen, cottony black smears overlapping to form a box of smoke so thick that he could not see beyond it. Red detonations lit the murk.

"Shit, you think they knew we were coming?" Broben asked.

"I think they're gonna know we were here," Farley replied. He looked away from the thickening barrage ahead of them. "It's not a girl I know," he told Broben.

Broben looked at him as if he'd sprouted antlers. "It's what?"

"Not a girl I know." Orange light lit Farley's face.

"Don't go flak-happy on me, Joe. Not now. I'm begging you here."

The cockpit shook from concussions dead ahead.

"The nose art," said Farley. "It's not a real girl. I see her in my head sometimes. In my dreams. She looks just like that."

"Ohhh-kay."

Farley shrugged. "I thought she'd be good luck," he said.

"Well I'll be goddamned. College Joe Farley is just as superstitious as the rest of us monkeys." Broben flinched at a blast ahead.

"If you tell anybody, I'll fly your side of the bomber into a steeple."

"It's about the only way you could get me into a church."

"Switching to automatic pilot," said Farley. "Asshole."

Now the scene before them was a demented artist's landscape of a mad god's Hell. A massive floating bin of coalblack smoke that seethed with sullen red pulses as more 88 shells detonated within its lethal demarcations.

"Here we go," said Farley.

Four dozen Flying Fortresses in tight formation hurled themselves into that ravenous and indiscriminate maw. *Fata Morgana* began to buffet as the sunlight dimmed and the smell of cordite filled the freezing air. They flew within a thunder now, constant hammer-blows of detonating flak in all directions. A sound like gravel thrown against the fuselage.

Farley's head turned like a man watching a tennis match as he eyed the instruments and the *Wrecking Crew* in front of them just off the right wing. The lead B-17 shook with the artillery shells' concussion, and Farley saw that she had already taken hits along her left side.

* * * * *

Garrett and Everett were hunkered down in the waist. Enemy fighters would not engage around the flak pattern, and there was little for the gunners to do but ride it out. Outside the thin skin of the bomber was the sound of battling Titans, mindless fury bent on their destruction.

A hunk of jagged metal punched through the hull by Everett's right

71

boot, ricocheted off a ceiling spar, and shot out the window on the other side not a foot from Garrett's head. Neither gunner even saw it.

* * * * *

Someone screamed in Farley's headphones. It sounded like Shorty, and Farley was about to order Garrett to the radio room when Shorty's voice came on the interphone.

"Radio operator here. I'm all right. I got some kind of awful static on the radio. Felt like someone stabbed me in the ear."

"Roger," said Farley. "Navigator?"

"Two minutes to the IP," Plavitz said immediately. *"The flak's so thick I'm losing ground markers."*

"Bombardier?"

"I'm having trouble adjusting the bombsight," Boney reported. *"The gyros are acting funny."*

"Well, you better unfunny 'em. I need to hand this crate over to you in about a minute."

"Working on it."

A shell burst by their right side and knocked forty-eight thousand pounds of laden bomber to the left like a bathtub duck.

Broben sat up straight and said, simply, "Joe."

Farley glanced at his copilot and his copilot was looking wide-eyed out the right window.

"They lost the tail," Broben said woodenly.

Just ahead and to the right the *Wrecking Crew*'s nose lifted and the massive Fortress planed up into the wind. Farley saw what was coming and yanked back on the yoke and turned the control wheel to ten o'clock and prayed he'd acted fast enough.

The *Wrecking Crew* went tail-down. The enormous metal cross of her hung in the air in front of them, then dropped. Farley had time to see the on-end bomber sliding back toward them before the *Morgana* responded to his maneuver and lifted up and banked left, taking the plunging bomber out of view and leaving him gritting his teeth and white-knuckling the wheel as he waited to feel an impact.

* * * * *

In the ball turret Martin hung in the midst of exploding flak shells and watched the *Wrecking Crew* take a direct hit from an 88 shell that sheared off the left elevator and half the vertical stabilizer. The tail immediately dropped and kept dropping. The crippled fortress stood in cross section above and ahead of the *Fata Morgana*, then dropped toward her flight path.

"No," said Martin. "No no no no."

The *Morgana*'s nose lifted and the bomber veered left and Martin hung within an impossible panorama of a Flying Fortress crucified in the air before him. He sped toward it like a suicidal bird toward a building. The mortally wounded bomber grew larger as it slid down the sky, grew and dropped until Martin saw red smeared across the cockpit window, dropped below the *Fata Morgana* as Martin pitched his turret until he stared straight down into the front bubble not thirty feet away, stared down at the bombardier pinned to the bubble by the plummeting craft, close enough to see the certain knowledge in the doomed man's face as the massive bomber dropped down tailfirst like a sinking ocean liner corkscrewing to the bottom twenty thousand lethal feet below. Down until the *Wrecking Crew* was swallowed by the lighting clouds of detonating flak that had destroyed her.

* * * * *

There were no parachutes.

"Plavitz, get us back on the run." Farley glanced over to see how

Broben was holding up and Broben looked back. Ashen-faced but okay. "Boney, you're lead bombardier now," Farley said. "Are we on or not?"

"The gyros won't spin." As ever, Boney sounded as if he could have been taking down a phone message. *"It doesn't make sense."*

"Boney—"

"Switching to manual," said Boney. *"Give me the aircraft."*

"Hold on. Plavitz?"

"My compass looks like a roulette wheel," said Plavitz. *"I got no landmarks to go by in this chimney."*

"I don't care if you have to drop crumbs. Get us back on the run." Farley muted his mike and glanced at Broben. "Could the Germans be doing this?"

"Knock out the compass, the radio, and the gyros?" Broben shook his head. "Brother, if they can do that, then we're all screwed."

"Navigator to pilot," Plavitz broke in. *"Right ten degrees."*

Farley repeated the instructions and turned the bomber. The flak grew thicker as they neared the target. The ship rocked with the concussions and the shrapnel slammed the hull.

Broben glanced at the altimeter. "Up five hundred," he said.

Farley pulled back on the yoke. Bright red flash of bursting shell outside. The left window starred but held. Farley tried not to flinch. Flinching wouldn't do any good. You couldn't evade this, you couldn't outrun this. You sat there and you took it.

"The formation's following us," Francis reported from the tail gunner position. *"B-17 going down at six o'clock. She's on fire. I see three parachutes. Four. I think it's the* Dollar Short.*"*

"Left five," said Plavitz.

"Left five, roger," said Farley.

"You're on rails, captain," the navigator said.

Farley hit the automatic pilot and flipped the controls to the bombardier station. "Pilot to bombardier. You have the aircraft, Boney."

"Bombardier to pilot. I have the aircraft," Boney confirmed.

In the top turret Wen saw a bomber in the flight group take a direct hit on the Number Four engine. The bomber veered, narrowly missing the front Fortress in its echelon, and dove.

"*B-17 hit at six o'clock,*" he said. "*They've lost their Number Four.*"

"*Copilot to flight engineer. Which bomber, Wen?*"

"*Can't see. She's under control but the engine's on fire. They're off the run for sure. I'm heading to the bomb bay to monitor the drop.*" Wen hooked his oxygen line to a walkaround tank and climbed down.

At his navigator's table behind Boney, Plavitz looked out through the two square ports on the left side of the nose. Engines One and Two looked good. He strained to see the ground through the veil of flak smoke. Plavitz made out wooded countryside ... low white concrete buildings and straight gray service roads ... a railroad line to the right. He looked down at his recon map and thumbed his throat mike. "*Holy moly,*" he said, "*we're right on the button.*"

Timpani rumbled all around them. The *Morgana* shuddered.

"*Looks good,*" said Boney. He stared through the bombsight as his left hand uncapped the red drop button. "*Lining up. Opening bomb bay doors.*"

In the ball turret Martin turned to twelve o'clock and watched the doors swing down in front of him. Sudden turbulence jostled him. Behind him the trailing B-17s in the flight group would be opening their bomb bay doors as well.

Martin glanced down. Through the flak smoke he saw rhythmic flashes of antiaircraft guns firing nearly five miles below. The concrete sprawl of the munitions factory just ahead. *Here we go,* he thought.

In the copilot seat Broben pulled the Very pistol from behind the pilot's seat and fitted it with a fat shell. He put a hand on the right-side window and held the gun ready. "*Copilot to bombardier, ready with the signal,*" he said.

In the nose bubble Boney hunched over the Norden, right hand calibrating. In the sights a long white concrete building drifted into view. "*I'm on the AP,*" Boney reported. He turned the dial a notch and pressed the red button. "*Bombs away,*" he said.

Broben opened the window six inches and stuck out the flare gun and pulled the trigger. *"Bomb drop signal fired,"* he said.

Seven heavy bombs dropped from *Fata Morgana*'s belly in twin columns, waggling like mindless swimming tadpoles and whistling lewdly as gravity pulled them toward their wholesale annihilation. Farley felt the bomber lift half a foot as the payload dropped.

"Flight engineer here," said Wen. *"One bomb still in the rack. Right side."*

"Boney, free that rack up," Farley ordered. "Plavitz, give me a secondary target."

"Right away, captain," Plavitz said.

Broben shook his head. Farley saw him mouth *Shit.*

"The railyard's just off our current heading," Plavitz came back. *"Turn right five degrees."*

"It'll put us out of the formation," Broben told Farley.

"Five degrees out, five back. Unless you want to come in at Thurgood with a thousand pounds of bomb in our belly."

"Drop it over the Channel."

Farley looked grim. "Only if I can't drop it here first." He turned the bomber and pressed his mike. "Boney, what's the status on that orphan?"

"He's jumping up and down on it, cap," Wen reported.

Broben rolled his eyes, and Farley couldn't help smirking at the image of the lanky and serious bombardier stomping on the stubborn bomb like a man tamping down a dirt-filled hole.

"Roger," Farley said. "Be sure just the bomb drops out, all right?"

* * * * *

Martin watched the area around the concrete buildings far below erupt with smoke. He strained to see if any bombs scored direct hits on the buildings themselves, but they were quickly engulfed in roiling columns of gray smoke that climbed skyward.

"Ball gunner here," he said. "I saw hits on the Aiming Point, but that thing should have gone off like a powderkeg. I don't think we—"

The back end of the bomber slewed to the left and Martin heard a thunderclap behind him.

"We're hit," Everett's voice yelled in his headset.

* * * * *

"Tail gunner, report," said Farley. He tried to bank right and suddenly the bomber didn't want to go. The others were yelling on the interphone and he told them to can it and again ordered Francis to report. The tail gunner didn't reply.

"Wen, get back there."

"On my way," said Wen.

Now Farley had to muscle the control wheel to keep her from veering right. That dive once started would become a giant arc that slammed into the world five miles below. Farley didn't intend to give it the opportunity. "Jerry, give me some elbow grease here," he said.

Broben grabbed his own control wheel. "Holy crap," he said. "Right elevator?"

"Feels like," said Farley.

"Jesus Christ, we're two for two." Broben shook his head. "What god of flying did we piss off?"

The wheel felt alive in Farley's hands as it pushed against him. His forearms ached from the struggle. The bomber shot from that remorseless country of flak and all grew bright. Farley blinked at the sudden stinging in his eyes. He wanted to put on his Polaroids but he didn't dare let go the wheel.

"Flight engineer to pilot," came Wen's tight Southern drawl. *"The rear canopy took a bad hit, the whole thing's shattered. There's a lot of debris and I can't get back there to see what the damage is. I don't see how Francis could've made it."*

"Are we on fire?"

"Don't look like it."

"Roger. Shorty, get Boney out of the bay and tell him to close the doors. We'll dump that last bomb over the—"

"Bandits, eight o'clock level," called Garrett.

In the ball turret Martin swung to eight o'clock and saw black specks in formation just above the horizon. *"Confirmed,"* he said. *"There's dozens of them."*

"Wen, forget the tail and get up top," said Farley. "They'll come at us from behind when they see the damage." Farley glanced at the instruments. The azimuth indicator was cartwheeling. "Navigator, what's our position?"

"Compass is still spinning like a top," Plavitz reported. *"Looking at the rail line ... we're headed southwest. Right fifteen degrees, captain."*

"Right fifteen, roger."

"Easier said than done," said Broben as he helped Farley manhandle the controls. Behind him Wen clambered into the top turret.

"Bombardier to pilot," Boney said. *"Closing bomb bay doors. One still in the rack."*

"Roger," Farley said.

"What the holy hell?" came Everett's voice. *"Can you see the flak field, captain?"*

Farley looked past Broben. *Fata Morgana* was nosing down as she arced around the flak field. Farley saw other bombers in the flight group emerging from the flak in formation, some damaged, some trailing smoke, but nothing especially—no, wait. There was something odd about the flak field itself. At the bottom of the box, the smoke was being drawn down and condensing, like water down a drain.

Farley tabled it for now. They were no longer in the middle of it, so he didn't give a damn if the flak field started dancing and playing "The Star Spangled Banner." They had bigger fish to fry right now. "What's the story on those bandits?" he asked.

"Still closing," said Martin. *"I'd say half a minute out. They're—*shit!"

"Ball gunner, report. You hit, Martin?"

"Something just shocked me. I've got some kind of short circuit here."

"Unplug your suit," said Broben.

"I did, but I can still feel it."

"Well, try ... out ... tight."

Farley glanced at Broben and yanked down his oxygen mask. "Your mike connection's loose," he told him.

Broben took a hand off the wheel and worked the throat-mike plug. *"How ... out ... ow?"*

Farley shook his head.

"Cap—" from Shorty. *"There's ... prob ... elec—"*

Broben snatched off his headset. "Son of a bitch!" he yelled. "I got shocked."

Farley frowned. He held the wheel with one hand and clamped the other under his arm to pull off one of his wool-lined gloves and the thin Rayon glove beneath. The cockpit air felt like ice. He tapped the throttle with a bare finger—and *saw* the bluewhite flash just before he felt the shock.

He glanced at the instruments as he put his gloves back on. The azimuth indicator was rolling like a hamster wheel. Every level indicator was topped—oil, manifold, fuel, batteries.

"We're picking up some kind of static electricity," Farley said. "Everybody keep your gloves on and be careful what you touch."

Broben pointed to his throat and shook his head. The interphone was out.

Then Farley felt the drumming of two sets of twin .50s as Martin and Wen began to fire.

* * * * *

The interphone went dead and Martin realized that there would be no coordinating with the crew on targets. And no help getting out of the ball. He was as isolated as he could get. Procedure now was to shoot at anything that moved and spoke German. But even as he worked the range finder pedal and sighted on the closing fighters and felt his thumbs slide above the red fire buttons, he could not rid himself of the memory of the *Ill Wind*, of an image of the crew above him all dead at their stations, the *Fata Morgana* a ghost ship sailing Martin toward the landing he'd evaded once before.

For a few seconds the world dissolved. Martin had seen horses walleyed and crazed but until that moment he had not understood that *blind fear* could be a literal truth. And then it cleared and he was screaming as both thumbs mashed the fire button at the Bf 109 fighter closing on the bomber's tail so straight and fast it looked like the son of a bitch was going to ram them.

Above him the bomber began to shake. The fuselage was ringing like a bell.

Martin's tracer rounds were falling short. The bandit was still out of range. Martin's suit was still unplugged and he couldn't feel his feet. Frostbite would be the least of his worries if he didn't smear this joker.

The German pilot would likely fire a one-second burst at the last possible moment and then veer off. The Messerschmitt was flying level behind the bomber because the tail gun was no longer a threat. Two others hung back in formation behind it, waiting their turn. Martin could not fire upward and Wen, in the top turret, could not fire down. The bastards were going to be hard to hit.

The yellow-nosed fighter in the lead began to glow as if some powerful spotlight were being trained on it.

The bomber shuddered so violently that Martin could not get the bandit in his sights. The ringing grew louder, and underneath it rose a deep thrumming that shook Martin's bones. A sudden migraine throbbed in time with whatever rhythm made the bomber tremble. Bluewhite lines glowed along the turret framework. Through his little window Martin saw the single-engine fighter lined in lightning.

The bomber bucked so hard that Martin thought they had slammed into something. Martin tasted blood and heard gurgling in his oxygen mask. He yanked it down and felt warm blood turn to frost upon his face. His nose was bleeding. If it froze, it would block the hose and he would die. He eyed the closing bandit as he banged blood from his mask.

* * * * *

Farley and Broben saw it at the same time. Dead ahead the flak-smoke funnel Everett had spotted drained down to an abrupt ending, a shaded pencil drawing suddenly erased at its base. Colors flickered at the bottom of the truncated cone, yellow flashes and bluewhite lightning, dull reds pulsing like a wound, a glowing violet outline that was somehow dark and bright at the same time. It hurt to look at but the two men could not look away.

Farley and Broben were fighting to level the aircraft. Their arm muscles felt like they were being squeezed in a blood-pressure cuff. Crackling bluewhite outlines traced the F-shaped throttle handles, tabletop lightning that grew to filigree the cabin. Farley felt the hairs on the back of his neck stand up, felt a sudden panicked urge to run, smelled sharp metal. The hull began to thrum around them like an oscillating fan thrown out of balance.

Ahead of them a hole yawned open in the sky.

Farley's head ached with a sudden piercing migraine. Warm wetness filled his oxygen mask and quickly grew painfully cold. He whipped off his mask and banged it against the seat to knock out the bloody slush, then scraped the frost of blood from his face.

Broben was bad off. His head lolled and his eyes rolled back and bright blood crystals rimmed his rubber mask. Farley spat out blood and put his oxygen mask back on and pulled off Broben's. He set it on Broben's lap and slapped his face. Jerry's head went straight and his eyes focused. He nodded at Farley and banged blood chunks out of his mask and put it back on and grabbed the controls.

81

Both men fought to steer the bomber but the ship would not respond. Farley tried to push the yoke to dive beneath the coruscating maw before them in the air but the yoke would not move. The bomber was a tiny bug drawn down a swirling drain.

Farley jabbed the button for the bail-out bell. Nothing happened. The thing before them pulsed with purple light that shot dull pain into Farley's eyes. His splitting headache throbbed in time.

This is what killed the gyros. This thing fried the radio and screwed the compass. And now it wants us. Farley thought it was some kind of storm and he thought it was a weapon and he thought it was alive and he thought all three were true.

Now the yoke shook in his hands as the bomber bucked like a marlin on a hook. Farley yelled and Broben yelled, but Farley couldn't even hear himself against the resonating thrum that felt like something pushing out within his chest.

I won't let you kill me, Farley raged. *Not me. Not my men. Not my ship.*

Fata Morgana and her ten crew and one pursuer dove into that awful gullet—

SIX

—and crossed over.

* * * * *

The engines died. The instruments died. The controls did not respond.

All went quiet in the cockpit.

Farley's migraine vanished. His stomach lurched as if the ship were in a power dive. He lowered his oxygen mask and blew blood out his nose. The red spray broke apart to form bright globules that floated in the bluelit cockpit.

An arclight glow came from everywhere. There were no shadows. Beyond the windshield all was white.

The recon map floated in the air above the instrument panel.

Farley looked at Broben and jerked back in his seat. Bright-red blood crystals glinted on the copilot's face around his oxygen mask. Above the frozen blood his eyes looked sunken and hollow and his skin was luminous. Through it Farley saw the bone of Broben's skull.

I've been hit, he thought. *This is what you see before the lights go out. What everyone sees who ever lived. No evading, no outrunning. You sit there and you take it. We're all dead.*

83

* * * * *

Squadron Commander Hauptmann Adler opened fire as the American bomber in front of him flew into the whiteout tunnel in the sky. The violet-edged opening irised shut on his Messerschmitt and sheared it in two at the instrument panel.

Adler stared stunned beyond the telling at the sudden vista before him. The front of his aircraft was gone. Propeller, cowling, engine, leading edge of both wings—simply *gone.*

His thumb still rested on the fire button. Freezing air screamed into a cockpit inexplicably open to the sky in front of him.

The fighter nosed up and began to spin.

Adler unbuckled himself and pushed forward and stepped out of his plane as if stepping from a city bus. Windblast knocked him backward and he tumbled. He yanked his parachute cord and then realized what he'd done.

The drag line shot up and the chute deployed. Adler was yanked like a marionette. He hung in air alive with flak and fighters and receding bombers. Freezing and without oxygen. His country five long drifting miles down below his boots.

* * * * *

Inside the silent tunnel the front end of the Messerschmitt began to tumble on two axes in the weightless white, propeller still turning, bright metal edges of severed engine and yellow cowling glinting where they had been cleanly cut. Spilling fluids separated into drifting spheres.

Far ahead the heavy bomber *Fata Morgana* hurtled mindless and unpowered through the weightless void, speeding without motion across a span that was not space. A twenty-ton projectile fired from the world to pierce a membrane unimaginably vast, immeasurably thin, imperceptible because it did not exist by any marker for determining existence.

And yet. And yet.

Fata Morgana hurtled mindless and unpowered across that barrier—

PART TWO: THE DETOUR

SEVEN

—and out the other side.

* * * * *

The sky went dark. The floating bloodpearls splashed down. Air rushed through the fuselage. *Fata Morgana* pitched forward and began to dive.

* * * * *

Farley pulled back on the yoke and the ship responded. The damaged elevator was still monkey-wrenching everything, and he kept the bomber in a shallow dive. He glanced at the panel as Broben toggled the batteries. Every indicator was zeroed out.

"Jerry," Farley said calmly, "give me auxiliaries and see if you can restart Number One."

Broben flicked the auxiliary generator and got no light at all, red or green. "Negative," he said.

"Feather the props."

Broben tried to lock the blades in place and pivot them edge-forward to reduce drag. None of the propellers would respond. "No soap, Joe," he said.

"Do we have any lights on the board at all?" Farley asked.

Broben surveyed the main panel, the center console, the overheads. "Negative."

"Okay, so no power and no hydraulics." He looked at his copilot. "Unless we get a restart we'll be deadsticking this brick in about five minutes."

"You looked out a window lately?" asked Broben.

Farley looked out the window. The sky was jet black shot with hard unwinking stars, yet the sun was visible as a harsh white circle like a spotlight in the sky. It looked like what Farley imagined outer space looked like.

The bomber flew above an enormous jagged canyon that looked like a crack in the foundation of the world. The crevice walls were sharp-edged and obsidian black, descending to a valley floor in shadow far below.

"It looks like we blew up all of Germany," said Broben. Farley didn't look away from the window as he asked, "Altimeter working?"

"Hey, it is!" said Broben.

"Fuel?"

"Just over fifty percent."

Farley nodded absently. "So everything electrical got knocked out. Fuel gauge is mechanical and the altimeter works on air pressure. What's our altitude?"

"Sixteen five."

Farley frowned. "That plateau can't be four thousand feet below us. Where the hell are we?"

He turned his head and raised his voice. "Wen, you back there?" With the engines out, buffeting wind and creaking metal was all the noise there was.

Wen climbed down from the top turret and stood in the pit behind Farley and Broben. The bottom of his face was streaked where he'd wiped blood from his nose. "Here, boss," he said.

"Tell Everett to crank the turret and get Martin out of there," Farley ordered. "You get the gear crank and start winding the wheels down when I give the word. Get some help with it. And send Shorty up here."

"I best check out that rear wheel."

"Get to it."

"You got it, cap." Wen dropped down into the lower cockpit.

"What the living hell just happened to us, Joe?" said Broben.

"No idea. But it's still happening, and I need you in the game. All right?"

Broben nodded. "I'm in," he said.

"Good man." Farley glanced out the window again. Everywhere he looked the ground was black and featureless as a sheet of smoked glass. The canyon directly below was a darker crack, some violent interruption in what otherwise would have been a vast smooth plain.

"You see anything out there?" Farley asked.

Broben shook his head. "Looks like an eight-ball," he said.

"I'm gonna try for the canyon, then," said Farley. "Maybe there's a river on the valley floor where we can ditch. Or maybe it opens out into a broader space. In any case it'll buy time."

"Hell of a gamble," said Broben.

"If we land on that plain we'll still be at twelve thousand feet. You see anything to live on down there? Any objective to reach?"

"I don't even see a rock."

"All right, then."

The bomber began to buffet as it caught updrafts spilling over the sheer cliff tops. *Fata Morgana* descended silent as a balsa glider into the enormous crooked canyon. The fissure looked to be about a mile wide. The bottom lay in shadow and Farley saw no gleam of water. He kept the aircraft centered between the sheer cliff walls and muscled her along the sharp contours.

Shorty stuck his head up from the lower cockpit. He was carrying the second of their two walkaround oxygen bottles. He lowered his mask and said, "Radio's out, captain."

"So's everything else," said Farley. "You're my relay, got it?"

Shorty swallowed. "Got it," he said.

"Tell Boney and Plavitz to stay in the nose and look for a place to land. We're coming in unpowered, so we're gonna need some room. Jerry, call out altitude."

Shorty nodded. He relayed Farley's order, breath smoking in the freezing air, while Jerry announced their altitude as fifteen thousand.

At his desk behind the bombardier station in the nose, Plavitz looked up from his charts and compass and lowered his oxygen mask. "Do we have any idea where the hell we are?" he yelled.

Shorty looked up at the command seats. "Navigator says he can't get a fix on our position," he said.

"It doesn't matter where we are," said Farley. "We're landing on it."

"Fourteen five," said Broben.

Shorty saw Everett undog the hatch and swing it back. Martin struggled out and Everett helped him into the cabin. "Martin's out of the ball turret," Shorty called up.

"Fourteen," said Broben.

"Tell Martin to get on the oxy feed in the radio room and stay put," said Farley. "Tell Everett to seal the turret and crank it till the guns are level. Ask Wen if that rear wheel's gonna lower."

Shorty relayed the orders calmly but with growing horror at their predicament.

"Thirteen five," said Broben.

"Bombardier wants to blow the Norden," relayed Shorty. "Navigator sees lights ahead."

"Affirmative on the Norden, but wait till we're at a thousand feet. Some detail on the lights would be nice."

Shorty felt faint and realized his face was numb with cold. He had to remember to keep using the walkaround. "He says it's green pinprick lights on the valley floor in the far distance straight ahead," he replied. "He doesn't think it's an airfield."

"Thirteen thousand," said Broben.

Farley held the bomber level as he could to keep the glide ratio as high as possible. More speed would give him more control, but would also put them on the ground sooner. Luckily a steady updraft of warm air from the valley floor was helping to keep their glide path shallow.

The cockpit darkened as the bomber descended into shadow. The stark sky now a crooked path between black borders of mountain-high cliffs.

"Twelve," said Broben.

A few miles ahead the dark edges of the massive cliffs framed a large open area, and Farley thought he could make out tiny pale-green lights in the far distance on the opposite side. Plavitz had good eyes.

They were going to break out into the open area at around eleven thousand feet. Another stroke of luck. The surface would be sunlit and Farley would be able to order the crew off oxygen and get the landing gear cranked down while he found a place to set her down. He hadn't relished setting twenty tons of aircraft on the floor of a pitch-black canyon on zero engines, no lights, and an unexploded thousand-pound bomb stuck in the bay.

At eleven thousand feet they broke into the open and everything went to shit.

Vortex winds that curled around the fissure entrance assailed the heavy bomber. Farley fought for control. The aircraft banked a sharp right and Farley felt the right elevator barely hanging on. He sailed her in a wide right turn and straightened out and then had to take her left because more cliffs rose dead ahead. The open area in which they now glided was a vast bowl ringed by sheer, planed walls with jagged peaks. A circular mountain range. In the center of the bowl rose a conical mound with a flattened top.

"Navigator says negative on a landing site so far," reported Shorty. "Bombardier says we're in a bomb crater."

Broben looked back at Shorty. "Bomb crater? This thing must be ten miles wide."

Shorty shrugged. "It's what he said."

Broben looked at the altimeter. "Nine five," he said. "Those turns were expensive."

"Everybody off oxygen," said Farley. "Get those wheels down."

He glanced at Broben as Shorty relayed the order. "It's going to be close," he said.

Broben nodded. It would take several minutes for a team working furiously with the hand crank to lower the landing gear one at a time. "When isn't it?" he said.

"We're still flying and we're still in one piece," Farley pointed out.

"Well, look whose glass is half full."

"Look who still has a glass."

Broben snorted. "You win."

Farley nodded at the front window. "Unless you have any better ideas, I'm heading for Plavitz's lights on the other side of the bowl there."

"All my better ideas involve being somewhere else right now."

"Roger that."

Shorty popped up again. "Martin says there's a bandit shadowing us at eight o'clock level," he said.

"You gotta be kidding me," said Broben.

Through the control wheel Farley felt a faint shudder. The slowly lowering landing gear was adding drag.

"Get Martin on a waist gun and tell Boney to get in the top turret," Farley ordered. "If it's not one of ours, it's history, got it?"

"Seven thousand," Broben said.

"And tell Wen I need an engine, dammit." Farley steered the bomber across the enormous bowl while Shorty relayed his orders. The surface looked rippled in places, waves hardened into rock formations splashed out from a common center. A crater? Ten miles wide? More like the caldera of some inconceivably large volcano. But this was no gouged mountain, it was a huge hole ripped out of a vast plain and radiating cracks bigger than the Grand Canyon.

He heard Boney climb into the top turret stand behind him.

Reflections played off the front windshield, and Farley realized he was looking at a shimmering column of air above the shadowed center of the crater. It looked the same as the disturbance in the air beneath the flak field above Zennhausen, and he didn't want any part of it. He pointed it out to Jerry and turned to glide around it even though it would cost them even more altitude.

Above and behind him Boney called, "Bandit! Bandit eight o'clock level!" as Martin yelled, "What the hell is that?"

The jackhammering of .50s filled the cockpit.

"Shorty," Farley began, and then something hit the bomber so hard it tore the controls from his hands. *Fata Morgana* slewed sideways and pitched right and began to plane down toward the ruined surface of that shifted world.

EIGHT

Wennda crouched behind a rockfall on the valley floor and studied the vast translucent wall of the massive Redoubt a kilometer away. Sunlight gleamed the wall's top third. Canyon shadow slanted across its gridded surface below. The wall was made of large rectangular panels of some dense glasslike substance with a faint green tint. Panels here and there were cracked and chipped, some missing outright and covered with metal or plastic.

The Redoubt wall ran the width of the fissure, and rose up five hundred feet. The wedge of canyon behind it had been roofed over with the same material.

A cluster of tall buildings rose within that space. As if some enormous dam of pale green glass across the canyon had drowned a city and left it on display like some cruel god's aquarium. Random lights glowed steady in the stark towers.

Wennda glanced at the other three members of the small reconnaissance party crouched beside her. Arshall and Sten were good soldiers and hard workers, fast, efficient, and skilled. Arshall farmed a plot with his older sister and their parents. Sten was a machinist who fabricated replacement parts for old equipment. Reliable men who trusted her to lead. They did their job and didn't argue. Well, not much. In any case, they weren't a worry.

The fourth member of their party was the worry.

Yone leaned against the rockfall and studied the translucent wall with Wennda's priceless binoculars. He was small and thin and dark-haired, absorbed in his surveillance. Among them but not of them, as likely he would always be.

Wennda frowned at Yone's back as he surveyed the place where he'd once lived. *Will I really kill him if he runs? Will I have a choice? Maybe that's why I brought Arshall and Sten. Because they won't hesitate if it comes to that.*

She glanced at Arshall and saw him frowning at Yone, and wondered if he was thinking something similar.

Yesterday their small recon team had quietly left the Dome and made the crater crossing. There was no foraging to be done. No game lived here, and none of them would have known how to hunt it if it had. Sparse weeds and vines had taken root in carbon-rich patches of crater floor, but there was nothing to eat or drink except what the team brought with them. It was unforgiving going. They slept in their clothes in the shelter of oddly undulant rock formations, smooth curved berms that once had briefly moved as ripples until they'd cooled to stone. At night the party lit no fire, and by day they traveled in the narrowing arc of shadow that crept eastward on the canyon floor until high noon, then thickened west to east as the unremitting sun shrank toward the blunt horizon. They followed the perimeter because no one dared go near the mound at the center of the crater. A vast well lay in its middle like a hole punched through the world. By day a column of air shimmered above it, as if a pillar of heat rose from the pit, or some great agitation in the deep churned what lay above. At night the vast bore glowed a faint pale green. Over it the insubstantial column glimmered in the nighttime air, distorting the hard sprawled stars that passed behind it.

Everyone knew what lived down in that well. If it *was* alive. A weapon from the old world, protecting something stored deep in the well like a dragon guarding treasure. Sometimes it emerged to soar across the blighted air. The Typhon, it was called. Parents warned their children, *Behave or the Typhon will come after you,* and its vague menace stalked their dreams.

These were the fixtures of their bleak and fractured landscape, rough-hewn icons in a broken world: A living machine guarding a deep well in the center of a vast crater radiating canyon cracks. Opposing cities on opposite sides, self-contained and struggling to survive a world stripped bare. This dire tableau a rude-carved history of catastrophe.

But in the last few days there had been odd changes in the shimmering column. Flickers and flares and undulations. Brief solidifications like some textured shaft of coruscating glass. Wennda thought it could be an indication that the Redoubt had managed to defeat or evade the Typhon and gain access to the crater well. Something down there was powering that vast display, perhaps the thing the Typhon protected. And if the Redoubt had got hold of that kind of power, there was no telling what they might unleash.

Two years ago the column had exhibited similar behavior. Wennda had wanted to lead a recon team then, too. But then Yone had arrived, escaped from the Redoubt to seek asylum, and the ensuing argument over what to do with him had eclipsed any suggestion of an investigative team.

Now the massive fixture of their landscape was acting up again, and the man whom many of her people thought might be a Redoubt spy was crouched before her studying the very place he might be trying to return to—and Wennda had practically escorted him here.

But no one knew the Redoubt as Yone claimed to, and if her people's ancient enemy had finally managed to gain access to the crater well, Wennda definitely wanted him along. If it turned out Yone had lied to them and really was a Redoubt spy, then only three of their party would be coming back. Wennda would have some explaining to do, but she was used to that. And she doubted anyone would grieve too much about the loss of a spy and an unplanned mouth to feed.

Yone flattened the binoculars and turned away from the Redoubt, frowning as he sat back against the shattered boulder.

Wennda held out a hand and Yone gave her back the prized binoculars. "See anything different?" she asked. "It can't have changed very much in two years."

Yone gave his characteristic quick nod and twitch of a smile. "Nothing I can see from here," he said. He had an odd accent and a precise way of speaking. People in the Redoubt were very different, Yone had said. Different speech, customs, organization.

"I want to go in," Wennda said. She ignored the startled looks from Arshall and Sten.

"That would be very difficult," said Yone. "They are always watching."

"It's amazing that you got away at all," said Wennda.

"Fortresses are built to keep things from getting in," he said. "Not from getting out. But yes, I was very fortunate."

"Can we get in the same way you got out?" Wennda waved at the bottle-green wall a kilometer away.

Yone raised an eyebrow. "It doesn't seem likely. I walked out the front door."

"You walked, or you were pushed?"

He shrugged, refusing to rise to the bait. "You have heard my story many times by now," he said. "I can tell it again, but you have already made up your mind. I came with you when you asked me to. I am trying to help." He held up a hand to stop her interruption. "Yes, I have my own interest," he said. "Anything I can help you learn about what they may be trying to do here will only aid my credibility. Anything I can do to help our city also helps me."

She started to say something else, to go after his use of the word *our*, which irked her. But Sten said, "Wennda, does anyone even know we're here?"

She felt her face grow warm. "I never said this mission was authorized," she said.

"You didn't say it was *un*authorized, either."

"By the time anyone got around to an official look, Redoubt troops would be banging on our airlock."

Now Arshall chimed in. "So far we haven't seen any reason to think they're up to something."

"So far," she agreed. "That's why we should go in there."

Sten blinked. "There's nothing wrong, so we should take a closer look?"

"Yes." Even to her it sounded ridiculous, but she folded her arms and dug in.

Arshall and Sten exchanged an exasperated look—one that Wennda should have been accustomed to, since she'd seen it most of her life. But such expressions—their very dismissiveness, their eye-rolling, *here we go again* nature—only made her even more obstinate.

Sten sighed. He knew Wennda better than the other two did—he had even requested a compatibility assay a few years ago, more out of curiosity than from desire—and now he appealed to her reason. "Look," he said, "I agree that it was worth scouting around, authorized or not. We don't have the resources we used to, and anything that looks like a threat from the Redoubt should be taken seriously."

Wennda nodded eagerly. "All right, then. So we'll—"

"*But,*" he interrupted, "going back and reporting that nothing's going on here would be a lot more useful than not going back at all." He pointed at the Redoubt wall. "And if we go in there, we won't come back out."

"My mother would be really angry," added Arshall.

Sten grinned. "And Arshall's mother would be really angry," he agreed.

Wennda looked at the three men. She was prepared to argue her case, but what good would it do? If they didn't want to go in, she couldn't make them.

"Fine," she said. "I'll go in myself."

"Oh, for—" Sten hung his head, gave Arshall a pleading look, and shook his hands at Wennda.

"Perhaps," Yone said, "we can learn more without trying to get in." He pointed to a series of low ridges like overlapping shingles. "From there we can get a closer look at their security placement and

100

their defenses. We can get a better idea if there's more activity now than the last time you sent a team." He turned back to Wennda. "The commander might go easier on us if we return with useful information."

Wennda frowned. Yone had a good point. But his perpetual helpfulness even in the face of suspicion annoyed her. She'd probably respect him more if he told her to go jump in the reverter. She also couldn't help noticing that the vantage point Yone had indicated would bring him even closer to the Redoubt. Was he helping her, or himself?

They were waiting for her reply, and she knew that she would only look unreasonable and stubborn if she insisted on trying to get into the Redoubt without at least pursuing Yone's compromise first.

Wennda nodded. "It makes sense," she said. She looked at Yone, and Yone gave his quick tight smile. *I almost hope you* do *try to run,* she thought.

Yone stood up from behind the rockfall. Something in his expression made Wennda think she must have said her thought out loud. His face was absolutely blank, but his eyes held an alarming intensity, as if he were coming to some realization. *Now,* she thought, *he's going to do it now, he's going to make his move.*

Wennda stood. Her hand went to the nerve gun slung on her back.

Yone squinted and cocked his head to one side. He frowned.

Wennda's hand paused on the plastic butt of the gun. Yone hadn't even glanced at her. Was it a ploy? If she fell for it would he kill her? Arshall and Sten would have no time to stop him. She glanced down at them and saw that they were craning their heads and frowning as well.

Wennda turned. In a moment she heard it. A faint drone, the distant burr of some giant insect on the wing. It came from back toward the northern fissure entrance. Yone paid Wennda no attention as he stepped up beside her. She saw a slowly dawning wonder on his face.

Now Arshall and Sten came up beside them. The four of them stood with their backs to the Redoubt and faced whatever was headed toward them. In half a minute they saw it knifing through the canyon air a mile away, winged and alight and roaring five hundred feet above the ground.

"The Typhon," said Wennda. She stood transfixed. All stood numb and pale and facing the perceived incarnation of their childhood nightmares.

"No," said Yone. He shook his head without looking away.

"What else could it be?"

"A machine," he said. "Look. It's a flying machine."

And it was. The winged object nearing them in the halflight of the canyon shadow was rigid, made of plastic or metal, with windows and canopies and a cockpit, and the growing drone they heard was a whining engine. Below its body were two wheels on metal stalks. A third slowly swung down.

"*There's* the Typhon," Sten said wonderingly. He pointed down the canyon corridor where something flew behind and slightly above the descending aircraft. No one in the recon team had ever seen it, but once seen there was no doubting what it was. The thing was larger than the descending air machine, but thin and dark with flat sail-like wings and a raked sharp head with dead white patches for eyes. The metal aircraft forced its way through the air; but the Typhon seemed part of it. Both objects beautiful and savage and signaling destruction in every line, yet utterly alien from each other.

Wennda unfolded her binoculars and pressed "record" and watched the Typhon rake back its wings and angle down toward the aircraft like a striking falcon. A brilliant streak shot from underneath the stream-lined head and sped over the aircraft like a meteor. The canyon lit orange and the cross of the aircraft's shadow flowed across the canyon floor. A soft thunder swept the fissure.

Thin streaks shot back from rods emerging from a clear bubble on top of the aircraft. They raced toward the diving Typhon and tracked right with its plummet. A rapid riveting echoed through the canyon.

Yone stared as bullets stitched across the Typhon's lower body. The Typhon cupped its wings and slowed its dive and arced up and rolled right. The sharp wings curled and the creature righted itself and rose and continued until it dove backward and away from the intruder that had unexpectedly damaged it.

"Is it coming back?" Sten asked.

"I think it is flying away," said Yone.

They watched amazed as the metal aircraft continued toward them. They saw now that it moved using four large propellers, and that three of them were not spinning. The hull was damaged all over, and one side of the tail section waggled as the aircraft descended. The machine's wheels met the valley floor and the aircraft sped roughly along the shattered stone, heading toward the rockfall sloping from the bottom of the cliff ahead. It slowed and began to turn but suddenly stopped. The engine coughed and died.

"Well," said Sten, "I guess we've got something to take back now."

Wennda nodded slowly. "They have a new weapon," she said. "They're trying to destroy the Typhon and get into the well."

"Maybe it's from the well," said Arshall. "The Typhon was chasing it out of there."

"Not from the well," said Yone. "From the column." He pointed back toward the distant fissure entrance, back toward the crater's center where they knew the vast column still shimmered above the enormous well.

Arshall snorted. "You think monsters live in there?"

Yone shrugged. "We came here because the column has been acting strangely. And now this." He nodded at the parked aircraft near the rockfall up ahead.

"The column has been acting strangely," Wennda argued, "because they've been doing something to it. Maybe that's the result."

"Oh, please," said Arshall. "They sent an expedition down the well, and they found that thing and brought it back."

"You saw those weapons," said Sten. "Wherever it's from, if that thing finds the Dome, it's over."

Wennda stared at the aircraft silhouetted against the faint green light of the Redoubt wall. Alien and dangerous and upsetting a long and precarious balance. She thought she saw motion and she raised her binoculars again and took a long look. "There are men getting out of it," she said. "I count six. They're wearing uniforms. I think they have weapons."

"So much for stealing it and flying it back," said Arshall.

Wennda lowered the binoculars and stared at him.

"Or blowing it up," added Sten.

"I think those options are no longer available to us in any case," said Yone. He pointed at the city wall, where a massive door had slid aside and two angular silhouettes were gliding out toward the parked aircraft.

Wennda raised the binoculars again. "Troop carriers," she said.

"Well, this just got even more interesting," said Sten.

"Let's see what happens," said Arshall.

Wennda lowered the binoculars. "I want to get closer," she said.

Sten and Arshall traded a glance. "Of course you do," said Sten.

NINE

In the alien quiet Farley and Broben stared at the wall of greenish glass that spanned the canyon ahead of them, its upper third gleaming, the rest in shadow. Through the glass they saw what seemed to be a city.

Broben looked at Farley. "What the hell?" he said. "What the *hell*, Joe?"

Farley only shook his head and unbuckled. "Come on," he said.

He started to climb down into the pit, then stopped. Shorty and Wen were already there, and they moved aside to let Plavitz and Boney crawl out from the nose into the cramped space. Every man had shed his flight suit and put on uniform and general-issue boots. Farley made sure everybody had a sidearm. His own was in its shoulder holster.

Plavitz pointed to the front of the bomber. "Did you see—"

"Stow it," Farley interrupted. "Everybody out."

Wen opened the forward hatch and swung out of the bomber. Farley waited while the others followed Wen, then he climbed down from the cockpit. At the hatchway he glanced back up at Broben. "Coming, Jer?"

Broben nodded. "It ain't a landing till you walk away from it," he said. He unbuckled and stood. Farley noticed that Jerry's hand shook when he lit a Lucky, but Farley only nodded at him and swung down from the hatch. His boots touched grit and he patted the aluminum hull. *Thanks, girl.*

The men were already lighting up, looking around, stunned and questioning. Eight men standing outside a battered bomber parked at the bottom of a steep and narrowing canyon before a massive structure like nothing ever built on earth.

Wen immediately went to the tail section, did a full walkaround, and came back shaking his head. "Can't believe this thing stayed up," he said.

Broben dropped out of the hatch. Farley saw that he had jammed the flare pistol into his waistband.

"All right, first things first," said Farley. "Plavitz, any idea where we are?"

Plavitz shook his head. "I didn't have any kind of readings at all, even before we went through that—whatever it was. Nothing in the sky to get bearings on, either." He pointed at the enormous city wall. "That's north. After that, your guess is as good as mine."

"All right. Shorty?"

The radio operator shook his head. "I picked up some kind of signal after Wen got the auxiliary generator going, but I never got anything out of it. It wasn't voices, German or otherwise."

Broben nodded at the faintly luminous city wall that spanned the entire canyon. "If that's Germany, the Allies have been awfully misinformed."

Farley gave him a sour look. Broben shrugged.

"What the hell did we just have a dogfight with?" Farley asked.

Wen folded his arms and looked at his boots. "Wasn't no airplane, I can tell you that."

"Then what was it?"

Everett and Garrett glanced at each other. Both men looked at Farley and shrugged. "We took turns firing on it when we weren't helping crank the wheels down," said Everett. "Wen's right. That thing wasn't an airplane."

"It was alive," said Garrett.

"It was bigger than our bomber," Farley pointed out.

"It was bigger than our bomber," Garrett agreed. "And it was alive."

Everett nodded. He looked embarrassed. "It looked like one of those big dinosaur birds," he said.

"Like a damn dragon," said Garrett.

Wen looked stubborn. "I know a machine when I see one," he insisted.

"All right," said Farley, "let's put a lid on it for now. We need to think about our situation."

Broben waved his cigarette at the city wall that filled the canyon's termination like a fairy-tale castle caught in an evil spell. "We just put on one hell of a show for whoever lives in that aquarium. I give it five minutes before they send out a Welcome Wagon."

"Then let's be ready for them when they get here," said Farley.

"I blew the Norden," said Boney.

"Good man. Wen, any chance of getting more than Number One going in the next ten minutes?"

Wen shook his head unhappily. "I misdoubt it'll happen in a day or two."

Plavitz pointed at the city wall. "You were off by four and a half minutes, lieutenant," he said.

They all looked to see a pair of vehicles approaching on the valley floor before the city wall—dark angular shapes moving before the faintly glowing structure. Long and van-like and black-windowed, unlit and utterly silent as they jounced along the rocky canyon floor on half-shielded balloon tires. Troop transports, Farley thought. Maybe twelve men each. They were going slow, maybe five miles an hour. Even at that speed they'd be here in a few minutes.

Farley frowned at the bomber's front wheels, effectively chocked by the depressions in which they had come to rest. He'd never get her out of there on one engine. With the tail destroyed, he wanted to at least turn her front toward whatever was coming their way. The crew could try to walk her around, but even if they managed it there'd be little time left to take stations. No, they were stuck in place with their shot-up ass to the unknown, and here was where they'd have to make a stand. If it came to that.

Farley turned his back on the approaching transports. "All right, listen up," he decided. "I want to give these people the benefit of the doubt, but if they pull up behind us instead of beside us, I don't think talking's going to be the first thing on their list. The tail gun's out of commission, and the nose and maybe the waist guns won't have a line on them." He clapped his hands. "So. Garrett, Everett, grab the .30 and an ammo can from the nose and take up a firing position on the rockfall. Stay low and don't shoot unless you have to."

"We can yank one of the .50s," Everett offered.

"You may end up hauling it farther than up that slope. Grab the .30 and get going."

They got going.

"Martin," said Farley, "see if you can get through that mess back there." He waved at the rear of the bomber. "If the guns still work, you're Queen for a Day if it gets ugly. If they don't, find cover and make sure you've got a shot."

"Understood, captain."

"You'll have to move Francis. And pull his tags."

Martin nodded grimly. "Only way to know if the guns still work is to fire them," he pointed out.

"If you can do it before those transports get here, go ahead. Once they pull up, it'll look like a warning shot."

"What's wrong with a warning shot?" asked Broben. "Those jalopies ain't the Red Cross bringing doughnuts."

"Let's don't give them room to say we started it," said Farley.

"I better hop to it," said Martin, and headed to the bomber.

"Plavitz, top turret," Farley ordered. "You're our main bet here."

Plavitz glanced at Wen, plainly wondering why Farley hadn't ordered the flight engineer to the top turret, his normal combat station. But he nodded and said, "Got it, cap," and hurried after Martin.

Farley watched him go, then turned to the rest of the men. "Shorty, grab water and rations from the ditch kits."

Shorty looked puzzled, but he nodded. "Will do, captain," he said. "I'll put 'em in a duffel."

Farley frowned at his flight engineer. "Wen, I hate to say it, but—"

"You want me to rig her so we can light her up."

"It might come to that. We're at the halfway mark on fuel, so leave us enough to get back."

Wen scratched his neck and looked over his shoulder, his giveaway that he disagreed with his pilot. "She's a pretty good bird, cap. We can't set a bomber on fire every time we fly one."

"I agree," said Farley. "Now take the flare gun and set her up to burn."

Wen scowled as Broben handed him the Very pistol. He tucked it into his waistband and dragged on his cigarette as he turned toward the bomber, muttering to himself.

"Toss your butts!" Broben called out. "This crate's about to be a *Hindenburg Junior.*"

Wen sidearmed the butt away and gave a two-fingered salute without looking.

"Boney," Farley said, "will that stuck bomb go off if we do have to burn her?"

"Doubt it," said Boney. "A small blast from the fuse booster is what sets off the TNT."

"Can you rig it so it does?"

"Jesus," muttered Broben.

Boney shrugged. "I can pull the fuse booster and rig that to go off if the ship burns. It'd do some damage."

"Go ahead and do it."

Boney nodded and turned back to the bomber.

Broben waited till Boney was out of earshot, then turned to Farley. "We fighting or running?" he asked.

"We're covering our bases."

"Well, if I'm not gonna help fly this tub, I better find somewhere to shoot from."

Farley turned back toward the approaching transports. "Maybe they're just bringing us the key to the city."

"Sure. And it's so big they need two trucks to carry it." Broben pulled his Colt and chambered a round. "I'll see you when the dust settles, Joseph."

Farley touched the bill of his crush hat and glanced up at the figure so recently painted on the nose of his new aircraft. He nodded at her, then hurried back to the main door.

* * * * *

The fuselage already reeked of spilled high-octane, and a spent fuel can lay where Wen had tossed it near the right waist gun. Shorty was pulling one of the rubber rafts from the overhead wing storage. A pounding from the rear of the bomber startled Farley until he realized it was Martin, trying to get back to the tail gun. Something clanged from in the left wing crawlspace and Farley heard Wen yell, *"God damn shit house mouse!"*

"Wen," called Farley, "find some cover when you're finished and hold onto that flare gun. Don't light her up till you have to, and don't wait a second longer than that."

"Ah-ight."

Shorty looked startled but said nothing. Farley saw that he'd got hold of a carton of Luckys to bring along with the water and rations he was pulling from the rubber rafts. He caught Shorty's eye and tapped his wristwatch, then hurried past him and through the radio room.

In the bomb bay Boney was already pulling the cylindrical fuse booster from the thousand-pounder stuck in the rack. Farley set a hand on Boney's shoulder and eased by him on the catwalk.

Plavitz stood in the top turret, swiveling the guns around to face the oncoming transports. Farley went around him and nearly got hit in the leg by the muzzle of a Browning M1919 .30-caliber machine gun as it

110

suddenly poked out of the crawlway from the nose. He danced back and Garrett followed the weapon out. The big man picked up the machine gun and straightened as Everett came out behind him, bandoliered by ammunition. With four men in it the pit was crowded as a rush-hour bus.

"Don't embarrass the Army, boys," Farley said, and climbed into the cockpit.

Garrett set the Browning on the deck and swung down from the forward hatch. Everett handed the weapon down to him, passed him the ammo, and followed him out.

In the pilot seat Farley switched off the interior lights. "Wen, Shorty," he called over his shoulder. "Time to go! Boney! How's that firecracker going?"

"Done," came Boney's nearly uninflected voice behind him. "I tucked it away."

"All right. Check your ammo and get behind a rock outside. Plavitz! How you making out up there?"

"Apart from not knowing where we are or who's coming after us," came from behind and above, "I'm ready as a pig at a luau, captain."

Farley snorted. "All right, then." He climbed back down into the pit and looked up at Plavitz. "It's you and Martin on board once Wen and Shorty clear out," he called up. "I'll direct fire outside. You know the drill."

"Press the shiny red button till they go away."

"Only once it's clear they want to make us go away first."

"Roger that."

Farley took one quick look around and then knelt and grabbed the bar and swung down from the hatch to the alien ground.

* * * * *

Broben faced away from the bomber in a half crouch with his pistol drawn. Farley's first thought was that the transports had arrived and unloaded, but a quick glance showed them still approaching. They

111

had slowed to a crawl. Farley unsnapped his holster and stood close to Jerry and drew his own .45. "See something?"

Jerry shook his head, still scanning the twilight canyon. "Heard something. Some*one*. Plain as day, and close."

Farley widened his eyes and looked around. He couldn't even see the crew behind the rockfall cover they had taken, and all of them knew better than to make any noise. "Maybe you're spooked," he said.

He turned back to Jerry just as a woman's voice directly in front of them said, "Don't shoot."

Farley aimed and Broben aimed but there was nothing to aim at.

"Don't shoot," the woman said again. "We're here to help you."

"Prove it, sister," said Broben.

Four figures appeared out of thin air not ten feet in front of them.

Even as he squeezed the trigger Farley registered that the strangers all had their gloved hands high and wide and empty, fingers spread. The gun went off but missed its mark, though the tallest figure took a step back.

"Jesus Mary what the holy shit," said Broben. He held his fire but kept his aim.

The tall one stepped forward, hands still high. "Will your aircraft fly?" she asked in a lilting accent.

Farley raised an eyebrow at the anonymous figure. Like the others she wore some kind of tight-fitting black uniform set with thin and hard-looking panels, like a matte-black flak suit with a visored balaclava. The woman and two of the others had stubby weapons, bigger than a pistol and smaller than a rifle, slung bandolier-style and pointing down.

"We have very little time," the woman insisted. "Is your aircraft able to fly?"

Farley studied her. "Who are you?"

The one without a gun, who was also the smallest of the four, spoke up. "Please, she is correct," he said, and nodded at the approaching transports. "We must hurry." His accent was different from the woman's. Farley couldn't place either one.

"We can get you out of here," the woman said. "But we have to go now."

"I appreciate the offer," Farley told the woman. "But we're not leaving our aircraft."

"You can't fight the entire city," the small man said.

Farley looked him up and down. He looked like he was wearing some kind of padded dance leotard. "You should get your people out of here before it gets ugly," he told the small man. "I don't have time to—" He broke off.

The two who had not yet spoken were staring up at the bomber's nose.

He turned to see what they were looking at but saw nothing that seemed odd to him. The front bubble, the cheek gun, Shorty's artwork. Maybe it was the bomber itself.

Farley turned back. Now the tall woman was staring up at the bomber, and the other three in her party were staring at her.

Broben glanced back at the ship, then looked at the strangers. "What's the deal?" he said.

As if moving of its own accord the woman's hand came up to pull the top of her balaclava. The mouth hole stretched in some parody of astonishment as the balaclava slid off her head.

"You gotta be kidding me," said Broben.

Farley could only stare in mute wonder.

Shorty stepped out of the waist door clutching a canvas duffel. He saw the woman and stopped cold and said, very slowly, "Holy moly. I'm better than I thought."

The woman looked from the nose art to Farley. Farley felt a jolt of recognition and his palms grew slick. Long black windswept hair and pale green eyes in a pale face that was long and angular and determined. Stern and regal and refined.

The woman's face and everything around her lit with sudden bluewhite light as the transports parked behind the bomber in a V and turned on a bank of blinding spotlights. The twin .50s chuddered as Martin opened fire with the tail gun.

113

Farley didn't so much as flinch. Even as the firefight erupted all around him and the others moved to find cover he stood rooted to that foreign ground and stared at the face that also adorned the hull of the *Fata Morgana* right behind him.

Something shattered and the light went dark.

TEN

Farley stared numbly at the pistol in his hand. He pulled back the slide and saw that a round was already chambered. He frowned.

He was sitting with his back against a boulder. Broben crouched beside him with his own pistol out, peering past the edge of the rock and looking as if he wanted to shoot at something but wasn't sure what.

Farley looked for the four newcomers and couldn't find them. Then the girl moved and he saw that she was crouched behind a low boulder, peering over the top with her blunt weapon beside her. One of her confederates crouched down beside her, still in his ski mask. He had no weapon. Their outfits were no longer matte black. They had taken on the shadowed mottling of the rock they hunched behind. They were very hard to see unless they moved.

Beyond them Garrett and Everett lay prone behind the main wedge of rockfall, a little up the rise. They'd lugged the .30 cal up the slope and propped it on a rock, with Garrett sighting and Everett beside him to feed the length of ammo belt. Boney and Shorty squatted behind their own small boulders with pistols drawn. The remaining two new arrivals had taken up positions behind the rockfall. Their outfits now matched the landscape behind them as well. Shadows had stretched across the valley floor and it felt like night here by the canyon wall.

Farley frowned. He could not remember how he'd gotten here. There'd been the four newcomers. The pulled-off balaclava. The girl's face. The sudden spotlight. The following machine-gun fire. And then, and then?

He must have run with the others. But what he remembered was just standing there, staring at the girl. A stranger's face that he already knew.

He shook his head like a dog shaking off water. Your station's drifting, Captain Midnight. You'd better get tuned in.

He peered out from his side of the rock. The *Fata Morgana* faced him a hundred feet away. Directly behind her the two dark and nonreflective troop transports were parked in a V. They looked purely mangled. Both leaned out where their balloon tires had been shredded by gunfire. The metal sides were dented, dimpled, and holed. The spotlights on each transport had been shot out. Curiously, the dark front windshields remained intact. Hatchways had opened on the far sides of the vehicles.

"Jer," said Farley.

Broben did not look away from the tableau. "Yeah, boss?"

"Plavitz, Wen, and Martin still on the bomber?"

"Unless they got Houdini with 'em, they are."

Black-clad troops wearing matte-black helmets with dark face-shields came around the sides of the vans and sprinted toward the bomber. Their outfits had the same chameleon trick as the newcomers, and it was hard to draw a bead on them. Broben squeezed off a round and the lead man staggered back, looked down at himself, and kept going. Broben looked at his pistol.

Farley saw the bomber's top turret swivel, but Plavitz didn't fire. Farley realized that the vertical stabilizer was in the way and the turret's cutoff cam was preventing the gunner from firing.

The tail gun opened fire again and two helmeted men fell apart like cut dough. The others checked their advance and retreated back behind the angled carriers. Martin didn't waste more ammo on the vehicles.

"Welcome to the big leagues, assholes," Broben muttered.

Farley glanced at the girl behind her boulder. She had been sighting down her chunky weapon and now she brought her head up, apparently startled by the twin Browning's relentless firepower. Farley

116

noted her stance, her steadiness, the way she coordinated with her team. He felt her over there like a beacon and he knew he had to put her out of his mind for now.

He looked back at Broben. "Those people sound German to you?" he asked.

Broben frowned. "They sound something, but it ain't German. I'm not—whoah." He raised his automatic as two more helmeted figures carrying stubby weapons sprinted for the bomber from different directions. Farley fired. He was certain he hit the left-hand runner in the chest, but the man just flinched and kept going.

From his left Farley heard a rising, high-pitched electric whine that cut off with a dull thunk. The man he thought he'd shot suddenly stiffened and fell forward like a toppled statue. His helmet slammed the ground without his arms coming up to break the fall.

The remaining runner raised his weapon. Farley heard another whine like a dentist drill revving up. It cut off, and some instinct made him duck back behind the rock. Something crackling whooshed by him and the hair on his arms stood up. He smelled an odor from his childhood, the sharp metallic smell of a nearby lightning strike.

He peeked out again just as Garrett's .30 cut loose from the rockfall. Blood and bone exploded out the running man's back and he went down like a dropped sandbag.

Broben waggled his pistol. "I want to trade up," he said.

Now the crew and their new friends were firing at the transports. Pistol pops and guttural machine-gun fire and the weird windup whine-and-clack of the strangers' stubby weapons.

Motion caught Farley's eye. The girl was waving at him. She pointed forward but Farley didn't see anything. "You got field glasses?" he asked Broben.

"Nope. Got a Zippo, though."

Farley scowled. "I think there's another transport headed our way."

The girl leaned back from her boulder. "We have to go," she called to Farley. "Destroy your aircraft and come with us."

"Three of my crew are still in there," Farley called back.

She shook her head. "Their reinforcements will flank us and attack while the others target the aircraft," she said.

"I'm not leaving my men," Farley insisted. "And I'm sure as hell not setting them on fire."

"Do you know what they'll do to them?"

"We should burn them alive so they won't be tortured?" said Broben.

"We're grateful for your help," said Farley, "but it's not your fight."

"If your aircraft is captured it will be used against us."

"I'm not killing my own men."

"If I can get them out, will you destroy the aircraft?"

"Count on it."

She studied Farley a moment, then conferred with her team member lying prone now beside the rock and looking very naked without a weapon. Then she leaned out and signaled one of her confederates behind the rockfall. She made a series of complex gestures that reminded Farley of a baseball coach signaling an on-base runner. Her comrade replied in kind and she nodded and looked back at Farley. He thought she was going to say something, but she didn't. She turned and ran out into the darkness.

* * * * *

Farley could see the third transport coming now, angling off to the right. Moving to flank, as the girl had said.

"Now what?" said Broben.

"I don't even have a bad idea," Farley admitted.

They watched the bomber's top turret as its twin machine-gun barrels lowered and began to track the transport.

"Come on, Plavitz," said Broben. "Beat 'em to the punch."

Plavitz did. The moment the transport was in range he opened up. Hot streaks flew across the canyon air and struck the slowly moving transport. The vehicle rocked from the barrage, and a dull ring of hammered metal carried along the valley floor, as if an invisible giant were pounding the vehicle with a mace. The metal dented and dimpled and crumpled, but resisted the fusillade.

The transport stopped. Light spilled onto the canyon floor as a hatchway popped open on its far side. Brief silhouettes appeared as troops hurried out and ran for cover. Plavitz peppered the balloon tires and the transport lowered a full six inches. He kept hammering until he took out the spotlights and the metal hull looked like a cheese grater. It was purely awesome to behold. Their new friends in black could only gape at the devastation wrought by the terrifying weaponry.

Broben nudged Farley and nodded at the bomber. Farley looked just in time to see a dark figure sprint to the forward hatch, jump up, and swing inside.

"That your girlfriend?" Broben asked. "Think so," said Farley. "Man." Broben shook his head. "What I wouldn't give to see their faces when they get a load of her."

Farley snorted, imagining Plavitz and Wen seeing the girl climb aboard. *Hiya, fellas! I'm the nose art on your bomber! A kind wizard brought me to life, and I have come to save you with my toy ray gun.* Walt Disney with the DT's couldn't have tricked that one up.

The top turret stopped firing. Farley thought Plavitz couldn't have much ammo left. Martin either. Once they all were down to pistols this party would be over.

A hand holding some kind of device emerged from behind the newly devastated transport. Machine-gun fire erupted from the bomber's left waist hatch and the arm withdrew. From the bomber Wen's voice yelled, *"That's me wavin' back, you dumb bag of shit."*

Farley heard a motor start up inside the *Morgana*. He recognized the steady chug of the auxiliary generator. He wondered if Wen were trying to start the engines, but then the bomb bay doors whined down.

The waist-gun firing resumed in short bursts just as the girl dropped from the front hatch and darted to a cover position behind the right wheel. She fired on the rear transports while the waist gun covered her against the new arrival away to her right. She was efficient as hell, and smart: Fire, duck back, sight from a different angle, fire again, all without predictable rhythm.

She brought up a fist and yanked it down like a semi-truck driver blowing his horn, and Martin jumped down from the bomb bay. He turned back and reached up and Francis was lowered into his arms.

What the hell was that Indian thinking? Farley was about to yell for Martin to take the dogtags and leave the body, but then the ravaged sky went bright. A bluewhite arc of burning flare descended, wavering shadows as it floated down.

Farley saw two soldiers setting up some kind of apparatus behind the third transport. Maybe the bomber didn't have a line on them, but Farley sure as hell did. He pointed them out to Broben and both men aimed and fired, the twin pops overlapping. The two soldiers sat down hard and looked at themselves and then resumed their work.

"Stay dead, you son of a bitch," said Broben, and fired again. Either he missed or the shot had no effect.

The machine-gun fire from the waist port cut off abruptly as Wen jumped down and ran toward Plavitz and Martin struggling with Francis, waving Martin on as he came. Martin shrugged out from under Francis' limp arm and sprinted for the rocks when Wen took over, and only then did Farley understand that Francis was still alive.

Then a thin thread of red light ran straight as a ruler from the apparatus the two troops had assembled to the rock where Farley and Broben knelt. Farley frowned and Broben cocked his head at the pure red beam that swirled with dust motes.

Farley heard a hollow *whunk*. He turned and yelled, *"Mortar! Mortar! Down down down!"*

The ground erupted in front of his boulder. Even with the mass of stone before him Farley was thrown back. As he fell he saw another glowing red line leading from the number-two transport to the slope where Garrett and Everett lay prone with their machine gun. He heard another, more distant *whunk*. Garrett and Everett were already sliding down the scree with the .30-cal. Three seconds later their former firing position exploded. Rock shrapnel whistled off in all directions.

The girl stood up from behind the bomber's wheel and ran back toward the rocks, firing as she came. Beyond her Farley saw helmeted figures advancing. He glanced right. The troops from the third transport were taking advantage of their vehicle's cover to pin down Farley's men while the other troops went after the bomber.

The crewmen were out of the *Morgana* and now the girl looked imploringly at Farley.

Farley nodded at her. *"Blow it!"* he yelled. *"Wen, light it up!"*

Wen and Plavitz still struggled with Francis. Wen looked pained and let go of the wounded tail gunner, and Plavitz took up the slack. The smaller of their new friends in black jumped out from behind the cover of his boulder and ran to Plavitz and got a shoulder under Francis' free arm.

Wen turned back to the bomber and pulled the flare pistol from his waistband. He aimed it at the bomber. Farley heard another high-pitched whine. Wen held position and didn't fire. Farley was about to yell for him to shoot when Wen toppled over like a statue, still holding the flare gun out and not moving a bit to soften the impact as he hit the hard ground with a sickening thud like a ballbat hitting a watermelon.

Plavitz and the small man reached the rocks with Francis. The girl stood by them returning enemy fire. More black-clad figures ran to fortify the ones already taking up positions against the bomber crew. Another electric whine and click sounded nearby, and one of the approaching soldiers keeled over the way Wen had.

Farley was about to go after the flare pistol when someone gripped his arm. He looked down at Broben and Broben slowly shook his head. "We're in over our head here, Joe."

Farley's face went tight. He looked at Garrett and Everett, pinned down in a new position where they'd set up the Browning. At Shorty reloading his pistol behind his rock. At the girl returning fire while at her feet the small man pressed Francis' chest where bandages showed spreading dark as Martin jabbed a morphine syrette into Francis' thigh and squeezed. At Wen lying in the open with the flare gun in his hand. At the helmeted figures now climbing up the bomb bay into his aircraft. *His* aircraft, god damn it.

"Shoot it," Farley whispered. He cupped his hands by his mouth and shouted. *"Shoot the bomber! Light it up!"*

The Browning immediately chattered. The huge rounds slammed home and the bomber shuddered from the impact. But it did not burn.

"Jesus," Farley said, "what do you have to do."

"Never thought we'd complain about it," said Broben.

Farley tried to think about what else they could do but there was nothing they could do. All around him handguns popped and the machine gun jackhammered and those Buck Rogers guns buzzed like high-tension wires. Red threads from the troop transports incised the darkness. The girl was looking at him. The face painted on his Flying Fortress.

He made the call. *"Move out!"* he yelled. *"Move out!"*

Broben turned his back to the bomber. "Don't have to tell *me* twice," he said, and ran in a crouch, keeping the boulder in line with the first two transports.

Farley gave his Flying Fortress one last look. Raked, defiant, powerful, beautiful, dangerous, and wholly seized. He looked at the flying woman painted on the nose, pointing the way out. Then he turned and ran the other way.

ELEVEN

They ran doubletime for a solid hour, keeping to the shadows by the western canyon wall, before they stopped to rest. One of their four new friends immediately took up tail-end charlie position while the others checked their gear and tended to Francis.

The wounded tail gunner was bad off. Shrapnel had flayed the left side of his head and upper left chest. He'd lost an eye and a lot of blood. His breathing was labored and Farley was sure his left lung had collapsed. Apparently one of their new friends was sure, too, because the first time they stopped to catch their breath he fixed a needle to a tiny hypo, threw away the plunger, and jabbed it into Francis' chest. Farley heard air hiss into the needle and Francis immediately breathed easier. His respiration was shallow and he was in and out of consciousness. The morphine probably helped, but the man treating Francis didn't seem happy that they'd juiced him.

The medic, whose name was Sten, said he thought his people might be able to save Francis if they could get him back in time. It would mean running all night and stopping only long enough to catch their breath and quickly eat. Farley was all for it if it gave Francis a fighting chance, but it was also hugely frustrating. He had a thousand questions and no opportunity to ask them. For now he had to bottle it up and keep an eye on his crew and the four strangers and the terrain.

As Farley ran, a part of his mind that was purely Walter and Amanda's boy Joseph needled the rest of him like a playground bully. *You lost Wen to enemy fire,* it whispered. *You'll probably lose Francis. An hour ago you lost your second bomber in as many missions. You know how long you were at her controls? A whopping four, count 'em, four measly hours.*

No. Farley shook his head. No. In those four hours the *Fata Morgana* had flown through thick flak and swarming fighters and God's own freak storm. She'd deadsticked down into some Moon Man version of the Grand Canyon, dogfighted on one engine with a goddamn *monster,* for christ's sake, put down in the dark on unknown ground in enemy territory—and swung through every inch of it like Joe Louis with a white-hot grudge.

She sure did, Joe, the bully in his head agreed. *And you fell in love with her because of it. The* Voice of America *was a jinx ship, a flying curse from nose to tail, and you burned her for it. But when it came time to pull the trigger on the* Morgana *your judgement was clouded and you were too damned late, and now she's crawling with strangers and a good man's dead. How's that for bringing them through the fire, Captain Midnight?*

* * * * *

They took their next break near the mile-wide fissure entrance. The canyon floor had grown much darker and a faint green glow came from center of the crater off in the far distance. The girl, Wennda, stood point, and from where Farley sat she was skylighted against that sickly light. He studied her and the landscape beyond her but could make out nothing that told him anything useful.

Shorty had dug into his bag of rations and now he was making the rounds, offering water and smokes. All of Farley's men took some of each. Their new friends' outfits had built-in drinking bladders and sipping tubes. They just looked confused by the cigarettes.

Broben was huffing and puffing with his hands on his knees. He'd gone through Basic like the rest of them, twenty-mile humps wearing forty-pound packs, drop and give me twenty, dig this, climb that. But he'd gained back a lot of the weight he'd lost in training, and he smoked like a burning tire factory.

Boney simply sat down against a rock and waited till his breathing slowed. Garrett and Everett had been carrying Francis, trading off with Sten and the other one, Arshall, who ran with the .30-cal on his shoulder. All four of them were big boys in terrific shape and looked as if they could run in their sleep.

Farley watched Martin and Plavitz approach the unarmed man who had run out to help bring Francis back. They spoke for a moment and Martin held out a hand. He and Martin were nearly the same size. They shook. Then Plavitz shook the man's hand and patted his shoulder.

Farley went to the girl looking out at point. She glanced at him as he approached, and he nodded and showed his hands. "I just wanted to say thanks for helping us out of a tight spot," he said. "And for everything you're doing for my tail gunner, Francis."

"You really aren't from the Redoubt," she said.

"Never heard of it."

A crease appeared between her eyebrows. "Yone said you had to be from somewhere else."

"You have no idea how right he is."

The furrow deepened. "But he can't be."

"Why not?"

"Because there is nowhere else." She looked past him and raised an arm. Her colleagues immediately readied to march. Arshall came up from tail-end charlie, and he and Sten grabbed Francis up in the sling they'd rigged from some strong and super-lightweight material they used for a sleeping bag or blanket, Farley wasn't sure which. Garrett and Everett grabbed the Browning and the remaining ammo. The small man, Yone, hung back as rear spotter. Farley wondered why he didn't have a weapon. Maybe he'd lost it in some earlier engagement.

Broben touched his toes and coughed and quickly straightened up. He gave Farley a grim smile and a thumbs-up, and Farley realized he must have been looking concerned.

"You ain't got no friends on your left," said Broben.

"You're right," Farley replied.

* * * * *

They were barely out of the fissure and hugging the shadows at the western edge of the vast crater bowl when Yone signaled that they were being pursued. They were thirteen counting Francis and they scattered and took up position behind rockfalls and tumbled boulders that lined the crater perimeter. A few men shifted position after the group had established, and Farley noted with satisfaction that they had moved to widen the line of fire on anyone who might be approaching, without exposing their own men to friendly fire.

Farley held position alone and watched the girl work her way along the makeshift picket to Yone. They had a brief discussion. The girl turned back and studied the waiting array until she spotted Everett and Garrett. She signaled them with two fingers, mimed firing a big gun, and beckoned them to her. Garrett and Everett immediately came forward carrying the .30-cal and the worrisomely short ammo belt.

Farley felt Broben come up beside him. Both men stayed low and kept their eyes forward as they talked. The darker depth of the fissure entrance from which they had emerged loomed straight ahead. It all looked ancient, raw, foreboding.

"Another clown car?" asked Broben.

"Hope not." Farley nodded at Garrett and Everett working their way to Wennda and Yone. "We've got one gun that can take them out, and it can't have ten seconds of ammo left."

Broben looked up, then looked away quickly. "Jesus," he said. "I don't recommend doing that."

Farley glanced up. The crater wall rose up a distance his mind did not want to accept. He felt like a bug clinging to the ceiling of a vast cathedral and looking down at a distant floor that was the stripped-bare sky.

He looked away and blinked. "Don't get that dizzy doing barrel rolls," he said.

"Company," said Broben.

It rolled out of the dark wedge of the fissure entrance, angular and flat-black. It turned left and came toward them slow and steady. As it neared Farley saw that this was not a fourth transport, but one of the three they had shot up.

"Christ, their jalopies don't stay dead either," said Broben.

"They must've put the good tires on the heap in best shape and come after us," said Farley. "They don't want us going back for the bomber. Or they don't want these people getting back to their base with news of it."

The girl turned away from the approaching transport and made a lowering motion with both hands. Farley got down, but she kept making the motion. He and Broben slid down until they could barely see, but the girl kept motioning.

"I don't think so, sister," muttered Broben.

Farley agreed. Maybe she knew something they didn't—probably she did—but Farley wasn't about to let others do his fighting for him while he cowered blind behind a rock. He shook his head at her.

She turned away and huddled up with Garrett and Everett. Then the gunners put on Wennda's and Yone's balaclavas. Wennda adjusted one of them and nodded, and the two men rolled a foot-high rock to the edge of their boulder and rested the barrel of the Browning on top of it. Garrett lay prone and sighted the machine gun while Everett held the ammo feed.

Farley looked at the pistol in his hand. It might as well have been a slingshot.

The transport came on. To Farley it looked purposeful, unwavering, as if it knew exactly where they'd stationed themselves.

At a hundred feet a red streak shot up from the vehicle like a firework. A moment later it exploded and a bright blue star flare on a parachute lit up the ground below.

"I hate these guys," said Broben. "I don't even know who they are, and I friggin hate 'em."

Farley was about to make some reply, but a shadow streaked across them. He just had time to think that something would have to have passed beneath the flare to cast a shadow, when an angular, winged shape blurred into view fifty feet off the ground in utter silence. It banked left and shot skyward. Farley's head turned to follow it and the troop transport exploded.

Farley fell back and pulled Broben with him. The concussion slammed across them. Pieces of carrier smashed into rock or hissed past. Charred chunks pelted rocky ground. Farley waited a few seconds, then sat up and took a look. Where the carrier had been was now a burning and twisted metal chassis. Thick black smoke billowed up from the puddling remains of balloon tires.

Farley looked up at the sky. The star flare still descended and the flying thing was already gone. It had banked in, released, and arced away—the fastest strafing run Farley had ever seen. And the most accurate. There had been no rocket streak. That thing had gravity-launched some kind of bomb and hit a bullseye.

Everybody picked themselves up in the stark light, looking around as if they'd inexplicably come awake in this forsaken place. Even Jerry had no wisecrack. What they'd just seen had been too sudden, too fast. Too big. As if the sky had opened up and the hand of God had lowered from on high to smite their enemy.

Wennda glanced at Farley and Broben as she went by him to retake point. She had got her balaclava back and it was clenched in her hand like the skin of some small animal. Farley hoped his shaking didn't show as he held up a hand for her attention.

"What the hell is that thing?" he asked.

She glanced up at the empty sky. "Biomechanical aerial drone," she said. "We call it the Typhon."

128

"Will it be back?"

"I don't think so. Not if we stay by the rim. It's protecting something in the well, in the middle of the crater. It destroys anything it sees as a threat."

"Who's flying it?" Broben demanded.

She frowned. "No one. Its mission program is still running even though there's no more mission."

Broben shook his head as if trying to clear water from his ears. "Do you savvy any of that doubletalk?" he asked Farley.

Farley held two fingers a quarter inch apart.

Wennda went to talk with Arshall and Sten as Yone, Garrett, and Everett headed toward them.

"I'm telling you it was there," Garrett was insisting. "What do you think, it dropped a rock?"

"I'm not buying it," said Everett.

"It had a bomb under its wing," said Garrett. "It wasn't there before." He turned a pleading gaze to Farley and Broben. "You saw that thing," he said. "Did it—"

Farley held a hand up. "You take your orders from me," he said. "Got it?"

Garrett looked puzzled. "We were only—"

Everett elbowed him in the ribs. "We got it, captain. It won't happen again."

"No it won't." Farley moved aside. "Go on."

Broben watched them walk off and lit a Lucky. "You okay, Joseph?"

"Sure, why wouldn't I be?"

"You tell me."

Farley glanced at the popping wreck. The star flare finally landed and lay burning on the barren ground. "You're gonna have to put out the cigarette, Jer," he said.

Broben held out the Lucky and raised an eyebrow. "How come?" he asked.

"They can detect heat." Farley indicated the bonfire that had been a twelve-man transport. "That's why she kept telling us to get down."

* * * * *

They ran the dark perimeter of the crater and took five minutes every hour to rest. Farley followed the girl's lead and did not question her. Her team had fought alongside him and were going doubletime to get Francis to a doc, and that was good enough for Farley for right now.

Whenever they stopped, Farley checked on Francis and the crew members who were starting to flag. Whenever they ran, Farley tried to identify constellations or plan his next move or count paces, or anything but dwell too much on things outside of his control. Which right now was pretty much everything.

Several times he thought he saw the skeletons of enormous creatures in the distance. Each time they resolved to the burned and twisted frames of vehicles.

Soon Farley simply trudged like a mindless hamster on a treadmill, not thinking about much at all beyond making it to the next break. A tour's worth of action in the last half day had left him running on fumes. His A-2 jacket was driving him nuts. At first he tied the arms around his waist, but the leather kept working loose with his stride. Finally he put his belt through the arms and gathered the jacket like a curtain and buckled the belt and ran with the hem of the jacket tapping the backs of his legs. His boots were hot and heavy but there was nothing he could do about them so he ignored them.

False dawn found them near the entrance to another fissure. They'd passed several during the night, canyon cracks radiating from an explosion or a meteor strike or *something* that had blown a crater the size of Manhattan. The ground showed evidence of lava flow, huge ripples frozen in stone, clustered spheres where molten rock had hardened over air bubbles. The scale of devastation was too large for the mind's containing. In the soft gray eastern light the world around them was a pencil sketch of ruin.

The eastern crater rim reconstituted ragged against a paling sky and then a merciless sun swelled to stretch a vast crescent shadow

130

across the crater bowl. The silence was exquisite. Farley realized he had not seen or heard a bird in all the growing morning. No insect sounds had scored the night. Apart from people the only living things he'd seen were green carpets of lichens and dull olive patches of mold on rocks, paltry weeds struggling from cracks.

They rounded a ridge protruding down the length of the crater wall and Wennda raised an arm to call a halt.

Half a mile away a group was headed toward them. Farley counted four figures, all in black, all armed. No balaclavas, though. Farley kept an eye on Wennda. She pulled out something that looked like a large cigarette case and expanded it to a box with a fold-down eyepiece like binoculars. She used it to study the group and then collapsed it again and broke into a huge grin. It changed her face completely, fine-boned features suddenly coltish and unguarded. Arshall and Sten had set Francis down, and for the first time they visibly relaxed.

Farley's crew stood waiting. Depleted, disoriented, and battle fatigued, they greeted any new development with dull suspicion. Most took advantage of the break to light up and watch this new bunch come on. For his own part Farley felt like an emptied vessel as he waited.

One of the approaching group raised a hand. Wennda waved back. Farley thought they looked cagey as they approached, scrutinizing him and his crew. Of course they would be wondering what the hell was going on. A group of four had left, and a group of thirteen was coming back.

Wennda's grin grew wider as the new group stopped before them. Three men and a woman. They looked nervous. All of them had the chunky Buck Rogers egg-cooker guns slung on their shoulders and they kept their hands on them. None of them smiled back at Wennda.

Broben raised his eyebrows at Farley and Farley gave a little nod. Broben ground out his cigarette and folded his arms to put his hand near his shoulder holster. Garrett casually leaned the Browning against his leg. The length of trailing ammo belt rested against Everett's foot. Shorty stood with his hands against his lower back. Farley noted that his holster was empty.

131

"So," said Wennda, still smiling, "you found us."

The one who had waved nodded. "And then some," he said, indicating the crew.

"This isn't even the best part. I'll tell you about it while we head back."

The man shook his head. "I'm sorry, Wennda. I need you to turn over your weapons."

"Our—excuse me?"

"Your mission was unauthorized and conducted without the knowledge, order, or consent of the commander or the Quorum," he said formally. "My orders are to conduct the four of you back to the Dome for a hearing."

"Wait a minute," said Wennda. "We learned a lot of—"

"Tell the commander, not me," he said. "I'm just doing my job. Which I wouldn't have to do if you'd done yours." He held up a hand to stop her reply. "Your weapons," he said. He glanced at the crew. "Everybody's weapons."

Farley stepped forward. "Captain Joseph Farley, United States Army Air Force," he said. And waited.

The man frowned. "I don't know what most of that means," he said. "I'm Grobe. I'm a lieutenant."

"Well, lieutenant," said Farley. "My crew aren't part of any unauthorized mission, and we aren't anybody's prisoners. This woman offered us shelter in your city. One of my men is badly wounded, and we need to get him to a doctor fast."

Grobe glanced at Wennda. "She doesn't have the authority to make that offer," he said. "As I said, she's acting without permission here."

Farley felt detached from the whole scene, as if watching it in a movie theater. His heart wasn't even beating faster. He genuinely had no feeling for what was about to happen. "So you think we're your prisoners?" he asked.

Grobe hesitated. He looked back at one of his own team. "We'll sort that out when we get back," he said. "Meantime—"

"Meantime nothing. Do you think we're prisoners or don't you? I

132

have a vested interest in your answer." He drew his sidearm. "So do you."

Farley didn't have to look to know that his crew had followed suit. He knew exactly where Garrett was standing with the .30-cal leveled, because all four of the new team were staring at it. Their own weapons were readied, but their bearers were uncertain.

"That weapon you're all looking at is a Browning M1919 machine gun," said Farley. "It fires four hundred thirty-caliber rounds a minute, and it *will* turn you into something a cat wouldn't eat. Now I'll ask you one more time: Are we prisoners, or are we guests?"

Wennda stepped closer to Farley. She held both hands palm-up, her weapon hanging freely from its sling. "Please," she said. "Put down your weapons."

"Not on your life," said Farley.

"Please. This is all a misunderstanding. It'll be cleared up when I make my report."

"No offense, toots," said Broben, "but what I just heard sounded like you were gonna end up in the joint."

She looked at Farley. "You've trusted me this far," she said. She turned to Grobe with her hands out and slowly went to one knee. She brought her gunstrap over her head and set her weapon on the ground, then rose and stepped back from it. "Arshall," she said. "Sten."

Arshall and Sten scowled but removed their weapons. Two of Grobe's team came forward and collected them. They looked apologetic about it and Farley realized that they all knew each other.

"Now you," Grobe told Farley.

"Pound sand."

The two men regarded each other from behind their weapons.

"Grobe," said Wennda, "your orders cover the four of us, not these men. They aren't the enemy and they weren't on my mission. Please lower your guns." She turned to Farley. "Tell your men to holster their weapons," she said. "Nobody wants to shoot anybody here."

It made Farley angry that he believed her just because he already knew her face. What had that belief gotten them into?

He did not look away from Grobe as he lifted his shoulder-holster strap and slid his pistol in. Grobe looked like he wanted to argue about it some more, but he lowered his weapon and nodded.

"Stand down," Farley ordered. He smiled at Grobe and indicated the wasteland ahead. "After you," he said.

Grobe nodded uncertainly. He gestured to his squad and they took up positions in a diamond around the group. The woman in their party, short and dark-haired, shrugged at Arshall. Arshall shrugged back. Then he and Sten picked up Francis and the seventeen of them set out.

Farley walked beside Wennda. He had a lot he wanted to say but she was clearly occupied with her own problems.

Grobe nodded silently as Wennda and Farley caught up to him. After a moment he looked past Wennda at Farley. "What's a cat?" he asked

TWELVE

Farley had assumed they would head into another fissure, where there would be another fish-tank city. Instead they made their way up a gradual rise of dark stone smooth as poured concrete ramping toward the crater wall. There was a cluster of enormous bulges up the rise half a mile ahead where stone floor met sheer cliff. Smooth and round and the same color as the ground on which they walked. The largest of these was at least a hundred feet wide. Like balls dropped by some careless child god, fallen to embed here in this ruined place.

Wennda and her group bucked up at the sight of them. Farley figured they must be close to home.

They rounded the largest of the seemingly embedded spheres until they reached its juncture with the crater wall. Here a dark recess led into the rock, irregular in shape, ten feet high by ten wide. The entrance blended with the shadow that usually obtained along the crater rim, and looked like a natural formation when it could be discerned at all.

The group was ushered into this space. Wennda and her crew didn't look especially worried, so Farley stepped in and closed his eyes to help them adjust more quickly. The party stumbled against one another. The flat reverberations of their voices and footsteps told Farley that the space was long and narrow.

"Gee, the world's cheapest Tunnel of Love," said Shorty.

From ahead came a sound like a huge sigh. A warm breeze blew by as if a sleeping giant had breathed across them. Farley thought of Odysseus and his crew in the cave of Polyphemus the Cyclops.

A small bright light shone from what Farley had assumed was a watch on Grobe's wrist. It revealed what looked like a door to a bank vault. Beside it was a black glass plate. Grobe shone the wrist light on the panel and drew a pattern on the dark glass with his right index finger. A green square lit up on the plate and Grobe pressed his hand against it. A dull clack reverberated. Grobe glanced back at Wennda and pulled open the door. The inner side was heavily gasketed, several inches thick, and set with a wheel crank in the center.

Grobe and Wennda stepped through and cold blue light flickered on. Farley stopped short in the hatchway. Lighted ceiling panels showed a large bare metal room. On the opposite wall was a door like a heavy battleship hatch, with another black glass panel beside it.

Someone bumped into Farley from behind. He glanced back.

"What's cooking?" Broben asked.

"Keep them back," Farley told him. He put his hand on his pistol and looked at Grobe and Wennda. "What's the purpose of this room?" he asked.

Wennda glanced at Farley's hand on his sidearm. "It's an airlock," she said.

"Airlock."

"The Dome's a positive-pressure environment," she said. "Air pressure inside is higher than outside. It lowers our exposure. We can't have invasive insects or weeds or diseases."

"Show me."

"Everyone has to be inside first," said Grobe.

Farley shook his head. "You, me, and her."

"There's no reason to. Just bring your men inside and—"

"Just do it," Wennda told Grobe. "Clearly he's figured out our plan to flatten his men with our evil smashy ceiling."

Grobe frowned at her, but relented. "They can only throw you in the reverter once," he said.

Farley leaned back into the hatchway. "If I'm not in here when they open up again," he told Broben, "do what you have to do to get out of here."

"And go where, the Stork Club?" Broben snorted. "Never mind, I got it."

Farley stepped into the metal room.

Broben gave Grobe the stink eye as the man shut the heavy door and dogged it.

Wennda approached the panel by the inner door, but Grobe waved her off. "Your clearance was revoked," he said. "Sorry."

"I guess the old man's pretty shanked at me."

Grobe smirked. "You could say that." He drew a pattern on the console's glass plate and pressed his palm against the lighted square that appeared.

The air grille sighed. Farley yawned and felt his ears pop. A green dot appeared on the glass plate.

Wennda turned the inner door wheel and opened the door. She gestured for Farley to take a look. Farley stood in the doorway and looked out on a wide stone ramp that gently curved down and out of sight. Dim light beads shone near the floor.

"It leads to another access door," Wennda said behind him.

"Where you keep the real smashy ceiling," said Farley.

"I see why you're the one in charge."

Farley raised an eyebrow at her. "Okay, lieutenant," he told Grobe. "Once more around the park."

* * * * *

Broben was fascinated by the pinprick lights spaced along the down-curving ramp. "How do they make them so small?" he wanted to know.

"I swear if you were having brain surgery," said Farley, "you'd want to know where the doctor got his watch."

"If it was a good watch, sure."

Farley shook his head. "Just keep your eyes peeled," he said.

They marched down into the curving dark.

* * * * *

Another metal hatch. Another pattern drawn upon a glass panel. Grobe pulled open the hatch and sunlight flooded the rampway. Farley squinted and shook his head. He had a pilot's sense of direction, and everything was telling him that this couldn't be right, that they'd entered the chamber near the western rim and circled down a long and gradual quarter turn that ought to have placed them underground and almost directly beneath the rim wall.

He followed Grobe and Wennda through the hatchway and emerged blinking into a late summer day. The sky was pale clear blue, the sun was just past the horizon, the day was warm, the air was cool. A large cluster of adobe buildings rose ahead and to the right like some architecturally themed downtown. In the middle distance were patchwork fields. Beyond that, tall grass grew in a shallow marsh beside a rectangular reflecting lake that was the same size. Toward the horizon flat rock buttes emerged from a dense growth of enormous trees.

Then Farley's other senses caught up to his vision. The air smelled stale and slightly funky. He felt no wind. No grass waved in any breeze. No insects sounded from the fields, no birds sang, no traffic noises came from the downtown cluster.

He saw a group of people working in a field, and his sense of scale changed radically. The neatly ordered geometry of crops became tiny, maybe a tenth of a mile square. The reflecting lake was smaller than a football field. The adobe buildings were not a downtown skyline but a cluster of what looked like apartments and offices. The distant buttes were suspiciously regular and no more than a hundred feet high, and their surrounding trees were not enormous but low and dense with foliage. Everything had looked larger than it really was because the horizon was not three or four miles away but half a mile.

Farley looked up again. The sky was cloudless and its blue was oddly uniform. The sun did not shimmer or show false motion around its edges. It glowed steady as a nightlight. And it was not perfectly round. More like a hexagon with rounded sides.

He shielded his eyes from the sun and made out a faint geometry across the sky, a regular tracework like giant chicken wire revealing hexagonal panels.

The Dome. Of course.

Wennda and Grobe were conversing in low tones. From their body language and gestures it was clear that they were unsure what to do with their new guests. The absence of established protocol was interesting.

Finally Grobe nodded, though he didn't look happy about it, and Wennda turned away and collected Arshall and Sten. She pointed to Francis on his makeshift stretcher currently being carried by Garrett and Everett. "Get him to the Med Center and then report to the commander's office," she ordered.

Farley went to Francis as Arshall and Sten relieved Garrett and Everett. He bent down and put a hand on Francis' good shoulder. Half the kid's head and upper left torso looked like badly wrapped hamburger. The dressing stains had turned dark brown. The large red spot on the white wrapping where Francis' left eye ought to be was unnerving. His breathing was shallow.

"We're getting you to a doctor now, Francis," Farley told him. "You're going to be all right. I need you to hold on, okay?" He patted Francis' shoulder and stood.

"We'll take care of him," said Arshall. "Dr. Manday will have him back on his feet in no time."

Farley raised an eyebrow, but the man seemed sincere. "Thanks," he said.

Arshall and Sten lifted Francis.

"Got him?" asked Garrett.

"Got him," said Sten. Everett held up crossed fingers and the two men trotted away.

Farley watched them go and then saw Wennda watching him. He nodded his thanks and she nodded back and turned to lead them on.

* * * * *

They were herded along a narrow brick walkway between fields and marsh toward the pale brown buildings. Grass grew through the dark brown brick in places and the edges of the path were ragged, as if bricks had broken off and been removed.

Grobe and his squad resumed their guard formation. Wennda walked beside Grobe at point, followed by Farley and his crew. Yone walked beside Martin. They seemed to have struck up a friendship, which made sense when Farley thought about it. Martin had been through combat with the rest of the crew, and though he was their brother now they still hardly knew one another. Yone seemed to be a bit of an outsider as well, and like Martin he had risked his neck to help get Francis out of the line of fire. Farley noted the friendship without worry. He had enough sense of Martin to know the man was smart enough to keep his cards close. And maybe he'd find out some useful info in the meantime.

None of Wennda's people looked around as they walked toward the cluster of drab buildings. This was home base for them. Farley's crew, on the other hand, stared at their surroundings and nudged one another and pointed. They didn't talk much. Among uncertain allies in unknown territory they were instinctively tight-lipped.

They were also punch-drunk and exhausted. Thirty hours ago they'd been sleeping in their bunks in southeast England and trying not to worry themselves sick about a bombing raid on a munitions factory.

They had not gone very far before Grobe called a halt. He turned to Farley with an expectant look, as if Farley should know why he'd stopped them. Farley just waited.

Grobe waved at Farley's men. "Those have to be extinguished," he said.

"Extinguished? You're talking about my *crew*, you—"

"The things in their mouths," Grobe interrupted. He mimed smoking.

"Their cigarettes?" Farley blinked.

"The filtration units are already strained," said Grobe. "We can't afford the extra burden."

"Mister, I have no idea what you're talking about."

Wennda held a hand up to Grobe. "This is a self-contained environment," she told Farley, gesturing around them. "Everything's recycled. Food, water, air, waste. All of it's filtered, reverted, reused." She indicated Boney, who had raised his head to blow smoke while his pipe fumed in his hand. "Sustainability is our top priority. Everything we do affects the ecosystem."

Broben took a long pull and breathed smoke. "Heck, we don't want to affect anybody's ecosystem," he said. "We'll go smoke outside."

Farley shook his head. "Just put 'em out," he said. "We can live an hour without a smoke."

Broben scowled, but he dropped his cigarette and ground it out. He bent and picked it up and showed it to Wennda and Grobe. Then he put it back in its pack. "I'll save my own butt," he said.

Grobe turned away and motioned them forward without another word.

Broben shook his head in disgust, and Farley indicated the dome. "It probably takes a lot of rules to live like this," he said.

"Shit," said Broben. "I bet even the Nazis let you light one up before they shoot you."

* * * * *

Farley trudged along in exhausted silence. He had a thousand questions and concerns, but most of his energy and will were occupied with putting one foot in front of the other.

Wennda was looking more worried as they got closer to the buildings. If what Grobe had said was true, it was a good bet her team would be court-martialed for desertion, or unauthorized activity, or going outside without a hall pass, for all Farley knew.

Farley stared at two men and two women working in a field. Hoes, spades, a square barrow, light jumpsuits. Arshall waved at them and they looked surprised and waved back. They continued to stare at the party making its way across the miniature cropland.

"I got a bet with myself," said Broben, "that Boatman is gonna shake me awake real soon and tell me I got thirty minutes to suit up, chow down, and get to the briefing."

"Never thought I'd be homesick for those sardine cans," Plavitz said behind them.

Behind Plavitz, Garrett said, "I just want to get horizontal for five minutes. I'm all in."

"You can sleep in the next world," Broben told him.

Shorty's laugh was a curt bark. "Well, whadda ya call *this*?" he said in Jack Benny's voice.

* * * * *

As they neared the buildings Farley saw that many of them had missing windows covered with fabric, some of the makeshift covers drawn back like curtains. The dark brick walkways had potholes that had been patched and worn concave.

The crew were led to a two-story, U-shaped building, dun-colored like most others here. Farley thought it looked like a budget motor court. Between two unmarked doors a group of men stood watching two others on spindly folding chairs playing a board game, making comments and offering suggestions. All wore lightweight jumpsuits. On the floor above them a man leaned on the metal railing, foot tapping and head nodding in a rhythm only he could hear. They stopped and stared as Farley's crew approached. Farley glanced at Wennda and their escort. Wennda looked determined and led them on.

The man on the railing touched his ear and stopped moving in rhythm. He looked over Farley's crew and didn't seem overly impressed. "So you found her," he said to Grobe.

"I was never lost," Wennda called back.

"What about Sten and Arshall? Did they know where they were?"

"Not really the time for this discussion, Lang," Wennda said wearily. "Are their quarters ready?"

"Thanks to six of us doubling up they are." Lang nodded down at the crew. "These are the eight new mouths to feed?"

One of the game players looked up. "Nine," he called up. "There's one in the clinic."

"Nine," Lang echoed. He shook his head. "Reverter fodder."

"Nice to meet you, too," muttered Broben.

Farley caught his eye. "You see anyone radio ahead about us?" he asked quietly.

Broben shook his head.

"The commander appreciates your sacrifice," Wennda called up to Lang. Farley couldn't tell if she was being ironic.

Lang shrugged. "Nobody minds a temporary inconvenience," he said.

* * * * *

The room was long and narrow and completely bare. No bunks, no chairs, no storage, no windows. Plain walls with thin lines where panels met. Overhead air vents. A tile floor worn colorless down the center. Light panels glowed overhead. Several were unlit, and one flickered.

"Gee, I wonder what the budget rooms are like," said Shorty.

"It isn't moving and there's no one shooting at me," said Plavitz. "I like it just fine." He took off his boots and curled up near a wall and to all appearances instantly fell asleep. The others set down their weapons and their meager belongings and sat against the bare walls and relit their cigarettes. Boney took out his pipe and looked at it and put it back. Broben touched the pack in his shirt pocket and then reluctantly took his hand away. "Don't you bums come begging to me when you run out," he told Garrett and Everett.

Wennda stayed near the open door and watched with a kind of amused horror as the men blew smoke toward the ceiling. "Will this be sufficient, captain?" she asked.

"Sure, I guess," said Farley, looking around the bare room. "For now, anyway."

"Then I'd like you to come with me, please."

"I don't need separate quarters," Farley said.

Wennda raised an eyebrow. "I'll keep that in mind. But at the moment, the commander would like to see you."

"All right," said Farley. He went to the door, then looked back at Broben. "Try to keep them from burning the place down, okay?"

"Man can only do so much," said Broben.

THIRTEEN

Two of Grobe's team stayed behind to guard the crew's quarters. Farley thought about protesting but tabled it. Nobody was going anywhere right now, anyway.

Grobe and the short woman in his team flanked Farley and Wennda as they made their way through narrow pedestrian avenues. Everyone Farley saw wore the same oatmeal-colored jumpsuits, though some had been decorated with drawn designs or patterns. People stared at Farley in an unnerving way.

They entered a low, wide, dun-colored building and were ushered through a lobby the size of a living room, then went up a narrow and dimlit stairwell, their footfalls loud on the worn stone steps. On the second floor they emerged into a narrow corridor lit by small high-hats and painted a dingy yellow. Foot traffic had worn a dull path down the middle of the floor. Some of the lights were out. Farley figured it was probably a bit of a trek to get a new lightbulb around here.

Grobe opened a door. "You'll wait here," he told Farley. "The commander will see you after Wennda has been debriefed."

Wennda forced a smile. "Maybe we should give him some more time to calm down."

"He's over fifty and it hasn't happened yet," said Grobe.

"True." She nodded, then took a deep breath. "All right. Better to chop it off than saw on it, I guess."

"You'll be fine." Farley thought he heard a note of contempt in the comment.

The expression that flashed across Wennda's face made Farley think she was about to slap Grobe. It vanished as quickly as it came.

Grobe didn't seem to have caught it. He nodded at the short woman—whose name Farley never did learn—and she nodded back and took up station by the door. Grobe indicated the room to Farley.

"Good luck," Farley told Wennda.

A nervous smile. "I'll try to wear him out before he gets to you," she said. She squared her shoulders and went down the corridor, Grobe beside her.

* * * * *

Farley found himself in a small conference room, mostly muted grays and black. Half a dozen swivel chairs made of some strong black mesh around black tubing surrounded a rectangular table with a black glass top. The lighting was subtle and indirect, though some of the lights were out in here, too. The far wall was decorated with unobtrusive geometric patterns. All of it was unremarkable and understandable to Farley, yet it was also alien. Sophisticated and dilapidated at the same time.

He went back to the door and pushed on it. It gave considerably and Farley frowned. It wasn't wood and it wasn't metal. He tapped the wall beside it with a finger and produced a hollow, high sound. He thought he probably could punch through it.

There wasn't much more that the room could tell him, so he sat in one of the chairs. It was more comfortable than it looked, and adjusted in ways he wasn't used to a chair adjusting. It would even lie flat.

If the Army had taught Farley anything, it was that you should do blanket drill any time you have a chance to, if you aren't on R & R. And this was about as far from R & R as Farley could imagine.

He put his hands on his chest and closed his eyes.

* * * * *

He was the only boy in the world, and she was the only girl. Just like that old song his mother used to sing. There was no one else. They had the world to themselves; they were a world unto themselves. They stood across from one another, close enough that he could see her face. Every mole and line and freckle, all the little imperfections and disproportions that together comprise character. The intelligent eyes, the determined jaw. The contours someone else had drawn from his vivid memory of a face he'd never actually seen.

And yet it seemed that she was far away from him. Her expression and the set of her eyes made him wonder if she even saw him. He knew she would not hear him if he spoke. As if he were some ghost. As if she were. Or as if they both were real but the common ground they shared was not.

* * * * *

A quick dull knock brought Farley upright so fast he nearly keeled over in the reclined chair. He was startled to realize he had fallen asleep.

The door opened and Wennda and Grobe walked in. Both still wore their oddly insect-like stretchy outfits with the matte-black panels. Wennda's hair was tied back in a ponytail. She did not meet Farley's eye as she went to stand at attention behind a chair at one end of the black glass table. Grobe nodded woodenly at Farley and stood behind a chair at the opposite end.

Farley knew what was coming, and he quickly got to his feet as the commander entered the room. He was bald with graying stubble, not large but muscular and flat-bellied, and he moved confidently and purposefully with an athletic economy. Grobe had said the commander was over fifty, but Farley had the impression of someone a decade younger. He wore the ubiquitous plain jumpsuit, but Farley didn't need a military uniform to know command when he saw it.

Farley glanced at Wennda as the commander went to a chair on the opposite side of the table. Her expression didn't change, but her chin rose a trifle. *That must have been some ass-chewing,* Farley thought.

The commander nodded curtly at Farley and sat down. Farley waited for Wennda and Grobe to sit before he did so himself.

If the commander was amused or annoyed, his face didn't show it. "I'm Vanden," he said.

"Captain Joseph Farley, United States Army Air Force. You're in charge here, sir?"

"I'm head of military operations."

"I appreciate you taking us in."

"Your status hasn't been determined." Vanden raised a hand to forestall Farley's reply. "I need to know about your aircraft."

Farley took a deep breath. *Here we go.* "I need to know about our status," he said.

"What I learn about the one will determine the other."

"Is that a fact. What is it you want to know, exactly?"

"Was it able to fly when you abandoned it?"

Farley couldn't help wincing at the word. As if he'd somehow orphaned the *Morgana.* Walked away from her without a fight. "Not without a hangar party," he replied. "Two engines wouldn't start. One was intermittent. Number One was—well, I think my flight engineer could have fixed it, but without him—" Farley shrugged.

"Is that a no?" Vanden asked.

"That's a no."

"If you were able to make the repairs, how long would it take?"

"Couple days, maybe. If we had the parts."

"And if you didn't have the parts?"

"Maybe never." Farley shrugged. "My flight engineer could answer that better than me."

"Then perhaps I should be talking to him."

"I wish you could. He got shot back in the canyon."

Vanden frowned. "This is alarming news," he said. He didn't sound alarmed.

"You're telling me."

Vanden looked at Wennda. "You didn't mention this man's role when you made your report."

"I wasn't aware of it until now," she said stiffly.

"This just gets better and better, doesn't it." Vanden waved her off. "What is your aircraft's armament?" he asked Farley.

Farley folded his arms. "I'm really not at liberty to discuss that."

The commander studied him. "There's every reason to believe this weaponry will be used against us," he said. "That means against you, while you are here."

"That would be unfortunate. But the information you want is classified by the U.S. Army Air Force."

Vanden leaned back and tapped his mouth with thumb and forefinger and looked thoughtful. Then he nodded at Grobe.

Grobe tapped the tabletop, and a lighted rectangle appeared before him. It flickered, and Grobe banged the table with a fist. The rectangle held steady. Grobe tapped symbols within it, and on the table in front of Wennda a small panel lit. She frowned down at it.

Grobe looked at the commander and spread his hands.

"Wennda," the commander said.

Wennda's mouth went tight as she pulled her flat binoculars from a chest pocket and positioned them in the lighted square.

Grobe tapped his panel again. A green light glowed on the binoculars, and a few seconds later a twilit miniature of the massive, pale-green wall of the Redoubt formed in the center of the table. It looked absolutely solid, as if a model of a section of the canyon had been placed upon the glass.

Grobe slid a finger along the bottom of the panel and the image blurred. His finger stopped, and now Farley was looking at a miniature *Fata Morgana* parked on the canyon floor in the middle of the table, bathed in the eerie greenish light of the Redoubt. The entire scene expanded until the bomber was several feet long. Farley could not believe the solidity and detail. For all he could tell, he was looking at a meticulously detailed model of his B-17F as he had last seen her. Appraising the visible damage, he also could not believe he had managed to safely land her on a canyon floor.

A flat version of the image now occupied Grobe's control panel. Grobe drew on it with a finger, and a red halo formed around the twin fifties on the top turret. "Two weapons here in a rotating mount," he said. "Chemical firearms with high-capacity belt-feed loading systems."

Farley narrowed his eyes. He glanced at Wennda, but she continued to stare firmly down in front of her.

Grobe drew another red halo, this time around the ball turret. "Two more here on an X-Y axis," he said, "possibly remotely controlled." Red ringed the tail gun. "Two here." The cheek port. "One here." Floating circles formed around the empty port in the plexiglas nose bubble and the swivel mount on the right-side gunner station. "Presumably one here and here."

His finger traced a large circle around the perimeter of his monitor, and Farley was startled when the cross-section of landscape on the table rotated as if parked on a lazy susan. The floating red rings rotated with it. Another ring formed around the Browning in its mount on the left window. "And one here," Grobe finished, "for a total of seven emplacements. Most seem to be manually operated."

Farley's lips pressed tight. Son of a *bitch*.

"Combustible liquid fuel powers four reciprocating engines turning propellers for motive power at subsonic speed. Maneuverability and range projections indicate a strategic heavy attack aircraft and not a fighter. But there's this." Grobe dragged his finger along the panel in the opposite direction until the view on the table looked down a jagged length of canyon fissure. The cliff walls looked as solid as the little Redoubt had.

A speck entered the dusky air of the canyon diorama. Grobe dragged a finger up the edge of his panel and the scale enlarged until the speck resolved as an approaching B-17. Even though it was only a few inches long, it was easy to see that the bomber was bad off—shot to shit; right rear stabilizer askew; only one engine running, and the props not feathered on Two, Three, and Four; one wheel down and one still lowering.

Tiny tracer rounds streaked from the right-side gun port. The bomber banked right—and Farley got his first good look at the thing that had fought them through the canyon and annihilated the troop carrier that had pursued them on the valley floor. It appeared at the top of the diorama angling sharply down, and it streaked by the angled bomber from above and behind, firing some kind of weapon that hung beneath one wing. It was bigger than the Flying Fortress, though clearly lighter, and it flew like a bird and fought like a Focke-Wulf 190. More rounds streaked toward it from the B-17. The thing shot ahead of the bomber and arced up with a suddenness that would have torn a wing off any fighter plane. It spread sail-like membrane wings and snap-rolled right and out of the scene.

Garrett and Wen had argued about whether the thing had been a creature or a machine. What Farley had just seen was both.

He realized he was holding his breath. He let it out.

Grobe tapped the table again and the image froze. "The video shows the aircraft firing what appears to be a combination of targeting, incendiary, and kinetic ammunition at eight rounds per second," he said, "with a muzzle velocity of eight hundred meters per second."

"Enough to drive off the Typhon and destroy two armored personnel carriers," said Vanden, looking at Farley.

Farley made his face a mask and stared back.

Vanden turned to Wennda. "You said they used these directly against Redoubt troops."

She nodded. "From the aircraft and from a less powerful firearm they moved to a sheltered emplacement."

"It went through their armor?"

She glanced at Farley. "They might as well have been naked," she said.

Vanden stared at the bristling metal war machine suspended above the table. "They still use the same armor we do?"

"Networked carbon filament mesh," said Grobe. He hesitated. "I should mention that Captain Farley's crew brought one of the mounted weapons here with them," he said. "In addition to personal firearms."

Vanden glanced at Wennda. This time she met his gaze unblinkingly.

Farley leaned back in his chair and folded his arms. "What is your interest in my aircraft?" he asked.

Vanden raised an eyebrow—the most expression he'd shown since he came into the room. "Your aircraft defeated the Typhon," he said.

"You call that a defeat?" said Farley.

"You weren't killed."

"I think I have a different definition of victory."

"No one has ever gone against the Typhon and survived," said Vanden.

"You should see what we do to Messerschmitts."

Vanden regarded Farley blankly. He laced his fingers and pressed his palms tightly together. "Based on the reports from Wennda and her … accomplices … and based on your actions against the Redoubt troops, I have to concede that her theory that you've come here from somewhere else may have merit."

Farley rubbed his face with both hands. He didn't know how much longer he could stay awake. He felt worn so thin you could probably shine a candle through him. "Well, I guess that's a relief," he said.

"Why would that be?"

"Because we don't want to be here any more than you want us here. Maybe we did fly through some big hole in the sky, but we sure as hell didn't mean to. We just want to get our ship back and go home."

"And you think it will be that simple."

"I think the goal is. I couldn't tell you about achieving it."

"And that's your objective. To go back to where you came from."

Farley shrugged. "What else?" he asked, more testily than he'd intended. "You all seem like very nice people, and I'm grateful for your help, but we didn't mean to come here."

Vanden tapped the tabletop and the miniature *Morgana* reappeared between them. He turned his hand and spread his fingers, and the bomber rotated and enlarged and rotated until the nose art hovered in the air. "Then please explain to me," said Vanden, "how you didn't mean to come here in an aircraft with a picture of my daughter on it."

"Your—" Farley looked from the coldly furious commander to Wennda, who shrugged helplessly.

FOURTEEN

Farley opened his eyes and blinked up at a paneled ceiling. The light directly above him was out. Voices murmured in conversation but he couldn't make out what they were saying.

He smelled coffee. He sat up.

"Morning, sunshine."

Broben sat with Yone at a small table that hadn't been there earlier. Jerry was smoking a Lucky, and both men were drinking coffee. Jerry lifted his cup at Farley. "Still hot," he said. "I ate the last doughnut, though."

"Shit. If this place ever heard of a doughnut, I'll eat my hat." Farley saw that he had slept curled against a wall with his flight jacket rolled up for a pillow. He got to his feet and went to the table and sat down heavily in a folding chair. The table seemed to have emerged from the wall like a retractable counter supported on two thin folding legs. Farley pushed on it. It didn't feel as rickety as it looked.

Yone poured coffee from a plastic pitcher with a screw-on cap and held the cup out to him. Farley accepted it with a grateful nod. The stackable plastic cup was thin but did not get hot in his hands. He held it beneath his nose and inhaled. He felt the coffee lighting up his veins before he even took a sip. "That's the stuff, all right," he said.

He set the cup down and Jerry lit a cigarette off of his and handed it over. Farley saluted with it. He closed his eyes and dragged. Coffee and a smoke. Hell, he was practically back home.

He ran a hand over his stubble, then opened his eyes and frowned at Broben. "How the hell did you shave?" he asked.

"Razor in the survival kit. No soap, though." Broben rubbed a cheek. "My face feels like a peeled potato."

"You should see it from this side." Farley blew smoke up at the ceiling, enjoying the return of the nicotine rush. He glanced around the barracks. "So they brought us some furniture?" he asked.

Broben shook his head. "It was here the whole time. Show him, Yone."

Yone smiled his quick on-off smile and stood up. He went to the wall and pulled out what Farley at first took for a tall, narrow drawer. Except that the drawer kept pulling out, to reveal a kind of cross-section of a staircase. The hollows beneath the steps were storage units. Yone went up the steps and pressed on the wall, then slid a section of it aside to reveal a recessed bunk. "There are eight bunks in this unit," he said. He went to the opposite wall and folded down a section and pulled it out to reveal a boxy sofa. "Two couches." He folded it back and pulled out another drawer that had a flat top. Perfectly fitted beneath it were two tall chairs. More shelving and more storage was tucked away in other recesses.

"I don't know if it's a barracks or a cuckoo clock," said Broben.

"Where'd they hide the head?" said Farley.

"Down the hall," said Broben. "Wait'll you get a load of that."

Farley frowned. "Is it afternoon?"

"It's next morning," said Broben. "We let you sleep in. You were pretty loopy when they brought you back yesterday."

"Where are the men?"

"Outside playing catch, if you can believe that."

Farley snorted. "I can."

"Your girlfriend came by already. Said she'll be back later." Broben pulled on his Lucky, flicked ash into his empty cup. "So you got the third degree from the CO yesterday. Yone says he's a hardass."

"He is that." Farley stretched. "The girl's his daughter."

"You're shitting me."

"Not even a little bit."

"Well. You got some hurdles there, pal."

"Me and Jesse Owens."

Broben snorted. "So what's the skinny?" he asked. "They gonna help us get our ride back?"

Farley glanced at Yone.

Broben waved his cigarette. "Yone's on the level, Joe. He's been filling me in on this joint. You need to listen to this."

Yone finished putting away the room's ingenious slide-outs and collapsibles and foldables and joined them at the little table, smiling nervously.

"Thanks for the coffee," said Farley.

Yone ducked his head. "It is synthetic, I'm afraid," he said. "They don't have coffee beans here. But it is not so bad."

Farley sniffed his cup again. It smelled like coffee to him. He took a last deep drag from his cigarette and dropped the butt into the cup Broben was using as an ashtray. Time to clock in. Captain Midnight is on the air. "They have them where you come from?" Farley asked.

Yone nodded. "It's quite a luxury, though. There is little room for growing nonessential crops."

"What's nonessential about coffee?" Broben asked.

Yone smiled. "I certainly prefer to live in a world that has it," he said.

"You came from there?" Farley asked. "From the Redoubt?"

"Two years ago," Yone said, and shrugged. "But I will always be a stranger here."

"Because your city and this one are, what? Rivals?"

"One could put it that way."

"How would you put it? Competitors? Resources must be pretty scarce around here."

"The cities are almost entirely self-contained. They don't rely on their surroundings for resources, because there are none, other than power."

"Where does the power come from?"

"For the Redoubt it is mostly solar. Here it is geothermal."

"You don't say."

Yone smiled. "I don't really understand them either."

"So what's the beef?"

"Beg pardon?"

"Why are they shooting at each other?"

Yone considered him for a moment. "No one here would ever ask that question," he finally said, "because they have known the answer all their lives. The hatred between the Redoubt and the Dome is as much a part of their world as the air, the calorie ration, the conservation laws. It is a heritage." He smiled thinly. "A birthright."

"Well," said Farley. "I'm not from around here."

"But that is my point." Yone poured Farley more coffee. "No one is not from around here."

Farley waved at the room. "You mean no one in these bubbles ever sees anyone else."

Yone glanced at Broben, who nodded for him to go on. "I mean," Yone said, "there *is* no one else. The Dome and the Redoubt are the only two cities in the world."

Farley studied him. "How is that possible?" he asked.

"War."

"That's a hell of a war."

"Yes. It happened centuries ago."

"Centuries. As in hundreds of years."

Yone nodded. "The war lasted for decades, and it grew until it involved most of the world. At first it was fought with bullets and bombs, but as the stakes grew higher they used chemicals and diseases created in laboratories. They built machines that worked without operators, war machines that thought for themselves and adapted to their environments. That fought without fear or hesitation. Without mercy. Battalions of living machines that swarmed the cities and darkened the skies."

"That's hard to imagine."

"You have seen an example already. Fought with it."

Farley glanced at Broben. "That thing that attacked my bomber?" he asked.

"The Typhon is a remnant of that war," said Yone. "Blindly following commands given to it by men dead for two hundred years."

"To do what?"

"There is a powerful energy source still functioning beneath the ground. In the shaft at the center of the crater. The Typhon seems to be protecting it."

"From what?"

"Anything it thinks is trying to gain access. Anything it thinks is a threat."

"Then whatever's down there must be a pretty big deal."

Yone nodded. "It may be some kind of power generator. Or a weapon. No one knows, because no one who has tried to find out has returned. Whatever it is, it is powerful enough to disrupt the air for miles above the well. Now that you have come here in your aircraft, some people are wondering if that disruption is more … fundamental. A kind of breach in the universe. A tear in the world that you managed to find your way through. Commander Vanden's daughter, Wennda, has come to believe this."

"I'd say it's a load of crap, but—" Farley waved to indicate the barracks, the Dome outside, the devastation beyond "—here we are."

"I would not discount the possibility," said Yone. "The energies they were manipulating by the end of the war were beyond our understanding. Weapons that took apart the very building blocks of matter. That destroyed entire cities in seconds. The scale of butchery is unimaginable. Millions killed in a single flash. Until finally they developed weapons that could destroy entire worlds."

"Who in his right mind would use them?" Farley demanded. "It'd be suicide."

"It was suicide," Yone agreed. "As you have seen."

Farley stared. "The crater?"

Yone's quick nod encompassed inconceivable destruction. "An explosion so powerful it cracked the planet's crust. Earthquakes and oceans of lava that destroyed entire nations. Much of the life that

158

survived was killed in the ice age that came because the planet was covered by a cloud of ash. The world was in twilight for decades. Without sunlight the plants and trees began to die. The oceans died. Without these, everything else began to die."

"From one explosion."

"As far as anyone can determine, yes."

"And we thought the Nazis were assholes," said Broben.

Yone spread his hands. "Perhaps they didn't realize the power of what they had made," he said. "So much has been lost that no one is certain."

Farley rubbed his stubbled jaw. "And you've all been waiting two hundred years for things to recover?"

"Oh, no." Yone shook his head. "There will be no recovery. The explosion tore a hole in the atmosphere. So that when the cloud of ash finally began to disperse, the sun itself began to kill what had managed to remain alive. Beyond a certain point life could not recover. Too many links in the chain were broken. What remains is mosses, molds, lichens, many insects, some plants, perhaps a few small mammals such as rats. The atmosphere on the surface will no longer support human life. It is too thin. Too cold."

"I don't understand," said Farley. "We spent a full day in it just fine."

"We are at the bottom of a crater that is nearly three kilometers below the surface. Only here are the air pressure and temperature high enough to support life. That is why the shelters were built here."

"The Redoubt and the Dome," Farley realized.

Yone nodded. "There may have been others elsewhere, but only the two here could have lasted so long. And to this day they watch each other with great suspicion and dread across the heart of the thing that destroyed them."

"Jesus," said Broben. "Aren't you the lucky ones."

Yone looked at him. "People could not have survived in such conditions for centuries without being very clever and very strict, as well as being lucky," he said, not recognizing Broben's irony. "Resources are limited. There is no room for waste. Repurpose, reuse, repair. Every child is taught this so completely it is more like a law of nature than a set of rules. Life is highly regulated, and everyone must be useful." He shrugged. "It has to be that way."

"Two hundred years in a bottle," Farley mused.

"In a bottle meant to last a tenth that long at most. But yes." Yone considered them a moment. "Perhaps you can understand how shocking it is to see new faces," he said. "To interact with a new person, when everyone is someone you have known since you were born. I am always reminded that I am not from here. I earn the calories I consume, but I will never truly earn the trust of my hosts. A new person will always be a stranger."

"And then nine of us show up," said Broben.

"Nine of you show up," Yone agreed, "in an aircraft that can defeat the Typhon. And our enemies have it."

* * * * *

The crew had got hold of a gray ball the size of a softball and were throwing it around in the barracks courtyard. Without gloves there was no point in rifling it to each other, so they were throwing pop flies and bouncers.

Garrett snagged the ball and was about to throw it again when he caught sight of Farley watching from the doorway. "Hey, look who's up!" he yelled, and threw a long high fly his way.

Farley caught it. "Guy needs his beauty sleep," he said, and threw it back.

"Gosh," Shorty said in Jack Benny's voice, "I'm sorry you had to cut it so *short*."

Plavitz came around a corner, talking with the smartass joker they'd met here yesterday. Lang, Farley remembered. As Plavitz stepped into the courtyard he grinned at his crewmates and held up a stick like some conquering hero. The crew cheered, and Plavitz patted Lang's shoulder. They immediately started organizing a game of stickball, recruiting from the male onlookers among the barracks residents.

Farley watched a moment longer, taking in the excited chatter, the perplexed expressions of the drafted players, the close horizon and faint geometry perceivable in the sky. The bizarre normalcy of the scene before him.

"Screwy, huh?" said Broben.

"You read my mind."

"You want I should call a meeting?"

"No, let's let them run a while before we put the leash back on." Farley looked away from the incipient pickup game. "Where's that potato peeler you used on your mug?" he asked. "I want to hit the head and make myself look at least as civilized as the rest of these monkeys." He nodded at the crew.

Broben smiled knowingly and told him where he'd left the razor. "Have fun," he said.

Farley thought it was an odd thing to say until he saw the facilities. Room for two, no sink, no towels. A brief jet of something that didn't quite feel like water shot when you passed your hand through a gap in a vertical metal cylinder on one wall. The slanted toilet bowl held no water, and nothing stuck to the porcelain. Or whatever the hell it was. And it flushed itself when you were done.

Broben gave Farley a thumbs-up when he came back. "Say, mister," he said, "you didn't see an ugly, smelly guy dressed like you a second ago, did you?"

"Shit, shower, and shave," said Farley. "Couldn't figure out the shower part, though."

"Nobody could. But there's gotta be a garden hose around here somewhere."

Farley leaned close to him and sniffed. "Fire hose," he amended.

"Jeez, one shave and he's a hygiene film—hey, here comes your dreamgirl. For your sake I hope her sense of smell ain't so good."

Wennda had entered the courtyard and was watching the crew

trying to explain stickball to the men they'd drafted to play. Farley tried not to smirk at Martin showing Yone how to pitch. Wennda saw Farley across the courtyard and smiled and waved.

Broben put his hands on his hips and shook his head. "Well, will you look at that," he said. "Why is it always the pilots?"

"You don't see Clark Gable and Jimmy Cagney playing tail gunners, do you?"

"Would it kill them to play a copilot sometimes?"

Wennda wore a jumpsuit and not the skintight and paneled combat outfit she'd worn earlier, but someone—it had to have been Garrett or Everett—wolf whistled as she walked across the courtyard. Either she didn't hear it or she ignored it. Or possibly, Farley realized, she had no idea what it meant.

"Captain Farley," she said. She nodded at Broben. "Lieutenant."

"Broben," said Broben.

"Yes."

Broben smirked and Farley dug him in the ribs as Wennda pulled what looked like a wad of cellophane from a pocket. She snapped it like a washrag and it went stiff. She tapped it and it glowed to life. "I thought you'd want to talk with our doctor about your injured crewman," she told Farley.

"Very much, yes," said Farley, a bit perplexed.

Wennda touched the glowing panel a few more times. A red light flashed and a faint tone sounded. A moment later Wennda was holding a miniature and apparently solid bust of a fine-featured black woman in the palm of her hand.

The woman smiled. "Wennda," she said. "Good morning."

Wennda shifted her hand so that the miniature woman faced Farley. "Hi, Dr. Manday," said Wennda. "This is Captain Farley. You're treating one of his crew."

"I certainly am," said the lifelike image. "Hello, captain."

Farley glanced uncertainly at Wennda. Her expression said *What are you waiting for?*

He leaned closer to the woman on Wennda's hand. "Hello, doctor!" he said, feeling as if he were falling for some prank.

Wennda looked amused. "You don't have to shout. And she can see you fine, too." She made a little pushing motion and Farley stepped back, feeling his face go hot.

"Could you give us a status report?" Wennda asked the doctor.

"Of course."

Farley felt a sudden dread. "I'd like—" he started to tell Wennda. He stopped and looked at Dr. Manday. "Doctor, I'd like for my men to hear this, if you don't mind."

"Not at all."

Farley nodded at Broben, whose expression said *You sure about this?* Farley rolled a finger, and Broben gave a piercing taxi whistle. The crew quickly gathered around, making a terrific fuss about the lifelike image on the nearly invisible device in Wennda's hand. The doctor blinked and smiled patiently.

"All right, simmer down," Farley ordered. "This is Dr. Manday. She's about to give us the news on Francis, so keep it quiet. Go ahead, doctor."

Dr. Manday's gaze shifted back to Farley. "All right," she said.

"Holy moly," said Shorty.

"Pipe down!" Broben growled.

Dr. Manday was now looking at her own miniature version of the transparent device in Wennda's hand. "Your man was brought in with a punctured left lung," she said, "a fractured upper rib, severed ligaments in the left shoulder, shrapnel and lacerations along the left side of the head and upper left torso, shattered zygomatic arch and sclerotic puncture resulting in loss of vision in the left eye, critical exsanguination—"

"Can you do anything for him?" Farley asked quickly. He didn't think the crew needed to hear the gory details.

"He's in a regen tank right now," said Manday. "Vitals are stable, tissue's taking, hemo and O2 are up. I sampled his lung tissue and I'm printing up some more for him, should be ready in about an hour. I won't know about the eye until later tonight. I pulled metal fragments from every wound site. Was he near some kind of explosion?"

Farley's mouth pressed tight. He hated this more than any other facet of the war. Human bodies weren't made to be thrown into that chaos like bugs in a woodchipper. "Yes, ma'am, he was," he said. "I'm sure you're doing everything you can for him."

"I can't do more and I wouldn't do less," she nearly chanted. "It will still be a few days before I can discharge him, though."

Farley blinked. "A few days?"

"Well, there is that eye," Manday said, a bit defensively.

Wennda glanced at Farley. "Would you like to know anything else?" she asked.

Farley shook his head numbly.

"Thanks, doc," Wennda said. Farley added his thanks, but the image had already gone dark.

"He's gonna make it?" Everett blurted. "St. Francis is gonna make it?"

"You heard the lady," said Farley, not quite believing it himself. "He'll be out in a couple of days."

The crew cheered. If any of them had a problem with Francis' bacon being saved by a doctor who was a woman who also wasn't white, it wasn't evident.

Wennda did something to the thin clear panel and then crumpled it again.

Shorty gaped outright. "A cellophane telephone!" he said.

"Cellophone," said Boney.

"Where can I get one?" Shorty demanded.

Wennda raised an eyebrow. "I'll see what I can do," she said. She smiled at Farley. "I told you we'd take care of him."

"I'm a believer," said Farley. "Thank you."

She looked faintly embarrassed. "The commander wants to see you," she said. "And I'd like to discuss a few things while we go." She glanced up at the sun and frowned.

"Sure," said Farley. "I wanted to talk to you, too."

"I think that's our cue, fellas," said Plavitz. "We better fade."

"Dis-*missed!*" Everett agreed.

The men went back to their stickball recruits.

"These idiots couldn't organize a two-car funeral," Broben told Farley. "I better take charge before someone gets an eye poked out." He nodded at Wennda and left to join the wildly gesturing fray.

"What are they trying to do?" Wennda asked.

"They want to teach your people how to play stickball so they can get a game together."

"Why are they only teaching men?"

Farley opened his mouth. Shut it. Shrugged. "No reason I can think of," he said. He cupped his hands to his mouth. "Hey," he called. "Let some girls play, too."

He missed the look Wennda shot him. "We should go," she said. "It's not good to make the commander wait."

"I'll bet."

Shorty glanced at his watch and then squinted up at the artificial sun. He grinned and called, "Hey, captain! Want to see a trick?"

Farley saw the others grinning, too. Garrett nudged Everett and jutted his chin.

"Sure," said Farley.

Shorty looked at his watch and raised a hand. His lips moved as he counted down, moving his hand in time, and then he snapped his fingers.

The sun went out.

FIFTEEN

Farley's first thought when everything went dark was, *Air raid!* But no one was running or panicked, there were no shouts or alerts. Lights in many buildings were already on. Floodlights lit at the top corners of the courtyard.

"I *knew* I should've paid that power bill," Shorty said in Jack Benny's voice.

Some of the crew laughed. With the stickball game on hold, most of them were already lighting cigarettes.

"Cute," said Farley. "What now?"

"Now we wait an hour for the next panel to come on," said Wennda. She pointed at the dim sky. "Sixteen panels along the meridian are artificial sunlight. They get brighter from horizon to zenith. But the eleven o'clock panel doesn't work anymore."

Farley craned his head. With the sun panel unlit the dome above them reflected enough light from the buildings below to reveal itself for what it was—a pale gray bowl covering a thousand people like a cake tray. Starless, moonless, cloudless, and unnerving.

Farley shook his head. "So how long's this been going on?"

"Eleven o'clock has been out for the last eight years."

"Why not just jump from the ten o'clock panel to the noon one? Or keep ten o'clock lit for two hours?"

She looked impressed. "Good for you," she said.

"I'm a barbarian, not an idiot. So why won't it work?"

"It will work. In fact, that was the solution for a few weeks. But it turns out that the longer a panel stays lit, the more likely it is to fail. And we'd much rather deal with the dark for an hour than lose another panel." She shrugged. "We're very good at improvising. But sometimes things just wear out, and there's nothing anyone can do."

"Maybe my guys can think of something."

"We would name a yearly holiday after them."

"Don't be silly. A statue would be plenty."

Her brow furrowed. "Sometimes I can't tell if you're serious."

Farley grinned. "I'll keep that in mind. So what does your father want to see me about?"

"The commander would like to discuss a plan for recovering your aircraft."

"He'll help us?" Farley was elated but surprised. "What's his angle?"

"I think he wants to explore different options."

"Fine by me. Long as we don't just keep exploring them till those aquarium jokers come knocking here in my ship."

"If I understand you correctly, I don't think he wants that, either. Nobody does."

"Well, what are we waiting for?" said Farley. He grinned. "We're burning daylight."

* * * * *

He told Broben he was headed for a meeting with the CO and set out with Wennda, the midday night continuing around them as they walked beside each other on the amber-lighted path.

"No more armed escort?" Farley asked.

"What makes you think I'm not armed?"

Farley studied her. "Now I can't tell if *you're* serious."

"I'll keep that in mind."

Farley laughed. *"Touché."*

"I don't understand."

"It just means good point."

They walked toward the low administration building where Farley had been taken the night before. Farley saw dim shapes of people moving in the distance, but he and Wennda were essentially alone.

"So the CO's your pop," he said.

"If that means father, yes, he is."

Farley shook his head. "Boy, that must put a crimp in your social calendar."

"I don't understand."

"I just mean you probably don't get asked out a lot."

"Asked out. You mean asked to leave?"

"Just the opposite, really. When you take someone out, you go somewhere together. So you can get to know each other better." Farley shrugged. "Heck, I'd ask you out even with old Iron Eyes to answer to, if there was any out to go *to* around here."

She looked puzzled. "Are you talking about genetic compatibility assay?"

Farley laughed but felt his face get hot. "Well, let's not get ahead of ourselves. All I meant was that it must be hard for guys to, uh, take an interest, because your father's kind of a hard—kind of stern," he amended.

"Stern." She laughed bitterly. "You could say that. Stern."

"What kind of heat did you end up drawing for your little unofficial outing?"

"What punishment did I receive for my unauthorized reconnaissance?"

"That's what I said."

"I was put in charge of you."

"No kidding. Of me, personally?" Farley rubbed his palms. "This could be fun."

"I'm responsible for your crew."

"Good god. I wouldn't wish that on a lion tamer."

She looked at him. "Could two different languages have all the same words in them, really?"

"Search me."

She laughed. "I'll have to take that as a yes."

"Okay, I'll try to tone it down."

"Please don't. I'm enjoying translating it into regular speech."

Farley laughed. "Look, I'm not asking you to tell tales out of school, but I can't quite get a reading on your—on the CO."

"Do you mean you can't tell what he's thinking?"

"I mean that exactly."

"And you think I can."

"Well, I figure if anyone can get a fix on him, it's you. We're in a bit of a jam here, and I'll take what edge I can get."

"And here I thought you were interested in me personally."

"How could I *not* be? You're painted on my bomber."

"I'd be flattered if it weren't so disturbing."

"I can't explain it."

"Even more disturbing."

"I'd probably feel the same way in your position."

"It's there for luck?" she asked. "A decoration?"

Farley frowned. "Sort of. It gives an aircraft a personality. Not that they don't already have them."

She looked alarmed. "The aircraft is an AI?"

"Tell me what that stands for and I'll tell you if it is."

"Artificial Intelligence."

Farley's brows knitted.

"Inferential heuristics."

He spread his hands. "Like you said: Same words, different language."

"Idiosyncratic multipermutational correlatability?"

He cocked his head. "Are you having some kind of fit?"

"Tell me if your aircraft is an AI and I'll tell you if I'm about to have a fit."

"Well, aircraft starts with AI. Does that help?"

"It's a machine with a brain of its own. Like the Typhon."

"She's got a personality," said Farley, "but she doesn't have a brain."

"Well, no wonder you painted my picture on it."

"I didn't mean it like that."

"You think I don't have a personality, either?"

"I think anything more complicated than a paper clip has a personality. And you seem more complicated than a paper clip."

"Talk like that just makes me want to dispense with genetic compatibility testing altogether and get right to it."

Farley scratched beneath his crush cap. "Look, I'll level with you, okay?"

"Okay," she said. "Whatever leveling with me means."

"It means I'll be honest."

"Have you not been?"

"No, I've been straight with you."

"Is that the same as being level?"

"You're making my head hurt."

"Well. What do you want to level me with?"

"About the artwork," he said. "I don't believe in magic, or elves, or, or—"

"Inter-multiverse gateways?"

"—or whatever it is you just said," Farley agreed. "But I can't buy that it's just a coincidence."

"I don't think it's a coincidence either," she said. "But I'll bet that both of us are willing to believe more things than we would have a few days ago."

"I don't have to believe in them. They're right in front of me."

"I believe that it's foolish to ignore what the universe puts right in front of you."

"The universe put you right in front of me, so I guess it'd be foolish to ignore you."

She stopped walking and looked at him. Her smile was pure inscrutability. "And who are you to ignore the universe?" she said.

Farley stared at her. She really was quite tall.

The sun came on again.

"Twelve o'clock," Wennda said brightly. "We're late."

* * * * *

Two hours later Farley walked back alone—amazingly alone—so engrossed in his thoughts that he was barely aware of his surroundings. Commander Vanden had grilled him meticulously about logistics. *How would you go about retrieving your warplane with just your crew? What if I gave you weapons? What if I sent a team with you? If the aircraft is operational, how will you return to your own world? If it isn't operational, or if you can't recover it, are you willing to destroy it? Have you considered what would happen to you and your crew after that? Even if you make it back to the Dome, to live here you would have to be productive members of our society. You would have to offset your calorie intake. Could you do that? What are your men's skills?*

Farley had also been grilled by a man and a woman who seemed to be some kind of scientists. The commander had said they were going to work on the problem of getting Farley back to his own world. They asked long technical questions he didn't understand a word of. They wanted to know about the vortex Farley had flown into, what had it looked like, what happened inside it, how fast had he been going, how high had he been, what instruments were and weren't affected, what other details could he remember? Farley told them everything that had happened, from the radio static hours before they encountered the thing, to the electrical shutdown after they came out the other side. They found all of this fascinating, but had nothing useful to tell him in return.

Now Farley's head was humming with possibility, with intrigue, with doubt. He wanted the CO's help very badly, but he just didn't know how much to trust him. There was no denying the help the Dome dwellers had provided, but there also was no denying it had

171

been in their interest to provide it. Vanden might even want the bomber himself. Use it to blow up the Redoubt, get rid of the Typhon, gain access to the power source in the crater. Invade the castle, kill the dragon, steal the magic jewel from its hoard. He might send a team to help Farley retrieve the bomber, or he might send them to be sure that the bomber was destroyed if they couldn't, and that Farley's men would not be captured and interrogated about the bomber or the Dome. Given the narrow margins everybody here had to live within, it was even possible the old man wanted the bomber himself *and* wanted Farley and his crew out of the picture.

Farley couldn't really blame him. Strangers in a powerful war machine had crash-landed on one side of a scale that had been precariously balanced for two hundred years. If he were in the old man's position, he'd cover all his bases, too. But Farley's chances of getting the *Morgana* back were a hell of a lot better with more troops and advanced weapons. Even if he couldn't get a team to go with him, Farley wanted the gear. What would it do for the Allies if he could bring that chameleon armor back?

I need to make that hardnosed bastard trust us. Make him *want* to help us.

Farley realized he was back at the barracks. There weren't all that many buildings here—hell, Stanford had been a lot bigger—and Farley had a pilot's sense of direction.

The stickball game was still under way in the courtyard. Farley hung back and watched for a minute. Men and women from the barracks were on both teams, along with the *Morgana* crew. Yone was pitching, Broben was catching, a woman was playing third base. A small crowd watched from the courtyard perimeter and second-floor railing. That smartass, Lang, was taking a lead off the first-base cushion and grinning at Yone. Everyone looked like they were having a good time.

Farley shook his head. Two days ago his men had been fighting Messerschmitts and enduring the worst flak he'd ever seen. Today they were in a huge dome city on another world, cracking jokes and teaching the natives to play stickball.

But that's what we do, thought Farley. We put down our comic books and go to England and fight the Germans and drink warm beer and fix the tractors of the farmers whose fields are runways now.

"That's what we do," he said aloud.

* * * * *

"Okay, here's the situation," said Farley.

The crew sat on the ingeniously unfolded sofas, dangled their feet from the recessed bunks, sat at pull-out tables, sprawled on the floor. All of them were smoking. The air vents worked harder to compensate, but the crewmen didn't notice it.

Farley looked them over before continuing. "This place is basically one big lifeboat," he said. "It was built to keep people alive after a war wiped out the entire planet. It's been doing that for a couple hundred years."

Shorty whistled. The rest of them looked at each other.

"These people have been locked up in here like a castle under siege longer than America's been a country," Farley continued. "They're alive because of strict rationing and some pretty tough laws about wasting resources, and their enemies are on the other side of the crater, twenty miles away. The CO of this operation doesn't like the idea of them having our bomber, and he can't afford to put us up here."

Plavitz raised a hand. "So we get our ride back and get out," he said. "Birds, meet stone."

Farley nodded. "I've been working with the commander to figure out how they can help us do just that."

The men cheered. Farley held up a hand. "So here's the thinking," he said. "If we shoot our way to the bomber right now, chances are what we'll find is a lame duck. But if we give them two more days, odds are they'll have done a lot of our repair work for us, and we'll have a bomber that's a lot closer to being airworthy."

Broben shook his head and whistled low. "That's a hell of a gamble, Joe."

"I don't think so. The *Morgana* was pretty worked over. Wen said it'd take *him* a couple of days. These people have never seen an airplane before, much less a radial engine. They aren't likely to fix three of them—along with the tail section and god knows what else—and take her out for a spin in two days."

"So that's the plan?" asked Plavitz. "Wait two days and then go get the *Morgana* back?"

"If it was that simple," said Broben, "the captain wouldn't be making a speech."

Farley nodded. "Here's the catch," he said. "We can really use these people's help. Their guns, their gizmos, their armor. More eyes, more ears, and more trigger fingers. The whole ball of wax. They've got about a thousand people in this bubble of theirs, and we're asking them to risk six or eight of them. We'll have a lot better chance of getting their help if we help *them*. There's a lot around here that needs fixing." He blinked. "Make them love us."

"In two days?" asked Everett.

"You got them playing stickball in twenty minutes." Farley looked them over. "Sure, this place was built by some pretty smart cookies—"

"That picture phone's sure a killer diller," agreed Shorty.

"Picture phone?" said Boney. "They have a fake *sun*."

"Not at eleven a.m., they don't," said Martin.

"That's my point," Farley told him. "This whole place is like one big clock, and a lot of it's broken. So we're going to find out what needs fixing, and we're going to fix it. Wennda's been handed TDY as our den mother here. She'll help us figure out where we can do some good."

"Is she gonna figure out where you can do some good, Joseph?" Broben asked.

"I do not seek the nomination, but if elected, I will serve."

Broben leered. "God and country, pal. That'll get you through these dark times."

Farley ignored him. "Garrett, Everett—you're farm boys."

"I am," said Garrett. "He's from one of those combines."

"Yep," agreed Everett. "I'm a *big*-farm boy."

"You two visit with those toy farmers they've got here," said Farley. "They've been growing crops in this cake dish so long, maybe they've forgotten some things."

"Will do, cap," said Everett.

"Plavitz, I want you to find what passes for a library here and study some maps. I want you to know how to get through those canyons in your sleep. On foot and in the air."

"If they have them," said Plavitz, "I'll tattoo them in my brain."

"Boney, you're pretty mechanical," said Farley.

"Like a robot," Shorty chimed in.

"And Mr. Dubuque," said Farley. "You've got the electronics background."

"Fat lotta good that does," said Shorty. "I haven't seen a single vacuum tube in this dump."

"So learn what they use in their place and get to work with Boney."

"What are we working on, skipper?" asked Boney.

"I want you to fix the sun."

SIXTEEN

Garrett had his hands on his hips and Everett had his arms folded as they stood amid the squares of crops beneath the rounded hexagon of bright afternoon sun. Both men were warm in their uniforms as they looked in mild consternation at plots of trellised vines, neat lines of plastic sheeting sprouting bushy growths, even rows of stalks, orderly orchards of big-leafed trees. The arrangement was too big to be called a garden and too small to be called a farm, as they understood the word. Behind the fields were the dun-colored administration and housing complexes.

"You feed a thousand people with this?" said Everett.

Their guide nodded proudly. Her name was Evna and she was distractingly pretty, though privately both Americans thought she could use a little more curve. They grew them small and thin and pale here in the Dome. Evna had boyishly short brown hair and wore the standard-issue jumpsuit and slippers, though her jumpsuit had been expertly decorated—by Wennda, who apparently had a talent for such things—with drawn-on stripes and swirls and intricate designs.

"One thousand one hundred thirty-five," she replied to Everett. "Not with crops alone, of course. Fats and protein that aren't provided by the reverter are vat-grown from cloned tissue. Much more efficient."

Garrett nudged Everett. "*Much* more efficient," he said.

"We get fats and oils from peanuts," Evna continued, heedless. "Soap, soil conditioner, paper fabrics—there's so much you can do with peanuts beyond eating them."

"Sure," said Garrett. "Me and this monkey work for 'em."

"We have eighteen crops in intensive cultivation," Evna continued blithely, pointing at the little fields. "Wheat, barley, white potatoes—"

"Don't read me the whole menu, sweetheart," said Garrett. "Just tell me what's for dessert."

Everett looked skyward.

"Did you bring your own food with you?" Evna asked. "The bioprinters can reproduce almost anything they can sample, as long as we've got the raw materials for fabrication."

Everett looked away from the artificial sky. "Trust me, no one's gonna give us a medal for showing you how to make Vienna sausages."

"Well, I'd still be very eager to sample what you have. Anything new is extremely welcome."

"Who wouldn't get tired of having the same thing over and over again?" said Garrett.

Everett made a pained face. "Maybe you should switch off full auto, Romeo," he said.

Evna was pointing at the large rectangle of water surrounded by grass in the near distance. "In the marshes around the ocean we grow rice," she said.

"Ocean?" said Garrett.

"Ocean biome," she elaborated, unhelpfully. "Sea plants, algae, tide machine. It filters to fresh water on this end. We get water filtration, clean oxygen, nutrient yield for crop soil, humidification. There used to be fish stock for protein, but it died out a long time ago."

"Can we get back to the farm?" asked Garrett. "I'm kinda getting seasick."

Evna frowned but nodded. "Of course," she said. "What would you like to know?"

"What's giving you a pain?" said Everett.

She turned toward a field of plants a few feet high. "It's my legumes," she said mournfully.

"Gee," Garrett said behind her, "your legumes look pretty good to me."

Everett punched him on the shoulder. "Let's take a look at them," he told Evna when she looked back.

Garrett nodded eagerly, and Evna led them to the plot. Well before they got there the two men could see something was wrong. The majority of the bean crop was vibrant green and lush, but about twenty percent of the plants were a pale yellow-green. Stalks were desiccated and straw-like, leaves were drooping, bean pods were chalky and brittle-looking.

Evna knelt before one such plant and turned a leaf up. Everett and Garrett knelt beside her.

"These are pintos," Garrett said.

Evna nodded. "High-yield pinto beans in dry-bred cultivation," she said. "We don't have a lot of genetic variation, so they've lost a lot of resistance over the years. We try to keep the Dome as closed and filtered as we can, but we still get problems from outside."

"Present company excluded," said Everett.

She flushed. "I didn't mean to imply anything," she said.

"He's just ribbing you," said Garrett.

Everett frowned at the sickly leaves. "I know rust is a problem with these," he said. "But that's not what it looks like." He dug into the rich soil with his fingers and pulled up a wriggling purplish earthworm. He showed it to Garrett, who nodded.

"I haven't seen any birds in here," Garrett said.

"There haven't been any for a very long time," said Evna. "We use manual seed dispersion and some bee pollination."

"A world with no birds," said Garrett.

She shrugged. "They were gone before I was born."

Everett held up the wriggling worm. "No early birds for you," he told it. He put it back in the soil and covered it back over. Then he rubbed his fingers and sniffed them. He frowned and broke off a leaf and rubbed it and sniffed it. He asked Evna about watering, humidity, crop rotation, sun cycles, pests, temperature.

Evna told him how the rain forest biome, where the miniature cliffs were, generated water vapor to maintain humidity, how the ocean algae scrubbed the air and filtered water. Garrett managed to put the brakes on his blunt flirting, and both men listened and asked questions and did not wise off.

At one point Evna excused herself to make her rounds. She told them she'd be back in half an hour and left the two strange men kneeling among the diseased bean plants.

They watched her go, then Garrett turned to Everett.

"Did you understand a thing she said?" he asked.

"Some of it."

"Brother, you're one up on me. Genetic biome hydroponic cost-benefit cloned ecosystem molecular I don't know what else." He shook himself like a dog. "I'm just a dirt mechanic; I don't know if these people are farming or making rockets."

"At least you know you can love her for her brain, too," said Everett.

"She never saw a cow. What kind of farmer never saw a cow?"

Everett grinned. "The farmer in the Dome, the farmer in the Dome," he sang.

"Aren't you the comedian."

"Hi ho, the derry-oh."

"Give it a rest already."

Everett grinned. "The farmer takes a wife," he half-sang.

"Yeah, yeah, and the wife cuts the cheese." He didn't laugh, which made Everett laugh.

Garrett broke off a withered seed pod. "This isn't white mold," he said. "But it's still some kind of fungus. It's powdery."

"What would you do if this was happening back home?"

"For starters, I wouldn't grow pinto beans."

"Say, that's helpful. Thanks for solving the problem, bud."

"I already know how to fix the problem," Garrett said. "You'd know, too, if you'd grown up on a real farm instead of that cabbage factory your dad works for."

"He's a general manager and it's a combine."

"Don't get a run in your stocking. Now listen and learn."

* * * * *

When Evna returned she saw both men propped up on their elbows between rows of bean plants, staring at the sky and passing a cigarette between them. Her face went hard and she quickened her pace. Garrett hastily stubbed out the butt and got up with his hands out as if he thought he'd have to ward off a tackle by a woman more than a foot shorter than him and half his weight.

"It helps us think," he said before she could lay into him.

"How exciting that must be. What has it helped you think of?"

Everett stood up beside Garrett and brushed dirt from his hands. "What kind of soap do you people wash dishes with?" he asked.

SEVENTEEN

Broben and Martin trudged behind Farley and Wennda as they headed toward one of the larger buildings in the central cluster. The captain was engaged in animated conversation with the tall woman as they walked, both of them intent on each other, laughing sometimes, curious and questioning.

Broben frowned. Dreamgirl or not, he'd seen this movie a hundred times, and it rarely had a happy ending.

He glanced at Martin and waved at their surroundings. "I feel like I'm in one of those snow globes people put out at Christmas," he said.

"It's not exactly what the recruiting posters said I'd see when I joined up," Martin said. "Where is it we're going, again?"

"Fabrication."

"Sounds like we're gonna sew clothes."

"They're trying to find a use for us," Broben replied. "I don't know about you, brother, but I drive a truck when I'm not bombing Germans."

"I push a pretty good idiot stick," Martin said.

"Maybe we're gonna turn screwdrivers. Shame we couldn't bring Wen. That hillbilly'd be running this burg inside of a week."

"I'm sorry I didn't get a chance to know him better," said Martin.

Broben shrugged. "Truth is, he was like sandpaper when he didn't agree with you. But I swear there's nothing that damn yokel couldn't fix. Wen didn't repair things, he healed them."

"My uncle Dan is like that with horses," said Martin. "He just kind of talks them into feeling better."

"So you really grew up with all that? Riding horses and everything?"

"Hell no. Horses scare the daylights out of me. Never shot a bow, either."

"I think it's the arrows you shoot."

"Like I said."

The cluster of tan-colored dwellings and administration offices was a thick-stemmed, narrow-armed T. The stem divided ordered plots of crops, and the miniature environments they called biomes ran parallel to the arms of the T. There was a tiny rain forest, a savannah surrounding a rectangular ocean the size of a football field, a shallow spill of marshland. A narrow C of grassland ran along the left rim.

Fabrication took up most of a building near the base of the T. Many of the interior walls had been removed to turn the conjoined space into a warehouse. Seemingly random stacks and heaps of material formed confusing paths through the building. The sound was oddly muffled, baffled by the dense variety of materials. People scurried to and fro, a few of them hauling materials on little upright gizmos that looked like drivable handtrucks. There was a steady muted patter and a constant background thrum of machinery.

Wennda was leading them down one meandering row when they had to step aside to let a vehicle pass. It was the size of a motor scooter, rectangular and bright yellow with a little revolving yellow light, and silent on four odd tires that were a series of angled rubber cones set around a hub. A lift-loader in front made Broben realize he was looking at the smallest forklift he had ever seen. A woman stood on a little footstand at the back, staring at them as she glided by. In fact everybody stared.

Broben whistled at the retreating vehicle and gave a Scout salute. "Man, that was something," he said.

"How can you tell, with those outfits?" asked Martin.

"Huh?" Broben felt oddly embarrassed. "I was talking about that little forklift. I want one for my dollhouse."

Martin's look showed that he wasn't sure if he was being kidded, which made Broben flush even more. "My first summer job was driving towmotor for a ship-to-rail outfit," he explained. "I'da traded an organ for a little rig like that."

The noise level rose as they entered an area where the original floor plan had been preserved, smaller rooms crowded with machinery—pipe benders, stampers, things that looked like caulking guns that seemed to fuse materials, something that looked like a woodchipper that shredded garments and fabric remnants to powder that was deposited in plastic tubs, other things that made no sense to the airmen.

"I was expecting flashing lights and super-duper televisions," Farley told Wennda. "This looks like my high school shop class."

"Fabrication wasn't built into the original plan," Wennda replied. "This is all repurposed, refitted."

"So Fabrication is fabricated."

She grinned. "Exactly."

Broben tried not to roll his eyes.

They came to a series of conjoined suites where workers dumped the tubs of powdered fabric into a hopper on the side of a machine a little bigger than a phone booth. It looked like a still put together by a madman, with piping of plastic and various metals, condensers, release valves, dial gauges and digital meters. A sheet of oatmeal-colored fabric slowly extruded out the other side into a bin and was automatically cut to length.

The workers stopped when the airmen entered the room.

"Everybody," said Wennda, "this is Captain Farley, Lieutenant Broben, and Sergeant Proud Horse. Please don't let us interfere with your work."

The workers nodded uncertainly and resumed their tasks, but they continued to glance at the strangers. Broben watched a man wearing work gloves remove a newly minted length of fabric and carry it to another contraption. The fabric was threaded onto a compact rack like the film on a movie projector and fed into the gizmo, which buzzed and thrummed.

Broben looked around at all the jury-rigged piping and stopgap release valves. He wondered how often things blew up around here.

Across the room Wennda was talking to a wiry, scruffy-looking man who was frowning at the three crewmen. The man pulled a cellophone from his pocket and snapped it taut. He tapped it and his frown deepened. Then he shrugged and crumpled it again. Wennda smiled and squeezed his arm.

"Palto is looking at the task schedule," she told Broben and Martin. "Lieutenant, you said you have inventory-storage experience?"

"I can drive the wheels off of one of those little forklifts, if that's what you mean," Broben said.

The dour man, Palto, raised an eyebrow. "Can you repair one?"

"I can sure give it a shot."

Palto nodded doubtfully.

"Sergeant Proud Horse wants to try something with a bioprinter," said Wennda.

"I do?" said Martin.

"He'll explain it to you," said Wennda. "We have to get to a meeting with the commander right now."

"Don't set anything on fire," said Farley.

"Sure thing, boss," said Broben. "You kids scram. And remember, no fighting in the clinches."

Farley scowled. "If they give you a hard time," he told Palto, "you've got my permission to feed 'em to that thing." He nodded at the machine that turned powder into fabric lengths.

"The reverter is more efficient," Palto said. Farley didn't think he was joking.

* * * * *

Palto brought Broben to Samay, the woman he'd seen driving the little forklift. She was at least ten years older than Broben and intimidat-

184

ingly knowledgeable about her work. She demonstrated the forklift's steering and hydraulics, and Broben was startled when she turned it by leaning in the direction she wanted to go. She stopped the vehicle, slid it sideways, and turned while moving in a sideways drift.

Broben whistled. "So I guess now women can parallel park," he said.

There was no engine. Each wheel was its own motor. Power came from rechargeable batteries printed onto thin sheets. Broben couldn't even have imagined such a thing, let alone repaired it. But the problem wasn't that the loader wouldn't go, it was that the lifting arms were stuck in place.

"Our lives depend on machines," Samay told Broben as she opened a service panel on the faulty vehicle. "We've either kept them running for nearly two hundred years, or we've used them for parts like recombinant genes." She showed him a scrawl on the inside of the panel lid. "Every machine is an heirloom, with its own genealogy of repair records, good wishes, names scrawled on parts. I often encounter notes written by people I knew as a little girl, on machines I'm working on. Or notes from people they knew when they were children. All of them are long gone, but the thing itself is still here. So to maintain these machines is to commune with those ingenious and determined people. And so to love the machine itself. Do you see?"

Broben gaped at her. "Holy jumpin' jeez," he said. "A city full of Wen Bonnikers."

"I don't understand."

"He was a guy who loved machines like you do. But he sure couldn't have put it like that."

Samay was patient with Broben after it became clear she was talking to a man who understood machines and respected them, and not to some savage. Miniaturization, hard plastics, lightweight alloys all impressed him, but he wasn't awed by them. Electronics was foreign to him, but it wasn't magic. It was just something he didn't understand yet.

But he would not stop calling his teacher Sammy.

"My name is *Samay*," she told him for the third time. She opened a side access panel on the loader.

185

"Yeah yeah," he said, waving it away. "Don't make a federal case out of it."

"Samay. Why won't you say it right?"

"Look," Broben confided, "I'm already trying to get used to learning repairs from a dame. Throw me a bone here."

Samay pulled a board from a slot in the access panel. To Broben it looked like a road map. "A dame is a woman?" she asked.

"Yeah. You know, a broad. A skirt. Not that anybody here ever heard of a skirt."

She frowned at the panel and slotted it back. "Women don't teach engineering and mechanics where you come from?"

"Huh? No, women can teach whatever they want to, I guess." Broben shrugged. "Mostly they don't learn it in the first place."

"Why not?"

"Why in the world would they want to? What would they do with it?"

Samay didn't hear a bit of condescension in Broben's tone. The man was genuinely puzzled. "So where you come from," she said, "I wouldn't want to do something that I've done here for most of my life?"

Broben thought about it. "It's like this," he said. "There's things men do and things women do. Some places just belong to them, see? And if you go to 'em, you feel like you're trespassing. Like if I was to knit a sweater, or something, people would start to wonder if I was a little confused. Follow?"

"No. I don't follow."

"Well, maybe it don't matter. 'Cause to be honest with you the war's got everything pretty shook up and turned around back home. Like for instance, our crate was put together by girls. Our bomber."

"Your aircraft was built by children?"

"What gave you that idea? It was built by dames, like I said. Girls."

"But—" She shook her head. "Never mind. Your warplane was built by women."

He nodded proudly. "Built in half a day by a whole platoon of Rosie Riveters."

"So necessity is removing social sanctions," she said.

"What's that in English?"

"A war of survival changes cultural priorities," Samay explained. "It strips us down to fundamentals."

"What if I don't want to be stripped to my fundamentals?"

"You don't have a choice. The scale of your war demanded that your society's priorities change to accommodate it. Women entering the technical labor force. A nonprofessional military."

"Maybe so," said Broben. "But at least it hasn't got so bad that dames have to join the army and start shooting people." He shook his head. "Women are the ones we're supposed to protect, not the ones doing the protecting."

Samay laughed and turned back to the loader. "Our military has as many women as men," she said, folding down another panel. This one housed rows of little rectangles. "I did my five years."

Broben looked confounded. "You were in the army?" He mimed firing a rifle.

She nodded as she pulled a tool from a holder and used it to pull out one of the rectangles. "I still am, if they need me. Everyone is." She held the rectangle up to the light and squinted at it. "We're only eleven hundred people," she told Broben. "It's no more unnatural for me to serve than it is for your women to build warplanes. We're all protecting what we believe in."

"Well, I believe in dames."

She laughed and put the rectangle back in place. "I'll make you a prediction," she said. "When your war ends, those kinds of things won't go back to the way they were before it started."

"Ah, that's a sucker bet. I mean, how can they? Winning changes things."

"I'm not talking about victory. I'm talking about unwritten rules. The ways you live. Work. Mate. Your women won't go back to—what was it? Fabricating sweaters?" She shook her head. "Oh, some will, of course. Maybe most. But some are going to want to keep making aircraft. Or fly them. And some of those will try to figure out how to make them better. Make them more efficient, produce them more efficiently." She grinned at the look on Broben's face. "I predict much change in your future, lieutenant."

"Sister, there's already been too much change in my future."

She laughed. Broben asked what she was looking for in the little rectangles. "Broken circuits," she replied.

"They're some kind of fuses?" he said.

"And relays, yes."

"Try pushing on them."

She looked skeptical but humored him, quickly pushing all the little plastic rectangles in the fuse box. She stopped at one and frowned. She glanced at Broben, reached to the loader's dashboard, and moved a joystick. The forklift rose.

Broben looked smug. "You'll get my bill," he said.

She held out a felt-tip pen and indicated the fusebox panel. "Sign," she said.

"You fixed it, not me," Broben protested.

She shook the pen. "You're part of it now," she said. "Sign your name."

Feeling oddly as if he were setting his name to some historical document, Broben signed.

* * * * *

Much change in your future, lieutenant.

Broben wound through the maze of stacks, preoccupied with unaccustomed notions. Microminiaturization. Servo motors. Printed circuits. Printed *batteries*. Gyro steering. Women in the work force who weren't secretaries or schoolteachers. Women who built cars. Who repaired cars. Owned repair shops. Managed auto factories. Hell, you'd have to come up with a new word for that one; they sure as hell wouldn't let you call them *foremen*.

A war of survival changes cultural priorities.

Sammy didn't know the half of it. In Mobile, Alabama, Negroes were building warships right alongside white men. A lot of people weren't thrilled about it, but everyone knew it had to be done. And after the war was over, were they supposed to lay down their wrenches and go back to saying *Yassuh, Missah Benny*, like Shorty imitating Rochester? Because at that point that's what it would be: Imitation.

Hell, maybe it always was.

The war had yanked America out of the sinkhole of the Great Depression and initiated the biggest tooling-up the world had ever seen. You got so lost in its mass of cogs that you couldn't see the greater machinery that enabled it. Unheard-of levels of production, transportation, technology. Change. A country suddenly more powerful and resourceful than even its own people had realized.

And how was *that* gonna play out after Hitler ate a lead sandwich? Would America say *Yassuh, Missah Benny* after this was over?

Broben didn't think so.

It loomed before him, all that change. Its scale and its extent were unforeseeable, but it was big and it was certain and it would touch almost everything before this war was settled.

Sammy was right. There would be no going back.

Broben realized he'd been wandering aimlessly among the Fabrication stacks and workers. He grinned sheepishly and waved at the staring people and made his way back to the room with the Magic Jumpsuit Machine, where Martin stood before the humming contraption, deep in discussion with that hobo-looking guy, what was his name? Bigtoe? Palo Alto?

Palto, that was it. Martin and Palto stood side by side, looking down at one of those World's Fair television gizmos people here pulled from their pockets like road holes in a Bugs Bunny cartoon. Martin was holding out a cigarette and pointing to it as if explaining it to the man. He broke off when he saw Broben coming toward them. "You all right, lieutenant?" he asked.

"Sure. Why wouldn't I be?"

Martin shrugged. "I don't know. You just look like a faraway fella."

"I been working on a forklift," said Broben. "What're you two talking about? It looked very significant."

Martin smiled. "Mr. Palto here was explaining how the printer works." He indicated the jumpsuit-making machine still buzzing along. "That's what he calls it, a printer. I was asking if it could make things besides those jumpsuits."

"You looking to buy someone a dress?"

Martin looked embarrassed. "Well, that bunch really seemed to have fun playing stickball yesterday, so I figured there's ways we can help around here that aren't just work. Mr. Palto says if we can make up for the calories, they can probably print up some baseball gloves."

Broben was incredulous. "You want to make ball gloves?"

"They don't seem to require much material," said Palto. "We don't have anything like bovine leather, of course, but we have excellent synthetics. Nylon polymers, lightweight carbon filament. We do need an example to scan so that we can make a fabrication template."

"How's that again?" said Broben.

"They need a glove for a model," said Martin.

"Oh. Well, that's a shame. It was a great idea, chief."

Martin darkened. He reached back and pulled something from his waistband and held it out, not looking at Broben.

Broben stared at it in wonder. "You brought your glove?" he asked.

Martin looked at the floor and shrugged. "The captain said bring what we needed."

Broben laughed all the way back to the dorm.

EIGHTEEN

Shorty and Boney watched the technician, whose name was Berne, pull a clear wad from a jumpsuit pocket and set it on the table. He smoothed it out and it went rigid. He tapped it and it glowed white.

"You don't have an extra one of those laying around, do you?" Shorty asked.

Berne scowled and put a finger to his lips. "Start hash folder request," he told the device.

"Folder name?" the rectangle asked.

"Solar array sub schematics."

A grid of labeled icons appeared on the sheet. Berne began scrolling through it by flicking his finger. He tapped an icon and another row of icons opened up beneath it.

"Shoot," said Shorty, "I was hoping it'd be a picture phone again."

"I was only talking to the Library," Berne said. "There's no avatar."

Shorty looked at Boney, who shrugged. "I guess they didn't want to be seen," Shorty said.

"There is no *they*," Berne said testily. "The Library's an AI. Central data core."

"Can you pick up a good swing program?"

"I have absolutely no idea what you're talking about."

Shorty put his hands on top of his head. "Man oh man. We made it to you people just in time."

"Maybe we could focus a little," Berne suggested.

"How do they get parts in that thing?" Shorty persisted. "It's thinner than paper."

"And you can see through it," Boney pointed out.

Berne glanced up at them and sighed. "It's a holofilament weave embedded in memory polymer," he said wearily. "Happy now?"

"It remembers for you?"

"The polymer doesn't remember anything except that it's a polymer. The *filament* does the processing. You can't see it because it's too thin. Right now it's just a dumb terminal. The data core does the processing and the com panel displays the result. That's what I'm doing now." He scowled. "What I'm *trying* to do," he amended.

"Jeez, get all touchy," said Shorty. "I just like knowing how things work."

"Why don't I just tell you that it's *magic,* so we can get on with what you came here for."

Shorty looked at Boney. "He don't like us vewwy much, do he?" he said in Bugs Bunny's voice.

"He doesn't know us," said Boney.

"I *don't* know you," Berne agreed. "I'm sure you're model citizens, and you're very good at—at whatever it is you do."

Shorty saluted. "Radio Operator First Class, mac, and don't you forget it." He hooked a thumb at Boney. "Sergeant Mullen there's the best bombardier in the Army. He's dropped down more chimneys than St. Nick."

"Once again I have no idea what any of that means."

"It's magic," said Boney.

Berne laughed despite himself and tapped another icon. "Fair enough," he said. "But I'm good at what I do, too. And so are about twenty other people who've worked on the eleven o'clock panel. We didn't just sit here in the dark for an hour a day for the last eight years, you know. We've tested circuits and debugged environment code and spectrographed gases in the induction coils. I've crawled around on the dome more than once. We've tried everything we could think of, and we can't find anything wrong."

"You have to try things you didn't think of," said Boney.

"I'm so eager to hear your outside perspective."

"We just want to help, if we can."

Berne folded his arms. "You know," he said, "after we exhausted all the obvious and logical solutions, we started holding weekly group sessions to come up with the most ridiculous fixes we could think of. Lightning rods and noble gases. We still conference if someone gets some new idea."

"Sounds like you've covered all your bases," said Boney.

Berne looked at him and spread his hands helplessly. "Whatever that means," he said.

"And he thinks we got nothing to teach him," said Shorty.

Berne looked sour. "I don't think it's very likely that two—let's call you *well-intended strangers*—who think my com panel is the voice of God, are going to figure out what's wrong with a two-hundred-year-old inductive laminate geothermal helio cell."

"We might," said Boney.

"You don't even know what it *is*. Much less how it works."

"You give it juice, it turns the juice into light," said Shorty. "Somewhere something wore out or came loose. You find out where and you fix it or replace it. Sha-zam, everybody's back to working on their tan before lunch."

"God," said Berne.

Shorty grinned. "Maybe we'll strike oil," he said. "Besides, what *else* you got to do?"

"Would you like a list?" Berne shot back. But he showed them wiring diagrams and circuit schematics. He tried to explain the diagnostic software and the routines that regulated sequencing and illumination. He gave up when he realized they didn't even understand what software was. They thought the holofilament schematics were a wiring diagram. These people were savages. Analog savages.

Berne shook both hands at the dense tangle depicted on his

com panel. "These aren't *wires* the way you're thinking of them," he explained. "They're microminiaturized optical filaments that transmit photon signals in a holographic medium."

Shorty reached over Berne's shoulder and tapped a line on a diagram. It glowed green, highlighting a correct route through the incomprehensible maze. "*This* sends a signal from *here* to *here*, right?" Shorty asked.

"Yes, but—"

"Then it's a wiring diagram. Who cares if there's really wires?"

"You ... have a point."

Boney asked about physical connections. Berne explained that a layer of crawlspace ran between the hexagonal sky panels and the dome that housed the city.

Boney frowned. "They built two domes?" he asked. "One inside the other?"

"They didn't *build* the Dome, they found it," said Berne. "It's a lava dome, a huge air bubble that was left after the lava cooled. They're everywhere. It's one reason it's been hard for the Redoubt to locate us."

"Lava," said Boney. "From when the crater was made?"

Berne nodded. "They hung a framework shell inside the lava dome," he said. "There's crawlspace, access rungs, subsurface."

"And you've checked all the connections."

Berne drew himself upright. "Every piece of hardware and every line of code that has anything to do with how the sun panels work has been reviewed, repaired, replaced, rewired, or rewritten. It's all in working order now, except for the eleven o'clock panel."

"How do you check your wiring?" Shorty asked.

"Diagnostic applications," said Berne.

Shorty cocked his head. Berne waggled his com panel. "Cellophone," he said, slowly and deliberately.

"So that thing told you the other things are okay," said Shorty.

"We verified the diagnostic software, if that's what you're implying. We also checked the physical connections."

Shorty rubbed his hands. "Now we're cooking with gas," he

said. "So how do you know when the voice that comes from the cellophone is on the level?"

"We debug the source code," Berne said wearily. His fingers drummed the desk. "We verify hard cabling with a tap. We test conductive filament with a circuit tracer."

"*A* circuit tracer?"

"You only need one."

Shorty grinned. Even Boney had a bit of a smile going. Shorty put his hands behind his back and ducked his head and twisted a toe like a schoolgirl. "And could we see it?" he said coyly.

Berne started to argue, then stopped. He threw his hands up. "Sure," he said. "Why not? Like you said, what *else* do I have to do?"

"That's the spirit," said Shorty.

* * * * *

The cable tester was the size of a key fob. It had a socket for bare wire and a clamp for insulated wire and it lit up when it got a good connection. Shorty wasn't especially worried about the cable tester misreporting results—a dead wire wouldn't make the light glow—but he checked it out anyway.

The circuit tracer was another story. It was the size of a pack of cigarettes, with a slide-out zoomable screen for doing fine work with an attached stylus. Berne demonstrated, touching the conductive stylus to a circuit panel. The little screen immediately showed a schematic, then showed the tested connection as a bright green tracing in the pattern.

"You *do* realize that the circuitry on holofilaments and microprocessors is too fine for human hands, yes?" Berne asked. "And there are millions and millions of them. We have to trust the diagnostics at some point." He lifted the wand and the screen faded. "As you can see, this one's good," he said.

"Put it on a bad connection," said Shorty.

"There are no bad connections on this board."

"How do you know?"

"Because—" He waggled the tracer stylus.

"Because you checked 'em out already," said Shorty.

Berne nodded. "Really," he said, "there are other things I could be—"

"Here's the thing," said Shorty. "Any time I get a good reading on a tube I know for a solid fact is bad as a headline, I start wondering who fixes the tube checker."

"I don't understand."

"Do you have another circuit tracer?" asked Boney.

Berne raised his eyebrows. "Not here."

Shorty waved impatiently. "You got a spare one of these boards?" he asked.

"The one I just tested is a backup."

"Okay," said Shorty. He picked it up and flexed it, testing its strength. Then he put it on the floor and set a foot on it and bent it until it snapped.

"What if we need that?" Berne demanded.

Shorty handed it to Berne. "Test it again."

Berne didn't bother to hide his contempt as he touched the stylus to a thin silver line in the broken circuit board. The little screen glowed to life and a bright green path lit through the maze.

Berne flinched. He touched it to the circuit board again. Another silver pathway glowed green. He tried again. The broken connection showed as good.

Berne looked at the tracer stylus in a way that made Boney think the technician was considering stabbing Shorty in the eye with it. Then he set it down and covered his face with a hand and slumped in his chair. "False positives," he said miserably. "I don't believe it."

"And so," Shorty said in his Announcer Voice, "at the end of a grueling inning it's Cave Men one, Dome Men nothing. And now a word from our sponsor."

NINETEEN

The room was small, clean, subtly lit. A crammed work cubicle took up one corner, with a desk that looked like a junior version of the dark glass conference-room table. Working before it was a balding, gray-bearded man, a little heavy, his loose-fitting khaki jumpsuit drawn with intricate designs and concentric patterns. He saw Wennda and beamed. Then he saw Plavitz behind her and his expression grew serious. It wouldn't take a genius to figure that Plavitz must be one of the Helpful Savages from the Metal Sky God.

"I was going to hug you," the man told Wennda as he got up, "but this looks official."

"It is official," she said. "But hug me anyway."

The man grinned and took her up in a bear hug. Plavitz was amused to note that he was a good four inches shorter than Wennda. He lifted her off the floor and she squealed and pretend-beat his shoulder. He set her down and let her go, and she stepped back, delighted as a six-year-old.

Then she remembered Plavitz and blushed. "Uncle Jorn, this is Sergeant Plavitz," Wennda said. "He's the navigator on the aircraft that brought these men here."

"Oh, sure, blame me," said Plavitz. He held out his hand. The man looked at it as if he were uncertain what to do, then shook it. "I'm really just a glorified map reader," Plavitz told him.

"Jorn is in charge of data storage and retrieval systems," said Wennda.

Jorn smiled. "I'm really just a glorified librarian," he said.

"That's just ducky," Plavitz replied. "Because I'm here to check out some maps."

"I'd be happy to show you," said Jorn. "What maps would you like to see?"

"Got one with a route back to New Bedford?" asked Plavitz.

Jorn looked uncertainly at Wennda. "I'm not sure," he said. "Maybe if you—"

"He's joking," said Wennda. "They do that a lot."

"We do," Plavitz admitted. "So, Uncle Jorn, huh? Are you the commander's brother?"

The ensuing silence was very awkward.

"I've spent a lot of time here," said Wennda.

"She had a cot," Jorn confirmed.

Wennda colored again. "Jorn practically raised me," she said.

Plavitz sensed they were trying to back out of a thicket. "Yeah, I just saw him do that," he joked.

They looked confused, and Plavitz felt his ears get hot. "Raise you," he explained. He mimed lifting.

"Ah," said Jorn. He smiled. "You do joke a lot."

"Let's get to that map," said Wennda.

* * * * *

Plavitz's hand flicked around on the lighted panel as if he were brushing off crumbs. He chuckled as items on the display slid on and off the desktop.

"You seem to be enjoying our system," Jorn said behind him.

Plavitz grinned. "It's a gasser once you get the hang of it," he said.

Jorn looked pleased. "It's good to see someone who appreciates it. People take for granted that information like this is available, but storage and retrieval is quite difficult to maintain." He shook his head. "So much has been lost."

"What happened? Your books get burned, or something?"

Jorn smiled gently and shook his head. "We have very few books, in the sense that I think you mean. Information is stored digitally in centralized servers."

Plavitz shrugged. "Too rich for my blood."

"A long time ago we learned how to store information electronically," Jorn explained. "It takes up almost no physical space, and it can be duplicated or accessed with very little effort. But the system crashed in the first decades of the Dome and the data archive was lost. They managed to retrieve half of it, but—" he spread his hands "—the damage still affects us. So much information gone. Engineering. Science. History. Almost all literature and entertainment." He shook his head. "The power fluctuates, a conductor overheats, a memory card fails at exactly the wrong time, and half of what your race has fought and sacrificed for a hundred thousand years to learn is simply gone. And the only way to get it back is to learn it all over again."

"I can't imagine," Plavitz said, largely because he had no idea what the man was talking about.

Jorn nodded. "That absence is so much a part of our lives that it's become invisible to most of us, but I stumble over it every day." He shook his head. "My apologies. I'm complaining about my work and keeping you from yours." His smile was a little sad. "I'm alone here quite often, and I tend to save up conversation. And a *new* person, well—it's very exciting."

"Likewise, I'm sure." Plavitz swiveled back to the desk, where a solid-looking model of the crater occupied half the desktop. "Man, if we had maps like this I could put us over Hitler's kiddie pool and Boney could drop an egg on his moustache." He gave a descending whistle and drummed the table. "Bam—war's over, here's your medal and your ticker-tape parade, everybody pack up and go home."

"I'm delighted you find it so useful."

"It's so useful it's spooky."

Plavitz went back to looking for routes on foot to and from the Redoubt, best routes to elevation above the crater rim, ground they could use for landing fields, even places to stash the bomber, if it came to that.

At one point he halted the scrolling landscape and frowned. The scene on the table looked directly down on the well at the center of the crater. Most of it was in shadow. What walls he could see were not a smooth bore. There were faint concentric lines and sloping diagonals, large rectangular panels, and a speck that might have been a light.

Plavitz looked back at Jorn. "What's the story with this well?" he asked. "It doesn't look like any bomb crater I ever saw."

Jorn peered at the com table. "We're fairly sure it's the central shaft of an underground complex," he said. "What remains of a complex, anyway."

"They would have had to dig down for miles."

"It's clear they were trying to protect something from enemy attack. Possibly whatever the Typhon is still guarding."

Plavitz frowned and turned back to the hole that seemed to sink below the table. Absently he drummed patterns on his chair.

A few minutes he turned back again. "Say, how come I can't find the Aquarium on this thing?" he asked.

Jorn looked up from his handheld com panel. "Aquarium?" he said.

"The whatsit, you know. The Redoubt."

"Ah." Jorn smiled. "Aquarium, that's very good. Quite funny, really. I doubt anyone here has ever seen an actual aquarium, you know. Or a fish, for that matter."

"You're joking, right?"

"We used to have fish in the ocean, but they died out long ago." He missed Plavitz's incredulous expression as he touched his com panel to the table, then dragged a finger across the handheld device. On the table the well slid out of sight and the landscape blurred by until they were looking down at one of the vast fissures. Jorn pointed to where it tapered to a halt. "That's where your Aquarium is," he said.

Plavitz leaned forward. "I don't see it."

"It hadn't been built yet when this image was taken." Jorn spread two fingers on his com panel and the image on the table enlarged.

Plavitz gaped as he appeared to dive headlong into the fissure. "You can make it bigger? I've just been going back and forth."

"Of course. You can zoom in and out." He demonstrated.

"Holy jeez. I could read a newspaper on the ground."

"I believe the resolution is ten centimeters," said Jorn.

"Wait, the whatsit wasn't built yet? The Redoubt?" said Plavitz. "This map's a couple hundred years old?"

"Like everything else here, I'm afraid."

Plavitz touched the control pane with thumb and forefinger. He pinched. The landscape on the table rushed away from him. He pinched again. Now he was looking down on the gaping fissure. He zoomed again, and there was the vast crater on the left side of the panel. Once more, and he was looking down on a scene that belonged on the Moon: An enormous divot torn out of the world and radiating cracks so long and deep that entire cities could be hidden within them. From this vantage point the crater floor looked smooth as a lake. Faint concentric rings marked where spreading lava waves had cooled and hardened, a shock wave frozen in place as it had spread from an unimaginable explosion hundreds of years ago. The land around the crater and its radiating fissures was flat and featureless. Not even a ruin.

"What's the scale here?" asked Plavitz. He indicated the panel. "How big am I looking at?"

"I should think it's a fifty-kilometer field of view," said Jorn. "We can find out exactly, if you like."

"Fifty kilometers." Plavitz squinted, calculating. He sat up straight and pointed at the crater and its radiating cracks. "This thing is *thirty miles wide?*"

"Well, the initial explosion was comparable to an asteroid strike," said Jorn. "Literally extinction-level."

"It cracked this ball like an egg! I can't even picture—" Plavitz frowned. "Hey, wait a minute," he said. He leaned forward and stared at the massive scar before him. "I'm looking at thirty miles? Fifty kilometers?" He swiveled back to Jorn. "Nothing on earth could get a shot that wide. It'd have to be up in—"

He stopped. Turned back to the panel and reached toward the devastation spread across the glass-topped desk. Hesitated. And pinched. And pinched. And pinched. And sat looking in wonder and in fear at a broken world floating in the air before him, the whole scarred ball a murk of muddy browns, ochre yellow, burnt rust.

"You took this picture from *outer space*?" said Plavitz.

"From a reconnaissance satellite in geosynchronous orbit," Jorn affirmed. "They're all offline by now. But for some time they transmitted—"

"This is all just one big picture?" Plavitz interrupted, staring at the dead globe floating in the empty before him.

"It's an ultra-high resolution composite," Jorn said behind him. "That's why you can navigate it to that degree."

Plavitz watched his own arm reach out to the panel once again. Watched himself enlarge the image. Saw the broken world expand as if he plummeted toward the crater. He stopped the rush still very high above the world. He frowned and felt something akin to the awful thing that clawed its way up from deep down whenever he flew into a flak field and the 88s were thudding off outside the insubstantial hull.

Plavitz's chair shot back as he bolted to his feet. "We're still here," he heard himself say. His own voice sounded very far away. A frayed signal breaking up. Coming in from over some horizon. From an isolated outpost. From unknown space.

"Are you all right, young man?" Jorn asked.

Numbly Plavitz turned to him and pointed without looking at the ruined world hovering behind him. Like some eidolon indicating the route that all would one day follow. "It's Europe," he said. His tone a strange flat calm. "We didn't go anywhere."

TWENTY

Back in their reconfigurable barracks that evening the crew brought Farley up to speed about their day's Good Deeds—what they'd observed, what they'd learned, what they'd contributed. They listened to each other's accounts like citizens of some ancient country silent before returned travelers' stories of foreign peoples, strange customs, unlikely beasts, miraculous achievements.

Then Plavitz told them they were still in Europe.

Most of the crew scoffed outright. "I think we'd have heard about a crater the size of New Jersey in the middle of France, don't you?" said Broben.

Plavitz folded his arms and dug in. "My job is reading maps," he said. "What I saw was a map of Europe that was mostly hole where the N in Germany ought to be."

"Nobody on earth could take a picture from outer space," Broben insisted.

Boney cleared his throat. He was looking at the unlit pipe in his hand. "Nobody on earth in 1943 could," he said.

"Oh, come on," Garrett said after the silence became uncomfortable. "You saw what it's like out there. It's not Earth, it's a whole different planet."

"They speak English," Boney pointed out. "They grow *peanuts*."

They were still mulling it over when someone knocked on the door. It opened and Wennda came in, smiling like someone with a secret she couldn't wait to tell. "I brought you all a visitor," she said, and stepped aside to let somebody enter the room.

The room went graveyard quiet. A few men slowly stood.

Francis Owens, tail gunner on the bomber *Fata Morgana,* stood looking back at them. Uniform repaired and cleaned. Boots polished parade-dress bright. A white gauze dressing covered his left eye. He wore no other bandages or dressings. Not so much as a Band-Aid. No scars, scabs, scrapes, or scratches. Not even a bruise. Cornsilk stubble where his scalp had been flayed to bone above his ruined eye.

The crewmen stared at him in uncharacteristic silence. As if some certain ghost had come calling, pale and tall and blond among them like some revenant messenger. Their quick glances among themselves said more than mere words could. Even Farley hesitated. Francis had been *flayed,* more torn up by shrapnel than any man he'd ever seen who'd still been alive. And now here he was, three days later, all walking talking googly grin and skinny height of Francis Eugene Owens, white gauze neatly taped across one eye and not another mark on him. That wasn't a medical miracle, it was goddamn *witchcraft.* Surely even Lazarus' wife had pulled up short for a few seconds before giving him a hug and a *welcome back, honey.*

Finally Shorty stepped close to Francis and squinted at him like a man holding a counterfeit bill up to the light. He poked the coltish tail gunner in the shoulder as if testing his solidity. Then he put his hands on his hips and shook his head. "Well, hell," he said. "If they can fix you up this good, how come you're still so damn *ugly?*"

Francis flushed. "Aw, gee whiz," he said. "Lay off, will ya?"

The crew roared.

* * * * *

"I woke up," Francis told the crew, "and I was floating in a fish tank full of Jell-O! I was *breathing* it. Like a fish! Can you imagine? The doc had to come and calm me down. A black lady doctor, cap!"

"She did a fine job on you, Francis," Farley said. "You look good as new." He hesitated. "It's a tough break about the eye, but I'd say you're really pretty lucky."

Francis grinned and ducked his head. "Aw, heck, it's not so bad," he said. "The doc said the light'll bother me for a couple days after the patch comes off, but then it ought to be just fine."

"That's terrific," Farley replied, "I'm glad it won't—" He stopped. "She said the light will bother it?" he asked.

Francis nodded eagerly. "She told me it'll tear up something awful, but that just means it's healing."

"Healing." Farley stared at the patch. They all stared at the patch. Because what was beneath it five days ago had not been an eye. It had been a stringy, bloody mess clinging to Francis' flayed cheek like the tentacles of a jellyfish.

Farley tipped his cap back and scratched his head. "Doc say when the dressing can come off?" he asked casually.

"Oh, not till tomorrow, at least."

"Tomorrow." Farley looked at Wennda.

She shrugged. "I said we'd take care of him," she said.

* * * * *

Farley lay awake. The man who could sleep like a baby the night before a mission now found himself staring up toward the barely discernible ceiling while his mind hummed and sparked like an over-driven dynamo. Around him in the dimlit room his crew slept on their ingeniously designed bunks, a few of them fitful, a few snoring, most of them out like lights.

The day's events had gone well and the crew seemed confident that they could be helpful here, if not indispensable. Their stories were tiles in a mosaic that was forming a picture of who these people were, how they lived, how they'd stayed alive so long. All of it useful. All of it paling beside Boney's knockout reply to Broben.

"Nobody on earth could take a picture from outer space."

"Nobody on earth in 1943 could."

Farley realized that Francis' arrival had derailed any further discussion of the idea that they had somehow landed in the future. He also understood that this was how the crew had wanted it. The future, another planet, the sky over Germany, it didn't make a difference. What mattered was getting out. Getting back alive.

But the notion ate at Farley. Germany was just another country. Even a different planet was just another place. You could at least imagine getting back. But as far as Farley knew the only direction you could travel in time was forward, at a steady speed of sixty minutes an hour. The future was a one-way trip. An inevitable destination. But the past didn't even exist anymore. It wasn't another country, another planet. It simply *wasn't*. There was no more *there* there.

Farley felt a blind panic lurking, like some stalking beast outside a cabin probing for an opening, a weakness. Any way in.

He fought it down and frowned up at the darkness. Who knew how late it was? Three a.m.? Four? Would there even be dawn light in this alien and yet familiar place? Certainly there would be no growing birdsong, no morning dew, no rising breeze.

Wennda, he suddenly remembered, had asked him out.

As the crew had been passing Francis around like some kind of party novelty, scrutinizing his patch and his baby-pink skin, practically sniffing him like doubtful apes, Wennda had pulled Farley aside and asked, "Would you like to go somewhere together tomorrow? Before your meeting with my father?"

"Sure," Farley had replied, distracted by Francis, by the bombshell Boney had dropped into the discussion about still being in Europe. "Where'd you have in mind?"

"Well, there's no out to go *to* around here," she'd said, "but I can come pretty close."

Farley had absently agreed, not registering Wennda's faint disappointment, and they'd set an early date, and only now did Farley remember previously telling Wennda, *When you take someone out, you go somewhere together. So you can get to know each other better.*

Captain Midnight, you are one magnificent lunkhead, Farley thought. *Nobody on earth in 1943 could take a photograph from outer space.*

The welling panic threatened once again.

Tomorrow, Farley told himself, the commander's scientists will tell me more about how we got here and how we can get back. They'll have equations and gold-plated words. They'll have ingenious theories and speculations, clever solutions that will work as long as their hypotheses are true.

I'm a pilot, Farley told the dark above him. *Show me the route that gets my men back home. Show me the map that shows the way to 1943.*

TWENTY-ONE

Wennda led Farley along the strip of savannah bordering the rectangular ocean. She pointed out features and functions, explaining their role in the web of the Dome's ecology, as they headed toward the artificial cliffs built into the tiny rain forest. She had been worried that Farley would sense her nervousness, but he nodded mutely at her compulsive monologue. He seemed preoccupied, and he looked tired and distracted, as if he had not slept well.

Wennda hadn't slept all that well since discovering these strange men, either.

Someone checking a water condenser in the savannah waved to her. She squinted and saw that it was Ingra, pregnant out to here. She waved back. Ingra dropped her hand and continued to look. Staring at Farley, of course.

Lang and Grobe and several others had made it clear that they thought Farley and his crew were a danger in themselves. In this frail and tightly managed world, strangers burdened an infrastructure already operating near its limits—and these particular strangers were heavily armed soldiers of uncertain origin.

Wennda understood their apprehension but she didn't share it. She had spent more time with the crew than anyone else had, except possibly Yone, who seemed to have found a kinship of outsiders with them. They were loud and rude and blunt, but they were highly trained and highly skilled, disciplined when need arose, and admirable fighters. There was a kind of benign arrogance about them that managed to be charming and off-putting at the same time. If you were on their side they would help you, simple as that.

There was also something very *alive* about them. They were spontaneous, emotional, sentimental. They told stupid jokes and played childish gags. They laughed in the face of danger—literally laughed—even though they seemed perfectly aware of the stakes. Her own people seemed so deadly dull beside them.

She knew that her father's cautious approval of Farley and his crew masked an eagerness to be rid of them. She couldn't really blame him. Even if they were not dangerous themselves, they had certainly brought danger with them. The captured bomber had upset a long-running stalemate, and now costly and potentially disastrous action had to be taken. Wennda had been surprised when her father had assigned her to oversee the crew's integration, and was even more surprised that he had not caused some wedge to be driven between his daughter and the leader of these disrupting strangers. Perhaps he was less concerned because he knew they would be leaving soon.

Wennda felt a stab of unreasoning panic at the thought of Farley leaving. In a few hours he would be meeting her father and his team to put the final touches on the plan for recovering the aircraft and attempting to return to wherever they had come from. If the plan succeeded she would never see him again. Of course, if the mission did *not* succeed there was a good chance she would never see him again, either. Which was why she intended to be on the mission.

Meantime Wennda was convinced that the crew themselves weren't going to harm her city or her people. This morning two of them were back in the Ag fields, spraying liquid detergent as a disinfectant against crop mold. At Fabrication, one of them was re-coiling an ancient copper-wire motor while another brought new kinds of food to scan into the bioprinters. Dr. Manday was sampling DNA from the wounded soldier for cloning tissue cultures, blood plasma, organ budding, white-cell bacterial resistance, and other organics that would help their fragile population. And it was looking possible to get the eleven o'clock sun back.

Wennda looked up at the familiar facsimile sky. *But not today, please,* she pleaded silently.

Farley looked up at the Dome when she did. "Gosh," he said, "another nice day. Can you believe it?"

She sensed he was poking fun, but she wasn't sure exactly how. She felt that a lot around him. "It's a day," she said noncommittally.

"Don't you ever miss bad weather?"

"I can't miss it if I've never experienced it."

"Then you don't know what you're missing." He squinted up. "A good rainstorm's terrific if you don't have to fly through it."

"We have rain. Temperature differences between the top and bottom of the Dome create evaporation and circulation, and pressure differences move warm wet air from the rain forest to the more arid side. So precipitation spreads where it's needed."

Farley made a face. "That's not rain. That's, I don't know. Mist. Drizzle. You need a toad-strangler sometimes. Thunder. Lightning. The wrath of God."

"I've seen lightning outside," she said. "It's very dangerous."

"It's good to be reminded that someone else is running the show."

Wennda frowned. "But we are running the ... show." She gestured expansively.

He gave a little smile. "This show," he said, and held thumb and forefinger close together.

And *that* was what disturbed Wennda's sleep. Not Farley's crew, not their weaponry, not some danger that followed their arrival here. Farley himself.

All her life she had been restless—physically contained, mentally constrained. Her reason told her that the Dome was all there was. Her nature wanted more. Farley came from more. From somewhere unimaginably large, strange, free. Wennda glimpsed that wider world in his every move, in the texture of his speech. When she viewed her world through his eyes it was unfamiliar, enigmatic, clever. Yet it also became very small and rundown. Farley's very character seemed larger than what she had known, and it spoke to that restless imp in her that yearned for more. At first she hadn't listened. Now it was all she could hear.

* * * * *

The air grew humid as they left the savannah behind and entered the miniature rain forest. Three-fourths of the Dome's plant life lived here, breathing out oxygen, filtering water. A little recirculating river ran through it, feeding into the strip of marshland and eventually the tiny ocean. The city's only trees stood tall here. Lush greenery spread everywhere.

They came to the base of the russet-colored cliffs amid the teeming forest.

"This is nice," said Farley. "We should have a picnic."

"All right," said Wennda. "What's a picnic?"

He grinned. "It's a fancy word for sitting on the grass and eating lunch."

"I'm afraid there isn't much grass. Is it still a picnic if you eat in a tree?"

He laughed. She liked seeing the worry lift from his face. "I don't know another word for that, so sure, why not?"

"I used to come here at night sometimes," Wennda told him. "I'd run through the bushes and lie down in the grass and listen to the river."

He glanced around. "I can see why you'd like that. It's as close to feeling like you're outside as you can get in this bell jar."

"Outside's not a bit like this."

He nodded and looked sad. "Then that makes this place even more special," he said.

"I always thought it was strange," she said, "how it's the same age as the rest of the Dome, but it feels ancient."

"Maybe there's something old inside you that remembers it."

She grinned. "That's it. That's it exactly. Something older in me that remembers." She turned a slow circle in the greenery. "I never told anyone about it before. It sounds—" she spread her hands "—well, odd."

"'A long time ago,'" said Farley, "'when we all lived in the forest....'"

She clapped her hands. "You really do understand," she said.

"Well, all that book time had to pay off someday."

Her look grew serious. "I don't mean the trees. I mean me. You understand *me.*"

"I don't know that I'd go that far. But I'm working on it." His smile became sly. "So," he said. "What now?"

Something in her thrilled at his *now.* She resisted an urge to glance at her chronometer. There was time. It would be fine. But in truth there was no time. Every second brought his leaving closer.

Wennda pointed at the base of the cliff. "Now," she said, "we climb."

* * * * *

The cliffs rose a hundred fifty feet. They looked real, but there was a convenience to their structure that belied nature. Here terraces and tiers, gouges and cracks and outcroppings did double duty as steps, handholds, even a little amphitheater and benches. Farley admired their design as he followed Wennda along the narrow route up the artificial cliffs. He was glad to be alone with her, glad that by the end of the day a plan for recovering his bomber would be in place. Farley would be getting weapons, a squad, tactical help, technical help from the science boys on how to fly back through the vortex. Meantime his crew were earning their keep, and the CO seemed pleased by their participation and not even especially bothered about his daughter fraternizing with the Barbarian from the Sky. No one was dead, there was hope of getting home, and Farley was out in the sunshine with his dreamgirl. He couldn't stop worrying about getting back, about getting his men back—but when you thought about it, there were worse things than not being able to get back to the war.

* * * * *

Wennda looked at the ten o'clock sun panel glowing on the other side of the sky, then glanced back at Farley. He seemed lost in thought. She turned forward and kept going. At least they were alone up here.

She thought about when she used to come up here at night to run through the bushes and lie in the grass and listen to that lulling ancient voice. Often she would take her clothes off so that she could feel the world against her skin. Her skin against the world. Something old in her remembering. She wondered why she hadn't mentioned that to Farley.

* * * * *

The top was flat and bare and maybe twenty feet square. Farley took in the miniature city, the ordered plots of crops, the rectangle of ocean, strips of marshland and savannah, the clustered buildings. You could easily believe you looked out across a thoughtfully patterned vista from a thousand feet up, but the true scale quickly asserted itself. The sky's falseness was more apparent here, the nearer panels' geometry impossible to ignore. Several of them dully reflected light from the ten o'clock sun on the other side of the dome.

Farley put his hands on his hips. "I like the view," he said. He turned to her, already half grinning and intending to say, "And the city looks nice, too." He stopped.

The feeling he was standing in his dream of her was overwhelming. This place he'd never been before, never could have seen. A world unto itself.

"I thought a break would do you some good," Wennda said, and broke his sense of déjà vu.

"It's gonna feel like R & R on someone else's dime."

"I'll assume that's good."

213

"It's terrific."

She beamed. "Come on." She took his hand and led him to the cliff edge facing away from the buildings and fields. They sat with their feet dangling and they looked down on valances of mist among the bushes below. Farley's eyes told him he looked out over a vast space. Other senses told him that a massive wall was near.

Wennda leaned forward to look down at the mist and felt his grip tighten. His hand felt warm and strange and comfortable. "I won't fall," she said.

His face was a caricature of disappointment. "Not even a little bit?"

She rolled her eyes. There it was, in five words. Confidence, playfulness, protectiveness, and utter *difference.*

"I don't get to do things like this with people," she said, looking down at tendril clouds fifty feet below. "With men. I'm the commander's daughter."

"I can see how that would have its good and bad sides," he said beside her.

She snorted. "People think I get away with things. I'm always in some kind of trouble, but then I don't get punished."

"Or you get punished harder than other people who did the same thing?"

She nodded. "But usually I get into trouble because I did something that needed to be done! Things I couldn't get anyone else to do."

"Or couldn't get permission to do?"

"Maybe. Sometimes." She laughed. "Yes."

"Maybe sometimes yes," he agreed.

"But I'm *right,*" she said. "I fix things, I find out things that help everyone. Nobody talks about that part of it. They either talk about how I have it easy or they feel sorry for me."

"Because you're the CO's daughter."

She nodded. "No one ever tells him you're too easy on her, you're too hard on her. They're afraid of him." She laughed bitterly. "They should be."

"He seems like a pretty tough nut."

She pulled her hand from his and turned toward him. "I'm sorry," she said. "I didn't bring you here to talk about that. I brought you here because this place is special to me, and I wanted to be alone with you. I wanted—"

The sun went out.

Wennda let out a long sigh as lights winked on in the fields below, in the clustered buildings in the distance. "This," she finished resignedly. "Us, here. Alone. At eleven."

"Oh." He was quiet a moment. "Oh!" he said again.

"Oh," she agreed. "Some tactician, huh?" She folded her arms and looked down into the impenetrable dark. Maybe she should just lean forward and let herself fall. Just a little bit, as Farley'd said. With her luck she'd live through it.

"Can I say something?" Farley asked.

"I wish you would."

He drew a long breath. "Can we maybe scoot back a little? This cliff is scaring the hell out of me in the dark."

She laughed. "Something scares you? The fearless aircraft pilot who flies between worlds and fights off typhons?"

"There hasn't been five minutes in the last four days when Captain Fearless here wasn't scared out of his gourd. Anyone who wasn't would be crazy. Or lying. Or dead."

"Here." She reached out, touched his back, and moved to his arm. "I'll save you, Captain Fearless."

"I'm counting on it," he said.

She pulled him back and let him go and stood facing the dark sky with her back to the warming breeze. "'I'm counting on it,'" she repeated. She shook her head. "How do you do that?"

"Do what? Count on you?"

"*Talk* like that." She let out an exasperated breath. "You do things that ought to make me mad. Grab me like I'm too careless to stay on a cliff. Like I'm a child. And then say you're counting on me to save you, like—like I don't know what."

"I'm just being—"

"You open *doors* for me," she said. "Hold chairs for me, like I'm injured or something. You stand up when I walk into a room. I've seen you glare at your men for using language you think I shouldn't hear. Like I need protecting."

"That's the way I was brought up. My mom would take me apart with a can opener if I was rude to a lady. But if it bugs you, I guess I can—"

"I like it." She turned to face him and put her hands on her hips. "I *like* it. If anyone told me about some man doing those things, I'd say What, does he think you're sick? Did someone tell him you're dying, or something? But you do it and it makes me feel like a woman. You sit across a table from me and everybody's talking about tactics, and you're looking at me. Not at a soldier, or an expert, or any of that. You're looking at *me*."

"It's not as if it's hard to look at you, Wennda."

"Shut *up*." She was surprised at her welling tears and she forced them back. "I'm a good soldier," she said. "I'm a great data tech. People say they appreciate things I do. They train with me, they work with me, they game with me. They gossip and argue and complain with me. What they don't do is try to be alone with me in the forest in the dark. They don't ask me out. Because I'm the commander's daughter. Because everyone knows who he is and what he's like, and they're terrified of him. Because they feel sorry for me but they think I'm privileged, too."

Farley didn't say anything. She loved that he knew not to say anything.

"And then you show up," she continued. "And you don't know whose daughter I am, or what my history is, or any of that. But somehow you understand me. I try to tell you why I like coming up here, and you say it's because there's something ancient in me that remembers it. You know what I mean, not just what I say. You treat me some way I've never been treated. You make me feel pretty. No one ever made me feel pretty before. Even if they thought I was, they couldn't tell me. I'm the commander's daughter." She laughed bitterly.

"Well," he said. "I think you deserve better."

"I think so, too." She wiped her eyes and looked at him, and the naked ache in her face was heartbreaking. "I think I deserve better. And I think that's you."

"I'm not better than anybody," he said.

"And I'm not pretty. But you think I am." She looked up at the lying sky. "Why is this so hard?" she pleaded. "Why are we so afraid of what we really want?"

"Maybe because it came from another world with a lifesize picture of you plastered on its nose like a billboard. Anyone who wouldn't be afraid of that is crazy."

"Or lying," she said.

He smiled. "Or dead," he agreed.

She laughed. She found his hand and pulled him nearer. His face all there was to see. "It certainly got my attention," she said. "Maybe that was the point."

"How could it be? I didn't even know you existed."

"I didn't say you were the one trying to get my attention," she said.

Farley raised an eyebrow. "Who, then? God?"

Wennda shrugged. "The universe. Quantum entanglement. God. I don't know. But something went out of its way to bring you here from another world. Maybe we'll find out why."

"Last night," Farley said carefully, "I found out I didn't come from a different world at all. I come from this one." He held a hand up as she started a reply. "From the past," he said. "Hundreds of years ago. Before your war. Before all this." His gesture encompassed the Dome, the ruined world beyond.

She smiled. "Maybe that's why I'm on your aircraft," she said. "I'm a memory of the future. An echo across time."

"An echo."

She leaned away and looked at him. Traced his jawline with a hand. His expression serious. City light glittering in his eyes. "Another world, another time," she said. "You still were brought. It's not any crazier than your being here in the first place."

Now he smiled. "I've seen an awful lot of crazy in the last couple of years," he said. "And every bit of it was real."

She smiled back. "Farley," she said.

"I think you can call me Joe by now, don't you?"

"Joe," she said. "All right. So what now, Joe?"

"You know what now."

"Yes." She put a hand on his back and the other behind his neck. Muscle flexed against one palm. Stubble rough against the other. "Yes, I do." She leaned toward him.

The sun turned on.

Stark in sudden light they gaped at each other. Farley's hands fell.

"Damn it!" said Wennda. "It can't be noon yet!" She stepped back and looked up at the lighted sky. "I want more *time!*" she demanded.

Farley looked puzzled. He cocked his head. "Listen," he said.

Wennda looked away from the dome and stood listening as sound carried from the city below. Shouting voices. She frowned and glanced at her chronometer. "Eleven twenty-eight?" she said in disbelief. "This can't be broken."

"It isn't," Farley said. "They fixed the sun."

Wennda slumped. Now came the tears she had been fighting.

"What's wrong?" asked Farley. "You've been wanting this for years."

She looked up at him. "Oh, Joe," she said, "I didn't want it *now.*"

TWENTY-TWO

"Pitcher Proud Horse goes into his motion and sets. Here comes the throw to Garrett.... Swung on and missed, strike three. Impressive heat up and in from the big chief. And that ends the inning.

"So here at the bottom of the second it's still Typhons one, Daybreakers nothing. This is your old broadcaster Shorty Dubuque coming to you live from Big Dome Field here in the future, which is brought to you by the six delicious flavors of Jell-O. J-E-L-L-O—ask for it by name at a food printer near you."

* * * * *

Farley smiled at the unmistakable pop of a ball hitting a glove. At the players, at the day. At a thousand jumpsuited men, women, and children gathered beneath a six-cornered sun that had not shone at this time of day in eight years. Loud hubbub, raucous laughter, cheers and jeers. Everything but Cracker Jacks. The aluminum bats took some getting used to, though. Farley understood that there was no wood to be found in the Dome—maybe even in the entire world—but hearing a *bink* instead of a *crack!* when someone got off a good hit was just plain wrong.

Instead of bleachers there were rows of lightweight metal folding chairs. Farley and Wennda sat near the first-base line and watched the ragtag Typhons take the field. Even after two full innings, the Dome dwellers on both teams seemed unsure about where their positions were, here in the fresh-cut diamond of grassland near the Dome wall. Garrett, now at catcher for the Typhons, waved furiously for third baseman Arshall to get closer to the dense foam square that was third base. Arshall frowned but complied, his new black ball glove hanging from his wrist like a canned ham.

Shorty announced from a folding table made of the same super-lightweight stuff as the chairs. He spoke into something that looked like a notecard but apparently was a microphone. Farley couldn't figure out where Shorty's voice was coming from. He couldn't see any loudspeakers. Or wires.

Shorty had designed the Typhons' uniforms, a silhouette of a diving Typhon on paper jumpsuits printed special for the occasion. The Daybreakers sported a stylized, faintly hexagonal sun with a huge smile, thick-lined wavy rays, and a bandage on one cheek. Hard-edged tribal patterns ran up the sleeves and legs—all courtesy of Wennda.

Farley had been impressed. "So you have hidden talents," he'd told her.

"They're not hidden at all," she had replied. "You just need the time to experience them."

Time.

Farley glanced down at her hand on his, the feel of it new and yet familiar.

He saw Commander Vanden sitting farther down the row, ramrod straight and scowling. *The guy's face would crack if he changed expression,* Farley thought.

The commander spotted him, and Farley gave a slow, grave salute. Vanden's frown deepened, but he only nodded curtly and turned to say something to Grobe, who sat beside him, consulting an unfolded com panel.

Yesterday's final planning session with the commander and his advisers had yielded Farley everything he could have wanted. The science boys had gone into the expected technical, highly theoretical, and largely incomprehensible detail about what the vortex was, and how and where Farley should re-enter it—assuming he had an aircraft to re-enter it with. That part would be determined tomorrow morning when Farley and his crew set out on foot for the Redoubt with weapons, armor, supplies, and a team of six Dome troops.

The crew had whooped and hollered when Farley gave them the news. He could not have been happier himself, except for one detail: One of those six troops would be Wennda. At the meeting he had tried to object, and the commander had quashed it out of hand. "If I didn't have any say in the matter," he'd told Farley, "I highly doubt you will, either."

* * * * *

"And once again the Typhons take the field—man, you never thought you'd hear that *line in here.*

"Coming up to hit is Plavitz. He moonlights as the navigator on our aircraft, so he's probably the biggest reason why we're here with you today."

Plavitz twisted in his batting stance to glare at Shorty. But the crowd cheered, unaware of the announcer's intended irony. The cheering thawed Plavitz, and he doffed an imaginary cap and bowed to the crowd.

"On the mound Yone gets the sign from Garrett ... aaaand here comes the pitch. Ball, low and outside. Quite an arm on this brand-new pitcher; they must spend a lot of time throwing things at each other in the Redoubt.

"Yone sets ... and here comes the throw. It's a high-fly hit to left center field! Lang goes back—followed by Arshall at third, Pohl at shortstop, and Ryner at first. It's an exodus from the infield! Lang staggers back and makes the catch! From the look on his face, he's just as surprised as we are.

"So that's one out here at the top of the third, in what is without a doubt the best ball game ever played here in sunny Future Dome Field as Samay steps to the plate. I hear she can really make a fork lift over there in Fabrication. Sorry about that one, folks; the only fork I ever lifted had pie on the end of it.

"Samay's got a lot of choke on that bat, very uneven stance. Yone throws—and Samay jumps out of the box as a fastball rockets past the plate, strike one! Now Daybreakers catcher Broben calls time from the bench."

* * * * *

"He's trying to kill me," Samay told Broben as he approached her. "He's from the Redoubt, you know."

"He's not trying to kill you," Broben said. "He's putting it right across the plate. Here, look." He stepped close behind her and put his hands over her hands holding the metal bat, conscious of Garrett grinning in his crouch behind home plate. He moved Samay's arms in a practice swing. "Swing it like that and *blam,* it's outta here."

She frowned at the artificial sky. "That would be impressive, all right," she said.

"Broben at the plate now, showing his left fielder the old baseball adage that it don't mean a thing if it ain't got that swing."

Broben scowled at Shorty. "I'm just trying to get her to first base," he called.

"You've already got her way past that," yelled Everett from the bench.

Broben turned toward the bench and held a fist up to Everett. The big waist-gunner grinned and showed both palms.

"And third baseman Everett yields the call."

Broben turned back and glared down at Garrett. "Tell that whiz-kid pitcher of yours to lay off the heat," he snapped. "That's an order."

Garrett saluted with his glove and shrugged at Yone on the mound.

"Yone gets the sign.... And here comes an underhand *pitch that you'd have to call off-speed. Samay closes her eyes and swings—oh, it's a rocket comebacker to Yone!"*

The ball bounced off Yone's glove and into center field. On the third-base line, Broben did a funny little dance and made a shooing motion. "Go, Sammy, go! First base, honey! Shake a leg!" He ran to her and set his hands on her hips and pushed her into motion. Samay trotted to first base and kept going. The baseman, Ryner, snagged her arm and reeled her back. "I think you're supposed to stop here," he said as the anemic throw from center field rolled by behind him.

All of Farley's crew put their hands over their heads.

"Second!" Broben yelled. "Go to second!"

"He said stay here!" she yelled back.

"He's on the *other team*!" Broben called.

Samay frowned but began strolling toward second as Ryner's teammates yelled for him to get the damn ball, for the love of Mike. On second, Boney took pity on Samay and left his position to take her by the arm and lead her to the bag.

"And Typhons second baseman Boney Mullen gives the assist. I have a note here that the gang listening over in Filtration wants a clearer explanation of that last play. Fellas, I'm here to tell you that it can't be done.

"Up to the plate now is center fielder Berne, the big Dome brain who works on the Dome's big brains. Yes, I really said that. Give him a hand, folks; he's one of the reasons we aren't playing in the dark today.

"Pitcher Yone looks serious after giving up that last hit. Here comes the throw. Up-and-in fastball, strike one.

"Berne gives Yone the stink eye. Yone goes into his windup. My money's on the heater—oh, and Berne connects! It's going.... It is going.... It is ... off the sky and left for the Dome's first-ever home run! Man, that hit nearly ruined three p.m. for the next eight years! It's good for two Daybreaker runs, and the crowd goes wild as the local boy makes good on Super Sun Day."

* * * * *

Farley cheered along with everyone else as Berne trotted heavily around the bases. That was one hell of a hit. Samay jogged across the plate and Jerry took her up in a huge hug. Berne stopped before the plate, red-faced and sweating, and looked at the crowd. He seemed surprised to see them cheering. He gave a little wave, took a deep breath, jumped up, and landed squarely on home plate. The crowd shot to its feet.

"That's good, isn't it?" Wennda asked.

"Are you kidding?" said Farley. "Fixing the sun's one thing, but if you really want people to love you, hit a homer."

Wennda nodded uncertainly and resumed clapping. Farley laughed. Just another sunny day in the park.

He looked to see if the commander had cracked any semblance of a smile and was unsurprised to see him still seated, scowling as Grobe said something into his ear.

Farley frowned. Vanden was looking even more pissed off than usual.

Farley nudged Wennda and jutted his chin at the commander. "What's he so cheerful about?" he asked.

Wennda leaned forward and looked at her father. She stopped clapping. "Something's wrong," she said.

Vanden spoke briefly to Grobe and inclined his head at Farley. Grobe nodded curtly and hurried away.

Farley's pulse kicked up a notch.

A chime sounded and Wennda snapped out her cellophone and held it to her ear. "Sten," she said. "What's going on?" She frowned at Farley. "They *what*? How many? Just now? When did they leave?"

Farley studied Vanden and tried to stay calm as Wennda spoke. The commander stared back.

Wennda crumpled her cellophone and took a deep breath. "My father sent out a team to destroy your aircraft four days ago," she said, staring pure hate at the commander. "Two of them just got back. One's badly injured. The other's reporting in."

"Four days ago," Farley repeated numbly.

"Right after your first meeting with him."

The commander regarded him across the crowd. A rock in the rapids.

Farley nodded slowly. "Do I still have an aircraft?"

"Sten says they didn't even make it into the Redoubt."

Farley looked at his crew divided among the teams on the new-cut field. "We left our weapons back at the barracks," he said.

Wennda touched his arm. "I'm with you, Joe. What do you want to do?"

"Anything but sit here a second longer." He stood up and stepped out from the row of cheering people. Immediately a dozen people got up from different places in the crowd and began to converge on him. It looked like a magic trick.

The commander spoke into a com panel and the converging people produced nerve guns.

Farley broke into a run. *"Back to barracks!"* he yelled to the diamond. *"Morgana crew, back to barracks, now!"*

The players stood watching uncertainly. Farley waved them forward. "Get to your weapons!" he yelled. Knowing it was already too late.

Wennda ran behind him, talking urgently on her com panel. Behind her half a dozen troops ran full-out.

Something crackled past Farley and he smelled sharp metallic ozone. Heard the whine of the fired gun. Turned his head and saw Wennda on the ground. Felt an odd cold tingle spread across his back. Tried to move his legs and couldn't. Watched the ground rush up to meet him. Heard his head hit hard. Saw the sun and all the other light go out. Smelled fresh-cut grass. Felt all feeling drain away.

TWENTY-THREE

The pain woke Farley up. A nail driven into the back of his head. Jaw muscles sore from clenching and scalp too tight for his skull. His teeth ached and invisible bugs crawled on his skin.

He opened his eyes and light stabbed in. He turned his head away and heard his neck creak. Shorty lay face-up a few feet away, eyes closed and teeth clenched and lips drawn back from gums. His hands were raised, fingers curled into claws.

"He only looks dead," came Broben's voice. "When he wakes up he'll wish he really was."

Farley turned his head the other way. Broben sat against the wall, grinning at him like a guilty dog.

"Am I right?" Broben asked.

"You don't have to yell," Farley rasped.

The grin widened. "I'm whispering."

"Well, stop it." He tried to sit up and couldn't quite manage it. Broben came forward and offered a hand. Farley reached to take it and saw his own hand clawed like Shorty's.

"It wears off in ten or fifteen minutes," Broben said.

"How long have you been awake?"

"Ten or fifteen minutes." He grabbed Farley's forearm and helped him sit up.

Farley glanced around. They were back in their barracks, all the pullouts tucked away and the room bare except for the contorted bodies of the crewmen on the floor. "Jesus," Farley whispered. "I don't suppose they left our guns around anywhere."

Broben shook his head. "Not even a slingshot."

Farley stared at his clutching hand and willed it to relax. Stood up and leaned against the wall. "Slingshot or not," he said, "we're getting out of here. Help me wake them up."

* * * * *

The crew hunched forward on unfolded couches or slumped at the edges of opened sleeping compartments. To a man they winced when they moved or when Farley's voice got too loud. They looked like the dregs of some bachelor party that had overstayed its welcome, listening sullen and quiet like schoolboys on detention as their captain explained that the last four days here had been a sham, a distraction to occupy them while a six-member demolition team set out to destroy their only chance of getting home.

There was silence after Farley finished. Then Garrett said, "I say we bust down that shitty door and make a break for it, captain."

"That's one option," Farley allowed.

"It beats sitting here waiting for a firing squad," said Everett. "Or whatever it is they do."

"They chuck you in the reverter," said Shorty. "Boil you down to your parts and shovel you over the crops."

Everett shrugged. "They can't shoot all of us."

"They shot all of us an hour ago," Broben pointed out.

"I'll still take my chances."

Broben raised his eyebrows. "I bet those fry cookers won't be on low next time."

"I bet I don't give a pointy turd."

The door opened and they all looked as Grobe stepped in. He and his nerve gun surveyed the room.

"Dibs," said Everett, and stood up from his couch.

Grobe smirked and leveled his weapon and stepped aside to let Berne in. The software technician had a mesh bag in one hand and a lidded bucket in the other. He was breathing quickly and sweating. His gaze darted around the room. "Food bars," he said, jerking the mesh bag. He lifted the bucket. "Toilet."

"Why don't you just throw the food bars in the toilet and cut us out of the picture," said Plavitz.

Berne frowned at him. "I just want to help," he said.

"You wanna help?" said Garrett. He jabbed a thumb at Grobe. "Shoot this asshole."

Berne scowled. "You'll note I have no weapon," he said. He looked at Shorty. "There's an issue with the sun panel," he said. He set down the bucket and pulled out his cellophone and shook it taut.

Grobe frowned. "I wasn't told about this."

"Engineering sent it to me on my way here." Berne lit the panel and showed the screen to Grobe. "It's here, in the shutdown sequence." He turned to Shorty and held it up. "I was hoping you could—"

"Put the com panel away," Grobe said.

Berne wiped sweat from his upper lip. "But this man was instrumental in—"

Grobe trained his weapon on the nervous man. "Now," he ordered.

"I was only trying to save some work," said Berne. He looked up at Shorty. "Perhaps I should just press enter and hope for the best?" he said.

Shorty nodded back solemnly. "Say goodnight, Gracie," he said.

Berne twitched another smile and tapped the filmy screen, and the room went dark.

Shorty dropped from the upper bunk and landed on Garrett, who was already up from the couch and barreling into Grobe. The three men toppled over grappling. Grobe hit the floor hard with Garrett bear-hugging him. Shorty twisted the nerve rifle out of the stunned man's grip.

From outside the door came the sound of more nerve rifles charging up after being fired. The door flew open and bright flashlights swept the room. Shorty brought his commandeered weapon to bear.

"Don't shoot," said a familiar voice behind one of the lights.

"Yone?" said Shorty.

"Yes, it's me." The light reversed, and now the crew could see Yone pointing a nerve rifle with a slim flashlight attached to the side of the stubby, squared barrel. Beside him a stocky woman stood holding another nerve rifle.

"Sammy!" said Broben.

"Hello, lieutenant," said Samay.

Grobe lunged for the gun in Shorty's hands. Garrett yanked him backward so hard his teeth clacked. Shorty grinned down at the man in the faint light and trained the weapon on him. "I'll bet," he said, "you'll be happy to tell me how to turn this thing down now."

Grobe glared and folded his arms.

"There is a slider on the left side above the trigger," said Yone. "All the way back is the lowest setting."

Grobe gave him a look of pure loathing. "I was right about you," he said.

"Oh, shut up," said Shorty, and pressed the firing stud. Grobe went stiff and keeled over. No one moved to soften the impact when his head smacked the floor. The rifle whined its annoying recharge sound.

"You sure you pulled that thing all the way back?" Farley asked.

Shorty shrugged. "I mighta pushed it back up a couple notches," he admitted.

Plavitz and Francis dragged the unconscious guards in from the doorway. "Jeez, the whole Dome's out!" Francis announced. His eyepatch an eerie monster eye in the faint light.

"Yes," said Berne. "The hard part was turning the power off and leaving essential services running."

"Looks like you aced it," Shorty told him.

"Thank you. This has been the single best day of my life."

Plavitz and Francis removed the guards' weapons and handed

them off to Garrett and Everett. Garrett hefted the plastic rifle. "This thing's a toy," he said.

"Maybe from that end," said Everett.

Plavitz and Francis couldn't figure out how to get the smartsuit body armor off the stiff guards, so Yone and Samay took over and began removing sections.

"More troops will be here soon," Yone said as he pulled off a section. "We must hurry."

"Hurry where?" asked Farley.

"Out of the Dome, of course. You can't stay here." He pulled off a last section of armor and looked at it. "Neither can I, now," he said, and handed the piece to Farley.

Farley rubbed the dark fabric with his fingers. It was so light you'd think a breeze would blow it off, yet it felt strangely liquid. He looked at Yone and nodded slowly. "I'd say you earned yourself a ride," he said.

"Thank you," the little man said simply.

"Thank me when we're in the air," said Farley. He hesitated.

Yone shook his head. "I don't know where she is, I'm sorry. The commander's men took her away."

Farley imagined finding out where they'd locked Wennda away, shooting his way in, leading her safely out. Out of the Dome, across the dead expanse, into the Redoubt, into the sky and home. *That's a nice thought, Captain Midnight. Now put it away. You can take it out and cry over it later, if you live through this.*

He turned to the crew. "All right, everybody move out," he said. "We've got a plane to catch."

* * * * *

They made their way in the foreign dark like blind monks, single file and one hand on the shoulder of the man ahead. Around him Farley heard only footfalls and tight whispers. The occasional beam of a flashlight swept by like a little lighthouse beacon. The dead flat quiet made him realize how much background noise there usually was throughout the Dome—air circulators, power hum, turbine whines, distant machinery. Berne's basics-only blackout meant no air filtration, temperature regulation, communication, defenses.

Farley would have thought the place would become a stepped-on anthill with the power out, but then he realized everybody here must have drilled for this contingency. He saw small groups and individuals heading toward stations in orderly fashion, most of them carrying tiny but powerful flashlights. He ordered the men to stay tight, turn on their own flashlights, and walk fast but not to run.

They hurried along a narrow walkway adjacent to the main thoroughfare, following Samay's lead toward the agricultural plots. The stocky woman had no problem keeping a fast pace, but Berne was lagging. Farley was on the verge of suggesting the technician might be better off holing up somewhere safe, when the smells around them changed and he realized they were already in the crop grid.

Suddenly their shadows stretched ahead on the narrow footpath, and Farley glanced back to see pale orange lights glowing from the corners of buildings in the administrative and housing clusters. Emergency lights on battery reserves. Bad news: No more darkness to hide in. Good news: The Dome wall wasn't a minute away.

* * * * *

"Tell me there's another way out of this bowl," Broben said to Samay. Crouched beside her and Farley behind a low plastic bin, he frowned at the closed hatchway set flush into the Dome wall a hundred feet away. The rectangular access panel beside it was the only clear indication the door was even there.

Samay shook her head. "There's access to the gap between the inner and outer shells, but the only exit to the surface is through the one lock."

231

"That's nuts. What if you had to evacuate?"

"The Dome was built as someplace to evacuate *to,* not evacuate *from.*"

"There's two places I'd've sent troops the second the lights went out: Our barracks, and the other side of that door."

"Troops or not," said Farley, "that's our way out of here." He glanced around and was satisfied that he could not make out the rest of the crew lying low in the fields.

"The access panel won't work with the power out," said Samay.

Farley nodded. "Then we'll do it the Army way."

She looked puzzled. "The Army way?"

Broben smirked and punched his fist into his palm. "Subtle," he said, pronouncing the *b.*

* * * * *

Four crewmen emerged from the small geometry of crops in a low crouch and trotted through the dim orange twilight to the Dome wall. They followed its gentle curve until they stood before the door. The black glass panel beside it was dark.

Garrett and Everett took flank with their nerve guns while Boney went to work on the panel.

"There's gotta be a manual backup," Shorty whispered beside him. "You don't build something that traps everybody when the power goes on the fritz."

"Good thing you didn't pull sub duty," Boney replied. He felt around the edges of the panel, then put both hands on the right side and slid a recessed lever out from the edge. He glanced at Garrett and Everett, then pulled the lever.

The access panel swung open. Behind it was a circular metal plate with a hole in the middle, and a Z-shaped crank bar held by plastic clamps. Boney pulled the bar free and fitted one end into the metal plate. He tried to crank the Z-bar but nothing moved. Shorty set his hands on the crank beside Boney's and the two men worked the bar counter-clockwise. Grudgingly it began to turn. Metal squealed, and beside them the door began to inch open.

"Jesus," Shorty breathed. "Send up a flare, while we're at it."

Beyond the half-open door all was pitch black. Boney moved aside and Shorty held a fist up. Garrett and Everett moved to flank him at the door. The stubby nerve guns really did look like toys in their big hands, Shorty thought as he counted one two three with his fingers. Then he gripped the nerve gun he had borrowed from Yone and ran into the half-open doorway. He dropped low and turned on the flashlight clipped to the side of the gun as Everett and Garrett came in behind him.

Sudden bright light blinded the three crewmen. "Lower your weapons," said a calm voice not ten feet away.

* * * * *

Farley and Broben traded a glance when Boney beckoned them from the opened hatchway. "Maybe we got here first?" Broben ventured.

"That'll be the day," Farley muttered. "Come on."

They got up from behind the plastic storage bin and ran to where Boney covered the hatchway. Farley stopped halfway in.

Five stiff figures lay on the floor, spotlit by small but powerful flashlights held by Shorty, Garrett, and Everett. The five Dome troops had already been stripped of their smartsuits and weapons.

"How the hell did you manage this?" Farley asked.

Shorty grinned. "Wasn't us, cap," he said. And raised his flashlight beam to show three more black-clad figures armed and standing farther down the narrow rampway.

Farley reached for a gun that wasn't there in a holster he wasn't wearing as one of the figures stepped into the light.

"I'll save you, Captain Fearless," said Wennda.

TWENTY-FOUR

"You have to let me go sometime," Wennda told him, acutely aware of the others watching the two of them.

Farley stepped back but kept his hands on her shoulders. "Says who?" he said.

She smiled, and right then Farley knew that he was in for the whole ride.

"How did you get here?" he asked.

She jerked her head at Arshall and Sten, who were shaking hands with a grinning Garrett and Everett. "They were already hiding in my room when my father confined me to quarters," she said. "We came straight here. Well, we made one stop."

She turned from Farley's hands on her shoulders and bent to drag forward a duffel bag Farley recognized as the one Shorty had brought from the bomber. It clanked when she moved it.

Farley looked at her questioningly and she gestured for him to open it. He unzipped it and whistled. "You are just the whole shebang, aren't you?"

"If you say I am."

"I do." Farley's handclaps reverberated flatly in the narrow rampway. "Merry Christmas, boys," he called, and began pulling out service .45s, holsters, cigarette packs, several yards of .30-caliber belt ammo rounds, and the Browning M1919.

Garrett picked up the machine gun. "Hiya, dreamboat!" he crooned. "Did you miss daddy?"

Broben grabbed a pistol and glanced meaningfully at the doorway, which they had closed after everyone entered the rampway. Farley nodded at him. "All right," he called. "Let's line it up and move it out. Plavitz on point. Martin—"

"Captain?"

Farley turned. Samay and Berne stood before him. Berne looked at the ground and fidgeted. Samay looked eager, a racehorse at the gate.

"You're not coming," Farley said.

Samay shook her head. Her eyes were very bright. "We have to stay and finish this," she said.

"We didn't mean to start a revolt," Farley told her. "We only want to go home."

"You were just the catalyst," said Samay. "Many people have been unhappy with our present situation for years. The commander's become—" she glanced at Wennda "—let's say too unilateral." She shrugged.

"You don't have to be diplomatic on my account," said Wennda. "He's the reason I'm leaving." She looked at Farley. "One of the reasons," she amended.

Samay looked surprised. "You're not coming back?"

"Sten and Arshall will. But no, I'm not coming back."

Samay accepted this with a nod. "Well. I know better than to try talking you out of it. But we certainly could use you."

"Should I stay and help strategize his downfall?" She shook her head. "He's still my father. It's better this way."

"I understand." Samay shrugged. "We'll still miss you."

Wennda frowned. "He'll keep communications offline," she realized. "Except for his people. He's probably already got a subroutine ready to go."

Berne smiled wickedly. "Jorn cloned the key servers onto salvaged units a few years ago," he said. "He'll bring them online for us if the mains go down."

Wennda smiled but her eyes glistened. "Uncle Jorn," she said. "Tell him goodbye for me and I'm sorry I had to go."

"I think he'd be the first to say you should." Samay turned to Farley. "We'll jam the airlock," she told him, "but we can't stay here and hold them off."

"You've already done plenty." Farley held out a hand. "Good luck."

Samay looked at the offered hand. "Strange," she said. "We'll never know what happened to each other."

"I was just thinking the same thing," said Farley.

She clasped his hand. "Good luck," she said.

"Sammy," said Broben. "You can't do this to me."

"Oh, lieutenant." Samay gave him a sympathetic smile. "You can go back and be an agent for change without me."

"Sure I can," said Broben. "But it won't be near as much fun." He beckoned her to him and held out his arms. She slid her rifle aside on its strap and stepped into his awkward hug. He patted her back and then let her go. "Keep your fuses tight, all right?"

"And you remember to sign your work."

He chuckled. "You got it, kid."

Farley looked at Wennda. "You ready?" he asked.

She snorted. "No. But that's never stopped me."

* * * * *

The canyon floor was at least a mile wide, but the fissure seemed narrow because the cliffs were so ungodly high. Indigo sky and blazing sun, cliff shadow stark along the flat and barren wasteland of the valley floor. Not one rabbit, not one bug. A heritage of weeds.

The party had been quiet since they'd stepped from the concealed accessway and into honest daylight, squinting as they went from the dark passage to the scree-filled slope that led down to the canyon floor. For the last hour the only sound had been their rhythmic bootfalls on the hardbaked ground.

Plavitz had point and Martin had tail-end charlie. Just ahead,

Garrett slowed down to let Everett come up beside him and hand off the heavy Browning. Arshall and Sten ran near them. The four big men again were taking turns lugging the Browning and the ammo belt.

Broben stared at the ground and devoted every ounce of energy to putting one foot in front of the other. Shorty hooked his thumbs beneath the straps of his duffel. Yone trotted along near Martin, apparently having little trouble keeping up with the doubletime pace.

Farley's hastily assembled bundle of fatigues, A-2 jacket, and minimal gear bumped in time with his jog as he and his crew made their way single file in the cliff shadow along the ragged fissure edge. He barely even noticed the body armor he wore. The stuff was some kind of mesh weave, matte black and a quarter-inch thick, lighter than cotton and feeling as if it contained liquid. He would never have believed it could stop a bullet if he hadn't already seen it stop several of his.

Beside him—unexpectedly, unbelievably—ran Wennda.

* * * * *

Farley called a break just before the fissure opened out onto the broad expanse of crater.

Garrett set the Browning on the ground and flopped down beside it, chest heaving. Boney sat down, took off his boots and socks, and examined his feet. Broben practically fell down, then dragged himself up to sitting with his back against a rock. Francis had not wanted a smoke since his release from the infirmary, so he handed out his remaining cigarettes.

"No smoking in the crater, boys," Broben wheezed.

Farley was winded, too, but he knew better than to let it show. He remained standing and made himself take deep breaths. The sun was nearing the western cliff edge and soon the fissure floor would lie in twilight shadow. A thousand feet to the north the black canyon walls abruptly ended, framing the bright rectangular entrance to the crater bowl.

Farley ordered Martin to climb a nearby rockfall slanting from the cliff wall and look back to see if they were being followed. Wennda gave Martin her digital recording binoculars and showed him how to operate them. "Magnify, record, night vision, infrared," she pointed out. Martin frowned at the flat device as if he were being given a crash course in how to fly a spaceship.

"We should head left when we get to the crater," Wennda told Farley. "Assume there's a team coming after us. Stay in the shadows, but remember they can see body heat. So your crewmen who aren't wearing smartsuits have to keep something between and themselves and the people coming after us, if they can."

"Can we make the Redoubt before daylight?" Farley asked Plavitz.

"It's about ten miles across the crater," the navigator replied. "So call it fifteen going halfway around the rim. Maybe six from the north fissure entrance to the Redoubt. A twenty-one-mile hump." He shrugged. "We ought to get there with a couple hours to spare, if the guys coming after us don't cut across the crater and get there ahead of us."

"If they cut across," said Wennda, "they'll go by the well and the Typhon. So I don't think they'll get there at all."

Martin came back and reported that he hadn't seen anything. "These binoculars are something," he said.

"I thought you people just put your ear to the ground," said Garrett.

Martin nodded solemnly and cupped a hand to his ear. "Me think maybe twenty, twenty-five cavalry, kemosabe," he said.

Farley waved him away. "Jerry," he called. "Mission briefing."

"You got it, boss."

Farley led Broben away from the others and lowered his voice. "Listen, Jer," he said, "you need to know what the labcoats told me about how to get back, in case you're the one doing the flying."

Broben frowned. "Okay." he said. "I guess it's good to know they think we *can* get back."

"Well." Farley put his hands on his hips and looked at the

men taking advantage of their five-minute break. "They're not a hundred percent about it."

"I wouldn't trust it if they were."

"I hear you." Farley frowned. "They said I shouldn't think of the vortex as a tunnel between here and 1943. They think it's more like a hub of a wheel. The wheel itself is time—*all* time, from Creation to Armageddon and everything in between."

"I'm already getting a headache here," said Broben.

"It's like a roulette wheel," Farley tried again. "Only the numbers are years, and the *Morgana*'s the ball."

"And where she stops, nobody knows?"

"Where the ball lands depends on how and where and when it gets dropped in. So we can improve the odds quite a bit."

"Now you're speaking my lingo."

"Here's the dope," said Farley. "You have to come in level at sixteen-five altitude, bearing one sixty-eight degrees, at two two five knots."

"Sixteen five, bearing one sixty-eight, speed two twenty-five."

Farley nodded. "I don't know how much wiggle room you have, but the white-coat boys went out of their way to stress that you want to go in as close as possible to the exact spot where we came out."

Broben looked worried. "We'll be doing great to be less than a couple hundred yards off the mark," he said. "What kind of difference are we talking about here? Miss by an inch and end up waving down at dinosaurs?"

Farley shrugged. "Maybe you'll get lucky and come out after the Germans surrender."

"Shit. Maybe I'll get luckier and come out before I ever joined up so I'll know better next time."

"You'd still join up."

"Yeah, I'm dumb like that."

Farley grew serious again. "It's a hell of a gamble, I know. But you're a hell of a gambler, Jer. And if there's any ship in the world I'd bet on, it's the *Morgana*."

Broben smirked. "That *is* lucky," he said. "'Cause it's the only ship in the world you *can* bet on."

* * * * *

Farley was taking one last look at the enshadowed western edge of the canyon floor when Wennda came up beside him. "You can't see them," she said, "but they're coming."

He nodded. "I know." He looked into her eyes. It felt like a long time but it wasn't.

Finally she smiled. "Time," she said.

Farley nodded. He turned and clapped his hands. "All right," he called, "everybody out of the pool."

* * * * *

They ran beyond the mile-wide portal of the fissure's end and out onto the vast and rippled surface of the crater. They turned left and followed the western perimeter, keeping to the thickening crescent of shadow as the naked sun sank in its damaged sky.

They were hard pursued.

TWENTY-FIVE

The Technician First Class made a final adjustment to the hydraulic array framed above the ball turret slung in the belly of the captured warplane. He stepped back and nodded at the Class One Weaponry Officer who stood waiting with obvious impatience, even though the proper functioning of the turret was in the WepOff's best interest.

At the nod, the WepOff immediately brushed past the Tech One and set his hands on the side edges of the little opened hatchway and lowered himself carefully into the tiny ball. The guns had to be pointed straight down before a man could enter the hatch from inside the plane, so the mod biobots had carved a divot from the stone floor below the aircraft to give the turret free rotation in all directions.

It was hard to believe the man could fit himself into the space. When they had first examined the turret, they had assumed it was an autonomous weapons node, or was controlled either by the ship's command center or by an interfaced pilot. When it became clear the ball had been built to contain a human being, they had assumed the operator interfaced with the onboard command center. When they could find no interface connector and no command center, they realized with fascination and not a little horror that the armed ball was meant to house a human operator who manually and independently controlled the steering, targeting, and weaponry—at altitude, without pressurization or climate control. Like virtually everything else on the aircraft.

When the Weaponry Officer One was situated in the ball turret, the Tech One sealed the hatch and touched his right collarbone. "Ready to power up," he said.

Across the cleared-off staging area another Tech One activated a power inverter that fed from the main solar array. The panel on his palm readout showed green. He touched his collarbone and said, "Power feed is on."

"Azimuth power clutch engaged," the Weaponry Officer replied immediately. *"Main power on."*

The Tech One on the warplane examined the ball turret hydraulic rig one more time, then glanced around the fuselage and shook his head in a combination of wonder and pity he had never felt before. What these people had done with the little they knew was simply ingenious. Water compressed in metal tubes that pistoned to drive crude whole-body aiming mechanisms on two axes. Metal cams that physically prevented chemically powered projectiles from firing into the body of the aircraft itself. And combustible fossil fuels powered all of it—the motive engines that drove the aircraft to lift speeds, the dynamo generators that supplied electricity to power communications, instrumentation, and the hydraulics that rotated the turrets. Everything was mechanical, analog. It was like learning that ancient humans had traveled to the moon using hot-air balloons.

And yet this machine had gone against the Typhon and survived. For all his people's technology, they had nothing that could match that feat.

The Tech One was eager for the aircraft to become operational again. Everybody was. This machine could be the catalyst of a long-desired chain reaction, the start of an event cascade that changed everything. Return the warplane to fighting condition, and use it to destroy the Typhon. Destroy the Typhon, and recover the locus. Recover the locus, and defeat those diluted culls huddled in their failing Dome. And then, free of their stalemating presence, begin the long and noble work of re-establishing the rightful empire of man. The grand dream had been the goal of his people since they had sheltered here centuries ago. A common cause, something to live for. But it had remained mostly dream until four days ago.

A diagnostic biobot scuttled by on spindly legs. The Tech One barely glanced at it. A dozen of the scurrying hemispheres were busily examining the warplane. Where they had already surveyed, another dozen mod drones tirelessly repaired, upgraded, modified. Modernized. When they were finished, this machine would still be an ape ancestor to the modern machines' *Homo sapiens,* but that ape would be smarter, more evolved. Ape sapiens.

The WepOff's voice again sounded in the Tech One's head, transmitted by bone conduction from his occipital interface. *"Weaponry Officer One. Gun selector switches on. Main sight on. All turret systems are powered up. Rotation mechanism check on your command."*

A new voice sounded. *"Begin."*

The Supreme! The Tech One felt his pulse surge and immediately suppressed it. Central received all biometric telemetry, and he did not want to give any cause to be removed from this assignment. Of course he knew that the dream of resumption would be realized by the collective labor of all. Every action was designed to push them forward, so every action counted. *What does not advance, hinders.* But *this* labor was direct. Its impact was immediate. Its consequences were demonstrable and dramatic. If it succeeded, the work he performed *at this very moment* would be instrumental in enabling the cascade that would lead to resumption.

Yet the voice of the Supreme had been unexpected. Of course he would be observing. But participating? Could he be physically present outside in the staging area? Somehow the notion was more intimidating than the idea of the Supreme observing the proceedings from Central. Failure would not be watched on a screen, it would happen in front of the Twenty-Seventh Supreme Commander General. Failure could not be part of the equation. The humiliation could not even be considered. No.

In the floor by the Tech One's feet the turret spun. The hydraulics whirred and clacked. The turret stopped and then reversed direction.

"Manual operation is imprecise and inefficient," the Weaponry Officer reported.

"Just fire on the target," the Supreme ordered. The Tech One thought he sounded irritated.

"Short burst," said a new voice. The odd thick accent nearly indecipherable. *"Thumbs on the red buttons and don't pull left or right."*

"Acknowledged," said the WepOff. *"Targeting."*

He doesn't sound the least bit nervous, the Tech One thought.

The turret rotated again. The Tech One pictured the twin bores swiveling toward the low-functioning clones propped up across the staging area. They had been repurposed from the organ tank and were considered expendable for this experiment despite their medical value. Anyone who needed a liver or a lung in the next few weeks would be out of luck. *Those who sacrifice also advance us.*

The Tech One glanced at the left-side gun port in the waist of the fuselage—a rectangle open to the elements, simply unbelievable. If he took two steps back he would be able to see the target. And the turret hydraulics would still be clearly in his view.

"Targeting is very coarse," the Weaponry Officer reported.

"You want me to come do it for you?" the third voice said. *"Maybe hold your hand?"*

The turret made a minor adjustment. "Targeted," the Weaponry Officer reported. The Tech One thought he sounded miffed.

"Well? You want an engraved invitation?"

The Tech One tried to control his breathing. He didn't think he would get into trouble for standing only two steps from his post. The turret would not move again, it would only fire on the targets. The hydraulics would not engage.

He took the two steps back. Through the waist-gun window he saw the upright clones across the stone-floored staging area, the high-speed cameras and ruled velocity scales beside the bullets' anticipated trajectory, the knot of Engineer Threes standing off to one side, their faces blued and shifting in the bioluminescence of their palm displays.

"Firing," said the Weaponry Officer.

The deafening staccato that pounded from beneath the airplane made the Tech One think the primitive equipment had exploded in the turret. He realized it was the ammunition's explosive propellant just as he saw two bright tracer rounds streak across the staging area.

One of the clones became a red eruption above the waist. The joined and naked legs stood a moment longer and then toppled.

The line of fire swept right as the chudder of the twin guns continued. Only two or three seconds more, but it was time enough to slag the measuring equipment and then tear into the clustered Engineer Threes. Even from here the Tech One could see pieces flying off them. Two of the E3s fell backward. A third toppled slowly, as if chopped down at his base.

One technician remained standing, amazingly untouched, mouth gaping, covered in bloody chunks. His readout hand still glowed before him.

"Abort," came the calm voice of the supervising Tech One, outside.

The Tech One in the bomber stood frozen a moment, trying to absorb what he had just seen. Medtechs rolled silently toward the shredded Engineers. The one still standing looked no more comprehending than the noncog clones.

The turret rolled until the hatch slid into view. The Tech One stared dumbly until he heard pounding from inside the hull. He shook himself and hurried to it. He knelt and undogged the hatch. It flipped back, and the Weaponry Officer surged out and knocked him backward onto the deck. The WepOff put his hands on the frame of the hydraulics rig. His foot groped until it touched the combination steering and trigger mechanism. He had not powered down the turret or closed the hydraulic valve, and when he set his weight on the left-hand grip and started to hoist himself out, the turret smoothly rotated and slammed the Weaponry Officer into the hydraulic rig's frame. The ball kept turning but the Weaponry Officer's torso stayed in place, and the moving hatchway cut him in two at the waist.

The gouting torso landed on the horrified Tech One. The arms flailed and then found purchase on the floor, one on the deck and one on the Tech One's stomach, and for a moment that would stalk the technician's dreams the truncated Weapons Officer tried to hoist himself up and walk on his hands, the dragging lengths of himself wetly mopping the deck. Then he fell back against the Tech One, who felt himself grow warm below the waist as he blinked up at aluminum struts and a diagnostic drone that had come to investigate. The two men lay like cuddling lovers studying the shapes of clouds.

The Tech One screamed. He pushed the body off him and heard it sigh and bubble as it sloughed aside. He stood. Warm soft lumps slid off him to plop softly onto the deck. He blinked at the open ball turret, hatch askew where it had struck the hydraulic rig frame. Blinking at the half body lying face-down in a metallic-smelling mush. At the patch of red glimpsed through the little hatchway where the severed legs and groin lay crumpled in the tiny metal ball.

The Tech One's body did a little galvanic dance and then he vomited copiously.

"Medtech," he said weakly. He touched his collarbone. "Medtech," he repeated. "Medtech needed in the aircraft."

The diagnostic biobot crept back and picked its way around the mess like a crime witness who didn't want to get involved. The Tech One heard it clattering toward the rear of the aircraft. He thought he might be sick again but he forced it down.

If the medtech got here fast enough the Weaponry Officer might be saved. But then the Tech One realized that the sources of the organs the man would need had just been blown to sludge by a volley of .50-caliber slugs unleashed by the Weaponry Officer himself.

The Tech One set his hands on his bloodsoaked knees and heaved again.

* * * * *

The Twenty-Seventh Supreme Commander General of Services and Forces of the Redoubt watched the three medtechs roll silently across the cavernous staging area, their nimble manipulators already at work on the Engineer Threes slung in their hanging bays. The Supreme was in a cold fury. He knew that the debacle he had just witnessed firsthand had been the sole fault of the idiot Weaponry Officer One, who had lost control of an unfamiliar system. But despite where the responsibility clearly lay, the Supreme was certain that his prisoner had played a role. There had been too many accidents in the round-the-clock repair and modification of the warplane. Too many biobots put out of commission or inexplicably reconfigured. Too many convenient delays. Missing or damaged parts. Personnel injuries. Miscommunications.

He knew that, in time, his people could repair the aircraft to combat status without assistance. But the captive seemed to have a complete model of the entire vessel in his mind. Every nut, strut, gauge, feed, and gear of the clever and stupefyingly complex Gothic clockworks that was the Flying Fortress. This lucky scrap thrown at them from the past, a bone offered up by the same incalculable power that had ruined their world. Many of his people were already whispering that the warplane's arrival was an act of providence, proof that resumption was at hand. As if some coughed-up tool were the reward for all the destruction, the centuries of hardship and cruel necessity, the attenuating generations lived without knowing whether their descendants would ever leave this box to reseed some bettered earth.

The Supreme would say nothing to counter this absurdity, though, because it was useful. It kept the remnant population bolstered as they toiled toward their common goal.

But destined or not, the warplane *was* a tool. A lever, accidentally dropped between the cracks of worlds, found by those most suited to take full advantage of its ability to move the world.

And the fulcrum?

The fulcrum stood beside him, arms folded as he regarded the quiet bustle, the organized response to unexpected mayhem.

Three Engineer Threes and a source clone shot to mere protein. Deliberate?

The Supreme looked back at his prisoner and felt his cold fury rise. The insolent slouch, the feigned indifference. *The organ tanks will be there for you as well when I no longer need you.*

Two repair drones dropped from the opened bomb bay doors, each carrying a bloody section of the Weaponry Officer One.

The man watched the biobots clatter off on multijointed legs in the direction of Medical Engineering and the organ tanks. He adjusted his dirty cap and shook his head. "Well, that's unfortunate," he said as he lit up a cigarette. "I musta tole that boy a hundred times to set that brake." He turned his head to spit a fleck of tobacco on the Redoubt floor.

TWENTY-SIX

The sun that had set over the top of the high cliff when they were in the fissure had come into view again as they progressed along the crater floor, shining merciless and unwavering in an indigo sky bereft of cloud, in air too thin to distort. A few hard stars shone through.

Even though Farley had passed through the crater's eastern perimeter not a week ago, the scale of the thing assailed him. It was the size of a large city, so big that it was hard to see it as a crater at all from within the bowl, so wide that the two-mile-high rim wall was a thin line at the horizon. Frozen lava ripples were ranges of low smooth hills, like folds in thick batter. Clusters of solidified air bubbles were the size of city blocks, some thin enough to have collapsed or broken open like bombed stadiums. The rubble of some final battle between warring deities.

And at the center of the crater five miles away, the flattened cone that rose above the well looked like an anthill at the bottom of a shallow bowl. Faint green light glowed from deep within the mound like something awful rotting in a bog. It looked ruinous and infected. The commander's eggheads had said it was a kind of friction caused by the fraying edges of reality itself, a byproduct of the cataclysmic energy produced by whatever was still functioning in the well. They thought it might be what the Typhon guarded. Some archaic remnant of the world before.

High above the crater well the constant vortex churned, a tornado sensed not through any feature of its own but through the

249

reality it displaced. A tear between two worlds, the violation that had brought them here. And their only hope of going back.

Europe, Farley thought as he ran. *We're still in Europe.*

* * * * *

Farley called another break at an outcropping a hundred yards from the knifecut wedge of black that would lead them off this soul-grinding crater floor and into the massive fissure that led to the Redoubt. Between here and the fissure entrance were small rocks, pebbles, a large boulder shaped like a sausage, and a narrow slope of rockfall at the cutaway where crater rim became cliff wall. This time the men collapsed where they halted, breathing hard and sipping water and shaking their heads. Boney took off a boot and tended to his foot. Broben just laid down in an X.

Farley posted Martin at rear guard again with Wennda's binoculars. If north on the crater face was noon, they had been near eight o'clock when the belly gunner had finally spotted the team sent after them as it emerged from the southern fissure onto the crater floor, though he couldn't say for sure how many there were. Five or six. Weapons fire had not yet been exchanged, but Farley knew it was only a matter of time. This break would be just long enough for everyone to catch their breath and tighten up their gear and move out again before their pursuers gained too much ground.

Wennda sat beside Farley and sipped from a tube in the collar of her smartsuit. She was breathing hard but not winded. "When we head back out you should remind your men to keep something between them and the team chasing us," she told Farley. "They forget that their body heat is visible if they aren't wearing armor. Staying in the dark isn't enough."

Farley nodded. "Hell, I keep forgetting it, too." He took a few deep breaths and slowed his breathing.

"So." Her smile was slanted. "What's our plan once we get to the Redoubt?"

"I was kind of hoping you could provide some info in that department."

"Sten and Arshall have a copy of the report from the team member who made it back yesterday. When we were there before, I was going to find out what I could from Yone." She nodded at the small man sitting on the ground a dozen yards away. "He's from there, after all."

Farley nodded and got to his feet. "I better talk to him," he said. "We have to move out in a minute."

"I'll come with you."

He helped her up and they headed toward Yone, who was fanning himself with the flaps of his partly unzipped coverall. Farley remembered Grobe telling Yone *I was right about you.* Who could blame the poor guy for wanting to come back with them? He would always be an outcast among strangers here.

Wennda stopped walking just as Farley heard it: Faint whistling high above that quickly grew louder.

"Mortar!" Farley yelled. *"Take cover! Everybody move!"*

He and Wennda were already running toward the big sausage-shaped rock. Halfway there an explosion shook the ground behind them like a drumhead. Farley felt heat on his back and was pushed forward. Beside him Wennda stumbled and rolled and came up running. They stayed low and ran like apes to the cover of the long rock while fragments of canyon floor pattered down around them.

Crouched behind the long rock Farley glanced at Wennda as he drew his sidearm. She already had her nerve gun ready and was leaning up against the rock's smooth curve. Farley risked a quick look at the crater floor and was relieved to see none of their party lying out in the open. Broben waved to him from where he lay prone behind a low flat rock fifty feet away. Martin lay beside Broben, peering south with Wennda's binoculars. Garrett and Everett were partway up the rockfall by the fissure entrance, already setting up the Browning.

A thin red thread of light appeared from the south and swung

251

toward Broben. The Browning spoke up, *chump chump chump.* Tracer rounds streaked toward the origin of the red light. The beam swung wildly, then disappeared.

Farley glanced at the darker fissure opening. It was an uncomfortably long hundred yards away, with little cover. He cursed himself for not calling the break after they had entered the fissure and posting a rear guard.

"It's gonna be a firefight if we don't get out of here soon," he told Wennda.

"If we can draw the mortar fire toward a heat source, we can run for the fissure," she said. "We could try—"

The rock she was leaning against bent in with a faint clunk. She jumped back and brought her rifle up. Farley dropped low and backed away from the rock and looked at its long, cylindrical shape in the canyon twilight.

"Jesus Christ," he said. "It's an Me-109."

"It's a what?"

"Me-109." He looked at her, astonished. "A German fighter plane."

* * * * *

The shape had not been readily apparent because the fuselage lay on its side and the front third looked partly embedded in the ground. Either the crater floor was soft here, or the Messerschmitt had broken through to some hollow space, maybe the top of one of those hardened air bubbles, when it impacted. The fuselage was crumpled and burned, the canopy had torn away, and both wings had broken off and were nowhere in sight. As if the plane had angled down into the crater floor and then tumbled when it hit.

There was no body in the shattered cockpit. The pilot had probably been thrown out when the fighter tumbled across the crater floor. Or he had bailed, but what would the poor bastard have done after

252

that? His body was probably out there somewhere, dead of wounds or dehydration. Whatever the case, the Messerschmitt had augered down onto the crater floor. Maybe the pilot hadn't been able to power back up or deadstick in. Or maybe he had dueled the Typhon and lost.

"Someone's coming," Wennda said. She nodded toward the western cliff.

Farley peered past the crumpled fuselage to see someone jogging toward them across the open crater floor. Martin? No, Martin was still beside Broben.

"It's Yone," said Wennda.

"What the hell?" said Farley.

"He's going to get killed."

"He's gonna get *us* killed." Farley waved the approaching man away, but Yone kept coming. "Take cover!" Farley called. "They can see you!"

A knifecut line of red appeared from the south and immediately swept right. An inch-wide dot found Yone and bobbled on his torso as he ran toward them.

"Go back, god damn it!" Farley yelled.

The Browning fired briefly from the rockfall. Two tracer rounds sped in the direction the red light was coming from. The targeting laser stayed on Yone. Farley clearly heard a distant, hollow sound, like a palm slapping the mouth of a Coke bottle.

"Son of a *bitch*," he said, and cupped his hands to his mouth. *"Mortar!"* he yelled. *"Get down!"* Now Wennda was yelling for Yone to go back. Yone kept coming and Farley looked around. There was nowhere else to go.

Faint whistling now from high above.

Farley pulled Wennda down alongside the embedded fuselage and prayed the plane's remains would shield them from the blast. He lay prone in the dirt with an arm across her and one hand absurdly clutching his crush hat. *Not now not now not now.*

The whistle grew. The round hit. The ground opened up and the world went dark and silent.

TWENTY-SEVEN

Farley lay in darkness. His head throbbed and his ears rang. He heard faint steady pattering, like rain on dead leaves, punctuated by irregular thumps and metallic squeaks. He felt sick.

He lay quietly and took stock. Sharp pains along his arms and back. Left upper ribs bruised where the shoulder holster mashed against him. His right ankle throbbed. The back of his head felt hot, and he thought he probably had a good-sized goose egg growing there. He didn't think anything was broken, though. Yippee.

He blinked and waited for his eyes to adjust. Faint light showed that he lay head-down on a steep slope amid rubble. More than that was difficult to make out because pulsing metallic afterimages trailed when he turned his head.

He eased himself up to his elbows and felt dizzy. He waited for it to clear, and when it did he was glad that he'd stopped moving.

A dozen feet upslope the buckled Messerschmitt fuselage lay on its side. It had fallen with them when the mortar round had blown a hole in the crater floor on top of what was clearly a narrow crack beneath the surface.

The ruined fuselage was covered with enormous bugs. Black, yard-wide hemispheres on six multijointed legs that picked their way along the foundered wreck or worked delicately at its burned metal skin, pulling out parts and taking apart the hull. They looked like ants swarming the corpse of some dead insect, an image reinforced by the line of creatures crawling to and from the aircraft. The slanting crevice was loud with taps and bangs and little shrieks of wrenching metal, and through it all a constant rustle of hundreds of dainty spider legs negotiating the fuselage and the rock-strewn passage.

The bugs were stripping the ME pretty fast. Sections of metal framework were already exposed. One bug had climbed to the top blade of the mangled propeller like some determined flagpole sitter. Another bug pulled off the cowling, and several others went to work on the now-exposed engine. The one with the cowling carried it away, even though the cowling was bigger than it was, and joined the line of bugs that crawled downslope like orderly looters.

On the other side of the bug line were Wennda and Yone. They sat upright against the crevice wall, a little downslope. In the dim light Farley couldn't tell if they were injured, or even conscious. Wennda's nerve gun lay by her feet. Two bugs stood in front of it.

Farley ignored the grinding pain in his upper ribs as he propped himself straighter. He eased his right hand to his holster and covered the strap with his palm as he pinched it open. The sound was just a tiny *tik* but it still made him wince. He slid the pistol free and held it against his chest. He thumbed the safety and squeezed the grip, then worked the slide.

All the bugs stopped moving. The carrier line, the bugs on the Messerschmitt, the two in front of Wennda and Yone.

Screw it. Farley raised the pistol. He brought his left hand to his right to steady his aim. The bug nearest him in the carrier line dropped the access panel it was holding and scurried to him, the faint patter of its nimble legs like light gravel on a tin roof. Farley could not believe how fast it moved.

The thing halted in front of him, its left-front walking leg six inches from his knee. Farley held the pistol steady. The bug studied him. That was how it felt. Farley saw now that the half-dome carapace was set with paler ovals that glittered as they subtly shifted. Insect eyes, inspecting him. Or camera lenses. The forelegs were as long as the other four legs, but they were whiplike and supple, not segmented and angled. Other than the light tap of its footfalls it made no noise as it moved. Even this close up Farley could not have said if the thing were a creature or a machine.

He looked past it at Wennda. His eyes had adjusted enough to see that she was watching him now. Beside her Yone watched also. A dark patch glistened along one side of his face.

The other bugs had not moved.

Farley tightened his grip on the pistol and took a deep breath and tried to watch the bug in front of him in his peripheral vision as he aimed at the bug in front of Wennda. He saw a spark from his pistol, then felt a shock through his wrist and heard something clatter on the ground. He thought the gun had gone off. But there'd been no flash, no recoil.

Then he saw that he was holding half a service .45. The front half lay on the ground between himself and the bug, which held a supple foreleg poised to strike again. The tip of the tendril now ended in two thin and narrow blades or claws.

Farley held completely still. Past the transfixed line of bugs he saw Wennda staring wide-eyed. She gave a small shake of her head.

Farley's fist shook as he lowered the cleanly severed hunk of sidearm. He set the pistol fragment in front of the bug and showed his empty hands. It looked like a gesture of surrender. It was.

The poised tendril retracted and the bug stepped closer. The tendril came up and swept steadily down Farley's body as if the thing were cleaning a windshield. The bug went still a moment, then stepped back and snatched up the pieces of gun and turned away. It returned to its place in the halted line, and the line resumed its downslope crawl. The bugs on the Messerschmitt returned to their methodical salvage.

The two bugs in front of Wennda and Yone turned toward one another and tapped their supple forelegs against each other like lodge brothers trading a secret handshake. Then they turned back to Wennda and Yone and swarmed them.

Yone yelled and tried to scuttle away. Wennda flinched, and the back of her head hit the sloping rock wall. Farley pushed himself to his knees and forced himself to stay upright as each bug swept a tendril the length of the trapped humans' bodies the way Farley's bug had done with him.

Wennda's bug slid both forelimbs around her nerve rifle and gently tugged on the chunky weapon as if taking a live hand grenade from a baby. The gunstrap across her back went taut and the bug stopped. It lifted the gun and tilted it experimentally. Then it dropped the gun and picked up Wennda and tucked her tight against its underside.

Farley jumped to his feet.

The bug joined the line, Wennda slung tight beneath it. She pounded and yelled and tried to grab the thin legs. The bug marched downhill unperturbed.

Farley went after them. His ankle screamed bloody murder and a fresh wave of nausea washed over him. He ignored it all and ran, passing bugs carrying airplane parts. The crevice quickly darkened as he descended. Something brushed the top of his head. He could no longer stand upright. It didn't matter. He was going to get to Wennda. Behind him Yone was yelling something but he couldn't make it out.

The work line slowed. Farley made out Wennda not ten feet ahead. She was no longer yelling or beating on the bug. The crack was now so narrow that Farley had to turn sideways to sidle between the bugs and the wall of the crevice. The bugs paid him no attention. Up ahead the clustered bugs were silhouetted by a crooked wedge of brighter light. They were crowded up against some constriction.

Farley dove between the legs of the bug behind Wennda and crawled forward like a sapper. He called out to Wennda and then he was sliding under her. Her back was to him and the tendrils bound her to the underside of the bug like cables. Farley grabbed hold of one and pulled. Nothing doing. He held on and let it drag him along.

"I'm here!" he said to Wennda's back. "I'm right behind you! Can you hear me?"

Her muffled voice said, *"Can't. Breathe."*

Farley glanced up. The wedge of light was three or four bugs away now. It looked to be an opening out into a larger space.

Farley dragged along the rough crevice bottom as he slid his free hand along the gunstrap across Wennda's back, following the strap to the metal clip that joined it to the stock of the gun wedged against Wennda's hip.

The bug dragged them through the opening and into some larger and brighter space.

Farley worked the clip free of the catch and the strap dangled free. He let go of the bug and hit the ground and grabbed the strap. The bug kept going and the strap grew taut and the gun began to slide out and then caught on something. Farley got to his feet and worked the strap from side to side as if playing some nightmare fish.

Then the gun came free and he fell backward. He lay there a moment, surprised. The oncoming bugs veered around him. Farley got up and ran to the bug that held Wennda and he aimed her rifle at it. The bug stepped out of the line and turned to face him. Beneath it Wennda's mouth worked silently.

Farley held his ground. The bug dropped Wennda and nearly pulled Farley off his feet as it snatched the weapon away from him. It turned back around and hurried off, holding the rifle high like a trophy.

Wennda curled up on her side and gasped for air. Farley knelt beside her and put a hand on her shoulder. "Are you hurt?" he asked. "Can you talk?"

She pointed to her stomach and Farley understood she'd had the breath knocked from her. He sat her up and held onto her and looked back at the line of bugs emerging from the narrow crevice in time to see Yone crawl out. Yone picked himself up and saw Farley and Wennda. Farley gave him a thumbs-up. Yone returned it and gave a pained smile. He looked like something beaten with a rake.

Then his expression changed and his hand lowered. He was looking past Farley. Bloodied and beaten and suddenly awed and afraid. Some unwilling heretic dragged to the temple of a vengeful god.

Farley turned to shield Wennda, assuming the bugs were coming back for them. But the bugs weren't coming back. They were marching in an orderly line that led across the level floor of a great and dimlit space, marching toward the vast and lethal bulk of the Typhon a hundred yards away.

TWENTY-EIGHT

Jerry Broben studied the faintly luminous Redoubt wall a thousand yards away, spread like a green glass dam across the canyon. He made out what might have been street lights, constellated geometries he supposed were buildings, and a gliding cluster of lights at ground level that was probably some kind of vehicle. City in a box.

In the center of the wall at ground level was a huge, recessed rectangle that he hoped was an equipment door. It certainly was big enough to admit a B-17.

Full night had fallen and the demolition team could not be more than a few minutes behind them, but Broben had left no rear guard to slow them down. The plan now was to let them catch up.

He turned away from the wall and dropped back down behind the rock where Martin knelt studying Sten's unfolded cellophone. Wennda's tricked-up binoculars were plugged into it, and on the filmy screen was an image of the Redoubt wall.

"Okay, smart guy, run through this for me one more time," said Broben.

"All right," said Sten. He fiddled with the binoculars and the image rotated.

Broben glanced at the crew. All of them so far past tired that they'd become some kind of meat machines that would numbly do their jobs till they broke down. All jokes and even grousing had stopped after they'd lost Farley and Wennda and Yone. These last few miles they'd started snapping at each other like whipped dogs. An overwhelming resignation colored every gesture. A sense of going through the motions. They watched the dark canyon behind them or looked at the lighted screen and they waited for a plan from their new commanding officer.

Broben had never wanted a job less in his life.

* * * * *

Yone had led the mortar fire straight to where Farley and Wennda had taken cover behind the cigar-shaped rock. The round had hit and they were gone. Farley, Wennda, Yone. Just gone.

The fissure entrance was a hundred yards away and there would be a firefight if they waited any longer. And there was nothing to wait for now. Just a deep gash in the ground. Even the rock was gone.

Broben gave the order and they ran for the fissure. Targeting lights had speared out but no more mortar rounds were launched. They had entered the darker fissure and stayed close to the left-hand side and they had kept on running.

The next five miles had been a cat-and-mouse game of sprinting in the dark and then taking cover and trading potshots. The pursuing demolition team had them on targeting but the bomber crew had them on range. Broben knew the game would change when they reached the Redoubt at the end of the fissure canyon, because there'd be nowhere else to run—and the Redoubt would start shooting at them, too. They had to gain some distance and buy some time. That meant keeping up the pace, ignoring their exhaustion and pain, and not stopping to catch their breath or exchange fire. Whenever there was good cover Broben posted a rear guard and left him to lay down suppressing fire while the rest kept going. The rear guard would shoot to pin down their pursuers, then high-tail it back until he reached the relief guard Broben had stationed. The relief would hunker down to stall the demo team while the one who'd caught up to him kept going and did his best to catch up to the group.

The tactic slowly gained them ground and time. It also strung the crew out along the fissure floor, wore them out even faster, and burned precious ammo.

Then they'd jogged around a fissure corner and there was the slab of the Redoubt wall glowing faintly in the distance. The ragged line of exhausted crew had put on a last fresh burst of speed. A thousand yards from the wall they'd taken cover while the rear-guard stragglers caught up.

And now here they were, hunkered down before the vast patchwork slab of the Redoubt and waiting on their new CO to put his stamp on some kind of plan.

* * * * *

"Okay, smart guy, run through this for me one more time," Broben told Sten.

"All right." Sten enlarged the image on the cellophone. "There are motion detectors at these points, and cameras here." Red circles appeared where his finger tapped along the Redoubt wall. "This shows the estimated scope of each sensor." Pale wedges spread from the red circles like shining headlight beams. Sten tapped again and several lighted wedges darkened. "These sensors have failed. Maybe they don't know how to fix them, maybe they can't." He shrugged. "But there's a gap—here." He indicated an unlit trapezoid to the left of the large equipment door. "It's very narrow toward the outside limit of the sensors' range, wider as you get closer to the wall."

"The team your CO sent out five days ago had the same info?" Broben asked.

"Probably."

"'Probably' didn't get them in."

Sten shrugged again. "I can give you the data. I can't tell you what they did with it."

Broben frowned at the image. "Okay, okay," he said. "I'm not trying to bust your chops. So you don't know how they tried to get in?"

Sten and Arshall traded a look. "No idea," said Arshall. "We weren't involved."

"There's this way that Indians would steal horses from forts," Martin ventured.

Broben looked at him as if he'd heard wrong.

The small belly gunner knelt beside Sten and indicated the Redoubt image on the com panel. "They'd wait till a party of riders was due back at the fort, and they'd get a couple of braves up by the wall. When the riders got in sight of the fort, the Indians would attack them from cover. The fort would send soldiers out to help the riders, and the two braves at the wall would sneak in before the gate closed. Everybody in the fort would be watching the fight outside, and the braves would round up the horses and then they'd just open the gate again and drive them out. The war party would break off their attack and go after the horses."

Martin looked up. They were all staring at him. "It just seemed kind of similar," he said after nobody said anything.

Broben looked down at the image on the com panel. "Can you make that bigger and show me where there's cover on this side," he asked Sten.

"Sure." Sten enlarged the image. Broben studied it while the crew glanced among themselves.

Broben asked Sten and Arshall questions about the smartsuit camouflage, about the narrow gap in the Redoubt's sensors.

"You're not thinking of doing this cockeyed stunt," Plavitz said, incredulous.

Broben gave him a withering look. "Unless your relatives were better at breaking into forts, yeah, we're gonna do this," he said.

"It wasn't really my relatives," said Martin.

"You said it's an old Indian trick."

"I don't know how old it is. I saw it on *Hopalong Cassidy.* Double feature. It worked pretty good."

Broben stared. "You are *the* worst Indian I ever saw," he said.

* * * * *

Broben crouched behind the lava berm and watched Garrett, Everett, and Shorty creep toward the massive wall in single file like cartoon characters tiptoeing past a bomb.

Much harder to see was who they were following. Sten and Arshall had activated their body armor's camouflage, and the stealth smartsuits were visually sampling their surroundings and minimizing the two men's heat signature. All five men walked perfectly straight, kept their arms close to their bodies, didn't look back. Sten had said his visor would show him the path, but to Broben it looked like three men and two ghosts creeping along an invisible but very narrow hallway.

The plan was for Arshall and Sten to lead Garrett, Everett, and Shorty to the wall. The crewmen would lie low while Sten came back for Broben, Plavitz, Francis, and Martin. Meanwhile, Arshall would head straight toward the blind spot out in the open in front of the main door and wait for the demolition team to arrive. When they did, he'd fire on them while the rest of the men stayed low. Broben was betting the fireworks would cause the Redoubt to send a troop transport after the demo team. When the door opened for the transport, Sten would make like the Invisible Man and slip in. From there he'd either find an access door or reopen the main one and admit the rest of the men.

Stage a fight to get the soldiers out of the fort, sneak in as they're leaving, round up the horses, and ride out while everyone's watching the shootout. That was the plan, anyway. But Broben knew that the first thing that gets thrown out when a plan commences is the plan.

He glanced at Plavitz and the navigator shook his head: No sign

264

of the demolition team. Broben wished they had another pair of binoculars. The super-duper ones were with Arshall.

A few nail-biting minutes later the men reached the wall and went prone beside it. Broben had to take it on faith that Arshall was crawling toward the huge equipment door while Sten was headed back to escort the second group; all he could see were three of his crewmen lying prone at the base of an alien fortress.

"Here they come." Plavitz nodded at the canyon floor. "Maybe half a mile down on this side. You can see two of them because their ballet suits aren't working. I think there's three more. You can see them for a second when they come out of the shadows. Those outfits take a blink to go from dark to light."

"Let's hope Arshall sees 'em too," said Broben.

"He's at the dead spot already," Francis reported. Sickly pale in the wall's dim light, the normally coltish tail gunner nodded confidently at the Redoubt. He had lost his eyepatch somewhere on the way here. "I see him moving."

Broben frowned. "That doctor fix that eye or trade it up?" he asked.

Francis just shrugged.

"Maybe we should get moving," Plavitz said. "They're gonna be on top of us in about two minutes."

"Wait till Sten gets here," Broben said.

"I'm here now," Sten said right beside Broben.

Broben jumped. "Holy Jesus effin—don't *do* that."

"Sorry." Sten deactivated his smartsuit and beckoned. "Let's go."

Broben, Francis, Martin, and Plavitz fell in line behind Sten and made their way toward the Redoubt wall. Broben knew he was walking between the lion's teeth right now, but he couldn't see it. He could not have felt more exposed if he were playing patty-cake with Santa Claus on a nudist colony parade float. Knowing that the demolition team was catching up behind them gave him an awful itch between the shoulder blades, and he dared not look back.

They were halfway to the wall when a familiar rising whine sounded from the canyon floor somewhere near the Redoubt's massive equipment door. Arshall had fired on the demo team, much sooner than they'd planned. He probably hadn't had much choice.

Bright red threads immediately appeared from the Redoubt wall. They swept the canyon, then angled in to converge near where Arshall had aimed. Broben imagined the demo team members desperately running for cover. He almost felt sorry for the bastards.

The watery ghost of Sten moved forward again. Broben quickly followed.

A bass-drum rumble filled the air and the Redoubt's huge main door slid partway open. A matte-black troop transport rolled out and sped toward the converging targeting lasers betraying the demo team's position.

Broben froze. How the *hell* could that heap have got sent out so fast?

"Go," he told Sten through clenched teeth. *"The door's gonna shut. Go!"*

Sten hesitated, then sprinted for the open equipment door. Targeting lasers swung toward him, lit him with red spots, lost him again.

The troop transport slowed.

"They're gonna see us," Plavitz hissed from the back of the line.

The main door began to rumble shut. The transport began to turn.

"They've got us," said Plavitz.

Broben was right about to give the order to run for it when a voice shouted from out on the canyon floor. At first he thought it came from the transport. Some warning to disarm. Then he saw the lone man standing a hundred yards behind the turning vehicle. Waving his arms at it and shouting. It was Arshall.

"Did his suit go dead?" Francis wondered.

Arshall jumped up and down and shouted again. Broben felt a sudden leaden certainty. "He turned it off," he said. "He's drawing their fire."

A trio of ruby-colored threads converged on Arshall. He ran weaving toward the troop transport. A patch of ground kicked up just behind him and he stumbled, rolled, and came up running.

The transport halted. It pivoted to face Arshall. Arshall yelled and waved it on.

"Go," said Broben.

No one moved. They watched the dead-black van speed toward the lone man luring it away from them. The silent play of coherent light from the Redoubt wall. The sudden small explosion from Arshall's side.

"God damn it, run!" Broben yelled.

They ran. Broben tried to keep straight on the path described to him by Sten. Maybe it didn't matter now, but it was all he knew to do.

The massive door shut tight with a dull boom. There was no way to know if Sten had made it in.

Broben glanced back at the transport. Arshall was nowhere in sight. The transport bucked over some obstruction and resumed its path toward the demolition team, and Broben saw Arshall drag behind it for a few seconds, then fall boneless to the ground.

Broben made the wall and dove down beside the three crewmen already there. All of them staring out at Arshall looking like a man-shaped hole in the dimlit canyon floor.

"Did Sten get in?" Broben asked.

Nobody knew. They watched the red lines track the barely visible figures of the demo team pinned down near the western cliff wall. The transport pulled up and the sides popped open and troops spilled out. They heard the faint ascending whines of the nerve rifles as the firefight commenced.

"They'll have to open the door to let it back in," said Boney.

Broben nodded. "That's our Hail Mary pass if Sten doesn't come through."

The ground around them brightened. Broben looked up, expecting a flare or spotlight, but there was just the flat horizon of dully glowing wall, bright-red spiderwebs cutting the avenue of night sky overhead.

Shorty tapped him on the shoulder and pointed, and he saw a man-sized oval in the wall at ground level fifty feet away. Bright light from inside. An armed silhouette appeared.

Broben drew his pistol. The figure lowered its weapon and beckoned with the other hand.

"Son of a bitch," said Broben. "He made it."

The crewmen turned and crawled like sappers toward the oval entrance. Broben hung back and let the others go by him. He glanced at the distant firefight. That demo team didn't stand a chance.

He took one last look at Arshall on the canyon floor. Then he followed his crew into the Redoubt wall.

TWENTY-NINE

The Typhon was parked head-first on an enormous slab centered on a groove that ran into a recessed bay the size of a warehouse, angular wings folded tight against its long body. Bugs crawled all over it like crabs feasting on a beached whale. A faint rumble sounded from it, a sound more felt than heard, the purr of a hundred-foot cat. But even without the deep vibration Farley would have known that this was not a dead creature being picked over. Perhaps the Typhon was not alive in any way that Farley understood, but though it swarmed with bugs and did not move he also knew it was not dead. Sleeping seemed as good a word as any.

The line of bugs carrying Messerschmitt parts from the crevice behind Farley flowed past the Typhon and out of sight. A sparser line of bugs returned from that direction. Some of these continued back to the crevice opening. Others veered off to join their fellow drones crawling on the Typhon. Whines and faint metallic keening carried across the dilapidated distance. Bright white flashed in tiny spots along the Typhon, and a flickering bluish glow from somewhere deep within the bay gave the space the appearance of some Dantean factory.

The bay in which the Typhon was parked was only one in a row of bays receding into the distance. Many were damaged—filled with rubble, roof collapsed. Most looked empty. More distant ones looked as if they held the flensed skeletons of other typhons.

Large and terrifying as the Typhon was, the thing was dwarfed by the sheer scale of its surroundings. This was the largest man-made space Farley had ever seen. The tunnel walls were slightly curved, as if some inconceivably large and powerful bore had dug them and melted the walls to a smooth gloss. A large groove that ran the length of the tunnel bisected large circular designs outside each repair bay. Another groove ran from each design to the bay itself.

The facility had to extend for miles, and for all Farley knew it descended for miles as well. He saw several open-framed, two-seater vehicles, and wheeled equipment sleds—from little upright carts the size of refrigerator dollies to slabs that looked as if they could have hauled a small house. In the bays were massive platform lifts and huge articulated cranes. Some of these still held components. Others had fallen with their burdens. The vast space was lit the same sickly green as the faint glow that emanated from the well in the middle of the crater. The air was musty and smelled of dirt, oil, faint copper. Time.

Farley and Wennda stared at the stream of bugs marching past the lethal body of the Typhon. Wennda was scraped-up by the fall and from being dragged, but she seemed otherwise uninjured. Farley put an arm on her shoulder and she put a hand on his.

"Do you think we can get back up the crevice?" she whispered.

"You kidding? I'll race you."

He helped her up, and they turned to see Yone still staring at the Typhon as he stood beside the line of bugs crawling from the crevice opening. One side of his face had been scraped raw in the fall, and the top of his jumpsuit was spotted with blood. As Farley and Wennda walked toward him, Farley could feel the Typhon behind him, like knowing that a sniper had you in his sights.

"Come on," Farley told Yone. "Let's take our chances back in the crevice."

"I quite agree."

The opening was just wide enough for one yard-wide bug, if it turned sideways to get through. The thought of going belly-to-belly

270

with the bastards to get back into the crevice made Farley's skin crawl, but he'd take rubbing bellies with the bugs over the Typhon any day.

He watched the bugs crawl out of the crevice opening. "Stay close behind me," he told Wennda and Yone, and headed for the entrance.

All the bugs stopped moving. The one that had just emerged from the opening stayed in front of it and raised its forelegs. Farley pulled up short and Wennda and Yone bumped into him.

"It doesn't look good," said Wennda.

"I'll go left," said Farley. "If our friend there moves with me, you two run in."

"All right," Wennda said after a moment.

"Okay." Farley displayed his opened hands to the bug and sidled to the left. Several of the eye lenses shifted to follow him. The rest stayed trained on Wennda and Yone. The bug did not move.

Farley lowered his hands and sighed. He stepped back and so did Wennda. The bugs resumed their steady stream.

Wennda nodded at the Typhon. "That's the only other direction," she said.

"Then there's no use crying about it. Let's go."

"We are just going to walk by that thing?" Yone asked.

"Well, I think we should tiptoe, but yeah," said Farley.

* * * * *

Don't think of it as mice sneaking by a sleeping cat, Farley told himself as they walked single file in the metal groove beside the line of scavenger drones that crawled past the Typhon. *Think of it as ants crawling in front of a lion. Lions don't care about ants. Ants aren't on the menu.*

The groove was five feet wide and at least that deep. Wennda walked in front, Farley at the rear. Farley wanted Wennda close, but Yone's injured leg meant that someone had to keep an eye on him in case he faltered.

Ahead and to the right lay the Typhon. Farley tried not to stare at the thing but it was impossible. They were trying to sneak past something longer and wider than the *Morgana* that had almost knocked the bomber out of the sky.

The sky was full of these bastards once. That's what Yone said. Battalions of living machines that darkened the skies. That fought without fear or hesitation. Without mercy. All you've got to do is walk by one of them without being seen. Nothing to it, Captain Midnight. Stay in line, keep moving, keep quiet, and maybe one day you can live to hold hands with a pretty girl back where you belong.

He almost made it.

* * * * *

Farley alternated between keeping an eye on Yone and Wennda and straining to take in as much detail as he could of what he had somehow come to think of as his nemesis. He saw that the Typhon's tail section was asymmetrical but aerodynamic, flaring into a kind of fluke that acted as a horizontal stabilizer, like the tail of a dolphin. The skin was dark and mottled and patched in many places. The bugs that swarmed it seemed to be repairing it. Arclights flashed from the tips of forelegs delicately spotwelding damaged sections. Other bugs opened the pliable skin to perform electrical repairs or surgery, or both. One bug swept a foreleg along an intake vent or a gill slit, then crawled inside.

Throughout it all Farley felt a sense of *breathing*, of extensive systems working to keep a very old and complicated thing functioning. It felt like standing next to a vast pressure cooker whose needle was well into the red. Farley's jaw ached from clenching his teeth.

He watched a bug run from the bay with a piece of equipment like a relay runner. He looked back at the hangar and did a doubletake.

The *Fata Morgana* floated in front of the Typhon.

Farley understood right away that he was seeing some kind of solid-looking projection, like the tabletop images in the Dome. But it was full-sized and it looked absolutely real. The bomber's right rear elevator was damaged. Flak and bullet punctures riddled the hull. The *Morgana* flew low in the northern fissure toward the pale rectangle of the Redoubt in the distance, a disorienting vista receding past the far end of the hangar bay.

From the foreground a bright orange streak shot toward the bomber and narrowly missed as she banked right. The top turret rotated and began shooting back. The image jolted as the rounds hit home.

The image froze.

The Typhon's enormous head cocked right.

The image enlarged. Farley could see Wen through the turret bubble as he fired on the Typhon.

On its massive metal slab the Typhon unfolded a wing. Something swelled on the underside near the creature's body. It swiveled slightly. Ahead of the Typhon, the image receded until the whole bomber could be seen. Streaks fired from what was now a rod projecting from beneath the Typhon's wing. Impact marks stitched along the top of the *Morgana*'s fuselage until they tore apart the turret bubble.

The image froze.

The Typhon turned its head and looked right at Joe Farley.

Farley went cold all over. His breath caught. Everything went far away. Nothing existed but that enormous streamlined head. No light but the pale dead ovals of its eyes. *It sees me,* Farley thought. *It sees me and I'm going to die.* He willed himself to move. He could not move.

Then he was falling backward and he hit the metal floor of the groove and saw stars and heard voices. Wennda? Yone?

All at once it all let go. "It saw me," Farley said. "We've got to go, we've got to move, *it saw me.*"

Wennda put a hand on his arm. "It's looking at its wing, Joe. I don't think it saw us."

Farley blinked at her. "Its wing?" he said.

"Look," she said.

He stared at her a few more seconds. She looked past him at Yone, and her expression was beseeching, and for some reason the idea that she was asking Yone for help because he'd gone flak happy snapped him out of it. He stood straight and looked out across the hard distance where the Typhon lay running simulation after simulation to teach itself how to destroy his bomber.

The wing was still extended. The head was still turned back. The re-created *Morgana* flew ahead of it again. The shape beneath the Typhon's wing was longer now, and bulbous, like some kind of engine.

The aerodynamic head turned back to face the resurrected bomber. The vista dizzyingly revolved until the *Morgana* faced the Typhon head-on. The Flying Fortress frozen mid-bank. Two figures dimly visible through the cockpit windows. One of them Joe Farley.

The scene zoomed backward. The frozen bomber retreated to a distant speck, a slanted line of wing. The image held a moment, and then the B-17 completed its mid-canyon turn and the walls streaked forward as the Typhon advanced. This time a full-out headlong charge. The bomber growing in the center of the lifelike vista. Small white flashes from the nose and belly as the guns began to fire. The top turret swiveling forward. Bomber and Typhon like jousters at some apocalyptic tournament. The *Morgana* banked again to swerve. A bolt of white-hot fire shot from the Typhon's wing pod. The Flying Fortress soundlessly erupted into a brilliant ball of particles that quickly dissipated and left no hint that in the previous second it had been a huge machine with men inside.

The image froze. The Typhon's head cocked, then cocked the other way. The landscape vanished and the long head lowered to the slab.

You figured me out, thought Farley. *You son of a bitch. You figured me out.*

THIRTY

With eight men in it the long and narrow room in which Broben found himself was stuffed like a rush-hour bus. Boney had to hunch to keep his head from hitting the low ceiling. The walls were white plastic panels. Light was indirect and glaring. The floor had a grated drain, and high up on one wall was a bank of shower heads. No furniture of any kind. The whole thing looked molded in one piece. Not exactly the vast aquarium-city vista Broben had been expecting.

A muffled klaxon brayed like a distant angry goose.

Sten touched a panel on the wall and the oval opening squeezed shut like a tightening muscle. Broben started to tell him about Arshall, but something in Sten's look made him realize that he already knew. "Where are we?" Broben asked instead.

"Clean room," Sten said. "Decontam."

"Anybody see you?"

Sten shook his head. "I don't think so, but they could have cameras in here. I would."

"Well, we're not gonna hang around to find out." Broben nodded at the inner door. "What's waiting for us in there?"

Sten hesitated. "It's easier to show you," he said.

Broben gestured impatiently and Sten turned to the inner door. Sten motioned Boney aside and Boney shuffled awkwardly out of the way. The men had to crowd even tighter against each another as Sten pulled the door wider.

In the distance, framed perfectly in the doorway, was the *Fata Morgana*.

"Oh, baby," Garrett breathed.

"Thurgood here we come," said Shorty.

"Are you kidding?" said Plavitz. "That ship couldn't be more of a trap if it was made out of cheese."

"You want to go back to the Dome?" said Broben. "Feel free." He stared hard at the bomber two hundred yards away. The bomb bay doors were open and the ball turret was pointing straight down into a divot scooped out of the floor beneath it. An arc of clean metal lay over the gouge that had been blown from the tail section. She was too far away to see what else might have been done to her, but from here it looked as if she were waiting for them on her hardstand. Nothing moved on or near her. Just looking at her lifted a weight from Broben's heart.

He pointed at the doorway and swept his arm to the left. "All right, everybody on this side, break left a hundred yards and then go for the bomber." He lowered his arm. "Garrett, you're up front with the Browning. I got the rear."

"Will do, cap—uh, lieutenant," said Garrett.

Broben's only acknowledgement of the slip was a slight nod. He looked at the men to the right of the hatch. "This side, break right, same thing. Sten, do your chameleon trick and provide cover from the rear."

"The suit battery is pretty low," Sten warned.

"I'll take what I can get." Broben looked around the cramped little room. "We're not attacking a fort, we're stealing a bomber. Got it? Keep it quiet. But you see anything that even *looks* like it's guarding our ride, you shoot it like a mad dog. I don't care if it's a blind nun with a tin cup; we're getting on that bomber and going home. Got it?"

"What do we do when we're on board?" asked Garrett.

"Firing positions. Shoot anything that moves that isn't us."

* * * * *

Garrett, Plavitz, Martin, and Francis bolted out the doorway and veered left. Broben had time to think, *This must be how those poor saps in Airborne feel when it's their turn to jump,* and then he was out the door and running on a rough stone floor inside a space so vast he didn't perceive it as *inside* at all. Full night had fallen in the fissure, and faint pale light like strong moonlight came from everywhere and nowhere. Ahead and to the left was a cluster of low structures. Behind them rose taller, lighted buildings with narrow roads between them. Here was the vast aquarium space he had expected.

Near the huge main door were stacked rows of large rectangular containers the size of semi-trailers. Parked near these was a wedge-shaped troop transport. Ahead and to the right, the *Fata Morgana* faced the main door in the middle of a huge rectangular staging area.

In the lead, Garrett cut right and made for the *Morgana* as ordered. Broben glanced at Everett leading the right-flank charge. Boney had fallen back and was limping so bad he looked like he was skipping. Broben looked for Sten in the rear but couldn't see him, which was terrific.

Where the hell were all these Redoubt bastards? Attackers outside, invaders inside, alarms going off like the end of the world, and not a soul in sight.

Shut up. Run.

The two flanking lines converged upon the bomber.

Man, the ship looked like a million bucks. The tail damage had been beautifully repaired. Broben saw no trace of flak damage, no oil streaks, no burn marks, not even bulletholes. Who'd bother patching bulletholes in a bird that wasn't flight-ready?

Fifty feet from the bomber Garrett pulled up short and raised the .30-cal, with its remaining yard of ammo belt. Broben clearly heard him say, "What. The. *Shit.*"

277

A spider the size of a St. Bernard dropped from the open bomb bay and scurried off in the direction of the nearest cluster of buildings.

Garrett apparently realized that machine-gun fire would only invite attention, because he lowered the Browning. The creature wasn't heading toward them, anyway.

Then another giant spider crawled out of the Number Four engine cowling and crept onto the wing.

Screw this, thought Broben. "Shoot it!" he yelled. "Shoot the goddamn thing!"

"I'll hit the bomber," Garrett called back.

"Then shoot the *other* one!" Broben raised his pistol.

Behind Garrett, Plavitz said, "But it's running away." His tone was amazingly calm.

"Who gives a shit, it's big as a goddamn Buick, for christ sake! Shoot the son of a bitch!"

"What in *the* hell is goin' on out there?"

Everyone stopped running.

The voice had come from the bomber.

Something dropped down from the bomb bay, and for a moment Broben thought it was another spider. But it straightened as it emerged from underneath the fuselage and walked beneath the wing on two legs.

The crewmen raised their guns.

The figure stepped out from the shadow of the wing.

"Jeez Louise," said Francis.

Wendell Bonniker pushed back his A-3 cap and turned his head and spat on the floor. "Never met her," he said.

THIRTY-ONE

Farley, Wennda, and Yone hurried along the groove in a slight crouch. They were well past the Typhon now but Farley couldn't let go of what had happened back there. The thing had looked him in the eye, or so he'd thought, and he had gone completely rabbit.

It's just a glorified fighter plane, he told himself. *It's what a P-47 will turn into in a hundred years.*

They crossed one of the lines that marked where the groove bisected the circular design outside a repair bay. Wennda suddenly called a halt and frowned down at the line.

"You all right?" Farley asked.

She looked up at him. Then she climbed up out of the groove.

"Wennda?" Farley tried to keep his tone calm. "What are you doing?"

"Come up," she called down. "The Typhon can't see us now."

Farley looked at Yone and Yone shrugged. Farley climbed out of the trench, then pulled Yone out.

They stood before one of the repair bays. This one held a massive framework gantry from which hung hooks and claws and cables meant to move across a hangared typhon to effect repairs. But there was no typhon in here, just an empty platform centered on the ditch-like groove that led toward the tunnel's central groove. The bay that housed the Typhon was far behind them, near the wall that marked the end of the enormous tunnel.

A drone skittered by, carrying a metal box in that direction.

"Look here," said Wennda. She indicated the large circular design on the ground in front of the repair bay. The circle was paler than the rest of the floor, and outlined in a ring of metal. The main groove ran through it; another groove ran from the outer ring to the repair bay.

"What am I looking at?" Farley asked.

"These circles turn ninety degrees," Wennda said. "So that the sleds that hold the typhons can move out onto them. Then they rotate back to line up with the trench."

"It's a transport system," Yone realized. "To move the typhons to other repair hangars. Or to where they took off and landed."

"I think it *is* how they took off," Wennda said. "It's a magnetic accelerator."

Farley frowned. "Come again?"

"A launch rail." She waved at the bay. "That's where they housed them, repaired them, programmed them. Then they moved them to the main rail and launched them, one after another. I'd bet my next ten dessert shares that this tube comes out somewhere in the crater."

"The well," Farley and Yone said at the same time.

"We have to go that way," said Wennda.

"Whatever causes the vortex is still operating in there," Yone said doubtfully.

She shrugged. "It's still the way out."

"Perhaps we will find a third way."

"I'm all for it," said Farley. "So long as we keep moving."

Yone indicated his injured leg. "You should leave me behind. I will only keep you from reaching your aircraft."

"I don't leave my people behind," Farley said.

"Even without me slowing you up, you know that you will only catch up to your crew if something goes wrong on their side of things."

"I also know that things go wrong a lot more than they go right, so we've got to try. And if everything goes perfectly and they make it out with the bomber, we still have to try. No one ever made a flight by giving up."

Wennda smiled a Mona Lisa smile. "Are they all like you where we're going?" she asked.

Farley smirked. "I'd have to say most of them are like me, but less so." He pointed down the vast tunnel. "Get moving, soldier."

* * * * *

They stopped to check out one of the open-frame buggies. The little vehicles weren't much more than two molded bucket seats in a hard plastic framework on four balloon tires. A storage box behind the seats. The tires were dry-rotted.

Wennda pressed a button on the steering wheel and shook her head. "The only things that have been maintained here in the last two hundred years are the Typhon and the launch rail. I'll be surprised if we find anything that powers up."

The repair bays continued. Perhaps their typhons had been operational after the destruction, but had gradually worn out over the years, until only the one remained. The bugs—repair drones, Wennda called them—must have cannibalized whatever was closest first, then begun to work their way down the line.

At one point they encountered a bug that had broken down. Its belly lay on the floor and its tendrils moved fitfully as the four rear legs tried to lift it but could not. Even as it struggled to rise it was swarmed by other drones. By the time the three humans drew even with it the faulty bug was half stripped and no longer moving.

"Are these things alive?" Farley asked as they gave a wide berth to the bugs savaging the body of the damaged bug. "Is the Typhon alive?"

"What you mean by *alive*?" said Wennda.

"I mean is it an animal or is it a machine?"

"Your question is binary," Wennda said. "It only lets the Typhon be one or the other."

"Well—isn't it?"

"It's not that simple." She indicated the vast facility around them. "These people made machines the size of germs that used organic chemicals for fuel. They fed, they made little machines, they combined to make more complicated machines."

"So they were cells?"

"*Manufactured* cells. Entire machines made out of millions of little machines. Independent pieces programmed to work together."

"But were they alive?"

"Is a baby alive? It's just a bunch of chemicals that organize into cells that combine and grow and reproduce."

"The Typhon isn't a damn baby."

"The Typhon was made to be exactly what it is, Joe. By people. Hating it is like hating a hammer."

"A hammer that decides what it's going to hit."

"You fly a machine that drops bombs. Aren't you a hammer that decides what to hit?"

Farley frowned. "All I can say is that I know I'm not," he said. "I'm more than that."

Wennda raised an eyebrow. "How do you know the Typhon doesn't feel the same way?" she asked.

* * * * *

Overhead lights came on as they advanced. The first time it happened it scared the hell out of Farley. He thought they'd been spotlighted from above, but Wennda was unconcerned. "It looks like I was wrong about things powering up," she said. Then she saw Farley about to bolt. "It's okay, Joe. It's reactive lighting. There's a motion sensor here somewhere."

"So we're being tracked?"

"If we are, I doubt there's anyone reading it. It's just an automatic system to save power."

Farley looked skeptical. They went on. Another overhead light came on. The one behind them went out.

"Okay, that's just spooky," said Farley.

Wennda smiled. "I won't let it hurt you, Joe."

"I'll hold you to it."

The farther they went, the more Farley felt like an archeologist exploring some buried tomb built by an unsuspected civilization. Ancient, mysterious, indecipherable. Haunted. He became aware of faint thrumming, some vast dynamo spinning beneath the ground for centuries.

Soon the sporadic parade of repair drones veered to the right, down a lighted corridor between two repair bays.

"Where do you think they are going?" Yone asked.

"Some kind of fabrication shop?" said Farley. He indicated the few bugs headed their way from the corridor. "*Something's* making replacement parts for the Typhon."

Yone looked worried. "Then there are people here?"

Wennda shook her head. "I don't think so," she said. She smirked at Farley. "But that doesn't mean there's nothing alive down here."

"Gotta love an optimist," said Farley.

* * * * *

A mile later the repair bays ended. The maglev launchway tunnel continued smooth and featureless until it ran into a blunt white wall a quarter-mile ahead.

"End of the line," said Farley.

"It didn't occur to me that the launch tube would have a door," said Wennda.

"Gotta keep the bad typhons from getting in somehow."

"There has to be some way to open it," said Yone.

Farley nodded. "Or a people-sized way out."

Past the final repair bay was another lighted corridor, plenty large enough for human beings, but looking like a gopher hole beside the enormous hangar. Empty, motionless, with evenly spaced doors. It curved slightly to the left. Across the launchway another corridor led in the opposite direction, curving to the right.

Farley frowned at the launchway door. "The well's on the other side of that?" he asked.

"There's every reason to think so," said Wennda.

"I think this corridor circles it." Farley indicated the curving corridor on the other side of the launchway. "That's the other end."

"This facility is a wheel," Yone realized. "We are in a spoke, and that corridor is the hub."

"I'll bet the important stuff's in the hub," said Farley. "Command and control, communications, administration."

"Power," Wennda added.

Yone closed his eyes. "The vibration is stronger," he said. "Can you feel it?"

Farley could. The thrumming hummed through him now like engines oscillating in unison. He could not tell whether he was hearing it or feeling it.

He didn't realize he had shut his eyes until he opened them. Wennda and Yone stood facing the corridor with their eyes closed, mouths open, faces relaxed. Wennda looked peacefully asleep, her face free of worry for the first time Farley could remember. There was something lulling in the thrum. Despite his urgency Farley thought how easy it would be to close his eyes again and bathe in that sound. To rest. He was so tired.

He opened his eyes again. What the hell?

"Wennda," he said. She didn't move. Farley grabbed her shoulders and shook her. "Wennda!"

Her eyelids fluttered open. "Joe," she said, and looked surprised. "I was—was I dreaming?"

Farley pointed at Yone. The sleeping man's eyes were moving beneath the lids.

Wennda frowned. "I think we should keep moving," she said.

THIRTY-TWO

Wen still wore his grease-smudged fatigues and his beat-up A-3 cap and a pissed-off expression. A filthy rag flopped in his back pocket and a smoking Lucky drooped from the corner of his mouth. He looked for all the world as if he were at home in a hangar at Thurgood, and he looked completely unsurprised to see the crew.

"You knew we'd be here?" Broben asked, after the arm-punches and insults subsided.

Wen took a deep drag of his Lucky. "'Course I knew," he said. "Cap'n wouldn't just leave her here." He looked around at the crew, paused at Sten, pulled the cigarette from his mouth, and waved it. "Where *is* the captain, lieutenant?"

The men glanced at each other and looked down.

"He didn't make it, Wen," Broben said.

Wen nodded slowly. All that showed on his face were lines where his mouth went tight.

"Sten here is from—you know about the Dome?"

Wen nodded again.

"He helped us get here," Broben said. "He's on the level. He lost people too."

Wen took one last laconic pull from his Lucky, then dropped it and ground it out with his boot. "We should get on the ship," he said, and turned toward the bomber.

"Hey," Broben called. "Where the hell *is* everybody here?"

Wen stopped and looked up at the distant grid of roof. He took a deep breath and turned back around. "Ain't that many," he said. "Three, four hundred maybe. They got a lotta gizmos, but they're barely holdin' on here." He squinted at the scaled-down city in the distance. "What works here works great, but half of it don't work at all. Everything's all patches and spare parts. Including them. They're a pretty scary bunch."

"So they leave you alone with a bomber?"

"Hell no. I'm chaperoned like a church dance." Wen put index and pinkie fingers in his mouth and let out a piercing whistle. The enormous spider-like creature on the wing scurried down the engine cowling with a multi-legged determination that creeped Broben the hell out. It dropped to the ground beside Wen.

"They call these things *biobots,*" Wen said. "They all over the place. This here's Abbott. That one that run off is Costello. Mostly they do repairs, but if I try to escape or sabotage the bomber, they're s'posed to stop me." A corner of his mouth drew up. "Something still goes wrong every time I about get her going, though."

Broben's heart sank. "You've been putting off fixing her," he said resignedly.

"You kidding? These little jaspers are the best grease monkeys you ever saw. They spoiled the hell outta me. You gotta train 'em up, but they learn pretty good." He fished the battered pack of Luckies from his shirt pocket and shook out a last cigarette. The spider extended a supple foreleg toward him and the tip glowed yellow-white. Wen bent and lit the cigarette against it. He straightened and blew smoke and turned to Broben. "I ain't been keeping 'em from fixing her," he said. "I been keeping 'em from knowing she's fixed."

Broben stared. "She can fly?" he said.

"Milk truck coming our way," Plavitz announced.

They all looked to see a large square vehicle like a delivery truck headed their way from the direction of the little city.

"Everybody on the bomber," Broben ordered. He looked hard

286

at Wen as the crew ran for the main door and the bomb bay. "She can fly," he said again.

Wen nodded.

"Okay," said Broben. "Okay." He ran to the main door and hurried into the bomber and pulled up short. Another spider was perched on top of the ball turret's hydraulic assembly.

"Rochester won't bother you," said Wen.

"He bothers me *now*," said Broben.

Wen waved it off as if a yard-wide spider on a Flying Fortress were something you saw every day. Broben tried to press himself flat as he sidled by the bug without taking his eyes off it. When he was past it he ran past Shorty at his seat in the radio room and hurried toward the cockpit.

"Hey, where's the ammo?" Everett called. He was scowling at the .50-caliber Browning on its swivel mount in the right-side window.

"I'm working on that," said Wen.

"Well, what the hell are we supposed to shoot with?"

"You got the .30 and a bunch of pistols. Improvise." Wen hurried after Broben.

* * * * *

Broben climbed into the pilot seat. It felt like years since he'd been in the cockpit. It felt like hours. He frowned at the controls as Wen climbed up to the pit behind him. The C-1 autopilot box below the throttle was gone. In its place was a white box the size of a cigarette pack, with a single button on one side.

He glanced out the window at the box truck heading their way. It was a lot closer than he wanted it to be. "How long before I can start her up?" he asked Wen.

Wen pressed a button on the white box and a light glowed green. "You can start her now."

Broben looked up at him in disbelief. "We can go," he said.

"Whenever you want."

"I want now."

"All right, then. I'll be up top." Wen dropped down.

Broben looked at the oncoming truck. It couldn't be a minute away. He glanced at the battery and inverter switches and verified that they were on even though he could hear their faint hum. The volt meter hovered around twenty-five. He engaged the hydraulic pumps and heard them whine. When they cut off he opened the fuel shutoff valves and engaged the booster pumps, then slid the red bar of the master switch to ON and flicked the ignition switches for Engines One through Four. He glanced out windows and saw that Wen had left the cowl flaps shut to warm the engines faster.

The milk truck was driving on the open staging area now and moving much faster.

Mixture-cutoff levers to Full Rich, throttle to ten percent, parking brake and tail wheel lock engaged. Prop RPM high, magneto switch One & Two on.

He hit the Number One engine starter switch for ten seconds, then flicked MESH. The engine caught right away. No bronchial wheezing, just the sudden deep cough of start. Broben glanced left and saw the prop spinning up. No smoke had coughed from the engine. The cabin vibrated gently and Broben smelled high-octane fuel. The fuel-pressure gauge began to climb.

The milk truck was two hundred yards away now. Broben slipped on his headset and switched on the interphone. "Pilot to crew," he said. "Skip the check-in, we're raising anchor. Bombardier, close the bomb bay doors."

"Close doors, roger," Boney said immediately.

Broben heard the whine from back in the fuselage as the doors began to close. He hit the Number Two starter switch, then hit MESH. Number Two started up like butter.

He remembered the belly turret guns pointing down into the floor divot. "Belly gunner, level the turret," he ordered.

"Belly gunner, I'm already leveled."

Fifty feet from the *Morgana* the transport cut left and stopped.

"Waist gunner here," said Garrett right away, *"I'm taking the .30 up front."*

Number Three started up without a hitch. Instead of the usual guttural roar and shaking there was a rich bass thrum and a steady vibration.

Broben started Number Four and motion caught his eye. A panel had opened on the roof of the truck and something shaped like a sideways bowl was rising up on a pole.

"Shoot it," Broben ordered. "Shoot whatever the hell that is."

"Thirty's not in the gun port yet," Boney said calmly.

The bowl swiveled toward the bomber and a keening whine began to rise, like a turbine spinning up. It reminded Broben of those nerve guns. The economy-size version.

Broben glanced at the closed main door across the staging area and looked at the throttle. God damn it. "Wen, I can't drive through that friggin door," he said. "How do we get out of this shithole?"

A quick burst of automatic gunfire came from up front, and rounds sparked off the bowl antenna poking out of the milk truck.

"Screw this," Broben muttered. He was reaching for the throttle when the bomber rang like a bell and the gunfire cut off. His vision went blurry and his eyes wouldn't move. His head wouldn't turn. His mouth felt shot with Novocaine and his ears rang. He couldn't talk. All his muscles went rigid. His face, his scalp, his toes. The cockpit went liquid and wavy. Lights smeared. The breath locked in his chest. Black fog skirted the edges of his vision. His thoughts were mud. The cockpit darkened and he felt a sense of pressure. Sinking to the bottom. Red flashes now. A white burst of adrenaline. Lungs on fire. Oh please I want to breathe please let this wear off so I can—

His muscles let go a notch. He pushed air out his throat, the tight hiss of it like a slow leak in a tire.

"Belly gunner here." In his headset Martin's voice came from far away. *"I think we're hit. I'm fine. Maybe because I'm in the ball? That*

truck just popped open. They're getting out on both sides. Maybe ten troops. Does anybody have a shot? Anybody? Over."

Breathe in. It's like sucking air through a wet paper straw, but you can do it. You have to do it.

"Anybody read me?" said Martin's distant voice. *"They're going for the main hatch. Ten men with zap guns and armor. They're right in front of me. God damn it. I'd have 'em all if I had a yard of ammo. Can anybody take these guys? Over?"*

Broben moved his fingers. The control panel swam into view. He could hear the props idling. He tried to release the brake.

"They're at the main hatch," Martin said. *"I've got my sidearm, can someone get me out, over?"*

Dimly Broben heard the hydraulics as the ball turret rotated.

"Main hatch is open. Main is open."

Broben released the parking brake and got a hand on the throttle.

"They're coming in. They're inside, they're in the bomber. Some still on the ground. They see me. I'll try to——"

The voice cut off.

"God *damn* you," Broben tried to yell. And couldn't.

Heavy footsteps on the deck behind him now. Accented voices. He tried to reach his pistol and felt hard hands on his shoulders.

Close. We were so close.

THIRTY-THREE

The gently curving hub corridor had white walls, white ceiling, white floor. Pale gray rectangles evenly spaced along the right-hand side seemed to float in a universe bleached of detail. Farley thought they had to be doors, but there were no knobs, hinges, keyholes, card slots, hand panels, or anything he associated with the idea of door.

Then they found one that had not shut flush. Farley hooked his fingers around the exposed edge and pulled.

"If these were sealed airtight, they might have been built to keep germs out," Wennda pointed out. "Or to keep germs from getting out."

Farley let go the door and stepped back. "Germ warfare?" he asked, scowling at the door.

"Why not? They built every other weapon they could."

Farley indicated the white corridor. "So a hundred doors around this thing and we shouldn't open any of them?" He banged the off-plumb door. "We have to get out of here somehow."

From the wall came a loud ratcheting like a missed gear.

Farley jumped back, one hand sweeping back to protect Wennda as the door grated open. The three of them stared at the entryway. Then Farley shrugged. "Hell with it," he said, and went in.

Wennda wanted to stop him but couldn't think why. She was having a hard time focusing.

Yone gave her a helpless shrug and his quick smile. With his scraped-up face, he looked frightening. "After you," he said, and swept a hand at the doorway.

"Oh, for crying in the sink," said Wennda. She brushed by him and stalked into the room.

Just inside she stopped. She stood in the center aisle of a small auditorium, molded chairs facing a stage with a sleek black lectern. A red-curtained backdrop bore a large design in black and white.

Farley stood transfixed before the stage. He was staring at the curtains.

"Do you know," he asked without looking back, "who they sent my bomber after, a couple hundred years ago? Who half the world sent millions of planes and tanks and ships and idiots like me to fight?"

Wennda eyed the curtain apprehensively. The design showed a stylized bird of prey looking to the left with wings outspread. Its talons clutched a wreath that surrounded a stark symbol made of four bent arms joined together.

"No, Joe," she said. "How could I?"

Farley climbed onto the stage and stood before the curtain. "These bastards here, that's who." He pointed at the *Reichsadler* clutching its swastika.

She glanced at Yone as he came into the room. He stayed by the door, staring at Farley on the red-curtained stage.

"We all keep saying that the war will be over in a year," Farley said. "But it won't. Not in ten years. Twenty. It'll grow until everyone has to pick a side. Until the entire planet's at war." He made a disgusted sound. "Man-made plagues, right, Yone? Fighting machines that think for themselves. Bombs that wipe out cities. Weapons that tear holes in reality itself. That think for themselves." He looked at Wennda. "Hammers that decide what to hit."

He pulled at the curtain. The gesture oddly like a child tugging at its mother's clothes. "These evil sons of bitches will hold out till there's nothing left to hold out for. And when they see they're going to lose, they'll take everything with them. The entire goddamn world."

He turned toward Wennda. "What do you think this building

is?" he asked, unnervingly calm, as if addressing a seated audience.

"I don't really know," Wennda said. "But I think we should go. There's something wrong with this place."

"A facility this size," Farley pressed on, "underground, hardened against attack, chock full of gear, with an entire division of typhons guarding it. And all of it at the very center of the blast that ended the world." He brought his fists up to his head and ground them by his temples. "Do you see it?" he asked. The hands lowered. "Do you see it now?"

"No, I don't, Joe," she said. "It was two hundred years ago."

"It was *last week*," he said.

He held up a placating hand. He looked like he was fighting for control.

Yone's voice came from the back of the auditorium. "This isn't where the weapon was meant to be used," he said.

Farley nodded. "It's where it was built," he said. "And something went wrong. Somebody pressed the wrong button, or forgot a decimal point. Or probably they all just bit off more than they could chew. And the rest is history." He looked at Wennda and laughed bitterly. "Your history," he said. "My future. They're the same thing." He was shaking.

"But the people who built the device were the only ones who survived it," Yone said from the back. He seemed reluctant to come farther into the room. "Because they were in the most protected structure in the world. And after the device was activated there was no more war to fight. No more enemies left, or allies either. Only a dying world."

"But they still wanted to live," said Farley.

"So they built the Dome," Wennda said numbly. She looked at the fierce black eagle on the red curtain. "Your enemies built the Dome."

"The Dome *and* the Redoubt," Farley said. "They were the only ones left, and the only place left on earth where they could survive was at the bottom of the crater their own weapon had made." Farley shook his head. "And I'm fighting like hell to get back so I can help make it happen."

Wennda saw that he was struggling not to cry. *He isn't angry,* she realized. *He isn't crazy. His heart is broken.* She tried to think what to do.

"But now you know what happened," Yone told him. "So perhaps you can make a difference when you go back."

"But it happened," said Farley. "So I didn't." He smirked. "Or maybe the difference I try to make is what causes all of this in the first place."

"Or you *not* going back is what lets it happen," said Wennda, walking toward the stage.

"But it doesn't matter," Farley said. "Here we are. Cause and effect."

"Captain Farley." Yone's voice sounded very flat across the room. "If you know the outcome beforehand, then you share responsibility for it if there is even a chance you could have prevented it and you did nothing."

"Cause and effect," Farley said again. "There's no getting away from it."

"Listen to me, Joe," Wennda said, feeling desperate. "It's not inevitable. Time's not an arrow. It's a shock wave. It spreads out in all directions at once. All possibilities. All outcomes."

"If *everything* happens, then what I do still doesn't make any difference."

"I'm trying to make you see that actions matter. What you do, or don't do, makes a difference every bit as much as chance or complexity. The future's nothing but potential."

He shook his head. "Not once you get there, it isn't."

"You are a stubborn man, Joe."

He snorted. "Maybe there's a world where I'm not."

"Then I don't want to go there. I want the world with the Joe Farley who said that no one ever made a flight by giving up. That's the one I want to be with." She climbed the steps to the stage and stood in front of him and set a hand on the curtain. "We can go back and try to prevent this. And if we can't prevent it, then we can live. The way everybody lives, even though they already know the end of everything is waiting somewhere up ahead." She took the bloodred curtain in both hands and pulled. The centuries-old fabric tore loose from its hooks and crumpled to the stage. A cloud of fine dust rose.

Wennda dropped the fold of curtain onto the soft red pile and looked at Farley. "We'll have time for all the things we don't have time for now," she said.

Farley cocked his head and looked at her as if she were a slumming angel. "Time," he said. Suddenly he felt oddly giddy, drunk with possibility, more capable because she was here with him.

"Time," said Wennda.

Farley gave a slanted grin. "Okay," he said. "We'll try to save the world. And if we can't, then we'll hold hands on the beach."

Her eyes were very bright. She had begun to sweat. "I'd like that," she said. "What's a beach?"

Farley's pulse quickened. He felt like he was running. "Something God made for people to hold hands on," he told her. "I'll show you."

"I look forward to it."

"Backward," he corrected. His palms were slick.

Wennda laughed. "I look backward to it, then."

Yone's voice made them look out at the auditorium, both of them suddenly feeling like actors playing a love scene on a stage. "I think we must be very near the energy source," he said. "I think it is affecting us in some way. I don't feel entirely rational."

"I feel…." Wennda frowned. "I don't know. But it's good."

"Invincible," said Farley.

"Optimistic," she countered.

"What should we do now?" Yone asked.

Farley looked at Wennda. She smiled and nodded and he grinned. He held his hand to her and she clasped it.

"We should finish it," Farley said to Yone. He saw Yone staring at the fallen curtain and he led Wennda off the stage and approached him. Yone looked startled when Farley clapped a hand on his shoulder.

"The curtain's down," Farley told him, "but the show's not over."

THIRTY-FOUR

The hand that reached into Broben's field of vision had an intricate tattoo that looked like a metallic roadmap. It reached past him and pulled the throttle back. The engines quieted and the vibration lessened.

Broben tried to force his hand to his holster. The roadmapped hand beat him to it and removed the weapon. Thick plastic bands were wrapped around his wrists and cinched painfully tight. His headset drew taut on its cord, then slid from his head as he was pulled from the cockpit and dumped beside the top turret footrest like a sack of concrete. A figure knelt beside him. Stretchy armor, form-fitting black helmet, chunky nerve gun.

The helmet regarded him blankly. Broben could not make out a visor, just a black glossy surface. Broben saw no rim where it reached the neck, and he realized that it wasn't a form-fitting helmet at all. It was the thing's head.

The soldier moved aside as another helmeted Redoubt soldier emerged from the nose crawlway unconcernedly dragging Plavitz by the collar. Plavitz's wrists and ankles were bound by thick plastic bands. Through the crawlway he glimpsed Boney in the nose, lying across his wrecked Norden bombsight, another of the anonymous troops standing beside him.

Broben looked into Plavitz's eyes as he was pulled along. He sensed the man behind them but all else about Plavitz was a rag doll as he was dragged into the bomb bay and along the narrow catwalk.

Broben's captor grabbed the back of his collar and dragged him through the bomb bay and radio room into the main compartment. Wen's pet bug, Rochester, was still perched on the bright yellow hydraulic rig above the ball turret, two legs wrapped around the post and a leg on each aluminum ammo can, whiplike forelegs poised. The soldier didn't even glance at the biobot as he stepped off the platform and dropped Broben to the deck beside Plavitz.

Broben could turn his head a little and move his eyes a bit. Wen, Garrett, Everett, and Sten had been dumped like cordwood alongside the upfolded seat boards. Redoubt soldiers in skintight armor combed through the aircraft. They were small and thin, but they had no trouble dragging a side of beef like Garrett. They moved silently and efficiently in the cramped space as if choreographed, and Broben wondered whether they had some kind of communication system. Headset radios, maybe. For all he knew they used a Ouija board.

The soldiers all went ramrod straight a moment before a figure entered the opened main hatch. At first Broben thought it was a man walking behind one of the spider things. Then he realized that both were one creature: A man from the waist up, a spider-like conveyance from the waist down. The steady taps of the articulated legs were heavy in the fuselage. It paused and surveyed the compartment. This man—or whatever the hell you'd call it—was larger than the soldiers, dressed in an angular, bulky, military-looking outfit that looked to be covering up a lot of tubing and machinery. His head was large and bald, and on one side of his scalp was a square of metal that looked like an access panel. A coiled cord emerged from under his stiff ring collar and plugged into a jack beneath the metal plate. He resumed his unnervingly smooth and alien walk toward the laid-out crew, and even as he neared them Broben could not have said whether he were looking at a man or some kind of robot.

The figure took in the aircraft, the bug above the ball turret, the twitching bodies of the crew. He pointed at Wen. Two soldiers picked him up and held him before the man. Wen fought to keep his head upright but it kept sagging forward like a man fighting to stay awake.

The man set a hand on Wen's chin and held his head up. A network of metallic tattoos disappeared into the man's sleeve. He turned Wen's head left and right, then let go. Wen's head drooped.

The man looked down at the inert crewmen. "Ten men," he said. His accent was harsh and difficult to understand. "And five more inbound." He looked again at Wen. "The organ tank won't need you now."

Broben heard a sudden meaty smack, and Wen's head snapped back. His nose was bleeding. It looked broken. Had the man punched him? Broben hadn't even seen his hand move.

"You thought I would not know that you had repaired your warplane."

This time Broben saw the blur before he heard the blow. Wen doubled over and the soldiers held him up. Blood dripped from his nose. His mouth worked as if he were trying to say something.

"You thought I would not know," the man said, as if reciting, "that all the accidents and delays were your little sabotages."

Wen's head snapped to the side. Broben heard teeth patter the hull. It had been a haymaker and it had come from very low and no human being could swing that fast. The lower half of Wen's face was covered in blood and his jaw was out of line.

"You thought that I would just let them come here and fly away with the means of our resumption."

A gut shot buckled Wen's knees. The thud of it like an axe biting into a tree.

"That there has been a moment," the man continued, "when you have not been watched."

Wen tried to duck the next blow and it caught him on the forehead. His head rocked backward and his eyes glazed as they looked up. Again he tried to say something.

A soldier grabbed his hair and made him look at the man. The man held his bloody fist in front of Wen and Broben knew that there would only be one more punch.

"You thought we were that stupid," the man said. "That I am that stupid."

Wen looked past the lethal fist and directly at the man. He coughed and spit blood. *"Muh,"* he said. *"Monkey wrench."*

The man cocked his head. Broben got the impression he was processing the phrase, waiting for something to tell him what it meant. Then he smiled and drew back the fist.

Two snakelike tentacles wrapped around his waist where it joined the multilegged life support, and tore him in two. The spider legs splayed. Blood and viscera splashed onto the deck, and Broben heard faint sputtering and saw bluewhite flashes from the severed spinal column. A wisp of pale gray smoke rose. The man's head turned. Perhaps he saw what had grabbed him. Perhaps some awareness remained in him as Wen's pet biobot dropped his sputtering torso into the warm red porridge on the deck beside his four convulsing multijointed legs.

Wen's biobot spider flowed down from the turret rig and swarmed the nearest soldier holding Wen. It reared up and reached toward the helmet and turned. The soldier's body toppled to the deck. The head hit next.

The second soldier holding Wen had let him go and was reaching for his weapon. The bug lanced his chest with both forelegs and then opened them outward as the other soldiers leveled their weapons at it and fired. The nerve guns had no effect.

Behind them another bug unfolded from the main hatch like a nightmare flower and swarmed the closest soldier with horrifying speed as yet another drone blossomed into the bomber.

Broben saw a service .45 in a sludge of bloody chunks two feet away. He reached for it, but his hand would only flop like a landed fish. He tried to get up but his legs only kicked stupidly.

A bug stopped with one leg planted in the slurry of blood and entrails and fine circuitry that had been the man who'd beat hell out of Wen. It turned toward Broben with a nauseating jittery motion. A foreleg came up.

Broben tried again to grab the pistol. The bug rushed to him and the thin, sharp-jointed legs straddled him. He looked up into glassy eyes or cameras above a delicate fringe of waving feelers. He tried to raise a hand against the looming thing, tried to will himself to stand. His body only jerked and flailed.

Something pressed against his neck and he felt a sharp sting. His muscles relaxed and he slumped over into the warm blood on the deck. He sat up immediately and raised his fists to the bug. It turned away and scurried into the radio room.

Broben looked at his hands. He had raised his hands. He had sat up.

He braced himself against the bulkhead and pushed himself up to his feet. The ringing in his ears had lessened. He had to piss so badly it burned.

Another bug unfolded through the main hatch. This one held a folded belt of .50-caliber ammunition and a bundle of flight suits. It picked its way past the mutilated soldiers and immobilized crew, tracking through the thick red curd that now runneled along the center of the deck. It stopped in front of Broben and held the ammo belt out to him.

Broben bent to take it but the belt was heavier than he could carry. The bug set it down beside him in a thickening tapioca of blood and organs, then skittered off toward the bomb bay.

The other crewmen were now struggling to their feet. Broben staggered to Wen. The flight engineer looked like something a mob had worked over with tire irons, but he was still breathing. It was more than Broben had expected.

Wen opened his eyes and blinked away blood.

"Monkey wrench?" Broben said.

* * * * *

The crewmen stared dumbfounded as the bugs speedily returned the ammo belts to their cans and convoluted feeds and expertly reloaded the machine guns.

"Just ignore 'em," Wen called out from the deck, where Broben tended his injuries as best he could from one of the bomber's rudimentary first-aid kits. The only pain med in the zippered canvas wallet was morphine, which Wen refused, so Broben couldn't do much more than mop him up.

A viscous soup of blood and organs and biomechanical body parts had collected down the center of the main compartment like bilgewater, and Sten was using a seatboard to bale the vivid slop out the reopened bomb bay doors. It smacked the ground with a sound like a wet mop slapped against a concrete wall.

"So you just say the secret word and your little pals know to come rescue us?" Broben asked as he taped a Carlisle bandage onto Wen's nose, which looked like a hammered tomato.

Wen shook his head. It looked like it hurt. "Not exactly," he said. "It just meant *Sic 'em*. Like an SOS to every bug in the place." He chuckled and then winced.

Broben sat straighter. "Wait a second. That's happening all over this joint?" He waved at the carnage.

Wen nodded. "Them poor sumbitches are probably busier'n a cat burying shit on a marble floor right now," he said. His grin was ghastly.

THIRTY-FIVE

Yone set his palm against a gray door in the white corridor. "Here," he said, and shut his eyes. "I can feel it. Can't you feel it?" His eyeballs moved beneath the lids.

Farley and Wennda traded a look, and each knew that the other was remembering Yone saying *I don't feel entirely rational.* To humor him Wennda went to the door and set a hand against it. The moment her fingertips touched it she snatched it back. She stepped back and frowned at her hand.

"Did you get shocked?" Farley asked.

"Not—shocked. It felt *alive.*" She kept looking at her hand.

"Wennda."

She looked up as if surprised to see him there.

"You all right?" asked Farley.

"I'm fine, why?"

"You're breathing hard. Your face is red and you're sweating like crazy."

She set the hand against her chest. Her heart was hammering like mad. "I feel like I just ran," she said. "No. Like I want to run."

"I think we better get away from here."

"It's here," said Yone.

They turned at his voice. Yone looked and sounded like a man talking in his sleep. "In here," he said.

"Good," said Farley. "It can stay there."

"Maybe you should touch the door," suggested Wennda.

"And maybe I shouldn't. Because from where I'm standing I'm the only one of us making any sense."

Yone slapped the door with a palm. "Here!" he said.

"I don't think that trick's going to work this time," Farley said. "We're looking for a way out, not a door that gives us the willies."

"Not the door." Yone pressed his raw cheek against the door. He looked purely crazy. Like a spurned lover haunting the porch of his obsession. "The locus," he said. "Can't you feel it?"

"Why on God's green earth would I want to do that," said Farley. But he stood behind Yone and put his hand against the door—

* * * * *

Farley had once donated plasma in the "Blood for Britain" drive. They'd drawn blood and centrifuged it to separate the plasma, then hung a bottle of his whole-blood cells on a stand and slid an IV needle into his arm. But the cells weren't body temperature anymore, and he could feel them coursing up his arm until they reached his heart. Like a cold wire drawn through the beating life of him. He'd felt a brief fear that his heart would stop, and then the cells warmed and his apprehension passed. But there had been that unexpected moment of mortal dread.

* * * * *

—put his hand against the door and something not electricity coursed up his arm. Some cold surge that vividly recalled those blood cells taken from his body and rendered strange and reintroduced. A snake in his blood sidewinding toward his core, and then a flooding in his heart both foreign and familiar. Pure and powerful and formless and mindless. And yet he sensed intent.

303

Beside him Yone laughed lightly. It seemed to come from far away. "They made a god," he said.

Farley's scalp crawled. He snatched his hand back from the door. The sudden painful silence made him aware that he'd been hearing a sustained ringing.

Wennda was looking at him. Her flushed appearance a bit reduced. Had she said something?

Shake it off, Captain Midnight. Farley turned and pulled Yone from the door. Yone flinched violently and said something unintelligible, then twisted his arm away from Farley and pressed himself back against the door like a frightened boy clinging to his mother's legs.

"Did you feel it?" Wennda asked.

Farley looked at his hand. "I felt something," he admitted. "I don't know that I'd say it was alive, but it was something. I think we're going to have to drag him with us." He stopped in the midst of waving at the door. It stood open and Yone was gone.

* * * * *

Curving rows of workstations faced a dull gray screen that occupied most of the front wall. An overturned tumbler at one station, its contents long ago evaporated. Farley would have bet his crush hat it had been coffee. It was the first genuinely human thing he had seen down here.

On the left side of the viewscreen wall was a door with a handle and a square window at head height. Farley tried the handle. The door was unlocked.

Farley looked at Wennda. She shrugged. He opened the door and stepped through.

Immediately he felt the overwhelming sense of invasion he had felt when he had touched the hallway door. A sense of power, of intent. A wash of bright green light, loud ringing in his ears. Urge to run, blind panic breaking through.

He stood on a small railed platform at the top of a narrow tread-plate staircase that descended at least two hundred feet along a sheer stone wall. It looked out over a space that would have fit a dozen typhon repair bays. The distant walls were crowded with pipework, beams, ladders, railed walkways, catwalks, stairs.

On the floor of that vast space was a machine the size of a battleship.

Farley felt sudden vertigo at the unexpected vista. The railed platform seemed precarious and insubstantial. He pressed back against the opened door.

Beside him a voice said, "Here." He looked to see a woman pushing a wheeled chair into the doorway. Wennda? What was she doing here? He hadn't seen her in years. No, that wasn't right. He had just been with her. Where had he been with her?

Wennda left the chair in the doorway and Farley stepped away from the door. It swung and stopped against the chair. Wennda stepped out onto the platform and gasped at the view. She clutched the railing and Farley grabbed her shoulders. They looked down upon the great machine.

It seemed to float above the flat stone acreage, an island unto itself. Countless components, disks, rings, cables, pipes, a band of something like giant pegboard set with evenly spaced staples the size of goalposts. The whole conglomeration forming a series of nested cylinders telescoping horizontally out into this vast space. The larger end was surrounded by a vertical octagonal framework set with jointed silver ducts banded with bright orange and wound around with miles of bare copper wire like an electric hub motor. The enormous octagon did not touch the cylinder at any point, and Farley saw nothing supporting it. It seemed to float before the huge machine. The green glow that now suffused everything was painfully bright in the empty center of the octagon, though from where Farley stood the nested cylinders blocked its source.

Wennda pointed down the stairs. Far below them a lone figure descended.

Motion made Farley glance at the door. He saw Wennda push a workstation chair into the doorway. He saw himself let go of the door. Saw the door stop against the chair.

Farley shook his head. *What the hell?*

At the rail he pulled Wennda closer. The smell of her hair. She turned her head and pointed down the stairs. Far below a lone figure descended.

Wennda motioned that they should follow. Farley nodded. Neither of them spoke. As if it were too loud to talk. He set a hand on the rail and went down the stairs as fast as he could. Wennda's steps behind him. There was no wind but Farley felt he faced into a howling gale. He slowed. Was he climbing? It felt like he was going up.

Far below Yone continued his descent.

Farley looked back at Wennda. She pointed down the stairs. The door stopped against the chair. The smell of her hair.

Farley halted and grabbed the rail and closed his eyes and took a deep breath. *I'm here. I'm Joseph Farley. Wennda is here with me. We are trying to get our friend Yone back so we can leave here.*

Pounding on the diamondplate steps. Farley opened his eyes to see Wennda catching up to him. Her eyes wide in surprise. "Joe?" she said. Not asking if he were okay. Asking if it were really him. How long has it been for her just now?

He heard himself say, "We should go back."

Near the bottom of the stairs Yone vaulted the railing. Farley watched him from far away on the field-sized floor, aware of the mass of the machine behind him. On the narrow staircase higher up stood two figures. One of them was Wennda. The other was Joe Farley.

When did we get down here? How did we get ahead of Yone? Of—ourselves?

"What's happening?"

Farley turned at Wennda's voice. The machine loomed like a metal cloud behind her. Cradled by a gantry that could have held a zeppelin. As Farley watched, the entire machine seemed to come apart like an exploded-view drawing. Millions of pieces and no two touching.

Farley felt drawn thin. The pieces came together. The door stopped against the chair. Yone vaulted the rail.

"It looks like a dynamo!" Farley told Wennda as they hurried down the stairs.

"I don't know what that is!" Wennda shouted back.

The green light was so much brighter here on the floor of the cavernous space. It flickered in the center of the octagon that floated at the wider end of the machine. Power. Distortion. Intent. Here was the source.

Farley looked for Wennda but she was gone. The machine was gone. He stood alone on the floor of an artificial cavern that was larger than any building he had ever seen. No pipes, no beams, no staircase slanting down the cliff of wall. Just green light and empty space and one man. And a sense of immeasurable time, brittle decay, inert dissolution.

"Wennda?" Farley said into the dark.

"Here." Wennda pushed a workstation chair into the doorway. There was no wind but Farley felt he faced into a howling gale. "Joe?" she said, but did not seem to know him.

Joe. *My name is Joseph Mayhew Farley. I'm right here. We should go back.*

The green light strobed and Joe Farley shielded his eyes and leaned into it as he struggled forward. Yone vaulted the rail. The door hit the chair.

Something touched his arm and it was Wennda and he loved her and he was an old man lonely without her all these years and he told Shorty how he saw the woman that he wanted painted on his bomber and he sat at the controls at the end of his long life and wondered if there lived still in the air some path that could lead back to her. "I'm a memory of the future," she told him. "An echo across time." And then the sun came on.

* * * * *

A small man stood before him. Scabbed face, limpid eyes, filthy jumpsuit. A weak man to all appearances, and yet Farley knew otherwise. He did not seem to see Farley but stared at some point past him, tracking something moving like a cat seeing a ghost. Farley turned to look but there was nothing there. Green light and an empty cavern and a sense of brittle time.

"Where are we?" Farley asked. "Where's Wennda?"

"We are at the heart of the locus," Yone said. "I am so glad you found me." He started to walk but Farley moved in his way.

"Why did you come here?" Farley asked. He waved to indicate the vast and empty space.

"I was called." A religious fervor on his injured face. "We were called here."

"You said they made a god."

"Did I? How embarrassing." He did not look embarrassed. His eyes were bright. "I believe I was not entirely in my right mind. The locus seems to be affecting us. Our brains. Maybe reality. How would one know which?"

Farley held up a hand. "Just help me find Wennda so we can get the hell out of here."

To Farley's surprise Yone put both hands on Farley's arms and bowed his head. "My friend," he said, "there is nothing in this world that I want more."

"But how do we get back?" Farley asked, glancing around the featureless space. "Where did everything go?"

Yone stepped back and looked up. Farley thought of Wennda looking at the artificial sky and shouting *I want more* time! He looked up at the cavern sky and closed his eyes.

* * * * *

You can't prepare yourself. There's no deep breath to take, no armor to put on. Whatever god you pray to when the flak begins to burst can hold no jurisdiction here. Here the time is all a box of jumbled letter blocks. You must hold on to your sense of sequence, distill *If A then*

B. Connect effects with causes to discern the proper order. The time fragments, reality fragments. You fragment. A bunch of chemicals organized into cells. A jumble arranged by the movement of time. Alive and aware and affecting. Actions matter every bit as much as chance. Hold onto that. To you. To Wennda. Your sense of her. Her face on the ship that brought you here. You are connected.

Go.

* * * * *

It hit him like a shot of whiskey on an empty stomach. Farley had to fight to stay upright. He looked up at the distant cavern ceiling and felt that he was falling.

Directly ahead the enormous octagon hovered just outside the rim of the largest cylinder of the vast machine Farley thought of as the dynamo. A conical projection from the middle of the cylinder pointed at the center of the octagon. At the point of the cone the green light was unbearably bright. Afterimages trailed when Farley looked away. He heard a steady noise like the soft buzz of a fluorescent light with dirty poles.

The windless gale roared silently. A hurricane inside himself.

He stood behind Yone on a small railed platform beside a wall of pale green light so bright that Yone was a silhouette before him. The platform rested atop a spindly metal pole like a cherry picker rising from a catwalk fifty feet below. The catwalk itself an insubstantial span a hundred feet above the ground.

Farley gripped the thin low railing with both hands. A ringing in his ears so loud it hurt.

Yone did not seem to see him but stared out at the wall of brilliant light. Farley shouted Yone's name but Yone did not react. Instead he braced himself against the rail and leaned out into that space and put his silhouetted hand out toward the coruscating sheet of light. On the other side of it Farley made out the dim shape of a long slim cone that tapered to a point, like an enormous spearhead that almost touched the wall of light.

Yone turned back and Farley put a hand on his shoulder. Yone looked at him like a man accosted by a stranger raving in a different language. Not a hint of recognition in his eyes.

"We have to find Wennda," Farley said.

Yone pointed down.

"There's nothing—" Farley broke off.

A hundred fifty feet away he saw Wennda's foreshortened figure walking toward the base of the machine. Her long shadow flickered.

"Wennda!" Farley's throat felt scoured as he shouted down at her. "Wennda!"

She kept walking and did not look back. Farley let go of Yone and ran. His leg still pained him from the fall into the crevice. Behind him he heard Yone's voice. Like a whisper in his ear but far away. He looked back but Yone was gone. Farley was on the cavern floor.

He felt dizzy and looked forward again. Wennda was no longer there. He stopped.

"It's here. The heart of the locus."

Farley turned. The voice had been Yone's but Wennda stood a few feet behind him. The two of them were on a railed catwalk a hundred feet above the cavern floor. A long, pegged pole rose high up from the center of the catwalk to a small railed platform. Like a cherry picker. Its bucket poised before a long, narrow cone that tapered to a point before a sheet of blinding green light in the center of the floating octagon. The cold light wavered and rippled like water, a vertical eight-sided pool.

He was on the machine.

Wennda brought her smartsuit's visor to her eyes and looked up at the curtain of light. "Can you feel it?" she asked.

Farley felt a plunging fear. "Wennda. We have to go."

She raised the visor and looked up at the curtain of light. "Can you feel it?" she repeated.

Farley stepped forward and grabbed her wrist. She turned to him and her face was all hard reflections and he was terrified and then he saw that she had activated her visor. *"Look,"* she said, and held out the visor.

"We have to go."

"Look," she said, and held out the visor.

The time was stuttering.

Farley took the visor from her and held it over his eyes. For a moment he did not understand what he was looking at. Then he realized that the view was highly magnified. He lowered the visor from his eyes and oriented himself on the point of the cone in front of the insubstantial platform on its spindly pole and raised the visor again. The green light was much dimmer, filtered by the visor. He could see something in the middle of the sheet of light, directly in front of the cone. A bug in the ointment. It wavered and shook, and Farley held his breath and forced himself still.

There. A small hemisphere with a stem emerging from one end, like a mushroom or a top.

"What am I looking at?" Farley asked.

"The thing that brought you here. To my world. To this room. To me. The locus."

"*That* thing?"

"Not a thing. An area. A set of equations. Coordinates. Instructions. Laws. It connects realities. Times."

"It's the size of a jawbreaker."

"It destroyed the world."

Farley pulled the headpiece off and stared at Wennda. She had sounded exactly like Yone when Yone had started sounding crazy.

Farley felt a sudden certain horror. "Wennda," he said. He glanced at the mote in the cold sheet of light. "Is that you talking to me?"

Near the bottom of the stairs Yone vaulted the rail and ran in the direction of the dynamo. Farley missed a step and grabbed the rail. He was certain he had just seen himself on the floor of the huge room, looking up at himself and Wennda running down the stairs.

Wennda nearly ran into him. "You all right?" she asked.

He pushed open the door and stepped out onto a small platform at the top of a narrow staircase bolted to a sheer stone wall several hundred feet high. A space that would fit a dozen typhon repair bays. Distant walls. A machine the size of a battleship. Sudden vertigo. Wennda pushed a workstation chair into the doorway. "Here," she said. Farley let go the door and stepped in. A small man stood before him. Scabbed face, limpid eyes, filthy jumpsuit.

"We are at the heart of the locus," Yone said. "I am so glad you found me."

"We have to go," said Farley.

"*Look.*" Wennda held the visor out to him.

He held it to his eyes and looked. The silhouette hand flickered as it reached toward the light. Floating in front of the cone was a small object shaped like a mushroom or a top.

"The thing that brought you here," Wennda told him. "Did you feel it?"

"I felt something. I don't know that I'd say it was alive, but it was something."

"A set of equations. Instructions. A bunch of chemicals that organize into cells that evolved to combine and grow and reproduce. Entire machines made out of millions of little machines. Independent pieces programmed to work together. A consensus. It connects."

Farley lowered the visor and looked at her. The jumbled letter blocks of time and event were spelling out a message.

"It's trying to communicate with us," he said. "Isn't it?"

"Is a baby alive? Aren't you a hammer that decides what to hit?"

She stood on the cliff top before the artificial sun went out. And she stood outside the door to the control room. And she held the rail on the staircase platform. And she pointed at the locus from the ledge of the machine. Can you feel it? And she looked at him and smiled.

And the green light flared and the world paled out to white.

THIRTY-SIX

Broben took a deep breath and pressed his throat mike. "Pilot to flight engineer. You're sure about this."

"Flight engineer here," came Wen's voice. He sounded like he had marbles in his mouth and the world's worst nose cold. He had insisted on manning the top turret even though his nose was broken and one side of his face looked like he was storing nuts. "The bugs'll come through for us, lieutenant."

"Uh-huh." Broben nudged the throttle underhanded and the *Fata Morgana* began to roll toward the huge blank wall of closed main door directly ahead.

"Tail gunner to pilot," said Francis. *"There's one of those milk trucks headed our way at six o'clock. It's got a big antenna on top."*

Broben looked up at the overhead panel and held his palms out. "Milk truck at six o'clock, roger," he said. "Open fire the second it's in range. Go for the bowl or the tires. Martin, get back downstairs."

"Back in the ball, roger."

Broben turned on the running lights and saw that the hangar door had begun to move. A slit of outside canyon slowly widened. Wen's crawly little friends had come through after all.

Beyond the opening door Broben saw the troop transport returning from its encounter with the demolition team. It was headed straight toward the *Morgana*.

Broben deathgripped the control wheel. God *damn* it. Friggin glaciers move faster than this door. He needed a hundred and four feet and it had opened maybe thirty.

A brief burst of loud jackhammering from the back of the bomber.

It'll have to do, thought Broben, and shoved the throttle full forward and let off the brake. The engines roared and the brake shoes squealed and the *Morgana* lumbered toward the widening exit. Broben gritted his teeth. It was going to be awfully—

The left wingtip brushed the door as it swept by. The bomber transitioned from smooth floor to canyon ground. They were out. They were out.

A bright red thread shot past the bomber and a patch of ground erupted ahead of them.

"Top turret here," came Wen's voice. *"We're taking fire from the wall."*

"Right waist gun," said Everett. *"Sten says it's their automatic system."*

Broben headed straight toward the approaching troop transport. "Come on, sweetheart," he told the bomber. "Just give me ten feet."

At the last second he pulled back on the yoke. The nose came up and the bomber lifted. The transport shot beneath the ball turret and the tail wheel rolled across the transport roof. Then the bomber dropped back down to the canyon floor.

"Holy crap that was close," came Martin's voice.

Broben steered past boulders barely visible in the bomber's up-angled wing lights and looked for a long stretch of level ground.

Something hit the top of the fuselage hard enough to rock the aircraft. Broben forced himself not to look away from the canyon floor. "Pilot here, what's the damage?"

"Flight engineer here, we took a hit, no idea what. Rochester's taking a look."

"Who the hell is—" Broben began, then remembered who Rochester was. "Roger," he said, and tried to focus on steering the bomber. They were jouncing hard now, and Broben had to back off on the throttle until he found ground he could use as a runway. The

Morgana may have been a great bomber, but she was a lousy bus.

There. A long flat stretch of level ground, right where he remembered. *Thank you, Jesus, I promise I'll stop gambling when I'm back.*

The engines didn't sound anywhere near loud enough, but the RPM gauges rose smoothly, the manifold pressure looked good, and the bomber was accelerating quickly.

"Top turret to pilot. That zap truck's gaining, lieutenant."

"Unless they got wings, I don't give a shit."

The throttle was full forward and the RPM hit 2500. The control wheel began shuddering. Broben surveyed gauges: Tachometer; fuel, oil, and manifold pressure; oil, engine, and carb temperature. Everything was sweet as could be, and the engines were purring like kittens. The airspeed indicator read eighty. *Now we're talking.* The ground ahead looked clear.

"Top turret to pilot. I dunno what they got under the hood, but they're catching up."

"Roger." Flaps up, rudder neutral, elevator trim minus nine percent. One hundred miles per hour, and the canyon walls were rolling by. One-fifteen.

Arrivederci, chumps, Broben thought, and pulled back on the yoke.

Nothing happened.

He pushed forward on the wheel and looked to see if anything lay in their path. "Shorty, get up here!"

"On my way."

"Boney, call out anything in front of us!"

"Roger," came the bombardier's laconic voice as he sat in the front bubble. *"Looks good up ahead."*

Shorty climbed up from the pit. The left wheel hit a bump and he grabbed at the copilot seat.

"Siddown!" yelled Broben. "Grab the folder by the seat and read the top page."

"Tail gunner to pilot," came Francis' voice. *"The truck's a thousand yards and closing."*

"Roger." Broben glanced at Shorty, who was frowning at the sheet. "Out loud, genius," he said.

"Um—" Shorty frowned at the checklist. "Form 1A—checked?"

"Skip it."

"Controls and seats—checked?"

"Yeah yeah."

"Fuel transfer valves and switch—off."

Broben glanced at the controls. "Check."

Boney's voice crackled in Broben's headset. *"Big rock, eleven o'clock, two hundred yards."*

Broben glanced out the forward window. "Bombardier, don't report anything unless we're gonna hit it or fall into it."

"Roger," said Boney. *"We're not going to hit it."*

"Mr. Dubuque?" said Broben.

Shorty tore his gaze away from the window. "Sorry. Uh, inter-coolers—cold."

Broben looked. "Check."

"Top turret here; they're five hundred yards and closing at six o'clock."

"Gyros—uncaged."

Broben didn't look. "Check," he said.

"Fuel shutoff switches—"

"Open," Broben interrupted.

"That antenna's aiming at us."

"Smoke 'em if you got 'em," Broben ordered.

"Roger," said Francis. The tail gun hammered.

"Gear switch neutral?" Shorty said.

"Yes, god damn it."

From the top turret Wen opened fire on the pursuing transport.

"Bombardier to pilot, there's a ridge dead ahead, three hundred yards."

Broben glanced out the window. A frozen lava ripple ten feet high and hundreds of yards long lay directly ahead.

"Elevators unlocked?" asked Shorty.

"Darn," said Francis. *"I'm jammed."*

"Say again, Shorty," said Broben.

"Um—" Shorty glanced at the sheet. "Elevators unlocked?"

"Bingo!" Broben reached out and unlocked the elevators. He pulled back on the yoke and the bumping stopped and the ground drained from the windshield as the *Fata Morgana* left the alien ground.

THIRTY-SEVEN

The cliff rose flat and smooth from dense white mist, too regular to be natural. Its top was flat and bare, too level and too square. Identical cliffs rose in the distance, little islands in an even fog, floating rocks on top of clouds. Castles in the air.

The sky was blank.

Farley sat on the edge of the cliff with his feet dangling and looked down on the undifferentiated carpet of mist, following it out until it blended with the jejune sky. No horizon could be seen.

Beside him Wennda said, "I like the view."

As he turned and saw her face he felt her fingers twined with his and knew she'd been here all along. Her hand cool and familiar and welcome in his. Her face home to his wayfaring heart.

He smiled at her. "I'm afraid there isn't any view," he said.

"There is from where I'm sitting."

He laughed and squeezed her hand and looked around. Their surroundings incomplete and unconvincing. "Are we really here?" he asked.

"I'm not sure that here is really here."

He turned toward her at a sudden fearful thought. "Wennda. Are we—"

She put a finger on his mouth. "I think we had to do a lot more than climb a hill to be alone this time," she said.

Farley kissed the finger and took it from his lips. "But—how can we be at the Dome?"

Her hair moved languidly as she shook her head. "More like somebody's bad memory of it."

"I don't understand." He held up a hand. "I don't want to understand. Just—" He made a leveling motion.

She smiled. "You don't want me to save you, Joe?"

"You already have."

She leaned against him. His arm across her shoulders. The smell of her hair. The solid reassurance of her the most convincing thing here.

They kicked their feet at the end of the world.

The last thing he remembered: Standing on the narrow platform at the heart of the machine that housed the top-shaped thing that frayed the real.

"We don't have long," Wennda finally said.

"We never did."

"Oh, Joe." The sad acceptance in her voice was heartbreaking. "I really hoped it would be your beach."

"It's all right." He pulled her tighter. "It doesn't matter now."

The mist below them began to darken.

Wennda's back went stiff beneath his arm. She glanced around and then stood up and went to the center of the squared clifftop. Farley quickly followed.

"It's not fair!" Wennda yelled up at the uniformly darkening sky. "Why'd you even bring us together?"

"Wennda—"

She looked at him. Her expression fierce enough to stop him. Then the anger melted but the intensity remained.

All was twilight now.

"Hold on to me, Joe," she said.

The naked simplicity of it. Here at the end of everything he took her in his arms and held her close, just as he had mere days ago forever back upon the clifftop in the Dome. The gesture conjuring their fearful wonder at that first admission.

"Yone was right," she breathed against his ear. "They made a god."

"I don't care," said Farley, and he didn't. Gods, machines, wars, duty, command. None of it. All he cared about was her, here, now.

"It's coming apart," she said, and pressed hard against him. "I don't know if we'll still be together when it's gone."

He leaned back and smiled as the prop of world grew dark around them. Her face a map of a country he would never fully know now. "It's okay," he said. "We're connected, remember?"

She laid her head against his shoulder. "We are. Thank you for remembering."

"Always."

She lifted her head suddenly and looked at him. "I want more time," she said. She looked up. "I want more *time*," she demanded of the artificial sky.

He set a finger on her mouth and leaned his head toward hers and closed his eyes and felt full dark enshroud their imitated world.

And shred.

* * * * *

"Captain? Captain Farley?"

Farley opened his eyes. The ghost of a tornado towered above him, pale green in its silent churning, distorting stars behind it as it flickered in an indigo sky. He lay blinking at it, thinking about gods and powers and manifestations. Pillars of smoke, pillars of fire, voices from whirlwinds, messages to reluctant prophets.

Someone shook him again. "Captain." Yone's voice.

Farley sat up. He was on a slope a hundred feet above the crater floor. Hard ground and grit against his palms. Cold air, no wind. Predawn light delineating the stark angles of a surrounding horizon of cliff and dark recesses of fissure openings miles away. Yone kneeling beside him, scraped face piebald with dried blood and

320

lined with worry. Wennda curled up on her side and stirring awake.

Wennda—

Symmetrical cliffs floating on thick mist. A white sky darkening. A kiss farewell almost.

Farley reached for her and she sat up gasping as if dashed with cold water and blinked uncomprehending.

"It's all right," said Farley. "It's okay."

Wennda stared at him. "Was I—" She looked around the crater floor, craned her head up at the coruscating vortex. Looked back at Farley. "Were *we*—"

"We are outside the well," said Yone. "Above the crater floor." He spread his arms.

Farley realized Yone had heard her ask *Where are we?*

"Outside the well," repeated Farley. He stood and looked upslope and saw that it ended abruptly not ten feet up.

Wennda regarded him with an expression he could not have named. "Were you there?" she asked.

"I think I was," he said. A slanted smile. "I'm just not sure if *there* was really there."

He helped her to her feet and helped Yone up the slope until the three of them stood on its rounded lip and stared down into the well. Its bore a quarter-mile wide at least and mostly dark. Isolated pinprick lights and hardplaned surfaces suggested many levels, a mosaic of scaffolds, stairwells, ledges, ramps, pipes, tunnel mouths. The core of some abandoned city faithfully abiding. "How did we get here?" Wennda asked. "I can't remember." But she cocked her head as if trying to reconcile conflicting memories instead of trying to retrieve the true ones.

"I am not certain, either," said Yone. "I only just woke up before you did."

"I remember a curving hallway," Farley said. "Running down a white curved hallway with both of you. After we left the machine."

"The machine." Yone's head cocked like the RCA Victor dog.

"Are you kidding me? Jesus, it was the size of a battleship." Farley heard the note of desperation in his voice.

Yone shook his head.

Farley turned to Wennda. "Tell me you remember."

Wennda squinted and frowned.

"The curving white hallway?" Farley pressed. "The chair in the door?" The details came back to him as he said them as if conjured by their incantation. He turned to Yone. "The stairs that went down two hundred feet? The locus?"

"A coffee cup!" said Wennda. And looked delighted at the memory's retrieval.

"A coffee cup," Farley agreed. "On a desk in a room that opened out into a huge space that held an enormous machine that held the locus. It was very small."

"But you just said it was enormous."

"The machine was enormous. The locus was small." He held his fingers an inch apart.

Wennda looked on the verge of tears. "I don't *remember*."

Yone looked away from the vast sink of the well. "But we are here," he said. "That is the important thing, yes? We are here! We are alive!" He nodded at the dark recess of the northern fissure. The upper line of the western cliff paling as the gradient of imminent day grew in the east. "We can rejoin your men," Yone told them. "It may not be too late."

"You don't have to talk me into it," said Farley. "Let's go."

* * * * *

Molten gold was welling in a foundry of ring-wall cleft as they walked down the slope with the steady knee-bend of descending hikers, their resurrected shadows leaning toward the west. A faint warm wind began to stir.

322

Farley stopped suddenly. His head cocked and his eyes narrowed as he took some inner measure.

"Joe?" said Wennda

Farley held up a hand.

Yone closed his eyes and stood listening. A faint drone grew in the distance.

Wennda glanced around. There was nothing to hide behind or under, nowhere they could run to except back into the massive well. "We have to find cover," she said. "We're too exposed here."

Farley looked at her like a man jerked suddenly awake. "We aren't exposed nearly enough," he said.

Yone opened his eyes and saw Wennda's perplexed look. "It isn't the Typhon," he told her.

Farley's grin was startling. "Not unless it grew radial engines, it's not," he said, and pointed north.

As if summoned by the gesture, the *Fata Morgana* shot out of the distant northern fissure like something fleeing the gate of hell.

THIRTY-EIGHT

"They are turning," Yone announced.

Farley lowered Wennda's com panel, which he had been using as a signal mirror. "They sure as hell are," he said.

A third of the way around the crater rim, the *Morgana* was banking hard right and peeling off from the rim wall. The unmistakable drone of four Wright Cyclone engines carried across the upcurved plain, the only sound there was to hear. Farley watched in mute wonder as his ship leveled off and headed straight for them. She flashed her landing lights and waggled her wings, and Farley felt his heart set sail. She was absolutely beautiful, and she was coming to take them home.

He turned to Wennda with his first carefree grin in what seemed like months. "Let's go hitch a ride," he said. They got on either side of Yone and practically carried him the rest of the way down to the crater floor.

A mile out the bomber banked to their right and descended. The landing gear lowered and Wennda and Yone let out a cheer. Farley laughed like a kid at a fireworks show. "Come on," he shouted.

He and Wennda skip-carried Yone toward the descending Flying Fortress like contestants in some picnic game. "We'll get sunburned on *ten* beaches back in the States," Farley promised Wennda. "We'll go dancing at the Avalon on Catalina. Artie Shaw, Glenn Miller. We'll drink a pint in this pub in Thurgood, Yone. English beer! It's like motor oil. You'll love it." He was babbling, giddy, nearly stumbling as he watched his bomber angle down toward the ground. He could make out someone standing in the right waist window. Everett? It had to be. Everett! Farley tried to wave and nearly fell. He laughed.

The *Morgana* touched down. Dirt kicked up behind her tires.

"Come on, come *on*!" Farley shouted. Wennda laughed.

The *Morgana* slowed to a stop and then turned smartly and began to rumble back their way. They were breathing hard by the time the bomber swiveled a quarter-turn right and came to rest a hundred feet away. Shorty's artwork nearly glowed beneath the pilot window in the early morning light. Floating rocks that looked like castles, the uncanny likeness of the woman who now stood beside Farley ethereal and impossible on the riveted hull. Worn out and beat up as he was, Farley could not stop grinning.

The pilot window slid aside and Jerry stuck his head out and doffed his cap. "Taxi, mister?" he yelled. His own grin big enough to unzip his head.

The crew came spilling out as if the bomber were on fire, Everett and Garrett and Sten from the waist, Martin and Shorty hopping out after them, Francis emerging from his own rear hatch. All the crew in thermal suits and headgear, Sten in cling-fitting body armor. Farley and Wennda and Yone were caught up in the press of bodies and grinning yelling faces and hard slaps on the back, and Yone was hoisted up by Everett and Garrett and carried toward the bomber like some visiting noble. Plavitz and Boney dropped from the forward hatch and waved at Farley and grinned at Yone upon the big men's shoulders. Boney bent to the landing gear and chocked the tires. Their own mother hen who saw to all the details.

Farley laughed and looked to Wennda to say something, but Wennda seemed to be having a serious talk with Sten in the midst of all the shouts and laughter.

Francis' goofy face filled Farley's vision, joyously yelling something Farley couldn't make out. His gauze eyepatch was gone and his eye looked perfectly normal, not a scar, not a scab, not even a bruise. Farley grabbed the lanky tail gunner's shoulders and gave him a good squeeze and shake. Past him Farley saw Wen hop down to the crater floor. *Wen!* Son of a bitch. He looked like he'd had the living hell beat out of him, face swollen and bruising. But Wen! Alive! Wen saw Farley gaping at him and he smiled his slanted smirk and touched his cap bill.

Everybody was telling Farley what had happened all at once. "Tell me at the Boiler Room!" Farley shouted. "First round's on me!"

Wennda was looking upset now as Sten spoke to her. Farley realized that Arshall was missing. Sten looked insistent and a little wild-eyed. He pointed north, toward the fissure that led to the Redoubt. Farley strained to hear.

Shorty saw his worried look. "He's probably telling her about that aquarium," he told Farley.

Farley looked at him.

"That joint's *kaput*," Shorty said. "Finished. They were barely hanging on as it was, and Wen got their repair bugs to turn against them. Can you believe it? It's all over but the mop-up."

Wennda turned toward Farley and looked at him in utter dismay. He felt the bottom drop out of his gut. "Not if her people don't find out about it, it isn't," he realized. "And there's only Sten to tell them."

He glanced up at the cockpit window. Jerry saluted him somberly, then grinned like a fox with a weekend pass to Henville. Farley felt the engine's guttural rumble through his feet.

He frowned. No. Not the engines.

He looked down. Glanced north and oriented himself from his memory of the underground complex.

The rumbling intensified. Farley turned toward the blunted cone of the well half a mile away. From its throat he heard a rising turbine whine, the voice of the devil calling from the Pit. He opened his mouth to yell a warning just as the Typhon streaked massive and hellbent from the well and up into the injured sky.

* * * * *

326

The men were turning toward the bomber even before Farley yelled for them to get on board. Farley glanced up at the streaking weapon banking as it climbed the sky and saw the great loop that the Typhon meant to make. They had a minute at the most before it hit its strafing run.

He waved for Broben's attention, then made a cranking motion. Broben raised a gloved hand.

"Everybody on board!" Farley yelled. *"Let's go let's go!"*

He saw Wennda and he stopped.

She stood rooted to the crater floor and looked at him from far away. From two hundred years away. Her expression a forlorn resolve that wrenched his heart.

Farley could not move. Could not speak. The engines revving up behind him. Crewmen calling to his back. In the air the living weapon reckoning the calculus of their destruction.

Wennda, Farley said. Thought he said.

They hurried to each other.

"I have to go," he told her.

"I have to stay," she said.

Farley's puppet heart unstrung. He looked back at the bomber. Everett and Garrett beckoned to him from the waist hatch. The languid motions of their arms like underwater fronds. Wen's silhouette in the upper turret. The twin guns slowly swiveling and angling up.

"Wennda—" he began.

She put a hand to his cheek and shook her head.

A wave of grief washed over him that nearly buckled his knees. He felt gutpunched.

"Doing the right thing feels lousy," he said.

"Doing what we want would feel worse."

"It still feels lousy." He shook his head bitterly. "We're not people who could sit on a beach while the world burns, anyhow."

"Maybe there's a world where we are."

"It isn't this one."

"No." She shook her head again. "This is the one where duty wins."

From the cockpit Broben slapped the metal right above the painting of her face. *"For the love of God!"* he yelled. *"Kiss her, already!"*

Farley turned back to her. Tears brewed in her eyes and she smiled the most burdened smile he would ever see. "Time," she said.

They held each other close and closed their eyes and kissed. The promised moment finally fulfilled. The whole world halting. Warm wind on the crater floor. Insistent engines growling. Their artificial world dissolving. I want more *time.*

He leaned back and looked at her and fixed her firmly in his heart. "I'll never forget you, Wennda," he said.

She took his hand and kissed his fingers and then set them over her heart. Then they let each other go and turned to shape their separate paths. Goodbye. Goodbye.

Farley glanced at the sky. He held a hand up to Jerry and started running.

Broben pulled his head back into the cockpit and slid the window shut. "Thank Christ," he muttered.

Everett reached out to hoist Farley on board. For a moment just before he stepped up into the hatch Farley let his hand linger on the thin metal hull.

THIRTY-NINE

Farley skidded in a congealed mess on the deck. Bright red blood was splashed all over the main compartment. The smell was unbelievable.

Near a bulkhead Yone was pulling on a smartsuit one of the crew had given him as he warily eyed a spidery repair drone that seemed to be manning the right waist gun.

Farley accepted this without question and hurried past Shorty at his table. There was blood all over the radio room floor. He moved carefully over the bomb bay catwalk and saw blood splashed on the bomb doors. It looked like a cow had been butchered in the lower pit.

Broben was already preflighting in the copilot seat. "Left throttle at fifty percent," Farley said as he climbed into his left-hand seat and reached for his headset. "I want—"

He stopped. Glanced around.

"Captain?" Broben said. He was already walking the left throttle forward, and One and Two were smoothly revving up.

Farley shook his head. Something felt different. He'd sensed it the moment he sat down. But he couldn't place it and there sure as hell wasn't time to hash it out. "I want your hand on the brake," he finished. "When I say *now,* release it and give her full right throttle."

"Release the brake, full right throttle, roger," said Broben.

Farley checked the props and cowlings on Number One and

Number Two. Not a hint of smoke or oil. Wen had done a hell of a repair job. Or someone had, anyway.

Through the window he saw Wennda and Sten running toward the rising cone that ringed the well. He craned his head and saw the Typhon. Seven o'clock high and coming hard around into its strafing dive.

"Top gunner to pilot," came Wen's voice.

"I see it," Farley snapped. "Everybody quiet."

The distant wedge of living weapon grew with frightening speed. The wings cupped and went rigid and the Typhon came even faster. A thin beam of bright green light stabbed out from one curled wing and held steady on the fuselage.

"Joe?" said Broben.

Farley could make out features now. The curved raked wings, the sweptback head, the pinioning patches of eyes. *You hate me, don't you, you son of a bitch.* The green targeting beam held steady as the mythic Fury plummeted. *You hate my airplane.* Something bulged from beneath the Typhon's right wing. *Nothing ever hit you back before, and you don't like it one damn bit.*

The extrusion lit up white from deep within the bore.

Farley gave the bomber hard left rudder. "Now," he said.

Broben released the brake and the bomber wheeled left and rolled forward in a narrowing turn as the right throttle came up to full.

White light bleached the world. The ground behind them erupted into dust. The blast wave lurched the bomber forward. The Typhon streaked overhead and arced away.

"We need to be in the air before it comes around again," said Farley. *And pray like hell there's nothing in the way, Captain Midnight, because this is your runway now.*

"Speed eighty-five," said Broben.

Farley glanced at him in disbelief and then checked the gauge himself. Eighty-five. "How much did Wen hotrod this thing?" he asked. "She's driving like a Cadillac."

"Shit," said Broben. "Wait till you *fly* her."

A few seconds later Broben called out one fifteen. "One fifteen, roger," Farley said, and pulled back on the yoke.

Fata Morgana regained the sky.

* * * * *

The instant she was back in her element and Broben brought her wheels up Farley understood that he was leaving with a lot more bomber than he'd arrived with. She climbed faster. Her engines ran smoother, cooler, quieter. But the more important difference wasn't something that the gauges showed. It was something he felt. A difference in the metal body that his brain controlled. He didn't muscle her, he didn't even steer her, really. He *suggested*. The *Morgana* he had flown here had been a dependable draft horse. Now she was a thoroughbred.

* * * * *

In the top turret Wen tracked the Typhon with the twin .50s as it banked right, climbing skyward like a rocket-powered mockingbird. He reported this to the captain and the B-17 immediately banked left.

"*That thing's gonna have another go at us,*" Farley announced. "*I'm heading for the canyon to cut down its options. Things are probably going to get hairy, so everybody stay sharp.*"

Wen patted the metal beneath the plexiglas blister. "Don't you embarrass me, now, girl," he said.

* * * * *

"So you got a plan?" Broben asked as fissure walls shot by on either side and the *Morgana* flew into twilight.

"I wouldn't go that far," said Farley, and thumbed the mike. "Everybody listen up. That thing's going to come in high and behind. We're going to hang a U and head right down its throat. Everybody strap in, tie down, and hold on." He eased the aircraft close to the right-hand cliff wall streaking by. "Call in when you get a sighting. Martin, it's your turn in the barrel."

"Roger that, captain," Martin responded from the belly turret. *"What do you need me to do?"*

"I want you to shoot the son of a bitch in two," said Farley. He banked a tight left in the steep corridor of jagged canyon. Broben nervously watched the cliff face blurring by. Pilot training hadn't covered hairpinning a bomber in a friggin hallway.

Farley looked at Broben as he told Martin, "Be ready and be quick."

"Nine o'clock high," came Everett's voice. *"Holy gosh it's fast."*

Farley gripped the wheel and brought them around tight and noted as they lined up on the fissure that the bomber was squarely in the center of the canyon. She had turned with tons of room to spare.

"Balls to the wall, Jer," he said.

They walked the throttles forward. The *Morgana* leveled off and sped to meet the diving Typhon. Farley saw it now, a distant wedge framed in the ragged strip of canyon sky.

"It's gonna hit us high, Joe," said Broben.

Farley shook his head, remembering the simulations the Typhon had run in its hangar bay. *You figured out what the Luftwaffe pilots learned, didn't you?* Farley thought at the oncoming shape.

The Typhon plunged below the level of the bomber, then shot up with a suddenness that would have killed a human pilot.

Farley held steady. *We've got one gun up front and we can't get out of the way. That's what you know.*

The Typhon leveled off and came straight at them, wings raked back and level.

You can come in faster and hit harder and veer off closer than a Messerschmitt can, Farley thought, and thumbed his mike. "Pilot to belly gunner," he said, and heard the measured calm of barrage flying in his voice. "On my signal."

The Typhon was two miles off and growing in the windshield.

Farley took a deep breath. Held it. *And all we can do up front is shoot and pray,* he thought. *That's what you're counting on, isn't it?*

Farley made out the bulge of weapon pod beneath the Typhon's right wing.

Broben was pressing back in his seat as if he wanted to crawl over the back.

But you went up against a different bomber in your little game. That's what I'm *banking on.*

The black core of the pod sparked white.

Farley cut the wheel hard right and hauled it back as he mashed the right rudder to full. The twenty-ton bomber groaned its shuddering length and cut a quarter-turn snap roll to the right, broad wings going knife-edge vertical.

"Now," said Farley. He was already giving opposite aileron as the nose came down into the hard evasive right no bomber in Creation should have made. Broben heard rivets pop. The crew were pressed against the hull like clothes in a spinning washer.

No one saw the depleted-uranium shell tear past the belly of the bomber at five times the speed of sound. No one saw the Typhon roll to its right and veer in the opposite direction, both aircraft passing belly to belly like jousting gods.

No one but Martin. Curled in the ball turret like some creature waiting to be born, massive fissure walls rushing past him in a dizzying streak on either side, twin guns aimed straight ahead, grips in his hands familiar as the stitches on a baseball. Feeling the old worn leather of the medicine bag against his chest and thinking of his grandfather's words about Wakínyan Tanka the Thunderbird when he was a child. And praying to whatever gods there were that he would not let his crewmates down.

The world turned ninety degrees as the bomber snap-rolled right.

In his ears his captain's voice said *Now,* and as Martin pressed the firing button something shot along the bomber's length so close and fast it left a hole behind it in the air. Martin rotated after it, chasing vapor, shooting ghosts, and just as the guns rolled perpendicular to the belly of the bomber standing on its right wing, the entire Typhon filled his world, a prehistoric shark streaking by a minnow, itself planed right and veering, mottled belly nearly raking bomber belly. And Martin's guns still fired pulverizing rounds the size of grease pencils that stitched along the exposed length of living weapon, that ripped divots of metal and flesh and tore through the elegant engineering of the thing's insides—

—and past.

* * * * *

The Flying Fortress peeling off and arcing down into the chasm.

Martin panting. Staring at an empty space. Medicine bag rising and falling underneath his thermal suit. Twin barrels hot and cutting through the empty air.

* * * * *

The nose dropped down and Farley kicked the aileron left and gave her hard left rudder and pushed forward on the yoke, the bomber falling sideways out across the canyon in a massive peel-out. He righted her and brought the rudder to neutral and kept her diving to pick up speed as she headed toward the western cliff wall half a mile away.

"Pilot to belly gunner, report."

Farley brought her around in a broad and gentle curve, losing height but gaining speed. He still had a thousand feet to spare.

"Belly gunner, report," Farley repeated. "What's the story, Martin?"

Everybody heard the belly gunner breathing in their headphones. Then:

"Up and in, captain."

Farley exhaled. "Nice pitch, chief."

"Nice call, sir."

"Tail gunner to pilot," came Francis' adolescent voice. *"That thing's at six o'clock low and headed away down the canyon. It's pretty low. I think it's kind of busted up."*

The sudden cheering over the headphones made Farley wince. "Roger that," he said. "We did some fancy dancing there. Everybody report in. Wen, give me a status check."

He glanced at Broben. The copilot was staring at him in total disbelief.

"What?" demanded Farley. He glanced at the air speed indicator and leveled off.

"'What?'" Broben looked around: *You believe this guy?* "You can't *do* what you just did, is what."

Farley shrugged. "I hear bumblebees can't fly," he said.

* * * * *

Jogging south along the sunlit crater floor, Wennda suddenly paused. Sten slowed and looked back questioningly. Wennda frowned and held a hand up.

A faint drone grew in the distance.

Sten looked around the bare and sunlit ground. No shadows and no cover.

"We have to find cover," Sten said. "We're too exposed here."

"It's not the Typhon."

Sten frowned. "It's not?"

"Not unless it grew radial engines," Wennda said. And smiled.

"Grew what?" asked Sten.

Wennda wiped her eyes and pointed north. Five miles away the *Fata Morgana* flew out from between the northern fissure walls, morning sunlight glinting from her cockpit windows, and began to trace the crater's rim, and began to climb.

I'm with you, Joe.

She kissed her fingers and patted her heart, and turned to start the great work of shaping her new world.

FORTY

"Sixteen five," called Broben.

The gyros were out, the azimuth indicator rolled, the compass spun, and every indicator was topped out except for altitude. Wen had said the ship would come through better this time out, and Farley had no choice but to believe him.

"Sixteen five, roger," Farley said. He looked from the crazed instrument panel to the violent colors traced with frozen lightning in the air three miles away. His eyes hurt with the colors' throbbing and he looked away. Below, the vast bowl of crater curved up to the notched rim wall.

"Speed two two five."

"Two two five, roger." Farley looked at Broben. "You ready?"

"You're kidding, right?"

Farley smirked. "Pilot to crew," he said. "We've got no reason to think that going back will be any different than getting here was, so get ready. Someone'll probably want to give Yone a hand." He paused a moment, thinking how to put what he wanted to say. Finally he just said, "If anybody wants to pray or do their lucky dance, now's the time. I'll see you on the other side."

"There's a couple ways you can take that," Broben pointed out.

"I mean all of them," said Farley. He brought the ship around to bearing one hundred sixty-eight degrees and headed for the maw of crackling light.

* * * * *

Yone sat on the canvas duffel cradling a green walkaround oxygen bottle. The temperature was zero degrees Fahrenheit at this altitude, and the lethal cold reached through the insulating smartsuit Shorty had given him. His teeth would not stop chattering and the scrape along his face felt pressed by a flatiron.

Garrett handed him a strip cut from a handkerchief and lowered his oxygen mask to show how he had twisted the ends of another strip and shoved them into his nose.

"Listen!" Garrett shouted. "You're gonna get a splitting headache and your nose is gonna bleed like you got punched!" He pointed at the U of fabric hanging absurdly from his nose. "If it gets into your mask, it'll freeze and you won't be able to breathe!"

Yone nodded and began twisting his handkerchief strip. Garrett patted him and yelled "Attaboy!" and Everett gave him a thumbs-up.

The fuselage began to shake. Bright blue threads of light crawled on the right-side machine gun.

Garrett lowered his mask again. "Interphone's out!" he announced.

The bomber bucked hard. Yone lifted up from the deck and nearly landed on Garrett. The light outside the ship was bright and shot with violet and dull red.

Yone winced at a sudden splitting headache. The hairs on the back of his neck stood up. He tasted metal and realized that his nose was bleeding heavily.

Everett made a pained face and lifted his mask and spat an alarming clot of red.

The hull around them shuddered.

The repair drone, Rochester, flowed into the compartment from the radio room. The bug was lit up with webbed lightning like a madman's Christmas tree. Suddenly the drone stopped moving as if it had hit a wall.

An all-consuming roar as the bomber slammed out of the world.

PART THREE: THE MISSION
(continued)

FORTY-ONE

The Flying Fortress was, as the Americans would say, a sitting duck.

The squadron of Messerschmitt Bf 109s circled high above the deadly array of exploding antiaircraft shells, and when the Allied bombers completed their run on the high-security munitions plant and turned out of the dense flak field, the fighters were ready.

Squadron Commander Adler dove down to take on the lead bomber. Oberleutnant Jürgen Große followed a hundred meters behind his commander's left wing. The third in their group, Leutnant Jaeger, flew behind Große in line with the commander's right wing.

Flak had crippled the huge enemy aircraft. The rear gunner's canopy was shattered and the right-side elevator was a dangling amputation. Evasive maneuvers were out of the question for the laboring bomber; the German fighters would be able to take their time and pick their damage.

Hauptmann Adler lined up on the tail of the wounded bomber. Große and Jaeger hung back to let him draw first blood. The Flying Fortress and three trailing Messerschmitts looked locked in place as they made a sweeping right turn that brought the flak field back in view above and ahead of them.

A shock went through Große's gloved hands. He flinched back and saw bright blue lines come alive across his compact instrument panel like a little lightning storm. All the gauges were in the red and the indicators were going crazy. At first Große thought that the panel had short-circuited. Then he looked up from the instruments and saw the damaged bomber caged in lightning.

Directly behind it, Adler fired his wing guns. The rounds shot past, a low near miss. The ball turret spun and returned fire.

Große's earphones screeched piercingly. Große winced and raised a gloved hand to tear the headset off. The hand stopped.

Angry colors churned the air ahead of the descending bomber. Hauptmann Adler's Messerschmitt was outlined in bluewhite light.

As Adler fired another burst the struggling bomber vanished.

An instant later the entire front section of Adler's fighter simply disappeared. The Messerschmitt looked sawn in two across the wing line in front of the cockpit. The open front end of the severed fuselage lifted in the sudden barrage of air and began to spin.

Große stared as Adler unbuckled from his seat and climbed up from the truncated cockpit and stepped out into empty air. Adler shot backward in the slipstream and tumbled. A ribbon of lines and drag chute deployed above him and a white parachute blossomed in the thin and freezing air.

A slit formed in the air in front of Große. The edges parted like the gaping mouth of an ocean predator scooping prey—and the Flying Fortress he had been pursuing erupted back into the world from the opposite direction, shedding molten sparks like some feral hound uncollared by an angry god of war.

Große yanked the stick and snap-rolled right to corkscrew over the looming Flying Fortress impossibly hurtling toward him. As he spun he looked up at the bomber below him trailing embers like some awful metal comet streaming fire into the world, looked up to see two men in the cockpit gaping back at him in similar astonishment.

* * * * *

Farley and Broben stared up as the German fighter corkscrewed overhead and past, the hard roar of its overthrottled engine fading in an empty vista of pale blue sky.

For a moment the gliding bomber creaked in a bed of wind. Then came a sound like distant popcorn popping, followed by a steady thud of 20-millimeter cannon fire.

Farley made a gentle turn and the sky ahead became full of approaching American bombers and streaking German fighters and exploding flak. Wisps of black smoke hung suspended in the air like flimsy jellyfish.

"Son of a *bitch*," said Broben.

Guttural coughing from the left side made Farley look to see Number One prop spinning up. Number Two engine suddenly belched and fired up.

Broben looked right. "Three and Four are coming up," he called.

On the instrument panel all the gauges topped out and then swung to measure correctly.

"We got juice," Broben announced.

Farley felt the bomber come alive around him, felt it supple through his gloved hands on the wheel. He increased their dive to pick up speed and head below the oncoming bomber formation—the formation he'd been leading seven days ago.

Huge columns of smoke roiled from the ground ahead. The bomb target. They had made their run above it half a life ago, it seemed, and now there it was ahead of them only seconds after the drop. He saw that Martin had been right when he'd reported that the munitions plant had been hit but not seriously damaged.

Static screeched in Farley's ears. Then Everett's voice was yelling, *"Bandits bandits five o'clock high seven o'clock low!"*

The waist-gun Brownings started hammering.

"I'm on the high one," Francis called out.

"Top turret here," came Wen's harsh twang. *"Those two Me's are comin' back around. Another one's spinning down to the deck. I see a parachute."*

Farley looked left to see if he could glimpse one of the fighters coming around for another run at them. Beside him Broben said, "Hey, what are you doing up here? You gotta get—"

A gun went off two feet away from Farley's head. He flinched, and the bomber lurched. A warm pistol barrel was shoved beneath his jaw. Farley went absolutely still.

A tight voice spoke in his ear. "Lower your wheels and turn on your lights," said Yone.

* * * * *

"Are we hit?" Wen called in Farley's headphones.

The blunt barrel remained against the underside of his jaw but the pressure lessened. Farley carefully turned his head to see Yone standing in the pit behind him, holding a service .45. Broben slumped against the right window, crush hat fallen over half his face as if he were taking a nap.

"Flight engineer to pilot," Wen said again. *"Did we get hit?"*

The top turret was behind and above them; Yone could hear Wen without a headset. "Tell him everything is fine," he said.

Farley could not look away from Jerry's lifeless body as he pressed his throat mike. "Pilot here," he said tonelessly. "Everything's fine."

Yone brought the gun away just long enough to pull the headset from Broben's head. Broben's crush cap tumbled to the cockpit floor and Farley saw his friend's slack features.

The gun pressed the soft underside of his jaw again. "Tell the men to stay where they are."

Farley's face was stone. "Stay at your posts," he said.

Yone quickly slid the headset on. "Now turn on your lights and lower your wheels."

"Go to hell."

Yone looked genuinely upset. "I know how hard this is, captain. But I can land this aircraft without you if I must. I would much prefer if you did it. You have been very kind to me. Lights and wheels, please."

Farley glared at the windshield. The pistol stayed on him as he leaned forward and watched his right hand flip on the landing lights and hit the left and right wheel switches. He sat back.

"Belly gunner to pilot. Captain, the wheels are lowering."

The pistol barrel pressed. "Shorty and your flight engineer must go into the main compartment and close the door," Yone said. "If it opens again, I will shoot whoever comes out."

"Wen," said Farley. "Go into the radio room and take Shorty into the main compartment. Shut the door behind you and keep it shut."

"What's going on, cap?" Shorty asked.

Wen ducked out of the top turret and looked down at Broben's body and the gun trained on the captain. His nose was purple and his lip was split and scabbed from the beating he had taken not an hour ago. "I knew something wasn't right about you soon as they tole me you was from the Redoubt," he said. "I shoulda said something."

"Go on, Wen," said Farley.

Wen glared cold hate at Yone and then went across the bomb bay catwalk. In front of the radio room he stopped and looked back. Yone shook his head at him. Wen spat on the deck and went in.

"Tail gunner here," said Francis. *"Those bandits are back on us, five and seven o'clock, but they're hanging back."*

"The landing gear's down," said Martin. *"They think we're surrendering."*

"Hell with that," from Garrett. *"I'll give 'em a burst so they know better."*

"Now you must tell them," Yone said.

Farley stared out at the horizon. "Pilot to crew," he heard himself say. "Yone's taken over the cockpit. He shot Lieutenant Broben. I've lowered the wheels to indicate our surrender. Do not fire on the enemy fighters."

Instead of outraged voices there was only bewildered silence. Then Shorty said, *"You're joking, right, captain?"*

Farley glanced at the .45 in the little man's hand. At the body of his best friend sagged against the window. "Everyone stand down," he said.

"Thank you," said Yone. "I'm sorry, but I need you to tip your wings."

Farley did as he was told.

A Messerschmitt came up to flank the bomber on the left. No one opened fire, and the fighter edged closer and drew alongside them. The goggled pilot studied the situation in the hijacked cockpit. Then he grinned broadly and saluted. He waggled his wings and moved ahead to take up shepherd position in front of the *Morgana*.

A shadow fell across the cockpit as another Bf 109 slid into place a hundred feet overhead. A third came alongside their right wing, and the lead fighter began a shallow dive. Farley followed. Far below was patchwork landscape crossed with roads. No hint of the fearsome weaponry unleashed in the air and on the ground behind them.

Farley's eyes narrowed. What was it Yone had said?

I can land this aircraft without you if I must.

Farley's knuckles went white on the control wheel. "That 109 on the crater floor," he said.

Beside him Yone gave a small and haunted smile. "I could not get the engine started after I came through," he said.

* * * * *

Another Messerschmitt drew up beside their left wing. The *Morgana* was bracketed by fighters now.

"I tried to make a life there," Yone told Farley. "But they were never going to trust me. I would always be the stranger. Then one day I heard a sound I had not for two long years. And you landed right in front of me. I thought, God has given me a way back."

Their escorts tightened their formation.

"I only meant to take a parachute and jump out once we were back. Even that was painful to consider. Because all of you had accepted me. The day you arrived you made me part of your crew. It would be a betrayal when I deserted. But I would be back where I belonged, and so would you. It was an honorable solution."

346

Farley saw an airfield in the distance now. All his options narrowed to a point. His future a stockade or a bullet.

"So what changed?" His voice was thick.

"Everything," Yone said. "Everything changed. Yesterday I was only a man trying to go home. Today I am a man chosen to bring back victory."

"It's just a bomber."

Yone barked a laugh. "Your aircraft? That thinking is the reason why you missed your opportunity, captain. I was brought to that world so that I could be given something incredible. As you were brought for me to bring it back. Our paths have been set by a force much greater than ourselves."

Farley glanced up at him with a look of wondering contempt. "You think God told you to do this?"

Yone was quiet so long that Farley thought he wasn't going to answer. Then he pulled an object from a pocket and held it out. "Something like a god," he said.

Beneath a gelatinous coating was an object the size of a quarter and shaped like a mushroom or a rounded top. It shimmered and blurred as if it were not entirely there.

Farley looked from the locus to Yone's triumphant face. "What have you done?"

Yone looked puzzled. "I have found an end to this terrible war. A way to save millions of lives."

"Yone. Listen to me. That thing's not a god. It's a weapon. An intelligent weapon. It's using you to bring itself back. It's making itself exist."

Yone shook his head. "You see only enemies and loyalties. You would rather fight your war than yield to a power that brings peace. The power to prevent the future we have seen."

A river roared in Farley's ears. He closed his eyes. "You've just *caused* the future we saw. The thing that ends the world in fifty years is in your goddamn hand."

"The thing that ends the *war*," Yone corrected. He smiled at the dampered locus in his hand. "You think I have not—"

The Messerschmitt in front of them exploded.

Both men flinched, and then the Typhon slid by like a passing battleship. The mottled belly gashed and bleeding fluid, the torn lengths staple-stitched and puckered divots rough-patched. Spindly repair drones clung to its savaged underside like ticks, methodically repairing even as the insane machine flowed by.

Yone gaped at it in mortal dread. "No," he said.

The Typhon rolled right and shed a dandruff of flailing repair drones. Farley glimpsed the seed-shaped weapon pod beneath the raked right wing, the sleek fury of the fearsome head as the unrelenting construct tore its damaged way across the contested German sky.

Farley looked up at Yone. "It's been guarding that thing you're holding for two hundred years," he said. "Did you think it would just let you fly away with it?" he said.

And Broben bolted upright in his copilot seat and pulled a steel plate from a flak-jacket pocket. He twisted around and rammed the plate into Yone's face. The blunt metal cracked the palate bone above Yone's upper teeth. His head snapped back and the headset cord tore from its jack and blood sprayed from his nose and mouth. His arms flailed and the gun went off. Wind hissed through the sudden hole in the top of the cockpit as Yone fell back into the lower pit—where Garrett knelt behind the bomb bay bulkhead, aiming his own service .45.

Garrett rushed to Yone and yanked him up and brought the small man's arms up into a full nelson. Broben dropped the metal plate and wrenched the pistol from Yone's hand. Farley glanced down at the steel plate and saw a flattened .45 slug in a dimple near the top.

Garrett turned Yone around and pinned him against the bulkhead and jammed his pistol up against Yone's eye. *"Why'd you do it?"* he yelled into Yone's bleeding face. *"Why would you do this?"*

Yone tried to say something and blood bubbled from his mouth.

"He's a Luftwaffe pilot," Broben said.

"He's a Nazi?" Garrett slammed Yone's head into the back of the copilot seat. "You're a stinking *Nazi*?"

348

A roaring wind tore into the bomber as the bomb bay doors swung open behind them.

* * * * *

"*Captain!*" Francis yelled in Farley's headset. "*That vulture's back, it's blowing everything out of the sky!*"

"Some details would be nice," Farley said automatically as he brought the landing gear back up.

"*Three miles back, seven o'clock level and coming back around. It's not flying so good, but holy jeez it's fast.*"

Farley turned ten degrees left and shoved the wheel hard forward. The *Morgana* dove. Dead ahead two miles away a massive column of smoke roiled above a cluster of low buildings. The munitions plant they had dropped on only minutes and a week ago.

A desperate idea formed.

"Come on, girl," Farley told his bomber.

* * * * *

From the radio room's opened doorway Everett and Shorty and Wen watched Garrett lurch toward the opened bomb bay. Yone hung bleeding from him like an untied butcher's apron.

The bomber nosed into a sudden dive and everybody grabbed what they could grab.

Yone began to struggle, and Broben climbed down and helped Garrett dead-carry him to the bomb bay entrance, fighting against the deafening wind and diving aircraft. Broben looked down through the opened bomb bay doors at a tree-lined road eight thousand feet below. He let go of Yone's legs and patted the writhing man's chest. "*Auf Wiedersehen*, Johann!" he yelled, and moved aside.

A voice cut through the raging wind. "Wait! *Wait!*"

349

Broben looked back to see Boney's lanky form unfold from the crawlway. He cradled a yard-long metal cylinder and struggled toward them. Broben saw a cotter pin in the top of it and recognized the fuse booster Farley had asked Boney to pull from the jammed bomb in case they had to blow the ship. Somehow he had hidden it where even Wen and his repair drones had not found it.

The bombardier raised the heavy cylinder high and pulled the collar of Yone's stretch armor and shoved the cylinder down the front. He looked Yone in the eye and yanked out the cotter pin.

Garrett heaved Yone out onto the little platform that led to the catwalk and dangled the bleeding man above a mile and a half of empty air. Yone kicked and screamed.

Boney leaned into the entryway and set a hand on Garrett's shoulder. "Not yet!" he said.

Garrett looked back in disbelief. Yone twisted in his grip and Garrett shook him like a terrier with a rat.

Boney squinted past the big man at the countryside sliding past below. He seemed to be performing some internal calculation. He closed his eyes and held up three gloved fingers and silently counted off, *three, two, one,* and then he opened his eyes and pointed. "Now," he said.

Garrett let go. Yone dropped screaming from the bomb bay and shot back in the slipstream.

Broben cupped his hands to his mouth. "Take *that* back to Hitler, you Nazi fuck," he yelled.

* * * * *

Farley plunged toward the climbing pillars of smoke. The engines strained, the airframe shook, the rushing wind sang off the wings. Farley's senses filled the metal and the bomber spoke to him in a language of rudder and flap and engine.

350

The smoke column towered before the diving bomber like a warning from a wrathful god. Craters clustered around the damaged factory at its base.

"*It's on us cap it's right behind us!*" Francis yelled in Farley's ears. "*That cannon on its wing is lighting up I think it's—*"

Farley pulled the yoke with all his might. His nose came up. The blood drained from his head. His wings creaked like cracking timbers. Red lace webbed his vision.

Hold on. Hold on.

* * * * *

In the shaking belly turret Martin hung like a bug in amber and watched the munitions factory grow before him with terrifying speed. They were going too fast and getting very low, and Martin couldn't see how they could pull out of the dive.

The bomb bay doors swung down in front of him. The crew was going to bail! They would leave him bolted in this metal coffin while the captain slammed the ship into the target and pulled the chasing Typhon with it.

Martin was about to yell for them to get him out when someone dropped out of the bomb bay and shot back under the turret. Martin swung around to look for a parachute—and saw the Typhon two hundred yards behind them. Wings swept and planed head straining forward. Beneath one wing the weapon pod sparked deep within the barrel, then blazed.

The falling man was scooped into that white-hot bore.

A jet of flame erupted from the rail-gun core.

The weapon pod exploded in a swell of light.

A giant's hand pressed Martin down. His vision clouded as the horizontal stabilizers bowed. The turret strained within its socket. The captain was trying to pull the *Morgana* out of the dive.

Too late, thought Martin as they screamed toward the cratered ground.

He set a gloved hand on the lump of medicine bag beneath his flight suit and watched the thunderbird die.

A chain of explosions erupted across the Typhon's engulfed body. One delta wing tore off and spun away. The Typhon slanted and began to fall. A stump grew where the wing had broken off. It thickened, extended, and burned. The Typhon plunged blazing like a thing cast out of Heaven, furiously altering its structure to find some ideal form, to claw its way up from the abyss. Crowned by fire now the planed head swept from side to side as if in denial.

The Flying Fortress shot into the pillar of smoke and then shot out again, coiling billows following and treetops whipping past two hundred feet below. In its wake the burning Fury sank into the welling smoke and struck the damaged weapons plant. The building detonated and a ring of shockwave spread across the landscape like a pond ripple. A brilliant hemisphere swelled out from the blast. The smoke column coalesced into a curling boil.

The overpressure wave caressed the bomber as she climbed above the German countryside.

* * * * *

Farley kept her climbing and turned northwest. "Pilot to tail gunner," he said, remotely glad to hear that his voice did not betray his pounding heart. "What's the status on the target?"

"What *target?*" Francis came back. *"The Typhon hit it like a rocket and blew it into next week. Jiminy Christmas, you couldn't fill your pockets with what's left."*

Farley took a deep breath and closed his eyes. Crewmen yelling and cheering in his ears. Hands firm on the wheel. This moment. This moment.

He opened his eyes and looked out at the seamless blue. The round sun. The unbounded dome of real sky.

* * * * *

Broben climbed back into the right-hand chair. "They're going apeshit back there," he said as he slipped on his headset. He held up the connector and squinted at the exposed wire where it had been yanked out of the jack. He snorted, then plugged it in anyway and turned to Farley.

The captain was staring blankly out the window. Broben stayed quiet until Farley blinked and then looked at his copilot like someone just waking up. "Anything unusual?" he asked.

Broben raised an eyebrow. "Really?"

"Right," said Farley. "Sorry."

The bomber climbed the German sky.

"They'll be back at their posts in a minute," Broben said.

Farley nodded absently. "I know they will."

Broben surveyed the instruments. "Engines are running a little cold," he said.

"Wen said they would."

Broben let the deep drone play another minute. Then he said, still studying the gauges, "She's something, huh, Joe."

A sad smile ghosted Farley's face. "More than I could have imagined."

"Um, captain?" came over the interphone. *"Tail gunner here."*

Farley frowned. "Pilot here," he said. "What's wrong?"

"Sir, we're not—I mean, we...."

"Jesus, Francis, spit it out," said Broben.

"Well—we're not surrendering anymore, are we?"

Farley and Broben gaped at each other. Then Broben put a hand over his face and started laughing.

Farley shook his head in wonder. "That's a negative, Francis," he replied, and looked forward again. "We're not surrendering anymore."

FORTY-TWO

Here's where I'm supposed to say that we limped back all shot up and dangling pieces, with one working engine that was running on fumes, and I had to belly her in because the gear wouldn't lower and Martin was stuck in the ball turret. That's the big Hollywood ending. But it wasn't like that. We had some hull damage from the 109s and flak, but nothing important had been knocked out. The engines purred like kittens and we had plenty of fuel left, because they were a lot more efficient than they had been.

Rochester, Wen's repair bug, wouldn't power up again. Wen wanted us to bring the thing back to England so we could take it apart and figure out how to make more of them, but I nixed that idea. We were going to have enough problems explaining things as it was. I made him throw Rochester out over the Channel. I swear to god, he teared up. A guy who wouldn't cry at his mother's funeral, unless her coffin had a screw loose. But that was Wen.

Once we were out over Holland the crew started trading stories about what had happened after we broke through, and we pieced it all together. I thought they'd just thrown Yone out of the bomber, and my last-ditch power dive was what had put the Typhon into the target. Martin set that straight. He was the only one who saw the whole thing, so we all got to hear another crazy story from him on the ride back.

Then we talked about what we should do when we got back. The idea of telling what really happened didn't even come up. We'd have been grounded, hounded, and Section Eighted. They'd have thrown away the key. But some crews had to have seen us suddenly heading the other way as the formation came out of the run, like we'd hung a U. We had to account for that. We figured a lot of bombers had been affected by the vortex, so we cooked up a story that our electrics went haywire and I lost my bearings and the wheels went down by themselves.

We arrived back at Thurgood right on the heels of the stragglers from that mission. I couldn't believe it. *Goodnight, Sweetheart* had blown a tire when she touched down, and they hadn't cleared her off the runway yet. I had to circle around and come in again.

It turned out we didn't have to tell our fib about an electrical storm. We'd been seen going the other way after the bombing run, all right. But everybody'd figured we'd cleared a bomb jam and gone around for another run on the target. That kind of thing wasn't unheard of, but it's still a crazy thing to do. The eighty-eights have your altitude dialed in by then, and if you don't kiss your ship goodbye you're almost certainly going to lose some crew. I'd heard of men who wouldn't fly with pilots who'd gone around again on a target.

So they locked me in a room and grilled me about it for half a day. I reckoned I was going to be court-martialed for being a damned idiot. Instead they did something else they do to damned idiots: They awarded me the Silver Star. Gave it to the whole crew.

The *Stars and Stripes* made a lot of hay over the story, and the papers back home got hold of it and we were flavor of the week. The Little Bomber that Could. We took some heat from the other crews, because no one likes a damn hero, but mostly we just did our job and it all blew over—until some reporter noticed that we were going out on missions and all of us were coming back, and he wrote an article about *that*. The No-Hitter, he called it.

We used that idea to keep people from poking around the *Morgana*. It's bad luck to talk to a pitcher who's throwing a no-hitter, and nobody wants to be the one who brings breaks the lucky streak of a bomber crew. We flew fifteen more missions and we didn't lose a man.

Don't go thinking any of this was a picnic. We weren't bulletproof, bombproof, flak-proof, or anything-proof. But we had an edge. I can't explain it any better than that. We had the *Morgana.*

The hardest part was not sharing what we had with the other crews. Bombers went down because we kept a zipped lip. Crews got killed, or spent the rest of the war in prison camps. It ate at us. But we'd all seen where this war would lead if we weren't careful—and maybe even if we were—and letting that happen was a whole lot worse. It got us through the war, I think. Plus, we'd all been through something nobody else had, not even other crews who'd seen terrible action, and we couldn't tell anyone about it. We only had each other. The *Morgana* got us through the missions, but we got each other through the war.

The double shot of the Little Bomber that Could and the No-Hitter was the kind of story people at home liked to hear, so the Army put us on a big morale-boosting bond tour. Brass bands, dancing girls, flybys, speeches, the whole nine yards. Plavitz got to meet Glenn Miller at one of those, not long before Miller went missing in England. Told him that "King Porter Stomp" was his favorite band tune. Miller just looked puzzled and said, "Sorry, I don't know it." We ribbed Plavitz for a solid week about that.

And Shorty met Jack Benny! It was at a USO show, and Shorty did his Benny imitation in front of him. Benny loved it, and he cooked up a bit with Shorty where Benny did his act, and said he'd met some guy backstage who sounded almost as good as him. And Shorty walks out and stands right next to Benny in the exact same pose, hand on his cheek and everything, and says, *"Almost?"* The crowd ate it up. So Benny demanded a showdown and put it to a vote, and Shorty won. It was hilarious. Benny told him to look him up in Hollywood after he killed Hitler.

People wanted to see the Little Bomber that Could, so we did our bond-rally tour in the *Morgana.* I was worried about that. We'd gone to all this trouble to keep what we'd brought back from influencing anything, and here I am, flying goddamn Chitty Chitty Bang Bang from one whistle stop to another. So I told the brass I only trusted Wen to work on the ship. Everybody thinks pilots are spoiled and superstitious, and sometimes you can put that to work for you. So we hid our hotrodded bomber by showing her off to everybody and his brother.

One day we were at a rally selling war bonds, and some wiseacre shakes my hand and says, "So I guess you boys got your meal ticket without having to fly your twenty-five, huh?" It really got under my skin. It's not that I wanted to go back. No one in his right mind would want to be in that mess. But I was a bomber pilot, and they had me barnstorming to sell bonds.

But if I went back to combat duty, my crew would go back, too, like it or not, and that didn't seem fair. So one night I called a crew meeting and told them what I wanted to do. Said I didn't expect everybody to feel the same as me, and that it was a crew decision, not a command decision, and I wanted it put to a vote. I'd stay on with our bond push if that's what they wanted.

But every one of them wanted to go back. Even Garrett and Everett, who were getting girls like movie stars, just nodded their heads and said they'd rather be on the roster. I was proud of them, but a little surprised, too, and I said so.

That's when Shorty stood up. I never saw him so upset. He looked at everybody and said, "You all know why you want to go back, and it's not just because we have a job to do. It's because we don't belong here." He looked at me, and I got the feeling he wanted me to stop him from saying what he was about to say. But I didn't, because I thought I knew what that was going to be.

He said, "I don't mean we don't belong the way vets feel when they come back home. And I'm not talking about feeling like we ought to be back in the war instead of smiling for cameras. I mean just what I said. We. Don't. Belong. *Here.*"

He talked about how he'd been joking around with a bunch of reporters right after he won his Jack Benny contest. He'd done his

Rochester impression, and they just looked at him. One of them said, "Who's that supposed to be?"

Now, Jack Benny had one of the most popular shows in America. Rochester was his—well, I guess you'd call him a valet. That's why Wen named the bug after him. The second you heard that voice, you knew who it was—and *everybody* had heard that voice. And Shorty's Rochester imitation was dead-on.

Shorty just figured they'd been gaslighting him and put it out of his mind. Then after our last USO show he was flirting with some girls, and he did a Benny line, and he was about to do Rochester saying "No, *suh,* Mistah Benny!" But some know-it-all interrupted him and said, "Oh, I *do* take exception, sir!" in this hoity-toity Limey accent. And everyone around him cracked up laughing. "I asked the guy who that was supposed to be," Shorty told us, "and he said, 'You're kidding, right? That was Winchester—Benny's butler.'"

So Shorty made sure to catch the next Benny broadcast, and there it was. "Winchester, did you take my car out?" "No, I only take *exception,* sir."

Shorty pointed at all of us like a prosecutor at the end of a murder trial. "And you all know it's not just me," he said. He brought up Plavitz's gaffe with Glenn Miller. Plavitz nodded and looked upset. "I looked it up, but I couldn't find it," he told us. "But 'King Porter Stomp' was the last song I danced to with my girl before I joined up. You don't forget a thing like that."

Then Garrett spoke up. He'd tried to buy a Snickers bar at a soda fountain, and the guy behind the counter had never even heard of them.

So I told them about my father's car. He was a doctor, and right before the war he bought a Nash 600. Doctors still made house calls back then, and he bought it because the 600 would go forever on a tank of gas. My last letter home, I asked him how the old Nash was doing. He wrote back and asked me who's this Nash person? He wasn't joking. He'd never heard of it.

Once it was out in the open it was scary. Things all of us *knew* we remembered were something else now. Or they weren't there at all. Not the big stuff. There were still forty-eight states, we were still fighting Germany and Japan. But things like that don't have to be big to make you think something's wrong with your head. And that is one scary feeling.

Leave it to Boney to hit the bullseye. We're still trying to figure out why things aren't adding up, and Boney leans forward and says, "We came back, but we didn't come back all the way."

I will never forget that moment. The way we looked at each other. Knowing that was it. That we'd come back to the past, but not to *our* past. And realizing that the mission hadn't really ended. That it never would. We were all getting back-slaps and free drinks and pretty girls, and not one of us wanted to stay there, because it wasn't our world. I guess it wasn't our war, either, but that's not how we thought about it. You expect to be frightened by the war. You don't expect to be scared of the world you come home to after it.

I told everybody that I would put in for a return to combat duty the next day. Then I went to bed and had the first good night's sleep I'd had in months. Two days later Germany surrendered.

* * * * *

Everybody got their orders pretty fast after that. Me and Jerry got falling-down drunk the day he got his. I re-enlisted. I didn't have a girl waiting for me—not in California, anyway. And where else would I get to fly the new jets that were coming?

They took apart the air bases in England so fast you'd think we got evicted. In 'Forty-eight the Russians raised the drawbridge on Berlin, and me and about a thousand other pilots airlifted supplies from Wiesbaden to Tempelhof. I'd spent a lot of time tearing that country up, and it felt good to pay some of it back.

Jerry and I kept in pretty good touch, and one day he wrote and told me he'd tracked the *Morgana* to a holding field in Arkansas.

The Army had brought all the bombers back to melt them down for scrap. I'd been worried what might happen if someone looked under the *Morgana*'s hood and got an education, so I should have been relieved. But that wasn't how I felt. All those mission stencils and girls painted on noses, blood in the metal, and then just stacks of aluminum bars. It breaks your heart.

Then Jerry wrote me that he and Wen had bought the *Morgana* from the Army for three hundred and fifty dollars. I couldn't believe it. I asked him what he thought he was going to do with her. He said he'd think of something. He did, too. Him and Wen went into business. Blue and Gray Technology. Yep, *that* BGT, and *that* Gerald Broben. They reverse-engineered the *Morgana* and figured out other things they'd seen in the future. I wouldn't be surprised to find out that Wen salvaged that damned bug from the Channel and took it apart, too. I was worried as hell about the can of worms they were opening, but they took it slow, released things in small doses. First thing they came out with was an omnidirectional forklift, the Sammy. It made them rich.

Damned if Shorty didn't go out to California and take Jack Benny up on his offer. He ended up writing for Benny's TV show, if you can believe that. They were having trouble with the guy who played Winchester because he wanted too much money, so Shorty created a new character—a black valet named Rochester. Ended up being more popular than Winchester ever was. So really Shorty was the only one of us who changed anything back to the way it had been where we came from. After he retired he started going to Eighth Air Force reunions and air shows, painting nose art on aircraft metal and A-2 jackets for vets. He sent me one. It's even better than the original.

Everett went back to his family farm, got married to some girl he met in Cleveland, and moved there to sell cars. He did all right. Garrett became a high school wrestling coach. Married another teacher and had five kids. He taught at the same school till he died of a heart attack in his mid sixties.

Francis got even more religious than he already was, thanks to his new lease on life. Resurrected like Lazarus. He became a deacon in his church, married a woman named Gail, a real knockout. Out of all of us, I think he ended up the happiest.

Plavitz had a rough go of it. Three marriages, a couple of failed business ventures. He was some kind of black sheep with the family business, shipping or something. He ended up with a bit of a chip on his shoulder, to be honest, and drinking didn't make it any smaller. He died in a car crash in 'Eighty-three.

We lost Boney first. He went into the woods with his service .45 one day in 1955. They found a note in his pocket with his Silver Star. He had a brain tumor, probably six months left by the time they caught it, nothing they could do. He apologized to his parents and the crew. We took it pretty hard. That apology to his parents had been for leaving. The one to us had been for letting us down.

Martin drifted off course for a while early on. You could see it when we all got together. He wouldn't look at you for long. Little things would make him tear up. He'd sit in a corner by himself and drink. Well, first the *Ill Wind* and then us. You'd be haunted, too.

One time, maybe the fourth or fifth time we all met up again, I got to talking with him. Asked him what he was doing with himself back in South Dakota, did he have a girlfriend, all that happy shit. I asked if he still played ball. He just laughed and shook his head no. I told him that was a shame. He shrugged and said he'd been out of the game too long. I said he'd sure be a great coach. High school, American Legion league, who cared? I guess it woke something up in him, because next time I saw him he showed me a picture of a minor-league ball club, him in a team jacket beside them, baseball in his hand and grinning his head off. Sioux Falls Canaries. Good for him.

As for me, I flew. Everywhere I could, every chance I got. Because the one place I knew I did belong was in the air. All those differences, you can't see them up there. They don't matter. It's the only place I feel at home. So that's what I did, for forty more years.

The crew reunions started about eight years after the war ended. I missed the first one because I was in Korea, flying Stratojets. Reunions like that hadn't really started yet for most vets. It was still too soon. The war was still too loud. But we'd gone back home and still not made it home. What we had left of the world we'd left was each other.

Eventually we had the internet for updates on each other, but that didn't stop the reunions. It made it so that when we did see each other, we could concentrate on what we really wanted to talk about instead of playing catchup. We'd wait till the sons and daughters and grandkids went to bed, and we'd talk about what was happening in the world, was it headed toward what we'd seen. As time went by we breathed a little easier about that, but I still see things that make me nervous. It doesn't seem like all that long a throw from those remotely piloted attack drones to the Typhon.

We'd compare lists of things that we remembered but nobody else did. We'd talk about our missions, of course, but mostly we talked about the Mission. And at the end of the night we'd ask the Question. *Have any of us told anyone what really happened?*

The answer was always no. No late-night drunk confessions, no diary entries. Not a word. It was easier to keep quiet about everything as time went on, because the further away from it we got, the crazier it all sounded. Like some fairy tale we'd all made up to get us through the war.

Around those dinner tables or on those front porches we were just a bunch of old guys reminiscing. Hearing aids and canes, eventually walkers. But we were also ten men keeping each other company on a lonely watch. And before we all went on our separate ways we'd make one final toast. It was always silent because what we were toasting was the things we couldn't say. And then we'd leave a glass behind for every one of us we'd lost, five glasses and then six and then seven, on down until two weeks ago, when I got the call from Michael Broben telling me I'd lost my copilot and my best friend for seventy years. Jerry'd dodged flak and bullets and weapons that haven't even been invented yet. Dodged cancer, too, for a while. But in the end he couldn't outrun it.

I didn't want to leave nine glasses behind at a house full of strangers. Or anywhere else. So after the funeral I deadheaded home, and I raised a glass to everything I thought would stay unsaid. I didn't have to ask myself the Question, because I hadn't told anybody. I didn't think there was anyone to tell. Our story would leave this world when I did, and that was okay by me.

But because it was just me now, and because I'm ninety-three years old, there was still a Question that I had to ask myself: *Did it really happen?*

And the answer is yes. Yes, it did. It really happened.

So that's the story of what me and nine of my friends did one summer a long time ago, when we were kids.

EPILOGUE

The old man rolled his cane between his palms and watched the F-shaped metal handle slowly turn. He did not look up when someone softly coughed.

A folding chair creaked. A whiskey voice with an East Texas accent said, quietly, "Captain Farley?"

The old man inhaled sharply and looked up from his cane. He blinked and glanced around the ten-by-ten canopy tent as if surprised he was not somewhere else.

A man and a woman sat facing him. The man was in his late sixties, sandy-haired, beefy, thick-necked, wearing Air Force dress blues with lots of chest candy, a silver star on each epaulet. The woman was heavy, kind-faced, late forties, narrow rimless glasses and a tan dress and low heels. Beside Farley was a tripod that held a tablet with the camera lens pointed at him. The tablet's black case bore a red-white-and-blue sticker. PROPERTY OF VETERANS HERITAGE FOUNDATION. Before the old man a small card table held a pitcher of icewater standing in a pool of its own sweat. The ice mostly melted, an empty glass beside it. Through gaps in the popup flaps the old man saw people passing, a quick glimpse of a child towing an American-flag balloon, patriotic bunting on a distant wall. Distant music sounded echoey and underwater. A live orchestra. They'd been playing big-band swing all afternoon. Right now they were playing Glenn Miller. Pretty good, but not a patch on the man himself.

"Captain Farley?" the man said again.

The old man looked back at the brigadier general—Andrews, he remembered.

"Are you all right, sir?" Andrews asked.

Farley gave a slanted smile. "Hell no," he said. "I'm ninety-three." He leaned back in his metal folding chair. It was hideously uncomfortable and his hips were singing an aria. He waved absently and let his double-handled cane fall back against his leg. "I'm fine," he said. "To be honest, I almost forgot you all were here." He looked at the woman. Kitchner, that was her name. Dr. Kitchner. History professor. "I do go on, don't I?" Farley told her.

"I could listen to it all day," she said.

General Andrews grinned at her. "You just did," he said.

Kitchner looked faintly alarmed and glanced at her cellphone. "Oh my goodness, I had no idea," she said. She got up and pressed the tablet and removed it from its tripod stand. She stopped in the midst of collapsing the tripod looked at Farley. "You've really never told this story to anyone, in all this time?"

"The people I'd have told it to already knew it. The rest?" He waved indifferently.

"No girlfriend? Never married?"

"Hell, I'm not a monk. I got involved a couple times, sure." Farley shrugged. "It never took."

"Well. That's a shame."

"Not to me." Farley's tired smile encompassed decades. "No offense, ma'am," he said, "but you people aren't quite real to me. I know I'm the one who landed here. I'm the ghost. But that's how it feels." He patted his chest. "I'm real. Wennda was real. The world I came from was real. The world I came back to?" He shook his head. "The others got with the program sooner or later, but I just never could."

General Andrews sat up straight. "Oh," he said. "*That's* why you kept flying."

365

Farley looked chagrined. "Took me ten years to figure that out," he said.

"All that seat time." Andrews shook his head. "All those years."

"I'm afraid I don't understand," said Kitchner.

Andrews raised a hand to the old pilot in the chair before them as if offering him as evidence. "He was trying to get back."

Farley looked away. "Still am," he said.

* * * * *

Last night the Blue and Gray Technology Gulfstream G550 had hummed a one-hour lullaby from Baltimore to the company airfield near Norfolk. The jet had a flight attendant, a medical technician with a crash cart, a sofa, and soft beige leather seats the size of Barcaloungers. Farley had been the only passenger. The flight attendant had brought him a soft drink and asked if he wanted anything to eat, then left him alone. The med tech had turned on a Kindle after takeoff from BWI, and barely moved again until they landed.

During the brief flight Farley's hand strayed many times to the letter that had been waiting in his mailbox when he'd finally gotten back from Jerry's funeral. Only once during the flight did Farley remove the letter from his coat pocket, carefully unfolding it in the cabin's dim to look down at the pale gray BGT letterhead. It bore two handwritten words, along with yesterday's date and a time. A limo had arrived at Farley's Inner Harbor condo at exactly that time.

The rest of the flight Farley had looked out the window at the crowded nighttime nation creeping by. All those differences, you can't see them up here. Unbidden, his fingers touched the contours of the envelope again and again.

* * * * *

Now Farley watched snippets of the Veterans Day crowd passing by outside the E-Z Up.

"Blue Skies," he realized. That's what the band was playing out there. "Blue Skies."

Dr. Kitchner was slipping her tablet into a small roll-on valise when Farley looked back. "Let me ask you something," he said.

She smiled. "Of course."

"I went along with this because Jerry arranged it," Farley said. "I figured if he of all people finally wanted it out there, I owe him at least that much. No one'll believe it, but what do I care by now?" He gave his slanted smile. "The general there started squirming about the time my bomber flew over the rainbow."

General Andrews started to protest and Farley waved it off. "Hell, I'd've squirmed, too. Who wouldn't?" Farley pointed at Kitchner. "But you didn't even blink. Didn't raise an eyebrow. Didn't even look at the general to see if he was buying it. Do you know what you *did* do, ma'am?" He folded his hands over the twin metal handles of his cane and leaned forward in his folding chair. "You nodded."

Kitchner tucked the cable into a pocket of the camera's case. "What's your question, captain?"

"Jerry never told our story to *anybody*. I'm as sure of that as anything I know. He left it up to me. He brought me here to tell it and he brought you here to hear it—and you weren't surprised by a word of it. So my question is, Who are you really?"

"Well." She colored. "I'm not a spy, if that's what you mean. My name is Doris Kitchner," she said. "I'm a volunteer archivist for the Veterans History Foundation. Mainly I'm a history professor at Georgetown. My specialization is statistical methodology of the National Socialist Party."

"Nazi bookkeeping?" said Farley.

"In a way. They were meticulous record-keepers."

"They were meticulous, all right."

"Yes. Well, five years ago a World War Two–era bunker was

rediscovered near the Czech border. They still show up from time to time, even now. This particular bunker was full of records pertaining to Allied bombing raids on German targets. Defensive arrays, flak patterns, target strike rates, casualties, numbers of downed aircraft, that sort of thing. Like the Allies, the German military tried to learn from every bombing raid."

Farley spread his hands: *So?*

"It was my good fortune to be involved in cataloging the bunker's contents," Kitchner continued. "But very soon after my work began there, the Air Force classified the project and brought in their own people. We—"

"The *U.S.* Air Force?" Farley glanced at General Andrews, who shrugged.

Kitchner nodded. "We were taken off the project and compensated for our time and made to sign nondisclosure agreements for sensitive but unclassified information."

"Gag orders."

"Pretty much."

"So what is it you're not supposed to disclose?"

Kitchner regarded Farley over the rims of her glasses. He stared back. She glanced at Andrews. The general put his hands up and said, "Hey, I can keep a secret."

Kitchner snorted. Then she adjusted her glasses and picked up her tablet and opened the cover. Andrews didn't bother to hide his watching over her shoulder as she tapped the screen a few times and then swiped across it. She stopped. The general's head craned forward and his mouth hung open like an ape beholding a magic trick. He put a hand to his mouth and he looked at Farley. "Holy god," he said.

Farley was about to make some smartassed comment when Kitchner worked the tablet again and held it out to him. A black-and-white image filled the screen. Farley leaned forward and saw mostly empty sky pockmarked by black wisps. A flak pattern, photographed from the ground.

Farley looked up from the screen. "Am I missing something?" he asked.

Kitchner set two fingers on the screen and zoomed the image until it showed an object blurred by motion and grainy with enlargement, but unmistakably a B-17 bomber in a steep dive, the ID number and nose art too motion-blurred to make out.

Farley studied it for one deep breath, then set his jaw and glanced up at Kitchner. He could not read her expression. He looked past her at the general.

"For christ's sake," Andrews told Kitchner. "Show him, already."

Wordlessly she dragged the plunging bomber to the bottom left of the screen.

The upper right now showed some kind of monster pursuing the B-17. There was no other word for it. Outspread sail-like wings that were wider than the Flying Fortress. A dark gray body that was thinner but much longer. A diamond-shaped head with a long snout and angular pale patches that might have been eyes. A dark gap at the bottom of the head that might have been an air intake or a gaping mouth. As if the creature were trying to devour the plummeting aircraft. Or screaming in rage as its quarry fled. Beneath the thing's left wing hung some kind of pod that might have been an engine.

Farley felt a mortal chill. Even now, eight thousand miles and seventy years away, he heard the keening air across the straining wings. The stuttering clatter of the .50s back behind him. The whump of flak exploding in the air ahead. Even now.

Farley reached for the tablet like a man receiving unsolicited commandments. Breathed fast as he regarded the plummeting shape he knew contained himself and nine other men. The arc of their lives beyond that captured moment. The estranging world beyond these walls. The unconveyable immensity still locked inside himself. The vindication in one impossible image. Here it is. Here it is at last.

The screen timed out and Farley looked down on his darkly mirrored face. Old and tired and struggling for control. He looked up at Kitchner and held out the tablet and she took it back.

"Thank you," they both said at the same time. And laughed in surprise.

369

"But how did Mr. Broben know to send *me* to record you?" Kitchner asked. "I never met him."

"The military buys a lot of hardware from Blue and Gray Technology," General Andrews said. "I had a lot of business dealings with Jerry over the years. Some of it was highly classified systems. We both had top-secret clearance and a lot of connections." He shrugged. "War hero, missions over Germany—something like this was bound to make its way to him."

"So Jerry sends Dr. Kitchner to hear our story because she's the one person on earth with evidence to support it," Farley said. "But he wanted you here, too."

"I have a pretty good idea why, now that I've heard your story," Andrews said. He nodded at Kitchner. "And yours, doctor."

Kitchner frowned.

Andrews leaned back in his chair. "When Jerry wasn't trying to sell me technology from the future, he was beating me at poker and drinking my Pappy van Winkle's. I would get him talking about the war, because my grandfather had flown out of Thurgood. He was a flight engineer on the *Rude Awakening*."

"*Rude Awakening*." Farley frowned. "She went down over—" He stopped.

"Over Zennhausen." Andrews nodded. "I never met him. When I was growing up I was obsessed with the Fighting Forty-Ninth, and the Zennhausen mission in particular." He shook his head. "I would pester Jerry all the time about it. He never let on there was anything odd about the mission, but some things about it just never made sense to me. The explosion was ten times the blast it should have been, even for a munitions plant. It went up like you dropped an A-bomb on it."

"We dropped a typhon on it. Maybe it amounts to the same thing."

"Maybe. But then Dr. Kitchner's bunker showed up." He looked at her. "Only one section of it was devoted to Allied bombing records," he said. "The rest was highly classified information about the Zennhausen facility."

"You were one of the people who took over the project?" Kitchner asked.

"No, ma'am. I only found out about it later, the same way Jerry did—through channels. People who knew my interests. I didn't know about your picture. But I did find out the truth about Zennhausen."

Farley felt an odd misgiving, but he had to ask. "What about it?"

Andrews glanced at Dr. Kitchner. "Most people know the Nazis were trying to build an atomic weapon," he said. "They actually came close to building a working reactor, they just ran out of time."

"And Nazis."

"Yes, sir. But they were also trying to invent high-energy weapons. Very sophisticated stuff—particle beams, directed-energy streams. Things we've only just learned how to build."

Farley's hands shook on his cane. "Zennhausen wasn't a munitions plant at all. Was it."

"No, sir," said Andrews. "It was an energy-weapons lab."

"Energy-weapons lab," Farley repeated dully.

Andrews nodded. "Huge. Underground. Blast-hardened. Self-contained. Heavily defended. And way ahead of its time." He spread his hands. "When I found out the truth I thought, well, now I know my grandfather's death really meant something. Because who knows what might have happened if that mission had failed? What the Germans might have gone on to invent."

"Who knows?" Farley whispered.

"You do, captain." Andrews pointed at him. "Jerry knew. Your crew. And now I know, too. If that mission had failed, the war would have dragged on, escalated, overtaken everything. Until the Germans invented the locus."

Farley nodded. Heart pounding.

Andrews leaned forward. "You and your crew didn't blow up a munitions plant. You prevented the future you had just escaped. You saved *billions* of lives."

Farley saw it. The jewel-like symmetry of it. The explosion

371

hadn't just destroyed the locus. It had destroyed the facility that would have *built* the locus.

Ever since the Mission Farley had worried about what might emerge from the knowledge they'd brought back, feared the discovery of the thing they had really dropped over Germany. A force immeasurably more destructive than any mere bomb. A thing that had reached across time to achieve its goals. But by attempting to manipulate events to guarantee its existence, it actually had prevented its own creation. Unmade the future Farley had seen.

All those years of lonely silence. All that private fear. All the awful dreams and sleepless nights. And all of it suddenly redeemed. They had prevented the end of the world. For one brief moment of raw apprehension Farley's troubled soul was given peace.

But he could not stop his mind from following the implications of the general's revelation, and fleeting redemption fell beneath the relentless machinery of consequence. Because Farley realized that by preventing that future, he and his crew also had eliminated the typhons, the doomsday crater, the Redoubt, the Dome—and Wennda.

A white-hot flare ignited in his chest. He fell back in his chair.

"Captain?" he heard Dr. Kitchner ask. "Are you all right?" From far away he watched the cane shake in his hands. Wake turbulence. The vortex left by the passage of something huge.

There had been no other proper course to take. One man's heart could not be weighed against the human race.

And yet. And yet.

Wennda.

Farley gripped his cane and fought inside himself.

All his life he'd held on to her eventuality. That she existed someday up ahead was a balm at least against the pain of not being able to find a way back to her. And now at last he knew he hadn't found it because it wasn't there. Had been unmade along with so much else. Wennda.

His hands would not stop shaking.

Don't you dare *lose your ship, Captain Midnight. Not now. Not after all this. It was* seventy years ago, *you stupid sap. You've steered through worse a dozen times and you're still here. It's just wake turbulence. Power up, push through, roll off. Do it. Soldier through, god damn it.*

Cold sweat chilled him. He loosened his collar and held up a hand. "Just give me a minute," he said.

"I'm so sorry," Andrews said. "I didn't mean to upset you. I thought—I was sure this was why Mr. Broben wanted me here."

"It is," Farley said. He coughed into his fist. He pointed at the water pitcher and Dr. Kitchner poured the rest into the glass and handed it to him, not letting go until he'd brought it to his mouth. "It's why all of us are here." He set the glass back on the little table and looked at the general and the professor. "We had the missing piece to each other's puzzles, and Jerry saw it. The big picture. God I miss him." He shook his cane at the ceiling of the tent. "I got you into a church after all, you son of a bitch."

* * * * *

Outside the E-Z Up Farley looked out on the enormous airplane hangar. The other tents were being taken down, their contents hauled away by BGT employees driving Signature Edition Sammy Juniors, mini versions of the forklift model their inventor had stolen from the future. Away went Veterans Day displays of flight suits and A-2 jackets and crush caps, mounted photographs of bomber crews and fighter pilots and aerial combat, machine guns and medals and flags.

At the far end of the hangar, near the Blue and Gray Technology Gulfstream that had brought him here, the huge swing orchestra was packing up. The circulating crowd and shouting children tugging patriotic balloons had dwindled to stragglers. A few hours ago long lines had snaked around the airfield, waiting patiently to tour the vintage aircraft despite the cold gray overcast November day. Because how often does a major corporation debut a mint-condition World War II warbird collection that its founders had maintained in a private hangar for decades?

Farley shook his head and smiled, thinking about Jerry and Wen and the surprise their company had unveiled today. A secret basement project that only outrageously wealthy men could have made a hobby of.

The Bonniker & Broben Collection looked as if it had rolled off the assembly line this afternoon. The Mustang fighter parked inside the hangar by the Aerial Combat display should have had a ribbon and a bow on it. The Mitchell and the Liberator bombers squatting off the taxiway looked like they'd been garaged straight from the factory. The C-47—a tireless draft horse Farley had learned to love during the Berlin Airlift—looked cherry as a showroom sedan.

And the main attraction just outside the hangar entrance. Even now his heartbeat quickened when he looked at her.

His hand went to the envelope in his breast pocket, but the tent panel rustled and Dr. Kitchner emerged, pulling her wheeled brown valise like a lapdog on a leash.

"Oh, good, I was afraid you'd already gone," she said. "Where's the general?"

Farley pointed at the row of blue Porta-Potties along the side wall. "Duty calls," he said.

"Oh." Kitchner frowned. "Well, I really must leave." She held out a hand. "Captain, it has been a unique honor. Thank you. For—well, *everything*."

Farley shook her hand. "One more question, doc," he said.

Kitchner nodded uncertainly.

"Do you think if we learn from the future, maybe we won't repeat it?"

She smiled and looked startled at the same time. "As long as there are people like you in the world, captain," she replied, "I feel certain of it." She grabbed the telescoping handle of her valise. "Give my regards to the general. I really do have to go."

"Have a safe trip," said Farley. He grinned. "And a good life."

Kitchner blinked up at him. "You really are quite tall," she said.

Farley was still watching the valise trail behind her when Andrews came up beside him.

"Sorry I didn't say goodbye," the general said.

"She asked me to give her regards," said Farley. "Think she has a plane to catch."

A young woman heading toward the hangar with an empty wheelchair waved cheerfully at Kitchner as she went from the structure's dusk into the waning day.

Farley turned toward Andrews. "Think she'll sell that video to the History Channel?" he asked.

The general laughed. "I think she'll just turn it in to the archives."

"Does anyone ever watch those?"

"I sure as hell hope so."

Farley snorted. "So is the Air Force officially done with me?" he asked.

The general turned to face him. "Captain Farley," he replied, "I believe it is." He saluted. "And I have never been more sincere when I say thank you for your service."

Farley returned the salute without thinking, back straight, shoulders square, eyes front, pain forgotten. His eyes stung and he swallowed. "Sir," he said.

Andrews broke the salute and nodded at the girl with the wheelchair, who had stopped a respectful distance away. "Looks like your ride's here," he said.

"I thought it was yours." Farley waved at the girl and she nodded and headed to them with the wheelchair. Farley let himself be helped aboard. He settled his cane against his leg and looked up at the general. "One more roll," he said.

Andrews nodded soberly. "One more roll," he replied, and toasted Farley with an invisible glass.

Farley regarded him a moment, then decided hell with it. "What else did they find in that bunker?" he asked.

The general raised an eyebrow. "As far as I know it's still classified," he replied.

"Well. I guess that answers that."

Andrews nodded at Farley's cane. "I keep meaning to ask you," he said. "That's a B-17 throttle, isn't it?"

Farley held the cane up before him. It was cherry wood, brass-banded near the tip, with an unusual **F**-shaped aluminum handle. Farley smiled at it, fond and knowing and sad.

"Goodnight, general," he said. Then he looked back at the girl and pointed the cane forward, and the wheelchair began to move.

* * * * *

Jerry had given him the cane at one of the crew reunions, Farley couldn't remember which one. Wen had made the handle from the *Morgana*'s left-hand throttle lever, Jerry'd told him.

Farley had hefted the cane, loving it instantly. *You sure you guys can spare it?* he had asked.

You do grateful lousy, Broben had replied.

* * * * *

"How are you doing, sir?" the young woman asked as she wheeled Farley across the hangar.

"I'm fine," said Farley. "Just taking it all in."

"The crowd was so much bigger than we expected. And you were great, the reporters loved you." Farley could hear her broad smile. "Can I get you anything?" she asked.

Farley nodded at the aircraft parked outside the hangar entrance. "You can get me over there, if you wouldn't mind."

"Glad to."

Farley kept his gaze on the familiar shape ahead as his hand went to his breast pocket and pulled out the Blue and Gray Technology envelope, the folded gray paper. He unfolded it and held it on his lap and closed his eyes and breathed in deep.

Oil and grease, high-octane fuel. And a metal smell hard to explain. Aluminum, iron, blood.

He opened his eyes and looked down at the letter in his hand. Below the printed time and date were two handwritten words painstakingly formed in shaky block letters. Two last words from Lieutenant Gerald Broben, hellraiser, wiseass, zillionaire, philosopher on wheels, and the best copilot this or any other world would ever see.

Farley smiled at that final message even as it blurred before him.

TAXI MISTER?

* * * *

She was skylighted against gray overcast, profile framed in the hangar entrance, angled upward as if eager to regain the sky. Pale light glimmered the contours of her graceful and aggressive frame, gleamed her cowlings and chrome and cockpit glass, glared the vivid painting on her nose. Undiminished by the decades, beautiful and sharp as she had ever been. A window looking out on 1943 in some other world than this.

"Hey beautiful," the old man whispered to his bomber.

The restoration was perfect. She was the *Fata Morgana* he remembered, nothing more and nothing less. He had no doubt that Jerry's drive and affection had made that happen, but Wen's hand showed in every bolt and rivet.

Farley was out of the chair before the girl could help him up. He only had eyes for the bomber as he leaned on his cane and walked closer and looked up in wonder at the painting on her nose. Shorty's artwork was even better than he remembered. The depth and subtle shading, the sharp clean lettering, the *trompe l'œil* floating rocks that might also have been flying fortresses. Above the artwork were sixteen stenciled bombs and six swastikas and one odd figure that looked something like a Thunderbird.

And Wennda. The figure's glamour just as he remembered. The

pose regal but sexy, features faintly stern. But this was no longer a painting that eerily resembled the woman he'd loved all his long life. This was a portrait of her. The likeness so perfect that it broke his heart.

Wennda. Her fretful expression concentrating on some problem. Her sudden and disarming smile when she solved it. The rich deep color of her eyes, glimpsed sometimes in a thin band on the horizon certain rare clear days at thirty-five thousand feet when the sun had dropped below the curve of the earth. The way she'd called him Farley until he'd said to call him Joe. The iron in her tone when she pressed home a point. The scent of her hair. The strength that had chosen duty to her people over feeling for him. The suspended moment in a hellbent chaos that permitted one brief kiss.

Farley had tried to tell himself that seven decades' time had burnished one week's memory of her like some bronze shield carried by a mythic hero. But he didn't believe that for a minute. What he yearned for with a marrow-deep longing that had shaped the life he'd led beyond their parting was nothing more and nothing less than Wennda. You don't misremember that.

Farley held his gnarled hand high to touch the underside of the bomber's fuselage like some weary penitent arriving at a shrine. His fingers slid beneath the painted signature.

Shorty Dubuque
August 1999

The hand stopped. The old man stood open-mouthed. Then he smiled. "Well, I'll be goddamned," he said.

"Sir?"

Farley turned at the voice behind him. He had completely forgotten about the girl. He looked around to see the crowd gone, the gates closed, the bunting being taken down. A crew was setting up to roll the Mustang back into the hangar.

"Would you like to go back to your hotel, Mr. Farley?" the young woman said. "It's been quite a day; you must be very tired."

"The day's got nothing to do with it," said Farley.

"I'll have them bring your car." She started away, but the old man grabbed her arm. The strength of his grip surprising.

"I want to take one more look," said Farley. He nodded at the bomber. "No crowds, no tours, no questions. Just me."

The girl looked doubtful, then suddenly smiled. "Of course," she said. "We're not on a schedule."

"That's the spirit," Farley said.

He let himself be helped as he went slowly up the portable steps below the waist door. In the hatchway he stopped and let his hand linger on the hull's thin metal skin. Hello? Hello.

He looked back at the girl. "Do you think we could be alone for a few minutes?" he said.

"We are alone, sir. Take all the time you need."

Farley gave a private smile. "I didn't mean me and you," he said.

* * * * *

The restoration work was utterly invisible. She was, simply, the bomber he had flown out of Thurgood in the last years of the war. The familiar mix of smells as much a part of her as the close-set aluminum ribs and rivets.

He glanced at Everett and Garrett's gun stations on either side of the waist. Two big men had stood here close as subway commuters and fired back in calm desperation at murderous fighter planes.

He made his careful way around Martin's ball turret bulging from the floor below. Someone had left a Coke can on the hydraulic rig where once a spider drone had torn apart a much-augmented human being. Farley pitched it out the left-side window and kept moving forward. He smiled at the hand-lettered sign on the door to Shorty's radio room. Goodnight, Mr. Benny.

In Boney's bomb bay Farley held his cane horizontal and made his way along the grab lines where those boys from long ago had done their desperate duty like construction workers treading I-beams five miles above the ground. In the pit he stepped around the top turret stand and looked up at the cockpit. His seat on the left, Jerry's on the right. The round footwells in the bulkhead in between where Wen had stood monitoring the instruments like an overseeing lioness.

Farley set his cane above the footwells and hoisted himself up. He had a bad moment where he didn't think he'd make it, but he told his body the hell with that. He picked up his cane and put both hands on the double handle and lowered himself into the pilot seat. The seat cushions stiff against his back and legs. It felt like being reunited with a missing limb.

Both throttles were in place now. Either Jerry had been bullshitting him about the cane, or Wen had replaced the one he'd supposedly used for the handle.

Farley looked at the empty copilot seat. The world was a better place with you in it, Jerry. Which means the world is worse without you. I know I sure am.

He leaned the cane against the bulkhead. Feet on the rudder pedals. Hands on the control wheel. Like putting on an old shoe. It felt like years since he had sat here. It felt like hours.

He closed his eyes and breathed the bomber in.

* * * * *

He dangled his feet over the edge and looked out across the vast blank white. She leaned against him and he put his arm across her shoulders. The warm press of her. Perfume of her hair.

She brought his hand forward to clasp in both of hers. The three hands old and spotted. He didn't need to look at her to know that she was undiminished by the decades, beautiful and sharp as she had ever been.

"Was I really there?" he asked. "Were you?"

"You were always going to be there," she said. "You remembered me before we ever met. An echo across time."

He shook his head. "There isn't any more time," he said. "Not in this world."

"Oh, Joe." She squeezed his hand. "There's nothing but *time." She leaned toward him and the sky paled white.*

* * * * *

Hands still on the wheel. Heart a cauldron alloyed with grief and fear and hope. The fierce unlikely wonder of every hot and bloody beat.

There's nothing but time.

Wennda you are not a forlorn hope. You aren't a desperate wish I'm making. You're as real as I am. Your face is painted on the ship that brought me to you. An echo across time. That future's still out there somewhere. Because time's not an arrow. It's a shock wave. It spreads out in all directions at once. From every possible past to every possible future. Someone I've loved all my life told me as much. Will live to say as much. Because she's waiting out there, somewhere. Somewhen. There is out there a hub around which all times turn.

His grip on the wheel. A shape he still felt in his dreams. Hull and engine and flap and line. The emblem of his yearning heart tattooed upon her metal skin. His last friend from the world before. Joe Farley twenty-two years old and brave and afraid and immortal and frail and very far from home.

Beyond the windshield the overcast was finally burning off and what remained of day was clearing. In some other future up ahead a bright soul's beacon shone. It would be beautiful at sixteen thousand feet.

He could hear the voices in his headset now. Boney and Plavitz and Shorty and Wen, Everett and Garrett and Martin and Francis. Everybody check in.

Gyros—uncaged.

Fuel shutoff switches—open.

Gear switch—neutral.

"Wheels up," the old man whispered.

He felt the cockpit tremble as the *Fata Morgana* began to pick up speed. Slowly at first, then in a rush. The daylight brightening to a blinding white as the world he knew all dropped away.

ACKNOWLEDGEMENTS

The experience, shared resources, and painstaking research of a huge number of historians, archivists, hobbyists, Youtubers, and forum members was invaluable during the writing of *Fata Morgana*. Listing all of them would amount to a lengthy bibliography; we can only offer our deep gratitude and appreciation for their work and their generosity in sharing it.

We'd also like to thank the following people and organizations:

The Collings Foundation (collingsfoundation.org), who maintain and operate the B-17G Flying Fortress *Nine-O-Nine*;

The creators of the website at *vintagetin.net/B-17Nine-O-Nine/G/*, for its amazing and invaluable panoramics of every location on the *Nine-O-Nine*;

The Experimental Aircraft Association (eaa.org), and the crew and volunteers of the B-17G *Aluminum Overcast,* for their hands-on approach and invaluable information;

Greg Kuster, Paul Hammond, and the March Field Air Museum (www.marchfield.org) for the generous loan of their beautiful B-17G Flying Fortress *Starduster* for our author photo;

Craig Good and Sean Bautista, for technical information related to piloting and large aircraft, and for catching manuscript errors large and small;

Jurgen Gross, Dave Williams, and David J. Schow, for answering questions as well as providing valuable input and unstinting support;

Adrian Smith and Lynn Bey, for their comments on an early draft.

If there is any level of detail and authority in this book, it's because of the people and organizations listed above. Anything we got wrong is most definitely our fault and not theirs.

Special thanks go to:

Richard Curtis, our agent, for his instincts, enthusiasm, and tough love;

Michael Carr, editor extraordinaire, for his diplomacy, acumen, and attention to detail;

Gigi Grace and Beth Weilenman Mitchroney, for unwavering support, patience, and faith.